AF424420

Blood

OF THE

Gods

WREN L. RIVERS

MIDIR

Anui
Midnorthern hub
Aurora Isle
Øsig
Western hub
Refuge
Avet
Central hub
Sekka
Redwood
Harbor
Biqana
Suhin-
Øsig
Southern Icecaps

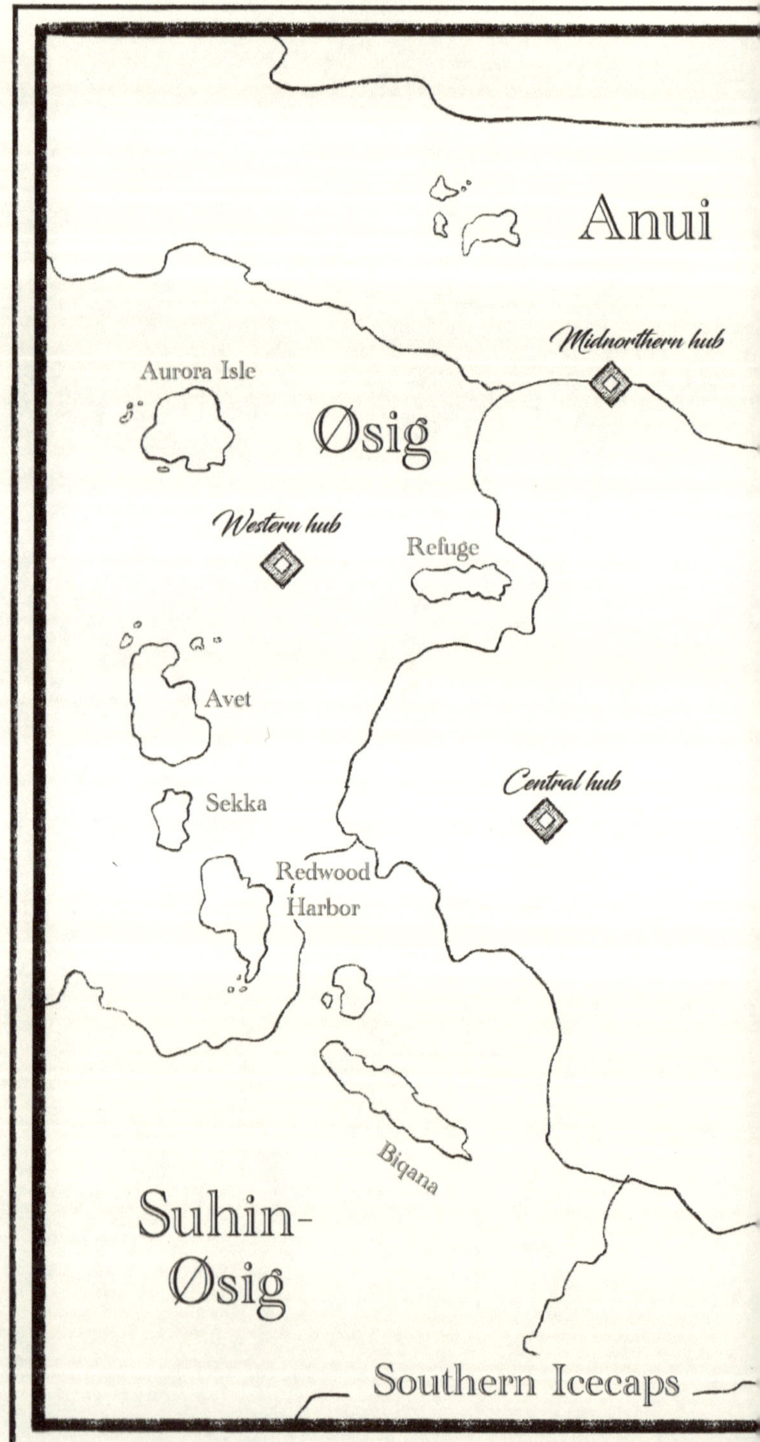

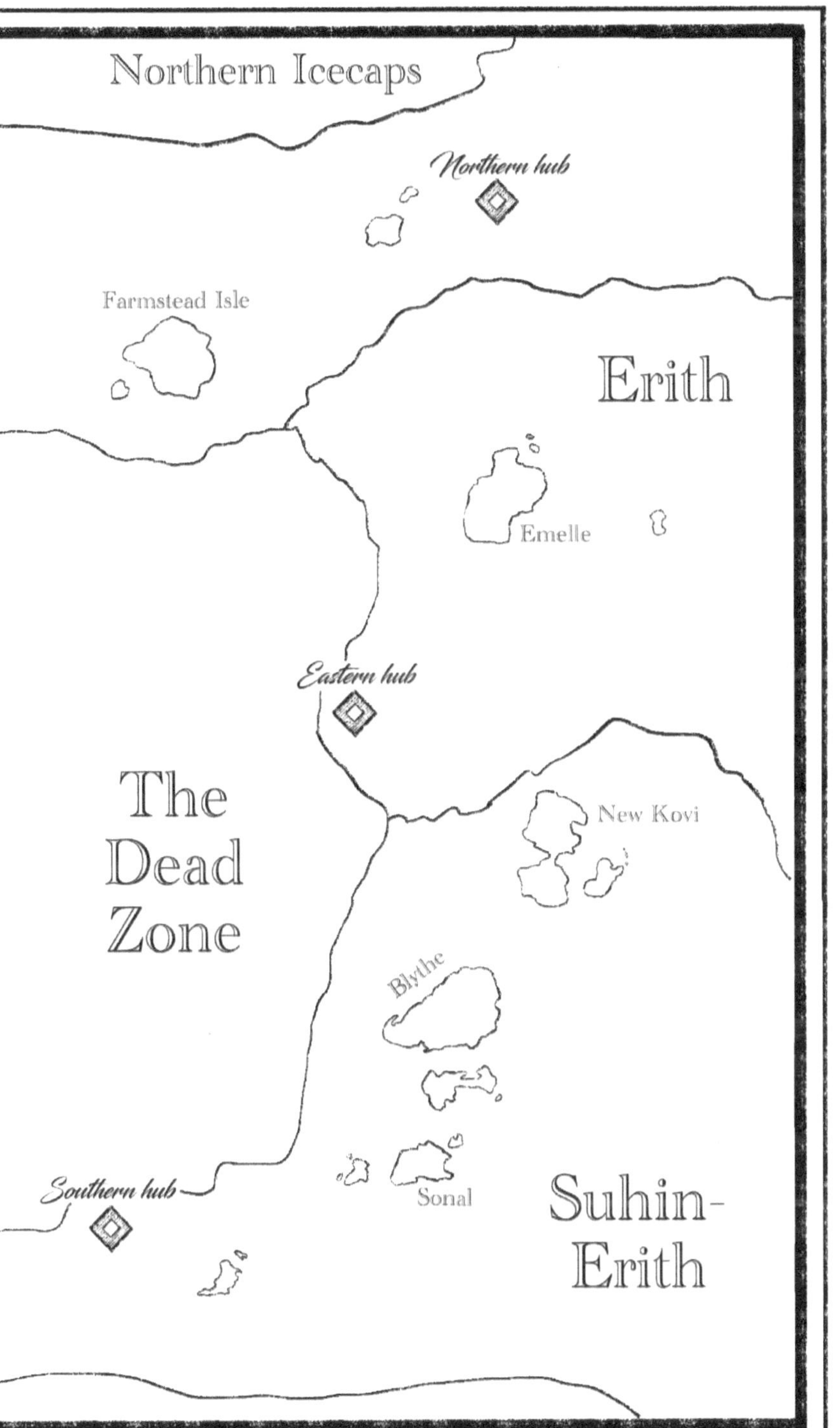
Northern Icecaps
Northern hub
Farmstead Isle
Erith
Emelle
Eastern hub
The Dead Zone
New Kovi
Blythe
Southern hub
Sonal
Suhin-Erith

CONTENT WARNING

This story contains content that may be unsettling to some readers, including blood, violence, gaslighting and manipulation, religion, pregnancy, and self-harm.

For anyone who has ever been made less than their true worth

1

"I'm unsure of whom I weep for more: those who have died or those who have survived. I have seen both sides. All that exists is misery."
—The Grand Catalogue of Last Words: Great Flood Era. Death #6,032,008,519. Drowned and resuscitated. Five weeks later, drowned.

5th Storm, Great Flood 1058

Captain Jonah Morgan was damn tired of taking in strays. The logic was simple: a larger crew meant solving more problems, and solving more problems meant caring about more people. The more people he cared for, the more he'd someday watch die.

When his gunner cried from above deck, "There's someone in the water!" and the subsequent pattering of feet knocked dust loose from the ceiling, his first instinct was to groan. This song and dance repeated far too often for Jonah's liking. Still, he shoved aside his weathered map and stomped from the lonesome safety of his cabin. Best to get the ordeal over with.

His crew was a measly four, minuscule for a square-rigged frigate such as the *Vengeance* but more than enough for Jonah's taste. They all huddled at the starboard hull. His first mate straddled the gunwale, one boot in the dinghy, the other firm upon deck. Her neck-length sandy brown hair caught the morning sun, casting unflattering shadows upon her round face.

"Don't bother," Jonah snapped.

Karina Thorne ignored him, heaving her other leg over the gunwale. *Typical.* The dinghy, suspended against the hull by old, fraying rope, settled under her weight. With the crank of a pulley, she lowered herself to the water.

Jonah peered over the edge. The person in question clung to a soggy chunk of driftwood, fighting to keep their eyes open. "They're good as dead," he observed. "Malnourished, pale. Let them drown. More merciful that way."

Karina shot him an unamused glance as the dinghy kissed the ocean's glassy surface. Trembling and weak, the person in the water reached out. They weren't close enough, and their sallow, seawater-slick fingers didn't catch Karina's. Having leaned their entire weight forward, they lost their grip on the driftwood and fell into the water with an insignificant splash.

Jonah figured that was that.

Karina had other ideas.

She dove in and did not resurface until she had her most recent pity project in her arms. A raven-haired head lolled against her shoulder as she pulled them onto the dinghy. Their limp body was no more useful than a paperweight.

The moment Karina hauled the sailor aboard, the patchwork crew of the *Vengeance* crowded around to catch a glimpse. "Back up," she said. The crew obliged, save for one. The gunner.

Jonah opened his mouth, ready to bark at her to scram, but Karina beat him to it. "Faye, fetch some towels, will you? They're soaked to the bone, the poor thing."

Faye swooped below deck, the vibrant shock of her tangerine shirt vanishing behind thick wooden doors.

Jonah eyed his first mate. "I'm not taking in anyone new."

"They were going to drown," Karina argued.

He knelt, rolling the sailor onto their side, lest they choke on any lingering seawater in their throat. Their body was as limp and pliable as a fresh corpse. A soaking wet mop of wavy black hair obscured their slack face, their cheeks too pale and yellowed to be healthy.

"They were cast overboard, I'd wager."

When Faye returned with a heap of ratty, fraying towels, Karina took one and brushed it over the sailor's damp skin. Their slender form shivered despite the storm season warmth.

Fat drops of seawater rolled from Karina's temple to her chin. She made no effort to wipe it away. "Or their ship sank. Have some sympathy, Captain."

Jonah felt none. But Karina was as whale-headed and stubborn as she was compassionate, and Jonah had the sinking feeling she would not budge. He sighed, begrudging. "Fine, whatever. We'll keep them aboard until they recover, and then they're on their own."

"Seriously, Jonah?"

"Yes, *seriously*. I'm done taking stragglers in."

Jonah rose and stalked away. He descended the creaky stairs, electing to ignore Faye's muttered, "Drama queen."

The cabin deck sat one level below. Here, a long passageway stretched toward the bow, doors to the crew's private cabins lining the bulkheads. The lights along the walls buzzed, their fixtures faulty but not yet worth repairing. Jonah hesitated at the base of the stairwell, his gaze drifting to the lone door at the end. He gritted his teeth and retreated to his cabin before that door could haunt him.

He returned his attention to his map. Tracing routes was a crucial job this far north. The *Vengeance* could not cross the 50° latitude. Any farther into Anui waters, where the churning ocean threatened to freeze, they'd be treading into pirate territory.

Jonah's mind drifted to Karina's rescue. A sense of profound wrongness radiated from her cabin. Who had Karina brought aboard? A pirate? A thief? A beggar? Regardless of who they were, they did not belong. He needed to get this person off his ship. From the look of things, the Midnorthern hub was two days' travel west—he could leave them there. The *Vengeance* was running low on supplies, anyhow. What was the phrase the ancients used?

Two birds, one stone.

Jonah dug out a sheet of half-used paper, old notes and reminders already scrawled upon it, from his desk's centermost drawer. As he pressed the nib of his fountain pen to the paper, a knock at his door jolted him. Ink splattered the page. *Great.* He wasn't going to get any work done today.

Karina stepped inside. Jonah jotted down his list before she could interrupt him again. Gunpowder, cleaning supplies, food...

"I hung their shirt to dry." Her voice was firm, demanding attention which, on principle, Jonah refused to give. He did not look up from his work as she approached. "I couldn't help but notice they were covered in scars."

"So, they've been in a few fights," he grumbled. "No surprise. This far north, they're no doubt a pirate."

"They weren't normal scars. They looked intentional."

"Surgical."

"Not surgical."

He glanced up. Karina's hazel eyes were soft with concern and curiosity. She wore dry clothes, but her hair appeared two shades darker than usual, thanks to the dampness clinging to it.

"Come. I want a second opinion, and I *happen* to value yours."

Karina took Jonah by the arm and tugged him from his cabin. Her fingers squeezed his bicep. Karina's muscle was less apparent on her stocky build than on Jonah's sharp, dense physique, but she had no issue lugging him across the passageway, despite his struggles to break free. She released him at the door, and he rubbed his arm.

Karina's cabin was far too cluttered for Jonah's taste. He couldn't see a speck of floor—a light pink shag rug blanketed most of it, and where the rug ended, shelves, crates, and trunks lined the walls, piled full of useless crap. Jonah had long since given up on his attempts to mitigate her hoarding tendencies—as long as her collection didn't spill *out* of her cabin, it was fine.

In front of a propped-open window, the sailor's sopping clothes hung to dry. Every time Jonah laid eyes on those damned windows, frustration rose within him. She and Mouse, the ship's engineer, had gone behind his back a few years ago to renovate, and they'd knocked out part of the hull to install big, garish panes of glass. Their project compromised the hull's integrity.

Atop Karina's cot lay her rescue, bundled in blankets. Jonah approached with caution. He pulled the blankets back. The skin on their flat chest was as pale as their androgynous face.

"Male, then," Jonah muttered.

"Don't make assumptions. Now, look here." Karina turned their right arm supine. Along the forearm were neat rows of parallel scars, almost scientific in their spacing and thickness.

Jonah frowned. "So, what? He's got self-harm scars." *I've got plenty, too.*

"In any other case, I'd agree, but I'm inclined otherwise. Look—see this, in the crook of their elbow?"

Jonah leaned in and narrowed his eyes. There sat a tiny, round scar right where one would find a vein, almost unnoticeable.

"A puncture site," Jonah muttered. "To leave a scar, it'd have to be a frequent offense."

"Whoever they are," Karina said with a frown, "someone's been drawing their blood."

2

"Our projections state the entirety of Zrila and its surrounding districts will be submerged in two weeks' time. The governor is issuing a mandatory evacuation. Again, the governor—hey, water's leaking into the studio! Don't let it touch any of our equipment—"
—The Grand Catalogue of Last Words: Great Flood Era. Death #0,000,418,350. Electrocuted.

7th Storm, Great Flood 1058

Long, interweaving coral-and-shell docks, their surfaces slick with seawater, rose and fell with the waves. Little stalls lined each row, some bland and simple, others adorned with colorful, attention-grabbing tarps and decorations. The stalls belonged to fishermen, artisans, farmers, and salvagers, many of whom travelled here from their cushy lives on Midir's tiny islands. Ships surrounded this tapestry of pathways, some merchants, most visitors. This was where the *Vengeance* found itself on this overcast morning, two days after Karina rescued the sailor from the ocean.

Karina basked in the salty air. Hubs were her childhood home, but they left bitter resentment on the back of her tongue, more so than any sweet nostalgia. Even so, she found the atmosphere, the crowds, exciting. Invigorating. Not so lonely.

"May you, steward of hubs, grant me a safe, fruitful visit," she muttered—a quick prayer to Syni, the goddess of commerce. Her parents had not contributed much to her childhood, but they had drilled the prayer into her. Even now, she couldn't break the habit. *"Let me find what I need. Let me resist the temptation of that which I do not. Savvan."*

Savvan. Ma and Pop always taught her to end her prayers with, "May it be so." In a small act of defiance, she adopted the Avetic word.

Savvan felt far more significant than its Midiri translation would ever be.

Meat, fruits and vegetables, flour. Jonah carried the scratchy burlap sacks, his arms trembling under the weight. To ease his load, Karina took a sack of oranges from the teetering pile and tucked it under her arm. Jonah's furrowed brow loosened a touch as they approached a booth at the end of the platform, run by a stout man with a kind smile. His eyes lit up when he spotted Karina.

"Good afternoon, Magnus!" she greeted.

"Karina! Always a pleasure. How have you been faring?"

"Well enough. Though, a few days ago I found a—"

"We're not here to make small talk," Jonah snapped.

Karina sighed. "Yes, we're looking to buy. Could you get us five fresh fish and ten salted? Salmon and tuna would be fantastic."

"What was it you found?" Magnus asked as he gathered the fish. "I've got no salmon."

"No worries. Cod is fine," Karina replied. "We found an overboard sailor. Have you overheard anybody talking about a shipwreck? Escaped prisoner? Any refugees?"

"Can't say I have." Magnus packed the fish into a reed basket. Jonah, beside her, wilted at the sight. Karina frowned. *He must have anticipated a bag.*

"I'll carry it," she whispered. Jonah nodded.

"Five shell coins for the lot."

"What? This should cost five *glass,* not five shell."

"The day I charge you full price is the day I die, Karina."

Jonah tapped his foot and fidgeted for only a minute more before he marched off. Karina made no effort to stop him. Though his sour attitude and thin patience left little to be desired, she sympathized. The crowds, the noise, the stench... Market hubs weren't for everybody.

Karina passed Magnus six shell coins. "Have you seen my ma and pop around?"

"They were selling at the Central hub last I knew," Magnus replied. He counted out the extra coin and held it out to her. She ignored it. "Six weeks ago, I'd say. Why do you ask? I thought you hated them."

"I do," Karina admitted. "Still, I don't know. Some closure would be nice."

"If I see them again, would you like me to mention you?"

"No," Karina said a bit too quick. Her stomach churned at the prospect. "Thanks, though."

"You'll be in my prayers."

She smiled, gathered her purchase, and hurried after Jonah. He was halfway between Magnus's stall and the *Vengeance* by the time Karina caught up with him.

"Jonah, a little longer wouldn't have killed you," she said.

Jonah fixed her with a flat stare. "You were asking for gossip. Why don't you talk to the mangy sailor you fished out of the ocean?"

"They haven't awoken."

"They haven't?"

"Not once." Two days, and the sailor remained dead to the world.

"They may be a lost cause. We'll leave them here while we have the chance. Conscious or not."

"No, we won't. Nobody is a lost cause. Were you a lost cause?"

Jonah paused at the base of the *Vengeance*. He looked Karina in the eye. "Yes."

She sputtered. "No!"

Jonah hauled the supplies up the gangplank. Karina, once she was confident he had the task under control, sought the one constant at the ever-shifting, ever-changing hubs: Willow.

Whenever the *Vengeance* stopped at a hub, Willow sold her art. Today she had paid seven glass coins to rent her stall. Two huge, vibrant paintings stood on iron stands behind her, the smaller ones lying flat on the stall counter. The hubworkers had shoved her between two salespeople whose fish was so rancid Karina gagged.

"How are sales?" Karina asked, holding a hand against her nose.

"Not great," Willow admitted. "Nobody's shown interest."

"A shame," Karina said. What Willow could do with a paintbrush was beyond anything Karina could ever dream of doing herself. Karina wondered, sometimes, if the god of art and music had blessed Willow's lineage. But her eyes didn't show any sign of blessing in their color, and there was no divine magic woven into her artworks. She was not blessed—she had trained for her skill. That, to Karina, was worth far more. "You'll get there. Someday, you'll be the most famous painter in Midir."

"I doubt it," Willow giggled. "But thank you."

"I'd love for you to teach me sometime."

"My door is always open."

Karina took a step back, knowing she should leave Willow to work, but her gaze fell on Willow's largest painting, and she paused. "Can I ask you a question?"

"Of course."

Karina gestured to the god of the sea's portrait. "I thought you hated depictions of Einari with blue skin."

"I do," Willow affirmed. "There's such a vast, beautiful range of natural skin colors—why do we have to depict him as *blue?* It's weird."

"Why perpetuate it, then? Why not paint his skin black? Or any other color, for that matter?"

Willow stared up at the painting, where Einari stood proud, surrounded by ocean and fish, with blue skin and sea-green eyes. "This is sinful of me to say," she muttered. "But black skin is far too beautiful to be wasted on a god like Einari. I will paint him with blue skin, and he will be ugly for it, because he is ugly for drowning our people."

Karina nodded. She met Willow's gaze. They were so dark it was hard to see any color at all, but they carried so much warmth and life in them.

"I'll wrap up in an hour," Willow said, checking her watch. "I think Jonah wants to get sailing."

"Of course he does." Karina chuckled. "Good to know, though—I'll leave you to it. Where's Faye? Is she helping you today?"

"On the *Vengeance.* She's fetching some water—she'll be back soon, if you want to see her."

"No, it's okay. I'll let you work." She glanced at the middle-aged couple who approached Willow's stall. Best not to be a distraction. She stepped away, and as she did, she prayed for Willow to make a sale.

Karina perused salvager stalls. The craft fascinated her. What all existed beneath the endless waves? She'd read tales of ancient buildings so tall they pierced the sky, lights so bright they competed with the stars, forests so large people got lost within them. She couldn't fathom it. The Great Flood had taken almost everything.

She couldn't resist buying an algae-covered bust of some scruffy old man. The stone sculpture was about as tall as her forearm was long. His nose and name were lost to time.

"What were the ruins like?" she asked as she paid.

"Cold," the seller replied, his tone flat. "Wet."

She tucked the bust under her arm and headed for the *Vengeance*. The lack of passion always disappointed her. There was so much history under the ocean! However, those who resigned themselves to the grueling labor of salvaging seldom cared for history.

As Karina walked, a hubworker one row over jingled a little bell—and when he did, the other hubworkers followed suit, until the entire hub lit up with the bright, cheery sound. Karina knelt upon the coarse surface of the dock and folded her hands. A small smattering of folks ignored the prayer bell.

At the end of the row, a priest wearing long, ocean blue robes stood on a steel crate.

"WE MUST REPENT!" he exclaimed, his voice deep and rich with devotion. "Our sins hold us back from salvation! Today, we stand upon Einari's beautiful ocean, and I beg he bless our doomed souls! Here, I pray, is where our goodness begins anew! We, upon the Midnorthern hub, will create a new humanity! Theft, apathy, greed: we must vanquish these sins from Midir if we wish to see land! Be pure, be good, so Einari may hear us and lower the floodwaters. My Lord, hear us now, we *will* be good! May it be so!"

As the others around her echoed, "May it be so," Karina whispered, *"Savvan."*

After prayer, she hurried back to the *Vengeance* for roll call.

The unconscious sailor showed no sign of waking.

Karina knocked on Jonah's door. Without waiting for a reply, she nudged her way inside. Jonah was at his desk with his nose in a book. He glanced up at her, but he was quick to return to his reading when she bypassed him and made for his library.

Spanning the entire length of the backmost bulkhead, Jonah's impressive library was one of the few things he splurged on. Karina encouraged his collection. It gave him reason to keep living. It gave him purpose. He'd struggled with living, with purpose, plenty in the past.

Books sat fitted tight on each shelf, secured with an iron guardrail to keep them from falling whenever the ship rocked. She brushed her fingers over the spines as she eyed each title.

Three minutes of searching passed before Jonah asked, "What are you looking for?"

"Medical books."

"Second-to-bottom shelf, third section from the right."

Karina's gaze fell to where the captain pointed, and she knelt, pulling a few books from their cozy homes. She tucked them under her arm. "Thanks."

"Anything to get you out of here faster." His tone was not malicious. Quite the contrary—it carried a subtle trace of humor.

She stuck her tongue out and slipped out without another word.

Back in her cabin, she flopped onto the beanbag chair in the corner, one of her favorite ancient finds. Its orange plastic coating flaked off in spots, but whoever took it from its underwater home had refurbished it well. One book at a time, Karina searched for useful information. She found nothing noteworthy. Finding answers was a challenge when she didn't know the problem.

An hour later, she glanced up to find Jonah hovering in the doorway. How long had he been standing there? She waved him in. "Boots off, please. You always track grime on my rug."

Jonah complied with a sigh. As he stepped in, his gaze flitted over to the pile of blankets on the floor, where she'd been sleeping for the past few days. He didn't comment, so neither did she. He sat on the edge of her cot, poking and prodding the stranger for a short while, his brows furrowed. Then, resting his elbows on his knees, he faced her.

"Karina," he said, "Even if they aren't a pirate—which I doubt—we can't help this person."

"Even if they *are* a pirate, which I doubt," Karina argued, "you were one, too, once. Do you have so little sympathy?"

Jonah avoided her gaze.

Karina pressed on. "I know it scares you, but this person needs us. What happened to the Jonah who picked up and helped each member of this crew, one by one?"

"Building a crew was your idea."

"Semantics. You helped. Listen, I know you don't want to consider it," Karina said, cautious, knowing she treaded dangerous waters. "But it's been eight years. The cabin at the end of the passageway is a waste of resources."

Jonah's eyes fell dark. He said nothing, his amber eyes glued to the floor at his feet. Karina knew she couldn't push him. The best she could do was plant the idea in his head.

"I'm not finding anything useful in the books," she said. The tension in Jonah's shoulders settled a touch.

"Not surprised," Jonah grumbled, his mood irreparably soured. "How are you faring?"

"Rough," she dared to admit. "I hate sleeping on the floor, and I'm at a loss."

"We can relocate them. You could wash your sheets. Sleep in your cot again."

"I won't let you put them in the brig."

"Fine." Jonah stood, kicked his boots on, and walked out, calling over his shoulder, "Keep sleeping on the floor."

3

???

Everything was hazy.

For a while, they floated in this nothingness, where all they heard was the ringing in their ears, all they felt was warmth. Wherever they were, it was cozy. The vague feeling of being swaddled in soft blankets lulled them into a sense of security.

Resting a little longer wouldn't hurt.

Something nagged them to get up, though. They peeled their eyes open. As they blinked away the blurriness, fading evening sunlight and colorful plants in hand-painted pots greeted them. A pink rug decorated the floor, a small desk was littered with papers and knickknacks, a giant tentacle...

They snapped to attention as their gaze settled on the massive, wriggling appendage, which had shattered one of the windows along the hull. They scrambled to their feet and stumbled with the sway of the ship. Yes, this was why their subconscious wanted to get them up—they were in danger.

Above the door hung a decorative cutlass. Whoever owned it would be unhappy, but...it was for self-defense, right? They dragged a chair over, stood upon it, and wrestled the blade off its mount. Armed, they hopped down and pulled the door open.

They stood in a long passageway illuminated by buzzing electric lights. The bulbs flickered as a loud crash rattled the ship. As they made for the stairwell at the front of the passageway, the ship groaned and listed to one side. They stumbled. A barrel rolled down the passageway and crashed into the bulkhead. Wood splintered, and an assortment of sailing equipment spilled onto the coarse floor.

The tentacled creature screeched, and the ship settled upright. Balance once again tested, they tripped and fell. It was a miracle they did not stab themself on their borrowed sword. The steel edge ghosted against their cheek, a whisper away from slicing their skin.

They scrambled to their feet and sprinted above deck.

A gargantuan squid-like creature towered over the ship, taller than the highest mast. The small crew looked overwhelmed and terrified. Giant tentacles cornered five people by the bow. Gripping their borrowed blade, they ran headlong into the fray and sliced a tentacle clean off the beast's body. It howled. Icky violet blood sprayed the deck.

"They're awake!" a female voice exclaimed.

"Stay focused!" another voice, deep and gruff, snapped back. "Faye, cannons!"

They weren't sure who spoke—there were more important things to worry about than pinning a voice to its corresponding face. They slashed through another tentacle, trying to blink back their residual light-headedness.

"On it!" A tall woman with brown skin and boy-short, choppy chestnut hair crossed their field of vision. She hurried toward one of the few intact cannons. She primed, loaded, and fired. The cannonball blasted straight through another tentacle.

The sea monster reeled back, and the crew scattered. One, a chubby, fair-skinned young woman with sandy brown hair held back with a red and white bandana, grabbed them by the arm and yanked them away before another tentacle slammed onto the deck.

"You took my sword, I see."

"Sorry." Their throat ached as they spoke. Their voice was low, raspy. When was the last time they'd used it?

"It's okay! We're grateful for your help."

The sailor they assumed was Faye fired another cannonball, which slammed against the creature's skull. A few loud pops followed as another crew member fired a few rounds from her long-snouted rifle.

With the creature's attention focused on the gunners, they—much to the chagrin of the woman whose sword they wielded—hopped atop the tentacle and ran, using it as a slimy, undulating bridge.

"What are you doing!?" Bandana Woman yelled. They did not reply.

A single eyeball the size of their entire body, if not larger, locked its gaze on them. It flailed, and they scrambled to keep their balance. The tentacle was too slimy. Their foot slipped. They fell.

They drove their sword into the tentacle. It sliced through the flesh and slowed their downward momentum. They dangled as the monster screeched in anguish. Deep violet blood dripped down the length of the blade and stained their hands. Their skin seared as though they'd touched acid. With a grimace, they climbed back onto the sea monster's limb.

They sprinted for the creature's face and drove their blade into its eyeball. It screeched, high-pitched and ear-shattering. There was no avoiding the onslaught of blood that sprayed from the wound and burnt their sensitive skin, the sensation familiar for reasons they couldn't quite place. They dove away on instinct and hurtled toward the ocean below.

Scrambling to find a grip on something, *anything,* their hands found nothing but salty, humid air. They've fallen before, somewhere high, fast, wind whipping through their hair as they plummeted. The powerlessness, the impending sense of doom, was familiar. The dying creature collapsed into the water before they did—the resulting wave overtook them and pulled them under.

At least the ocean water washed away the acidic violet blood.

The ocean's current battered their body. They couldn't swim. They didn't know how. Each clumsy stroke sapped their waning energy, the surface growing farther from reach, the promise of air becoming a distant dream. Their lungs ached. They pushed for the surface, frantic, but their limbs were heavy like lead. Dark spots dotted their vision.

Someone grabbed them and pulled them upward. When their head breached the surface, they gasped and wheezed. They met Bandana Woman's worried gaze. She helped them to a rickety rope ladder, and with shaky limbs, they climbed. The rope was slick with seawater. Their foot slipped off a rung, and their forehead knocked against the hull. They caught themself, squeezing the ladder tight enough to render their knuckles pale, and finished climbing.

When they returned aboard, the tall ginger-haired man grabbed a fistful of their shirt collar, pulling it so tight it constricted their throat. They coughed. Choking was no better than drowning.

"Jonah!" Bandana Woman gasped.

"Who are you?" This was the voice who'd been barking orders. It was deep, gravelly, gruff. They flinched—they could see it in this man's eyes: he wished they'd drowned.

A strand of ginger hair fell in front of his face. It was long on top, parted down the middle, but shaved short on the sides. Jonah was tall, much taller than them, and his muscles strained against the sleeves of his black tee. He cut an intimidating figure.

"Um—"

Bandana Woman wedged herself between them and Jonah, forcing him to let go of them. "We would've sunk if not for them. Give them space."

Jonah grumbled something indiscernible.

The other crewmates, though wounded and exhausted, rushed over. The cannoneer, Faye, hugged them so tight she squeezed the air out of their lungs. *For one minute, could these people give me space?*

"Ohmygosh!" she exclaimed. "You were so cool!"

They squirmed. Faye snickered and released them. Their legs trembled, unreliable as their adrenaline faded. One knee gave out, and Bandana Woman caught them before they could collapse. She, at least, knew to be gentle.

"Hey, give them some space. Go clean up, will you, Faye? And Willow, patch up Mouse's cut." Bandana Woman ordered. "Let's go sit down, yeah? I don't want you falling over."

She helped them to a fire pit surrounded by iron. As they sank onto a bench, she struck a match, tossed it in the pit, and settled in the seat across from them. The flame illuminated her face in the dying evening light. The captain sat beside her with his arms folded.

Best to start by establishing a rudimentary layer of trust. They handed their borrowed sword to the woman. She smiled and wiped seawater off its blade.

"Okay," she said. "First off! My name's Karina, and the grumpy guy is Jonah, our captain."

Jonah scoffed. "Don't waste our time. They don't need to know our names. They'll be off our ship soon enough."

"I'm sorry about him." She shook her head. "He's standoffish, but his heart is in the right place. He doesn't take well to change."

They weren't sure what to say, so they said nothing.

"So," Karina continued, "tell us about yourself!"

They blinked. They hadn't thought much about their own identity since they'd awoken. Staring down at their hands, they dug as deep as they could.

Who were they?

They were silent for a little too long. Jonah and Karina stared at them. They were lightheaded and woozy. The ship's rocking didn't help their malaise.

"I don't, uh...I don't know."

Jonah stood. They flinched. "You don't know?"

"Jonah!" Karina snapped. "At least thank them for saving our lives!"

Jonah eyed them up and down. His frown showed no sign of relenting. "We could've handled it on our own."

"We would've been monster food!" Karina rubbed her temples, then turned back to them. "We'll start slow. Do you know your name?"

They squeezed their eyes shut and racked their empty, clouded mind. Did they have a name? They must. When they opened their eyes, they shot Karina a hopeless look and shook their head.

"We have to call you something," she said.

"We'll call them Stranger," Jonah muttered.

"What kind of name is that?"

"It's okay," Stranger piped in. "It's better than nothing."

Karina placed a hand on their shoulder. "We'll come up with something better, I promise."

"Sure."

Stranger paused to observe the crew. The sun had set, leaving the deck dark, though a few dim lightbulbs at the stern illuminated the space enough to discern silhouettes. The sniper, a young woman with deep black skin and long locs, finished cleaning up the blond boy's injured arm. She slung her rifle over her back and hurried downstairs. She returned with glass jars and gathered the blood seeping from the severed tentacles. Faye heaved a few tentacles overboard, though she dragged two of the smaller ones somewhere below.

Karina clasped her hands together. The sound jolted Stranger. "Is there anything you remember? Anything at all?"

Recalling memories made their head throb. "Not much. I fell, but I don't know from where. Someone pulled me out of the water and threw me in his brig. My memory gets hazy after that. Next thing I know, I'm breaking out and running. I dove into the ocean because I had nowhere else to go but needed to get away."

Stranger locked their gaze on the point where the dark ocean met the inky black sky. Silence reigned, and they were grateful neither Karina nor Jonah said a word.

"And then you..." Their voice came out no louder than a whisper. "You pulled me out."

"What did the man look like?" Jonah's frustration spiked the anxiety in Stranger's chest.

"I don't remember much. He was tall. He had a graying beard, and, um...missing a hand, I think. Prosthetic."

"Argo," both Jonah and Karina growled. Jonah looked off-put by the name, a heavy wince gracing his sharp face.

"Argo?"

"Nobody knows his real name. Most call him Argonaut the Lawless."

"He's a menace in the northern seas," Karina added when Jonah's explanation offered nothing of value. "Nastiest man any of us have ever met. Do you remember anything else?"

"No. Nothing."

"Sea monsters aren't supposed to exist," Jonah muttered. "They sure as hell didn't before you showed up."

Karina frowned. "Now, now, Jonah. The Book of Death says—"

"Fiction."

The moon and stars glowed overhead. Stranger stared up at them. Tracing patterns in the stars soothed them. "The Book of Death," Stranger said, their voice airy. The title struck them as familiar. The fog of amnesia obscured it, but it was less out of reach than any detail about their own self.

"One of four holy texts," Karina said. "The Books of Death, Tide, Fire, and the Wilds."

Something in the back of their mind nudged them toward each god's name: Death, Einari, Elaine, Novika. Midir's dwindling population revered them.

"Farmstead Isle is close," Jonah snapped, cutting the conversation short. "We'll go into debt to pay the docking fee, but we're getting repairs, and we're leaving Stranger on the pier."

"Jonah! This isn't their fault!"

"Karina, get some rest. I expect all hands at first light. We need to get as many repairs done as we can ourselves. And *you,*" he said. "You're coming with me."

Jonah gripped Stranger's bicep and pulled them to their feet. Stranger had no energy left to struggle, so they stumbled behind him. He took them two levels below deck and shoved them into a cell. They braced for pain, like fire flowing through their veins: agonizing, brutal, debilitating.

But pain never came.

As Jonah vanished from sight, Stranger curled up on the cold iron cot, yearning for the soft blankets they'd awoken in. They'd taken great risks to escape from... What was his name? Argonaut. And yet, here they were, on a different ship, in another brig.

Were they fated to never know themself? To never know freedom?

4

"Wait—I'm slipping!"
—The Grand Catalogue of Last Words: Great Flood
Era. Death #2,614,326,001. Head trauma. At the gates
of Judgment, she stated, "My uncle was a mountain
climber. Now, we have all become mountain
climbers."

14th Storm, Great Flood 1058

Jonah took immense pride in his wooden ship. Most in the Great Flood era were built of steel. The vessel had once belonged to his adoptive father, before he died of cancer ten years ago. He had inherited the ship, and for two subsequent years, he and Soph alone sailed it. At the time named *Charlotte* after some woman Jonah didn't know, the ship became the most valuable thing Jonah owned.

But now, as the *Vengeance* limped toward Farmstead Isle, the wooden vessel was a burden. Trees were as rare a commodity as the land they grew on, and repairs would cost him most of his savings. Making the money back would be a pain. He shuddered at the idea of selling at a hub.

Jonah categorized damages based on urgency. The hull was top priority, and the deck needed to be walkable. Something about the rudder's alignment didn't seem right—the *Vengeance* drifted westward when the wheel sat straight. Everything else deemed nonessential, however, could wait until landfall.

Jonah spent his morning patching a leak in the hold. Water gathered at his shins, soaking his slacks. The nagging musk of mildew was already pungent in the air.

He struggled to wrap his mind around it all as he hammered a slat of spare wood steadfast against the leak. Whatever sea creature it was, Jonah knew of no documented name. The ocean was vast and unexplored, so Jonah wasn't quick to jump to a conclusion of monstrous origin, though it was odd. Jonah had never seen a creature bigger than his own ship, save for the occasional whale.

He couldn't help but think of Soph. If she'd seen this creature, what would she have thought?

Her excitement wasn't difficult to imagine. Sophie Morgan had always loved fables. Tales of heroes and monsters, of gods and their divine golden blood. Jonah seldom shared her sentiment, but on many an occasion she would sit him down, tell him her favorites. He loved her, so he listened. Sometimes.

She seemed to most adore the story of the Great Flood. He remembered, clear as day, one of the countless times she sat him down to recount such a tale. Soph was nothing if not persistent.

"The God King Einari once walked vast continents in a mortal body," Soph told him. *"Continents! Land as vast as the oceans! Wouldn't that be so cool to see?"*

"I guess so."

Soph wore a cheery blue dress that day, her long ginger hair held away from her face with a headband in a shade of green Jonah would never dare wear. He preferred muted reds and browns and grays, but Sophie couldn't stand any color that wasn't bright and eye-catching.

The Book of the Tide sat in her lap, unopened. The tome was thick, dense, and heavy. She had no intention of opening it, but she kept its comforting weight in her lap.

"You know the whole story about the collapsing building, how he saved the little girl, how his blood healed her wounds, blah blah blah," Sophie rambled with a playful roll of her eyes. *"The main takeaway is the blood. I mean, the stuff can cure wounds! Heal illnesses! Prevent death! It's amazing!"*

"You still believe that? Nothing can magically cure death. Mixing blood is unsanitary, anyhow."

"I didn't say cure death, I said prevent," Sophie said. *"You'll believe it, too, one of these days."*

Maybe, if Jonah had a vial of God's Blood at the time of Sophie's murder, she would still be with him. But he hadn't. Gods and monsters didn't exist, and they never would.

Jonah drove another nail into the slat of wood.

Faye bounded in and out with a bucket, draining the hold of its accumulated water. Jonah was grateful for her presence. Her arrival snapped him from his thoughts before they could spiral too far.

"Faye," Jonah addressed as she sloshed through the water for another bucketful. "Could you pass the tar?"

On a shelf to Faye's right was the metal tin, its exterior coated with drips of old dried tar from previous uses. Some of it, dried around the rim, ensured the lid did not sit firm atop it. She passed it over. He dipped two fingers into the tin and slathered a generous amount around the repair site to seal it. The tar was gritty and sticky. He grimaced.

Jonah handed the tin back. Faye placed it on the wrong shelf, then scooped another bucket of water to take outside. Jonah gestured to stop her. He dipped his tar-covered hands into the bucket and scrubbed the filth from his skin. Once his hands were as clean as he could get them, he waved her off. He moved the tar to its proper place one shelf higher and stepped out of the hold.

Two flights of stairs had never been so exhausting. Jonah's legs burned with each step. The hot, humid storm season air was no more refreshing than the *Vengeance's* stuffy hold.

Jonah observed his crew, not eager to get back to work. His slacks were still drenched with seawater, and the rest of him, with sweat. Faye dumped her bucket's contents over the side of the ship. To port, Willow futzed with the cannons, and at the helm, Mouse recalibrated the rudder. Beside the mainmast, Karina sat hunched, riveting steel sheets to the damaged deck. All crew accounted for.

A flash of movement from above caught his eye. He turned his gaze upwards, landing on a form perched atop the mast, far above the crow's nest. Stranger.

"What the hell are they doing?" Jonah stalked over to Karina. His gaze flitted up to Stranger, then back to his first mate, fixing her with a hot glare.

"They wanted to help."

"You can't—" Jonah groaned and rubbed his temples. "Take them back to the brig. They're our prisoner."

"No."

Loath as he was to admit it, Karina was right. The *Vengeance*, unlike most ships in Midir, did not have an electric or combustion engine—Mouse wished to remedy the issue, but his success had been slim thus far. For now, the ship relied on the wind.

The sails were torn and falling loose from their rigging, and the yards had splintered, rendering it a treacherous climb. Jonah didn't have a single crewmate who enjoyed climbing the mast. The prisoner's labor solved the problem.

Stranger dangled from the main topgallant yard by a fraying rope tied around their waist. They wore a scrap of white cloth on their head to catch sweat and prevent overheating.

"I figure," Jonah said, changing tack, "we can sell the remnants of the animal." He couldn't bring himself to say *monster.* "Someone who believes in it will pay well. Maybe we can get by without going into debt."

"I don't think we should."

"Why not?"

"It might get into the wrong hands. I know you don't care, but you've at least heard the most famous story from the Book of Fire, haven't you? About the blood of a monster?"

"You're right," Jonah said. "I don't care. There are more immediate concerns. Would you rather be indebted to the land folk?"

"I suppose not."

"Let them believe something mythological is going on. It'll get us the money we need. Now, quit gawking. If Stranger falls, it's their problem, not ours."

Jonah craned his neck to watch Stranger work. Their stitches were sloppy and poor, but they did the job. Despite the strain of such a task, they smiled. Jonah couldn't for the life of him figure out why. The masts were tall enough to prove dangerous, and fixing the sails was not easy work. His crew was smart to dislike it, and Stranger, Jonah wagered, was a fool.

"I'm not gawking," Karina said with a snicker. "You are."

Jonah gritted his teeth and tore his gaze away. He didn't trust them.

Nobody in their right mind rescued someone this close to Anui waters and expected them to not be affiliated with piratekind. Their claim of memory loss did not help their case. What was Stranger's angle? Were they Argonaut's spy? Were they pretending, hoping to catch the unsuspecting crew off guard? Was Jonah going to wake up one day with a knife to his throat? All Stranger claimed to remember was Argonaut. Anyone affiliated with him was bad news.

Jonah knew better than anyone. The year he spent dedicated to Argonaut's cause was a year of his life he'd never get back.

Stranger acted innocent. They had a handsome face and a skittish demeanor—they already had Karina wrapped around their finger. Jonah wasn't going to let them fool him. He'd rather have his crew hate him than have his crew dead.

Quit generalizing, Jonah could almost hear Soph say. *You don't know anything about them.*

Not knowing anything is reason enough not to trust them, he imagined himself arguing.

He spent the remainder of his morning trying to calculate the cost of repairs. When he reemerged from his cabin around midday, the crew had paused their work for lunch—and Stranger, for some bizarre reason, remained atop the mast. They sat in the crow's nest, their gaze fixed on the horizon. What were they doing up there? Scheming?

Do they look like they're scheming? Soph would ask. *No. They're enjoying the breeze. It's hot out. Give them a break.*

Today, Willow took up cooking duty. She loaded each plate with two slices of stale bread topped with tuna and pickled cucumber. Jonah was about to settle down and take a bite of his lunch when he spotted mold on his slice of bread. He scraped the tuna onto his shell plate and tossed the slice overboard.

"Karina," Jonah said. "We need fresh bread."

"I can bake some," she said. She stood behind the bench, her gaze trained upwards.

"Do we have flour?"

"Lots. Down in the hold."

"The hold flooded."

"Oh. We can get some on the island, then."

Karina's presence in his periphery irritated him. Why hadn't she sat down? He opened his mouth, ready to snap at her.

"Stranger!" Karina called before Jonah could get a word out. She waved for them to come down.

Jonah stifled a groan as Stranger descended. He wasn't eager to spend his lunch dealing with them.

"You haven't eaten anything all day," Karina chided when Stranger's feet hit the deck. She ushered them to the fire pit and pushed a plate of tuna into their hands.

Stranger was odd in a way Jonah wasn't sure how to put into words. They did not carry the typical demeanor of a pirate, but Jonah wouldn't let that fool him. It could be a performance.

Nonetheless, they *had* contributed to the repairs.

"Thanks to Stranger fixing our sails," Jonah admitted, reluctant to thank the prisoner. "We'll make landfall within the week. The remains of the creature we fought might pay our docking fee, but be prepared to surrender coin, as we'll need to pay for lodging and repairs, too."

"Yessir," the crew echoed.

5

Though the butterflyfish is a global symbol of authenticity, keep close watch for forgers. Counterfeit glass will have cracks from amateurish carving. Counterfeit shells often feature missed patterns, so keep a close eye on the number of scales...
—Midir International Treasury

18th Storm, Great Flood 1058

The morning before landfall, the crew went about their daily tasks with their heads hung low. Jonah seemed to be the only one among the crew in good spirits. He stood with a tall posture and a resolute expression. He wasn't *happy,* as Stranger doubted the man had any capacity to be, but he wasn't as sour.

They did not join the crew at the fire pit for breakfast, opting instead to linger at the bow, watching the looming island grow ever closer. Willow brought them a brittle shell bowl. The mushy oats and deep brown, gooey molasses gave the food an unappetizing appearance. They didn't touch it.

The *Vengeance* docked within the hour. As Faye lowered the anchor, three tall men dressed in ruffled white shirts dropped a gangplank into place. They boarded the *Vengeance* without permission.

"Novika blesses you this morning, boys!" The boisterous leader of the trio addressed the crew, despite half the crew being women. "Looks like you've taken quite a bit of damage here."

"Indeed," Jonah said, unfazed by the feigned cordiality.

"You have coin?"

"I can make a barter."

"We don't do trades. Coin, or you best be on your way."

Stranger expected more brutish people at the docks. These men looked...not soft, not weak, but they held a different kind of power.

From head to toe, they were drenched in wealth, from their silver necklaces down to the gold buckles of their custom-cobbled shoes. They intimidated Stranger.

Jonah said nothing as he retrieved three glass jars of deep violet from his satchel.

"Monster Blood," gasped the shortest of the three. He clasped his hands together and uttered a prayer.

Stranger strained to make out his words but caught nothing. They didn't need to hear, though, to know just how unholy this substance was, to understand why this man prayed. They felt it in the deepest recesses of their soul. They took a tiny step back, anticipating the acidic sting Monster Blood left upon their flesh.

When the dockworker finished praying, he said, "We'll take it at one-fifth of the going price for God's Blood. Three hundred glass."

"A fifth," Jonah echoed. "Why?"

The man shot Jonah a peculiar look. "Are you dense?"

"If *atheist* and *dense* are synonyms."

"I'd wager it's fake," said the second. "Can't trust oceanfolk."

Jonah tossed the leader one of the three jars. With a quick *pop,* the man uncorked it and dipped a finger into the thick, murky ichor. It coated his fingertip to the first knuckle. He brought it to his lips. Stranger winced. Didn't it hurt him?

"We'll take all three and allow passage for two days."

"Two days?" Jonah balked. "It's got to be worth more."

"Take it or leave it, *sea slug.*"

"Give us one week, and we'll throw in a few severed tentacles from the creature it came from. In case you're worried it's not genuine." He gestured for his crew to retrieve the trophies. Willow and Faye ran off.

Jonah stood firm. Stranger found it admirable. Few things seemed to scare the captain. Maybe nothing at all.

"Now, I'd hate to be *rude.* You asked why Monster Blood is less valuable," the leading dockman mused. "Its beauty is the harm it could bring a god. Thus, its value is limited to a narrow set of circumstances, and most folk are far too devout to fathom slaughtering a divine, should one set foot in Midir."

"Gods aren't real."

"Ah-ah-ah! Neither are monsters, huh, boy?" The leader wore a wide, sardonic grin.

Jonah shook his head.

When Willow and Faye lugged the tentacles across the deck, painting a long streak of violet in their wake, Jonah said, "Do whatever you want with them. I don't give a damn. Give us a week."

"I suppose it could be arranged," the leader agreed.

"And this," Jonah tossed him a sack of coins. "To pay for the repairs."

The leader produced one glass coin from the bag and inspected it. He traced his thumb over the carvings with great care, eyeing each shape upon the coin. He placed it back inside and tossed the sack in his hand, up and down, up and down, up and down.

Stranger nudged Karina with their elbow.

"Why is so much worth a week's stay?" they whispered.

"That's how islands fend off overcrowding."

Before Stranger could reply, Jonah turned to the crew and barked something about pooling together coin for lodging. The entire crew, save for Stranger, scattered.

They stood with Jonah. Alone. They shrank under his firm gaze.

"You," Jonah snapped. "Get out of my sight."

Stranger's heart caught in their chest. They opened their mouth to say something, anything, but their words died in their throat. They glanced out at the island. Farmstead Isle was so tiny, they could see the opposite shore.

"Go on. Shoo."

Tentative, Stranger crossed the rickety gangplank. When their feet settled on the pier, they wobbled, trying to find their balance on unswaying ground.

Stranger's feet dragged as they walked.

Stonework buildings lined the streets. The islanders squeezed farmland wherever there was space—tiny yards, terraces, and rooftops thrived with plant life. Oats, vegetables, wheat. Stranger veered off to the side of the path and knelt. The grass was soft, warm, and damp with dew. They brushed their thumb over a buttercup's delicate yellow petals. The islands didn't seem as horrible as Jonah made them out to be. They sure were pretty.

"Ugh." Someone's groan startled them. They hopped to their feet as two women in lavish, flowy dresses marched by, the *clik-clik-clik* of their high heels punctuating every step. "Has he never seen grass before? Yikes."

The second woman snickered. Farmstead Isle's beauty paled.

Stranger trudged onward, their head low. No matter how small they made themself, their presence was an eyesore. To the rich, the poor were a stain. Stranger yearned for the *Vengeance's* safety. The crew made them feel like they were worth something—even Jonah treated them like royalty in comparison.

That night, while the crew of the *Vengeance* slept in comfy beds at an inn, Stranger curled up under a bridge, using a rock as a pillow.

Frigid ocean water churned around them. The cold settled deep in their bones, so profound that their body could no longer shiver. They clung to a sheet of ice, floating upon the choppy waves, its biting frozen sheen their salvation from drowning.

In the foggy evening haze, a hand against their bare bicep burnt like hot embers. A man, tall and imposing, clung to a ladder descending a steel dreadnought's hull. Their rescuer hoisted them over his shoulder and hauled them aboard.

"You're lucky I found you," a deep, scratchy voice crept into their fuzzy, muffled hearing. "Otherwise, you'd be as good as dead."

A firm hand pressed them flush against the frigid metal deck. Something sharp poked at the crook of their elbow. They squirmed as much as their worn-out body would allow. Fear rose in their throat.

"Don't worry," the man said, his thumb pressing the syringe's plunger. "This won't hurt one bit."

Stranger shot upright with a shout as burning pain flowed through their veins. When they regained their bearings, they squinted into the blinding beam of a flashlight.

"This is private property," the flashlight's owner said. "I'll let you off with a warning. Get lost, slug."

A boot nudged them in the ribs, not aggressive but not friendly either. They forced their aching body to stand. The flashlight clicked off. Stranger rubbed their eyes. A man in a well-ironed shirt stared at them. His badge shone under the light of the moon.

"You have a home, boy? A job?"

"N-no, sir," Stranger whispered.

"Then get off my island. You don't belong here."

They wanted to.

Four dreadful days passed. Stranger found they most preferred the solitude of pre-dawn. At this hour, the streets were barren. They walked with no destination. Their legs ached and their eyelids drooped, but they would get in trouble for loitering again if they stopped.

Sometime after the sun made its ascent, Stranger stood before a tall, peculiar building, fitted with a bell tower atop one of the many spires. Large wrought-iron doors marked the entryway, the dark metal standing out against the white stone walls.

A wrinkled man with gray hair and a cane hobbled past Stranger, and in a rush of confidence, they cleared their throat. "Excuse me, what is this building?"

"This is our temple."

"Temple?" Stranger repeated.

"The temple." The man's words were slow as though he were speaking to a child, or someone who did not fully understand his language. "Where people go to pray. You ever heard of a god before, boy?"

"Oh. Uh, yeah."

"Then leave me be. I wish to get a good seat."

"Sorry."

Stranger's curiosity got the better of them. Knowing they risked punishment, they slipped inside and pretended they belonged there.

They stood in the entry, stunned. Rows upon rows of long pews lined the nave, occupied by people with their heads down in prayer. The pews were built of a rich, saturated brown wood—the kind of wood that boasted wealth all on its own. Stranger's gaze trailed up the arched walls to the ceiling, so high they felt as though they were gazing at the Heavens itself. A vibrant mural spanned the entire ceiling.

The mural featured, at the forefront, the goddess of the wilds, painted in the rich browns and greens of their Domain, their dark skin and braided hair standing out against the lighter, more muted tones surrounding them. Other gods knelt as though to praise them, the god of the ocean and the goddess of fire to each side. Another stood beside the goddess of fire, but the paint had worn away, leaving them unrecognizable. Time had taken its toll, and these folk did not consider that segment of the mural worth restoring.

The sun shone through massive stained-glass windows, casting shimmering yellow and green light upon their skin. Even as islanders shoved past them, annoyed they occupied the walkway, they felt safe here.

"Gorgeous, yeah?" A familiar voice snapped Stranger out of their reverie. Karina.

"Yeah."

She tucked her hands in the pockets of her slacks. "It's a shame land so pretty is inhabited by people so awful. The rolling hills, the architecture..."

"How are repairs?"

"They're ahead of schedule. The guys at the pier were impressed by the Monster Blood we gave them. They've been working through the nights." Karina let out a tiny sigh. "It scares me. I can't shake the feeling we're going to be the catalyst ending with a dead god."

Their gaze fell. Karina's latter remark did not strike them; they were too focused on the former. Once the *Vengeance* left, they would be trapped. They would starve and wither away and die.

"Hey, look at me," she said. Stranger met her gaze. "I'm going to do everything in my power to get Jonah on your side. Okay?"

They appreciated her effort, futile as it was. "Thank you."

"Sit with me."

Stranger followed her to the front of the nave and settled beside her in the second row of pews. Karina clasped her hands, closed her eyes, and prayed. Stranger, beside her, folded their arms across the back of the pew in front of them, resting their chin on their arms, and gazed ahead.

There was an altar upon the small stage at the front. Upon it was a glass case which protected an old book. A spotlight illuminated its torn, time-browned pages. *The Book of the Wilds,* they guessed. The scripture of Novika.

When Karina finished her prayer, she stood. "Come with me?" she asked, extending a hand. "I'll keep you company."

"I think I'll stay here a bit longer."

Karina nodded. "Keep close to the pier when you leave, okay? I want to be able to find you again."

"Sure."

Then, she was gone.

The last Stranger knew of the time was around noon. A priest climbed atop the stage and delivered a sermon about how building a culture of peace and love would prove they were worthy of the crops they grew. Stranger held back a bitter laugh. *How contradictory.* They loved each other, but they resented outsiders.

After the midday sermon, Stranger slumped forward and rested their head on their arms. The position was uncomfortable, but they managed to fall asleep. When they woke, their neck and back ached. They gazed at the book on the stage. People came and went.

An hour before sundown, a priestess stood upon the stage and gave a closing sermon, then urged patrons to wrap up their evening prayers. Stranger's heart sank. Even a place boasting safety could not keep its promise through the night. Stranger stood, stretched their legs, and trudged outside.

They lingered near the pier. Karina's request was Stranger's lifeline.

They hadn't seen her since morning. If the *Vengeance* wasn't so prominent on the shoreline, they would have worried the crew had left.

Stranger wandered the nearby streets. Nowhere seemed like a good place to settle, and they resigned themself to another sleepless night. Amid their thoughts, gaze glued to the ground in front of them, they spotted a single shell coin. They picked it up and turned it over in their hands. What was once a beautiful scallop had been filed down to a perfect circle. One side was smooth, and the other, ridged. On the smooth side sat a delicate carving of a fish. They tucked the coin in their pocket.

The inn wasn't far. Armed with some money, they could make their night a touch more comfortable. They approached the receptionist with shaky hands.

"Um," they tried. They presented the shell coin. "Can I get a room?"

The receptionist's face flattened into something unamused. "What is this? A joke?"

Stranger didn't understand. "I have money."

"A room costs one hundred of those, you know."

"This is all I have."

He scoffed. "Get lost, slug."

"Would you scorn Novika's gift of land by punishing those who need help?" they asked, recalling the earlier sermon. "Aren't they the reason you thrive? They wouldn't have wanted any of their patrons to suffer."

"Don't twist my faith against me, boy," he snapped. "Get lost, or I'll call the authorities."

Stranger ducked their head and trudged toward the exit. As they walked, they spotted Jonah on a couch in the common room. His amber eyes were trained on them, his mouth turned in a tight, ever-present frown.

They tore their gaze from the *Vengeance's* captain and slipped outside.

Stranger drifted back to the temple. They rounded the side of the building and sank against the wall. Exhausted, sore, and hungry, they closed their eyes.

6

"Damn this shoddy plastic kayak! What a piece of junk! I've barely been at sea two days, and it's already got a blasted hole!"
—The Grand Catalogue of Last Words: Great Flood Era. Death #4,136,572,093. Drowned.

20th Storm, Great Flood 1058

Karina stared at the ceiling from where she lay on the inn's firm, scratchy couch. Sleep was unattainable tonight, though Willow and Faye slept snuggled against each other on the bed across the room. Earlier, she spoke with Jonah about keeping Stranger around, but Jonah was stubborn in believing Stranger didn't belong on the *Vengeance*. He spouted his usual nonsense like, *"Stranger is a pirate,"* and *"we have no budget for an extra crewmate."* Karina saw straight through him. He wanted to justify his decision by making up convenient little lies. He didn't like Stranger's brand of different. He feared it, even.

Karina refused to let anyone be neglected. She knew the feeling. *Thanks, Ma and Pop.*

Her mind raced to come up with a way to convince Jonah. Stranger needed a home in the same way Faye needed a home when she stowed away; the same way Mouse needed a home when he broke free of his abusive family; the same way Willow needed a home when her ship was wrecked in a storm, all crew dead but her. Stranger needed a home in the same way Karina had needed a home, left to her own devices at as young as six. Jonah's big, beautiful ship was more of a home than she'd ever experienced before.

Willow and Faye slipped out of the inn at first light. Jonah knocked on the door fifteen minutes later. She knew it was him—his knock was rapid and firm.

"Repairs are finished. I'd like to leave soon," Jonah said when

Karina opened the door. His gaze shifted, peering into the room behind her. He frowned. "Where are Willow and Faye?"

"Outside," she said. Last she knew, they sat together on the bench out front, Willow's head against Faye's shoulder, hands clasped between them. Karina was not eager to disturb them—they seldom got time alone with one another amid the bustle of sea life.

Jonah nodded. He turned, but Karina wasn't so ready to let him walk off. "Hey, Jonah," she said. "Let's have breakfast together!"

Jonah eyed her—no doubt he sensed an ulterior motive—then nodded. Karina slipped on her boots and gathered the little satchel she'd brought ashore, which contained only a couple spare sets of clothing. She slung it over her back and hurried after him.

The little dining room was quaint and cozy, with wooden chair-rail molding and deep red walls. Karina chose a table underneath a crystal chandelier, no doubt salvaged from an ancient ballroom or casino. The table had space enough for three.

She leafed through the menu. While Karina always found the wealth of islanders to be distasteful, there was no beating island food. These folks had every resource at their fingertips. When a waitress came along, Karina ordered a breakfast pie, and Jonah ordered a slice of toast and an orange. Karina couldn't help but find amusement in his simplicity. *Classic Jonah.*

"So," Karina leaned forward, her forearms pressing against the table. "Let's dig into your psyche."

"I knew you wanted something. If this is about Stranger, the answer is no."

"Who did you grow up with?"

"My sister and my adoptive father. Never knew my biological father. My mother died in childbirth. Blah-blah-blah. Whatever."

"What would you say your greatest trauma is?"

He frowned. "Karina."

"Humor me."

"Watching my sister die." Jonah's blunt retelling was a sign of how far he'd come over the past eight years. The memory no longer shattered him. He still ached, but he had learned how to live with the ache. Grief never vanished—one adapted around it.

"And how did it affect you?"

Jonah stared.

"Come on," Karina urged. "Pretend I'm someone you're opening up to for the first time."

"I don't open up to new people."

"You opened up to me. I was a new person, once."

Jonah leaned back and closed his eyes, a grimace gracing his sharp features. Karina gave him time.

"Once you told me Argonaut was leveraging my grief," Jonah said, his words slow, heavy. "I didn't see a point in staying alive."

"Why?"

"Why the hell not?" She was my best friend! How the fuck was I supposed to go on?"

In the otherwise-empty dining room, his words echoed. Karina allowed the following silence to hang until the waitress brought them their breakfast. The breakfast pie was a triangular slice of egg, broccoli, and sausage. It was a marvel of baking. Karina wished the *Vengeance* had an oven. Maybe she could try to recreate it the same way she baked bread: in a covered pan over the fire.

"So," Karina continued. "Would you say losing Sophie is the root of your fear of loss?"

Jonah groaned. "I thought the conversation was over."

"It's never over, Jonah." Karina was surprised he had played along for this long. "Now, your fear of loss manifests how?"

"I don't know."

Liar. "Does it manifest in your resistance to forming new connections?"

Jonah said nothing. He peeled his orange.

"Is it why you refuse to allow anyone new onto your ship?"

"This *is* about Stranger," Jonah growled, his expression darkening. He stood, the legs of his chair scraping against the tile floor beneath him. "Knock it off."

Jonah gathered his breakfast and marched out of the room.

Karina found Stranger on the curb across from the pier. They sat slouched, elbows resting on their knees, their gaze pinned on the *Vengeance.* With no way off the island and no money, would the islandfolk throw them in jail and leave them to rot? She couldn't stomach handing them such a fate.

"Come on," she said. "I'm sneaking you aboard."

"What?"

Karina took their clammy hand and helped them to their feet. She led them to the pier. "We'll hide you in a barrel in the hold. Jonah won't know until we're far from shore. I'm not leaving you here."

"Karina," Stranger tried, "I appreciate the sentiment, but I don't want to impose. If the captain doesn't want me, I won't stick around. I'll be fine, I'll figure it out, okay?"

"They're right." Jonah's deep voice startled Karina. She gasped—she hadn't noticed him at the top of the gangplank. How long had he been there? "We're doing a headcount and leaving. Without Stranger."

Stranger offered Karina a smile, but it didn't reach their eyes. Behind their smile was fear.

"If you won't bring Stranger aboard," Karina snapped, "I won't work as your first mate anymore."

Jonah groaned. "Let's *go,* Karina. They'll charge us for another day if we're not out by the top of the hour."

She stomped aboard and took her post by the mooring lines. When Jonah gave the order to depart, Faye and Willow hoisted the anchor. Karina, though, stood by the lines and refused to untie them. If Jonah wasn't going to listen, she wasn't going to, either.

Jonah pushed past her and untied the lines. He shot Karina an icy glare.

Good, she thought, *be upset.*

A stiff breeze caught the sails, and they drifted to sea. Stranger sat cross-legged at the edge of the pier to watch them depart. Karina was surprised Jonah lingered by her side. Had he registered the gravity of his decision? Unease was written all over his face. *Good.* He was fighting with his conscience. His brow furrowed, and his mouth turned downwards. This wasn't an angry or an annoyed frown, though—this was the look he got moments before his directive flipped.

Come on, come on!

The pier grew smaller, farther away. Stranger remained there, and Karina figured they wouldn't move until long after the *Vengeance* was out of sight.

"What do you think the islanders will do to them?" Karina asked. "Lock them away? Force them into servitude? Sell them back to Argonaut?"

"Karina," Jonah growled through gritted teeth.

"They couldn't be a pirate, you know, because Argonaut isn't the type to keep his own ilk prisoner. He'd much rather *use* them, like how he used you. Remember?"

Jonah ignored her, his jaw set, his eyes fiery, intense. He glared at the pier for a little longer, then whirled around to face his crew.

"Drop the anchor," Jonah barked.

Relief rendered Karina's knees weak.

7

20th Storm, Great Flood 1058

What you're doing is wrong, Soph's voice echoed in the back of his mind. Even in death, she was his moral compass. *Stranger will die out there.*

They'll be fine, Jonah tried.

They won't. Imagining her crossed arms and the stern pout on her freckled face was not a difficult endeavor. It was haunting how similar Karina looked. In Sophie's stead, Karina Thorne had become something of a new sister. And oh, how swimmingly they would have gotten along...

Damn you, Soph. Damn you, Karina.

He dove off the stern and into the ocean. He threw all his strength into each powerful stroke. *This is uncalled for,* he thought. *Stranger can handle themself. Stranger will only cause problems. Stranger will be fine on their own.*

He lifted his head to take a gulp of air, and Stranger's surprised gaze locked onto him. Despite what Jonah considered to be his best judgment, he pushed onward.

He didn't need another crew member. He didn't need one more mouth to feed, one more voice adding to the hubbub of day-to-day life.

When Jonah reached the pier, he planted his hands on either side of Stranger's hips to stabilize himself. His nose brushed theirs. Their eyes were blue as the skies around them, glittering under the morning sun, wide with astonishment.

A million possible words swam through Jonah's head. *Karina was right. You can join our crew. If you put in the work, I'll give you a chance.*

"You look stupid sitting there," was what came out of Jonah's mouth. "You'll embarrass yourself."

"Oh, so you swam all this way to insult me one last time?" Stranger's voice was sharp, laced with the fear and hopelessness of a man abandoned.

"Don't flatter yourself," Jonah snarled. "I'm going to give you a choice."

"What—"

"Shut up. One: you stay here, and you figure your shit out on your own. If you're lucky, you'll starve to death before the landfolk sell you back to Argonaut. Two: you swim back to the *Vengeance,* and we'll... allow you to stay with us. *For now.*"

"I can't swim."

Jonah offered a hand. "Do you trust me?"

"No," Stranger grumbled. Nonetheless, they took his hand, and he pulled them into the water. Stranger's hands snaked tight around his waist. Swimming with another person clinging to his back was a challenge. His pace was slow, his movements hindered. He made do. Stranger's body trembled against him. What did they fear more: the prospect of drowning, or Jonah himself?

Willow tossed down the rope ladder. Jonah nudged Stranger toward it. They grabbed it like it was their lifeline and climbed. Once on the safety of the quarterdeck, Stranger braced their hands on their knees. Jonah ignored them as he pulled himself aboard.

Karina grinned.

"Shut up," Jonah snapped.

"I didn't say anything," she replied in a singsong voice.

"Let's get sailing. I'm sick of this place."

The crew hurried from the helm to the main deck, aware of their responsibilities. Good. Jonah wasn't in the mood to delegate. When Faye hesitated, Jonah waved her off with a stern glare.

Stranger wrung their hands. Jonah remedied their nerves by leading them down the quarterdeck ladder. When he reached the main deck, he thrust a mop and a bucket into their hands.

"Swab the deck."

The task wouldn't help them sail, but it would keep Stranger out of the way. Jonah stalked below deck. He left Stranger to stand alone, stunned, clutching the mop and bucket to their chest.

8

"I can't go on like this. We've lost everything to the Great Flood—our homes, our livelihoods. And... let's be honest. We're all going to die, anyways."
—The Grand Catalogue of Last Words: Great Flood Era. Death #0,045,752,598. Gunshot to the head. Self-inflicted.

20th Storm, Great Flood 1058

Sweat drenched Stranger's sun-hot black hair as they scrubbed the deck. They struggled with a grimy spot by the starboard hull, where water splashed above deck often enough to develop a thick layer of mildew. They didn't let the grueling labor discourage them—if they worked hard enough, they'd earn Jonah's respect.

After thorough scrubbing, the deck shone under the sun, though the unweathered wood from the repairs stood out like fresh stripes across the deck. *Could I paint it to match?* Jonah seemed the type to care about those details. *I could impress him.*

Reluctant as they were to bother the crew, they flagged Mouse down. He was the closest, and he looked as though he'd finished his work on the anchor's capstan. Stranger wasn't sure what exactly he had been doing.

"Is there anything I can use to paint the new wood?" they asked.

Mouse pointed to his ears and shook his head. He signed, "I'm Deaf."

Oh. "Sorry," they signed, quick and apologetic. Their fingers trembled—they were a nuisance even to the crew's youngest. "I'm looking for paint. So the new wood matches."

A tuft of wispy blond hair fell in front of Mouse's eyes, and he brushed it away. The teenager was overdue for a haircut. "You know Midiri Sign."

"I guess I do." Like spoken Midiri, the language came naturally to them.

Mouse smiled. "Come with me. We've got wood stain in the hold. Much better than paint."

Mouse led them to the hold. He approached a tall iron shelf in the back corner, obscured by a crate of potatoes and some sacks of flour. Standing on his tiptoes, Mouse reached to the back of the shelf and retrieved a half-used bucket of stain. He handed it to Stranger. "Brush it on," he signed once his hands were free. "Wait a bit, then rub the excess off with a rag."

Stranger nodded and got to work.

By the time they finished applying and wiping away the stain, evening loomed. They flopped on a bench by the fire pit, though they did not get more than a minute's rest before Jonah appeared above deck. Stranger took pride in the way he surveyed the deck, brows raised, thoughtful and, dare say, impressed.

Whatever he thought about Stranger's work, he did not express it aloud. Instead, he said, "Come with me."

He strutted below without sparing a glance to see if Stranger was following. Stranger scrambled to keep up.

Their destination was the door at the end of the cabin deck.

"You'll be needing a place to sleep," Jonah said. He pushed the door open and led them inside. "This... was Soph's room. I suppose it's yours, now."

"Soph," Stranger repeated.

Jonah grimaced. He hadn't meant to let the name slip.

Appease him. Don't be a nuisance. "I can sleep on the deck."

"No. You'll be unshielded from the weather, and you'd be an easy target should we get ambushed. Besides..." Jonah stepped into the cabin and trailed a finger along a white-painted dresser. His finger picked up no dust. "It's high time I sorted through her belongings."

Stranger looked around. The bulkheads were painted a playful shade of yellow, and the blankets upon the hammock boasted a gentle blue. The furniture appeared to all be in pristine condition, and the wardrobe was full of clothes, long unworn.

"I'll need an hour to clear it out," Jonah said with a flippant wave. "I just wanted to show you where it was. Go make yourself useful."

Stranger made for the door, though they faltered in the doorframe. "Uh, Captain?" they asked. They wiped their sweaty palms on their pants as Jonah gathered a handful of blankets and sheets.

"Hm?"

"Um, thanks."

Jonah did not reply, but he shot Stranger an acknowledging glance.

Stranger wasn't sure how to be useful, truth be told. They weren't a skilled sailor, as far as they were aware. What could they do? They didn't know how to load a cannon or rig sails. Jonah was right. They didn't belong here. As they made their way toward the staircase, they paused at what they presumed was Jonah's cabin. The door stood open. Stranger's curiosity got the better of them—they wandered in and peered around. Their heart hammered against their ribcage.

'I was familiarizing myself with the layout of the ship,' was the excuse Stranger practiced in their head as they snooped. They couldn't help but wonder: what made Jonah tick?

His cabin was tidy and sparse. A desk sat in the center, bolted to the floor to keep it from sliding with the rocking of the boat, and there was a small cot shoved off to the side like an afterthought. Behind the desk stood tall bookshelves, packed to the brim. Against their better judgment, Stranger snatched a book from the bottom shelf and hurried out.

Instinct told them to climb the mast. There, they wouldn't get in the way of those working on the deck. They settled in the crow's nest and made themself as small as possible. If anybody were to ask, they would say they were on lookout duty, though they spent their evening reading. The statement wasn't a lie. They kept an eye on their surroundings, though nothing but ocean stared back at them. The island they'd come from was a mere speck in the distance.

A bird landed on the floor beside them. It hopped around and pecked at the wood, searching for bugs. What a beautiful creature—it had crisp white feathers and a long beak. It stared at Stranger with beady black eyes, tilting its head as though to analyze them. Stranger watched it, enamored. *Peck, peck, peck.* They reached out with as gentle an intention as they could muster. Their fingers brushed over the soft plumage on the seagull's little head.

It cawed, spread its wings, and took to the sky once more. Stranger watched it with a smile.

The sun sank below the horizon. When it grew too dark to read, Stranger folded down a corner of their page and snapped the book shut. A stiff breeze ruffled their hair, bringing in the gentle cool of nighttime.

Below, Faye and Willow sparred with wooden swords. Karina and Mouse stood on the sidelines, holding a lantern with a dim bulb. From what Stranger understood about Willow, she was more attuned to fighting at a distance, using the long rifle she always wore slung over her back. Her instinct, Stranger noted, was to try to get away from Faye. But Faye exploited Willow's weakness. She stayed right up in Willow's face.

Swallowing their nerves, Stranger scaled down the mast and made their way to the group, taking their place beside Karina.

"Does this..." Stranger started. They faltered. "Does this sort of thing happen often?"

"When we can," Karina replied. "We try to do a different pair each spar. Keeps things interesting."

"Hmm."

"You want in? I could add you to the lineup."

"...I'd hate to impose."

"You're not imposing," Karina reassured, though her words did little to put them at ease. "I think it'd be good for all of us. We get too used to our own fighting styles, even when we try to switch things up. I think Jonah will be interested in seeing you in action again."

"I... Okay. Sure," they stammered. "Are fights—real fights—common?"

"They can be. We want to make a decent living, like most folks. But some have a different definition of *making a living* than others, so we must know how to defend ourselves."

"Oh." Stranger paused. "And how does one make a living?"

"Hub sales are the most common. Some people dedicate their lives to selling. I've seen it firsthand. It's not a trap I wish to fall into, so we sell as infrequently as possible. Fish, Willow's artwork, ancient trinkets from my collection... and Mouse does handiwork on other people's ships from time to time, though he doesn't get much business, because not many people trust a teenager with their engine system."

Willow had Faye in a headlock, and she held her there until Faye, who had spent all her energy trying to escape, tapped out. Willow released Faye and extended a hand to help her to her feet.

"Round two goes to Willow!" Karina exclaimed. "Congrats, girl! How do you feel?"

"Tired," Willow laughed. "Faye's good at wearing me out."

Stranger turned to Mouse and signed, "How many total rounds?"

"Three," Mouse signed back. "They both have one win. Next round takes the match."

"And what happens if you win?"

He shrugged. "Nothing, really. Loser owes the winner a small favor."

Faye downed her flask of water in four desperate gulps, and Mouse tossed Willow a towel to dry the sweat dripping down her brow.

"The third round is the most interesting," Karina said. "Everyone's tired, so it's a game of endurance more than strength."

"Unless you're up against Jonah," Faye chimed in. "Then you're hosed, because Jonah's got crazy stamina. It's inhuman. I think it's 'cuz pirates taught him to fight. He doesn't spar much, unless we ask him to, because he sorta... always wins."

"Pair me with Jonah," Stranger said before they could register it had come out of their mouth.

"Are you sure?" Willow asked.

"Y-yeah. I'm sure."

As Faye and Willow squared up to fight their third round, Mouse's inquisitive gaze found Stranger. "I'll see what I can do. He doesn't always *want* to participate," he signed. "Though I think he'd accept a spar with you."

Willow and Faye took their positions once more.

"You want to call it?" Karina asked Stranger. Stranger's nerves spiked. Inclusion was a strange feeling when all one had ever known was rejection.

"How do I—"

"Call out the round number and give a countdown."

"O-okay. Um. Round three!" Stranger called. "Ready, set... go!"

The combatants lunged into action.

Stranger crossed the cabin deck, their steps light and airy. Everyone else had long since retired for the night, but after the spar—which Faye had won—Stranger spent another hour or two leaning against the bow and reveling in the ocean breeze. Now, hesitant to wake anyone, they treaded with caution.

Once the cool night air came in and the excitement died down, their anxieties grew. In the silence, their mind wandered. Jonah had accepted them on board, reluctant as he seemed. They couldn't show any weakness, lest it give the captain a reason to change his mind.

Stranger bit their lower lip as they slipped into their cabin. Jonah hadn't seemed ready to clean the room out. There was no way he thought of Stranger as anything other than a complete waste of space. A waste of his time, too. The crew said Jonah has never lost a duel. Why the hell had they challenged him?

But if they were able to beat Jonah...

Maybe he'd find me worthwhile.

Stranger dumped their borrowed book on their shelf and climbed into the hammock. They'd finish reading tomorrow and return it before Jonah noticed its absence.

In the night, Stranger dreamt of falling.

Stranger joined Faye at the helm at dawn. They'd be damned if they didn't learn how to sail.

"Stranger!" Faye grinned at them. "Want to navigate?"

"If it's not too much trouble, could you show me how?"

They spent an hour with Faye. She explained how the helm connected to the rudder via a series of ropes running down through the

Vengeance's core. She taught them how to read a map and a compass. Stranger couldn't wrap their brain around reading a map, no matter how many times Faye explained it. The map was written in a language Stranger didn't recognize. Island names, hub names. One of the major regions, too, was undecipherable, but they recognized the other five. *Øsig. Suhin-Øsig. Erith. Suhin-Erith. Anui.*

Midir was nigh-endless ocean. The *Vengeance* could be anywhere. Yet, somehow, Faye seemed to know their location sat somewhere on the north end of the centermost region, which she called the Dead Zone. Based on the map in Faye's hands, it seemed this region had no islands—the reason for such a foreboding name.

Faye stepped out of the way to allow Stranger a chance to take the helm.

"We'll always be at the mercy of the wind," Faye explained. Stranger's arms trembled as they gripped the wheel. "For the most part, adjusting the angle of our rudders gets us where we need to be. We can't sail against the wind, though. Here—try turning."

Stranger turned the wheel sharper than necessary, overestimating its weight. The *Vengeance* listed toward starboard, and everyone aboard stumbled. Willow, who had to chase after a few renegade cannonballs rolling across the deck, shot Stranger an annoyed look. Stranger tensed, straightened the wheel, then backed away from the helm.

"Uh, m-maybe I'm not suited for navigation."

"Nonsense!" Faye chuckled. "You need practice. You should've seen me when I first learned. This was back when the crew was Karina, Jonah, and me. I'd never sailed an engineless ship before. I almost knocked Jonah overboard trying to steer around a wreckage site."

Stranger took another step back. They bumped into a warm body. With a sharp gasp, they whirled around to face Jonah, who stared, flat and unaffected.

"Ah, speak of the devil," Faye laughed. "You need to start announcing your presence instead of sneaking up like the first freeze of the year, dude. You're going to give poor Stranger a heart attack."

"Meet me in my cabin," Jonah said. Stranger didn't have a chance to reply before he stalked away, climbing down to the main deck and disappearing through the doors and downstairs.

"Oh, heavens," Stranger muttered, wiping their sweaty palms on their pants. "I'm in trouble, aren't I?"

"You're not in trouble," Faye laughed. "If he were mad at you, you would know."

"I'm pretty sure I know." Jonah's face was impossible to read. What was going on in his head? "He's mad, he wants me gone, I—"

"Hey, chill," Faye reassured Stranger. "You haven't seen him mad."

"I haven't?"

"You haven't. He just wants to chat. Don't keep him waiting."

Stranger hurried down the ladder.

"How's the book?" Jonah asked as Stranger stepped inside his cabin. He waved for them to close the door. They nudged it shut with their foot.

"I, um, I don't know what you're talking about." Their words came out sounding more like a question than a statement. Panic made them a bad liar.

"Sit."

Jonah gestured to the stool at the opposite side of his desk. Nerves coiled in Stranger's chest as they crossed the room and sat. They looked everywhere except the captain's face.

"My library is open to everyone," Jonah said, leaning back in his leather chair. "I can tell who took which books from my shelves. I know my crew. Mouse uses the technical manuals. He wrote most of them—he takes them to add more notes or for reference while making repairs. Karina's a fan of history books, Faye likes action-adventure, and Willow likes the texts about wildlife and art."

Jonah faced the bookshelf. He eyed it from top to bottom before landing on the little gap in the bottom shelf. He stared at it for quite some time.

"Tell me," he continued. "Can you read it, or are you looking at the illustrations?"

"Um...yeah? I can read it."

Jonah narrowed his eyes, then selected two books at random: the first was from the bottom shelf, next to the one Stranger had taken. He passed the book across the desk to Stranger. They took the book into their hands and ran their thumb across its damaged, dusty cover. No doubt this book, like most others on the bottom shelf, had seen better days.

"Tell me the title."

"Ashen Snow," Stranger read. They flipped it open and skimmed through the first page. "Looks like it's a collection of folktales from the Era of Fire, before Elaine's ascension."

Jonah gave them a peculiar look, something between confusion and interest. He extended his hand, and when Stranger handed the book back, he tucked it back into its spot on the shelf. He passed the second book to Stranger.

"Tell me the title."

Stranger didn't recognize this text. They flipped through the first few pages and eyed the illustrations of mountains and gemstones within. "It's...about rocks and landforms."

"The title, Stranger." Jonah's sharp growl startled them. With a squeak, they snapped the book shut.

"Um."

"You can't read this one."

"It's in another language," Stranger admitted. Under Jonah's firm gaze, shame surfaced. "No."

"Would you like to know the difference between these two books?"

"Well, one's about rocks, and—"

"Quiet," Jonah barked. Stranger winced. *"The Geological Essentials* is written in our common tongue, *Midiri.* But the other one? The one about, what did you say, the Era of Fire?"

Stranger nodded.

"The books I've placed on the bottom shelf are written in *Køveni.* The language of the ancients, Stranger. This language has been dead for millennia."

"Oh."

"I've been collecting them. I hoped someday I'd find a scholar who could translate them. Then you show up, and you can speak *and* sign Midiri with fluency, but cannot read it. Instead, you can read Køveni, and I presume you can speak it, too. Yes?"

"Um...yes."

"Say something." Jonah said, a brow raised in curiosity.

"Uhh," Stranger stammered, racking their brain for something to say. *"Fisig i seves lieni."*

Jonah stared.

"It... Um... I said, *'Your crew is kind,'"* they rambled, instinct urging them to fill the silence. "If you're interested in grammatical structure, though, a word-for-word translation would be more like, *'Kind is your crew—'"*

"Who the hell are you?"

"I don't know."

9

"How far, I wonder, will the sea rise? Einari, I beg you to show not wrath, but grace. I stand stranded upon my roof, and I pray you spare us..."
—*The Grand Catalogue of Last Words: Great Flood Era. Death #0,000,002,934. Drowned.*

24th Storm, Great Flood 1058

What started off as a calm Thursday morning atop the crow's nest turned hectic when Stranger glanced up from their book's well-worn pages. A ship drifted on the distant horizon, its trajectory toward the *Vengeance.* Until now, the seas had been empty. They tensed. Could it be Argonaut?

They scrambled down to the deck.

"Ship!" Stranger called when their feet touched down. "Ship on the horizon!"

Their cry startled Willow and Jonah, who knelt on the deck, weaving fishing nets. Karina hurried to the bow and held a spyglass to her eye. Stranger hugged their arms tight to their body.

"It's the *Burning Maiden!*" Karina exclaimed with a wide grin. "I'll send up a flare! Let's say hello!"

"Wait—" Stranger started. Karina whizzed past them, jogging to the quarterdeck. From there, she rifled through a crate and produced from within it a flare. Upon firing, a loud *pop* filled the air. Stranger flinched. Sunshine-yellow smoke billowed into the air.

Another, more distant pop echoed. Stranger's wary gaze turned to the unfamiliar vessel, and above it billowed the exact same shade. *A rudimentary language,* Stranger mused, intrigued. *A set of phrases or ideas, no more than ten, if the crew included black, brown, and white.* What did the yellow flare mean? Yellow was a friendly color—and judging by Karina's grin, the message sent must be one of welcoming.

Despite this, they couldn't help the anxiety pricking at their skin.

"Chill out, swabbie," Faye chuckled, clapping a hand on Stranger's back. "They're friends."

The allied ships pulled parallel to each other. Faye heaved a gangplank across, and someone on the other end tied the two ships together. Stranger clambered back up the mast. Instead of settling on the crow's nest, though, they opted to climb across the mainyard. There, they could eavesdrop but stay out of sight.

The *Burning Maiden* was a small sloop, driven by engine rather than mast, puny compared to the *Vengeance.* It looked agile and quick, but the lightweight build no doubt rendered its steel hull vulnerable. Stranger shuddered. They'd grown to hate steel.

Two women crossed the gangplank. They looked to be around Karina's age, somewhere in their mid-twenties. Their skin was brown, but not the same shade Faye's was, carrying a different regional undertone Stranger could not place.

"Nyx!" Karina exclaimed, pulling the shorter of the two into a tight hug. Nyx's glasses smushed against Karina's shoulder, offsetting them from her nose. "Oh, it's been so long! How have you been?"

"Quite well," Nyx replied. "The weather has been much too calm for storm season, though. Don't you think?"

"I'm happy to soak up the sunshine! Of course, between you and me, Jonah's the one who needs it more. He needs to quit sulking in his dungeon of a cabin all day."

She elbowed Jonah as he joined her side. He scoffed.

"And Ashe!" Karina turned to face the tall woman by Nyx's side. "You look different! Did you cut your hair?"

"No," Ashe chuckled. Her voice was deeper than Stranger expected it to be. "I've been styling it differently."

"Well, it looks pretty! Oh, and your vocal training sounds like it's been paying off!" Karina cheered. Her compliments left Ashe with a bright smile, bordering on giddy. "C'mon, it's almost lunchtime. Let's eat together."

Karina led the visitors over to the fire pit, gesturing for the rest of the crew to join them. Faye, Willow, and Mouse hurried over and found their seats. Jonah opted to stand, leaning his back against the railing, gazing away from the group.

The group gabbed amongst one another. Faye had taken the task of interpreting the spoken conversation for Mouse. The visitors didn't appear to know Midiri Sign.

"Wait, hang on." Karina looked around the deck behind her, searching. "We have one more."

Stranger winced.

"One more?" Ashe asked. "When you all took Willow in, I thought Jonah didn't want anyone else on his crew."

"Oh, trust me, he didn't."

Karina pointed up. When Ashe and Nyx's gaze followed, Stranger hoped the sail obscured the women's view.

"Stranger!" Karina called. "Come on down!"

They did not budge.

"I'm sorry about them," Karina said as she turned back to Nyx and Ashe. "They've been through a lot."

"Is their name really *Stranger?*" Nyx asked with a furrowed brow.

"They have amnesia. We don't know what to call them, so Jonah said to call them Stranger. It stuck, I guess."

"It's an unkind name."

"I've tried to think of other options, but nothing seems right," Karina admitted. "We'll find something. Right now, they need to focus on recovery. Their time on Farmstead Isle wasn't kind."

Stranger wasn't sure they liked being talked about. They shrank a little farther into the sail's shadow.

"They're a lot more skittish now," Willow said. She roasted a seasoned cod over the fire, which Nyx had ignited. Stranger hadn't seen any matches in Nyx's hand. "They didn't spend any longer than us ashore, but they had a rough time. You two know how it is."

"I see," Nyx murmured, sympathetic. "Land folk can be cruel—I left my homeland for a reason." Stranger frowned. *Nyx is from an island?* Why would she give up a cozy life in favor of toiling at sea?

Though Stranger was otherwise content to hide upon the mast, a pang of hunger eventually won over their nerves. They snuck down the mast and crept over to the fire pit, whose flame, at this point, was no more than a glow of embers.

"Have you heard about Argonaut?" Nyx asked, adjusting her glasses, which had slipped down the sharp bridge of her nose.

"What about him?" Mouse asked. Faye spoke his words aloud. "He's up to something new every week. It's hard to keep up."

"Rumor has it he's become a dealer of God's Blood," Ashe said. "Not a ton, but enough for word to get around."

"Nobody knows how he's going to use his profits," Nyx added. "Leave it to him to take something so pure and use it for something sinister."

"Oh, come on," Jonah growled. "What a load of shit. Gods don't exist, and if they did, their blood wouldn't have magical healing properties. It sounds unsanitary."

Stranger nabbed a steel skewer loaded with fish, which lay close enough to the dying fire to keep it warm. Stranger couldn't help but wonder if the crew had left it there with them in mind. As they reached for it, they bumped the skewer and knocked the fish from where it rested. They fumbled for it. After they managed to catch it, they looked up. All eyes turned to them, and they froze.

"Oh!" Karina exclaimed. "Come sit with us!"

"Uh."

"It's okay! Ashe and Nyx don't bite, I promise."

Stranger sank onto the bench beside Karina. Everybody stared at them. They did not say a word, instead pinning their gaze on the deck.

Nyx came to the rescue. "It's not a fairy tale, Jonah. My family was blessed by Elaine eons ago, though with each generation, our power fades."

"Blessed? Come on."

"Jonah, please," Karina grumbled. "You can't still be this apathetic, after the sea monster attack!"

"There must be a logical explanation. I'm not buying it. Some undiscovered deep-sea creature. Its blood is purple because of the pressure and lack of light at its native depth—"

"Oh, yeah? Then how was it alive at the surface?"

Nyx chuckled as the two leaders of the *Vengeance* bickered. Stranger met her pale yellow eyes. An odd color for a mortal.

Nyx seemed to read Stranger's mind—or she noticed they were staring. "I'd like to think my family's eyes were as bright as yours, once, back when Her Grace first granted us our blessing. My generation is the last to carry Elaine's power—look at Ashe. Hers are brown. She cannot carry the flame as I can." Nyx said. She held out her hand and pricked her finger with the nail on her thumb, which was longer than the rest of her nails, sharpened to a point. A bead of blood dripped down her finger, and when it reached her palm, a small flame ignited there. She closed her hand into a fist, and the flame extinguished. "With such a bright blue, your family could have been blessed, too. Must be a recent blessing. Perhaps by Einari?"

"Oh, *heavens* no," Stranger spat, revolted by the prospect. "I'd rather rot in Punishment for eternity than be blessed by *Einari.*"

They enunciated the god of the sea's name with a particular venom. Karina and Jonah quit bickering to stare at them in surprise.

"I... hate the ocean a lot, I guess." Even Stranger didn't understand where such malice had come from. They rerouted. "Why did you cut your finger?"

"To use the gods' power, I have to give over a little bit of my life force. It's a pact between divine and mortal."

"I see," they muttered.

Everyone stared at them. Deciding they couldn't bear the attention, they clutched the fish skewer tight in their hands and stood.

"I don't believe I've ever met someone with such animosity toward the God King," Nyx said as Stranger made their way toward the stern. Nobody stopped their retreat, and Stranger was grateful for it. "Many fear him, sure, but even those who fear him devote themselves to his name."

"I sure do," Karina replied. "If we don't devote ourselves, the Great Flood will never recede."

Stranger ate in solitude in their cabin. They resolved they'd spend the rest of their day down here, away from the bustle and attention. However, a mere hour of pacing around their cabin passed before they grew antsy. They didn't like being cooped up. It was too much like...

Steel. Cold metal walls and floors. It wrapped around their wrists, cutting off circulation to their hands. Patterned light cast upon them, shaped by the rows of sturdy bars. A bearded silhouette. A syringe, *pain, pain, PAIN—*

Stranger gasped and coughed. When had they collapsed? They sat upon the floor—*wood, oh, thank the gods.* A bead of sweat dripped down their brow as they forced their trembling body to get up off the ground. They stumbled to the washroom and splashed water on their face.

Stranger gripped a wooden training sword so tight their hand ached. About twenty paces away stood Jonah, and off to the side was the crowd of spectators, bustling with excitement.

I should back out, they thought. *I still have time. I could—*

No. No, they needed to do this. They *had* to win. They had to prove themself worthy.

"I'm not going easy on you because you're new," Jonah said. For the spar, he'd changed into a simple black tee. The fabric hugged his tall, muscular frame. "I expect you to do the same. I want to gauge your skills."

Stranger nodded.

"As a reminder," Faye called, "there are three rounds. If you get pinned for ten seconds, if you take a blow that would prove fatal in a real fight, or if you tap out, you lose the round."

Stranger struggled to pay attention, too aware of Jonah staring at them, analyzing them. His intense gaze made Stranger want to run and hide.

"Round one starts in three!" Faye yelled. She thrust her hand up into the air. "Two! One!"

Neither they nor Jonah jumped into action. They circled each other with slow, methodical paces. Above them, mottled gray clouds wove a dreary tapestry.

Stranger took the initiative. Had Jonah been waiting for them to? They charged and swung their sword. The momentum of Stranger's strike came to a screeching halt when it crashed against the flat of Jonah's blade. Stranger struck again and again, but Jonah was far more experienced, far more prepared.

"You're going to have to try harder," Jonah growled as he darted to the side. "You're telegraphing your attacks. You may as well shout what you're doing next."

Jonah struck, and Stranger struggled to block it. Jonah was a skilled swordsman, and Stranger wasn't sure what they knew. They could still give up, they figured. They could back off and forfeit the fight. But then Jonah would think them a coward.

They were no coward. They pressed on.

"Your form is sloppy," Jonah noted as they exchanged blows. "You're not confident. Come on. Show me the fighter who took down the so-called *monster*."

A gentle rain mixed with the sweat already forming on Stranger's brow. For a long time, wood clattered against wood, boots stomped against the deck, and otherwise, silence reigned.

"Are we placing bets tonight?" Ashe asked.

"We don't place bets on Jonah's spars," Willow replied. "He always wins."

Jonah kicked Stranger to the floor. Their back hit the deck with a loud thud. The collision forced air from their lungs. Stranger wheezed, fighting to regain their bearings.

"This is it," Karina said. "The end of the round."

As Jonah towered over Stranger, they swept their foot under his legs, using the slick, wet deck to their advantage. Jonah shouted as he fell. He caught himself with his left hand. As Stranger scrambled to their feet, Jonah shook his wrist off.

"I've got forty glass and ten shell on hand," Ashe said, pulling a sack of coins from her pocket. "I'm putting them all on Stranger."

"Are you sure?" Karina asked.

"I've got a good feeling. Anyone want to bet against me?"

"I'll put in sixty glass on Jonah," Faye piped in.

"May the best win," Ashe smirked at Faye.

"Indeed."

As Jonah moved to stand, Stranger planted their boot onto his back and shoved him face-first into the deck again.

"Ten. Nine. Eight." Stranger counted. A strange sense of pride swelled in their chest. Jonah snarled as he struggled under Stranger's foot. "Seven. Six."

Jonah pushed himself upward. Stranger threw all their weight onto him, hoping to force him back down. Stranger couldn't help but eye his biceps, the way they flexed, straining against his sleeve. He was strong. Stranger's body weight was as light as a sack of feathers. Not nearly enough to overpower him. "Five. Four. Three."

Jonah dropped down to the deck, sending Stranger stumbling, their balance upset. Jonah hopped to his feet, grabbed Stranger by the arm, and kneed them square in the back.

Stranger crumpled.

They knelt upon the deck, waiting for the throbbing pain to fade. Jonah paced, his attention glued to Stranger. Rainwater pelted them, cool and refreshing over their overheated skin. They stood, and lightning lit up the late evening sky, followed by a deafening clap of thunder. Stranger couldn't help but laugh.

Adrenaline was a funny thing. They rushed toward Jonah, who took a braced stance—knees bent, body tense—as he prepared for a head-on collision. Instead, Stranger danced around him and pulled him into a headlock. Their blade locked against Jonah's throat. They mimed slicing his jugular.

Both ships' crews hollered, some mixture of excitement, shock, and—in Faye's case—outrage.

"Round one," Nyx hooted over the crowd, "goes to Stranger!"

10

"And as it began, the god of the sky begged Einari to cease, but a fool such as Aeris had too simple a mind. So amusing, it was, how they believed mortalkind to be sinless. Einari laughed, deeming it a jest.

"'Should they prove their purity, I shall give back their land,' Einari decreed. 'Pray and repent, they may, and when I feel they've prayed and repented enough, I shall free them of their punishment.'"
—The Book of the Tide

24th Storm, Great Flood 1058

Jonah tracked Stranger as they rolled their shoulders and ambled toward the spectators. They took a long swig of water from a flask Karina handed them.

"Maybe we should call it a night," Karina suggested. "The weather's getting pretty nasty."

"Hell no," Jonah spat, slamming his own drinking flask, now empty, onto the deck. Willow ran off to refill it. "I don't care about the damn weather. You want to leave? Go ahead. I'm seeing this through."

Thunder rumbled in the distance.

"You guys ready?" Faye cut in. "Or do you need a break?"

"Ready," Stranger replied.

"Jonah?"

"There's no luxury of rest during real combat."

Faye nodded. "Round two! Current score: Stranger, one; Jonah, zero!"

Jonah eyed Stranger up and down. Stranger's challenge, when Mouse reported it, had surprised him. Their fear of Jonah was no secret. Somehow, someone so small had managed to overpower a beast fifty times their size. This was why he agreed to this duel—to see how much of Stranger's feat was raw power and how much was pure luck.

"In three! Two! One!"

Stranger and Jonah surged toward each other. As Jonah ducked away from a close swipe, he caught a glint of something in Stranger's stormy blue eyes. Excitement. This was the Stranger Jonah wanted to see. If they were going to be a member of his crew, they'd need to break free of the timidness that shackled them.

Stranger ducked out of his sightline. He didn't have enough time to whirl around before Stranger hit him at the base of his neck with the wooden blade's hilt. Jonah grunted and stumbled forward.

Why waste a killing blow? Jonah thought. *They could have ended the round.*

He opened his mouth, such a quip on the tip of his tongue. Words failed him when he turned to find Stranger snickering. They were toying with him. The bastard.

They stood perpendicular to Jonah, their posture more relaxed than he had ever seen. They held their training sword with a loose grip, its blade brushing the deck floor, and they gazed partway over their shoulder at Jonah with a lazy smile. Jonah knew he looked a wreck. His hair was disheveled, his arms were trembling in some strange combination of exertion and rage. Stranger—curse them—looked as though they'd stepped out of the washroom. There was no doubt Stranger enjoyed tossing the captain around like a ragdoll in front of his entire crew. *Humiliating.*

Jonah weaponized Stranger's newfound confidence. "Is that all you got, *prettyboy?*"

Stranger took the bait. Jonah dodged their next slash and slammed his heel into their knee. Stranger yelled, and while they were distracted, Jonah grabbed them by their hair, pulled their head down, and kneed them in the stomach.

Stranger crumpled. Jonah picked up Stranger's sword as he strode toward them. He wondered if he'd knocked them out. It'd be a shame if he had. There wouldn't be a third round, then. But as Jonah approached, Stranger stared up at him, wide-eyed and trembling.

Fear was a horrible look on Stranger, Jonah decided.

Nothing was more revealing than a fight. A fight could differentiate a pirate from an islander. This spar, if nothing else, would teach Jonah a bit about where Stranger came from. *Come on,* he thought. *Show me who you are.*

They hoisted themself back to their feet. They stood off-kilter, favoring their right knee. Lightning struck the ocean off the bow, and the whole ship shuddered. Everybody except Stranger flinched at the resounding thunderclap. In a heartbeat, the fear washed away, and the glint of electrical energy returned to their eyes.

There we go.

Without their sword, Stranger was at a severe disadvantage, but they threw a hefty punch. Jonah dodged, then raised the sword in his left hand—Stranger's—and feinted a strike. He then swept in with the opposite sword. He swung for Stranger's throat. It would be a killing blow. Jonah would win the round.

Stranger thrust their hand out and caught the blade. They yelled. A wooden sword, though lacking a sharp blade, was still a formidable weapon, and Stranger would develop a nasty bruise later.

"If this were a real fight, at best you'd be covered in blood, and at worst, you'd lose your hand."

"Good thing this isn't a real fight, huh?" Stranger taunted.

"You know," Jonah couldn't help but lecture as he struck with the other sword. Stranger hopped away. "You should always practice the way you'll perform."

Stranger snorted. "What's the fun in that?"

Jonah did nothing to stifle his annoyed groan. "Don't do it again."

Stranger skipped out of the way of another strike. They whistled as they moved.

"Take this seriously, damn it!"

"I am!"

Jonah charged, calculation by the wayside in favor of sheer, unbridled, blinding rage...

And before Jonah could even register what had happened, he stood bent over the gunwale. In Stranger's grip was a fistful of sweaty, rain-soaked ginger hair. It tugged at his scalp. Faye counted down from ten, but her voice sounded distant and muffled. Stranger's body pressed against his, pinning him from behind. The railing dug into his stomach. Heat spread across his face over such a compromising position.

Stranger released him and stepped away.

"Round two goes to Stranger!" Nyx shouted. A chorus of cheers followed. Jonah shouted in frustration, kicking Stranger's flask off the side of the ship. It splashed into the ocean.

"Alright, Faye," Ashe sang. "Pay up! Stranger won—"

"No!" Jonah barked, cutting her off. He grabbed Stranger by their shirt's ill-fitted collar. "One more round. All or nothing. If I win this one, I win it all. If you win..."

He shoved Stranger away from him. They stumbled a few steps.

"Well, newbie's luck," he spat.

"Deal."

Jonah hadn't expected Stranger to accept. Any wise combatant would take their win and run, but Stranger was a strange one indeed.

"No swords this round," Jonah declared, tossing the blades aside. "Same rules apply, but we fight hand-to-hand."

"Fine by me." Stranger's grin was much too smug for Jonah's liking. They cracked their knuckles. "Maybe I'll break a sweat."

Jonah screamed and tackled Stranger. He planted his hand upon Stranger's cheek and pressed their face against the deck. Stranger elbowed him in the jaw.

"Never thought Jonah would be such a sore loser," Faye laughed, which earned a feral glare from him. *You're next.*

His distraction proved to be a mistake. He had Stranger in a losing position. The moment Jonah cast the glare over his shoulder, Stranger planted a foot against Jonah's chest and pushed, sending Jonah stumbling back.

Stranger hopped to their feet. They threw a flurry of sloppy punches. Jonah held his arms to his face to block them, and Stranger threw a hook around Jonah's defense. He didn't duck away in time. Jonah staggered and sputtered.

He recovered slower than he would have liked. He shook himself off, then drove his elbow into Stranger's collarbone. He swept one leg out from underneath Stranger, offsetting their balance, then shoved, sending Stranger tumbling to the deck.

Stranger was short of breath now, Jonah noted.

They weren't down for long. Stranger sprang back up and awaited Jonah's next strike. Jonah stared, hands on his knees. He wiped rainwater and sweat from his brow. What went on in Stranger's head? Were they analyzing Jonah's every move? Or were they flying by their sails, acting on instinct and whim alone?

He had a feeling it was the latter.

Jonah broke the stalemate. He pulled Stranger into a chokehold, leaving them gasping and grabbing at Jonah's arms.

"There's no shame in tapping out," Jonah growled into Stranger's ear.

"No way!" Stranger gasped, and *oh,* what Jonah wouldn't give to see that conviction in their eyes outside of combat. They stamped their foot down atop Jonah's. In most circumstances, his steel-toed boots would have protected him, but Stranger's heel slammed right where the steel reinforcement ended. Jonah swore. He released them as pain radiated up his leg.

A punch to his temple sent him falling to his knees, the world spinning around him. Stranger hovered in his peripheral vision, wringing their hands, as though they feared they'd hit him a tad too hard. His head throbbed. He attempted to push himself back to his feet, but his body refused to cooperate, so overtaxed that his thighs cramped and his biceps ached. His breaths came in short, shallow puffs.

He thumped his palm against the deck once, twice.

"Stranger wins!" Karina exclaimed, as Faye was far too busy wallowing in her misery of losing the bet. Jonah did not put up a fight over the declaration. Stranger had won, fair and square. Not that Jonah had any fight left in him, anyhow.

"Looks like someone needs to hand over sixty glass," Ashe teased. Faye grumbled and pressed the money into Ashe's palm.

Jonah stood and met Stranger's gaze. He wondered which version of Stranger he faced now: the one who fought or the one who feared?

"Meet me in my cabin," he grumbled. He was eager to get somewhere quieter. All the chatter muddied his thoughts.

Karina rushed to Stranger and pressed her canteen into their hands. As they sipped, the spectators gathered around them, and Jonah walked off.

The crew would take a while to settle down, granting him time before Stranger showed up, so Jonah got changed. He tossed his soaked clothes into his woven reed washbasket, dried off, then slipped on a simple gray tank and some thin pants.

"...I could've made it here fine on my own," Stranger's voice floated into the room as Jonah settled at his desk.

"I know," Karina replied. Stranger pushed Jonah's door open, and Karina stopped them. Stranger turned to look at her, one pale hand planted on the doorknob. "I want to make sure you know it's okay to ask for help. You don't have to struggle alone—you're one of us now."

Stranger cast a glance into the room. They met Jonah's eyes, their gaze lingering, before turning back to Karina. "I appreciate it. Thanks."

They stepped inside and closed the door behind them. Limping across the room, they flopped onto the stool across the desk from him. Their rich black hair was matted with rainwater.

Jonah leaned back in his chair, legs crossed, arms folded across his chest. "Good work today," he said, fighting to keep his tone flat. "I'm impressed."

Stranger blinked. They didn't appear to believe him. The way they had opened up during their spar was like night and day. Now, they'd closed off again.

"Get some rest. I know I will be," he continued, filling the silence. "I suppose I owe you a favor. Take some time to think on what you may want."

"Okay."

"You have a solid foundation, but don't let it get to your head. Training is key." Jonah paused, hesitant. "I thought you were a pirate when we first found you. But your fighting style... It doesn't resemble a pirate's."

"What do pirates fight like?"

"They fight dirty. They cheat and exploit weakness. If you sparred like a pirate, you would have broken one of my legs. You would have tossed me overboard instead of pinning me to the gunwale."

"So, if I don't fight like a pirate, what do I fight like?"

Jonah contemplated this with a tight frown. "You... I don't know. You fight, and for a fleeting moment, I see *you.*"

Stranger nodded. They stared at their lap, and Jonah eyed them up and down. They needed to rest. He wanted to check them for injuries, but... they looked alright, for now. Nothing urgent. He'd check them over tomorrow.

"You're dismissed," he said.

Stranger nodded and stood on shaky, overexerted legs. They stumbled to the door.

"Crow," Jonah called before they disappeared. "Come see me in the morning."

Stranger froze. "Crow?"

"You spend a bizarre amount of time in the crow's nest," Jonah muttered. "And Nyx was right. 'Stranger' is unkind. I suppose, if you're to be a member of my crew, you deserve a proper name."

"Crow," they repeated. "I like it."

Jonah cast them a smile. It was small, showed no teeth, but Crow stared. Their eyes glittered even in the dim light, like two stars in the night sky.

"Go dry yourself off," Jonah broke the spell, his face falling back into his typical easy, gruff frown. "I'm sick of you tracking water all over my floor."

Crow flinched, then nodded. They disappeared down the passageway.

11

*"I pray Einari may know my faith shall never falter. I
beg the ocean spare those who love him. I am created
of love."*
—*Prayer #14 from the Book of the Tide*

25th Storm, Great Flood 1058

Crow's entire existence ached. The dull throb of their sore muscles was
not the kind of pain they were accustomed to. This was a satisfying pain.
Despite their body begging them to rot in bed for the rest of eternity,
Crow heaved themself to their feet and stumbled out of their cabin. The
hammock was comfortable, sure, but they yearned to feel the open air.

Soon enough, they would—but first, Jonah had wanted them to pay
him another visit. Their feet dragged as they walked, bone tired as they
were, but nerves still nagged at them. Could they delay the meeting?
Would Jonah get mad if they spent an hour on the mast first? The
answer was a resounding *yes.*

They stopped at Jonah's door and raised their right hand to the
smooth wood. The door swung open before they could knock. They
gasped and stumbled backwards. Flashes of needles in their veins, frigid
steel, and crooked grins affronted their vision. Their vision swam. They
couldn't tell which way was up. They—

It's the captain. He's not going to hurt me. I think.

"I was about to come get you," Jonah said as he urged Crow into
the cabin. "I wasn't sure if you'd try to sleep in. Or sneak away."

Crow sat on the stool by Jonah's desk. Jonah knelt in front of them.

"Take your shirt off."

Crow blinked.

When Jonah said nothing more, Crow unbuttoned their frumpy,
ill-fitted white shirt and let it slip to the floor.

Jonah placed a hand on Crow's bare shoulder, brushing his thumb over a fledgling bruise. It had blossomed a pale yellow in color and ached under the pressure. His palm was warm against their skin. As far as they were aware, they'd never been touched with such gentle intent before, and they weren't sure how to handle it. They shivered.

"What are you doing?" Crow dared to ask.

"I check in with everyone I spar," Jonah replied, flat and clinical. "I'm making sure you're not walking around with any untreated injuries. I didn't deem it pressing enough to check you last night, but it needs to be done."

His hand trailed across their skin, leaving a tingling sensation in its wake, to another yellowed mark under Crow's ribcage. He must have thought it alright, because he moved to Crow's wrist, turning their palm toward the ceiling. The bruise from catching Jonah's sword was dark, brown, and angry. Jonah stared at it for a while, his brow furrowed as he poked and prodded.

"Bruises shouldn't be this color," he mumbled. He fished through the medkit for a glass jar of what appeared to be some type of salve. He massaged it into Crow's skin, then wrapped it tight with a bandage. Crow winced. Unlike the soreness of their muscles, this pain was sharp, familiar.

Jonah gestured for Crow to swivel around on the stool. They complied. His hands found their back. "Your muscles are tight. You should have stretched beforehand. It's not hard to take care of your basic needs, Crow."

Was it? Crow had to keep reminding themself to eat and hydrate. Their amnesia clouded too much. Mere thought of the emptiness of their mind sparked a sharp frustration within them. No matter how hard they dug, memories slipped away like seawater through a net. They wished they could grasp onto *something* about who they were.

"...Do you think I'll ever get my memory back?" they asked, their voice small.

The calloused tips of Jonah's fingers traced across their shoulder blade. "I'm not sure," he said. "I'm no doctor, but I think amnesia is permanent."

Jonah worked his way down Crow's back, checking all their bruises one by one. Jonah nudged them to swivel around again. He wrapped a bandage around their knee, diligent and focused.

"Hey, Captain?" Crow asked. Jonah's eyes flitted to meet their gaze, then turned back to his work. Crow hesitated. Was he inviting them to follow through, or telling them to shut up? They wrung their hands. "Do you hate me?"

As Jonah's fingers traced down Crow's calf, he opted not to answer. Crow didn't push it. *He hates me, I'm a burden, I'm taking up precious space on his ship.*

Jonah finished his work in silence.

When he moved away, Crow picked up their shirt, took a sniff, then recoiled. "Hey, um, can I cash in my favor now?"

Jonah eyed Crow. They shouldn't have brought up the whole *favor* thing. Jonah would throw them in the brig for even insinuating—

"Sure."

"Oh," Crow muttered. A peculiar expression crossed Jonah's face, like he didn't quite understand why Crow was surprised he agreed. "Um. Can I borrow some of your clothes? 'Till I can wash these?"

"You want to borrow clothes," Jonah repeated. "You don't want me to wash your clothes for you? Or purchase more?"

"N-no, it's fine. I can take care of it. I don't want to be without anything to wear in the meantime, though."

"Fine."

Jonah walked over to his wardrobe. He, too, appeared stiff in the aftermath of their spar. He popped the wardrobe door open and tossed a shirt and slacks to Crow, both dyed a rich, deep black.

"Thanks. I...I'll get these back to you as soon as I finish."

Jonah nodded.

Crow hurried out. They took one boot off, then the other, then their socks, too, all without stopping their beeline to the washroom, save for the occasional stumble.

The washroom was simple in its design. It featured, in the center, an iron basin large enough to fit a body to bathe. A latrine sat in the corner, and, in front of it, a thin green mat, which appeared to be no more substantial than a towel, lay on the floor.

Crow turned the washbasin's spigot. The stream of water was pitiful and slow. While they waited for the basin to fill, they changed into Jonah's clothes. The fabric was comfortable and held the faint earthy scent of whatever soap Jonah used. The shirt's neckline slipped off their shoulder. The pants did little to cling to their hips. They searched the washroom, eventually finding an unused length of rope, which they tied around their waist as a makeshift belt.

When the basin filled, they cut the tap and scrubbed their clothes of all the caked-on grime. Island dirt. Sweat. Mildew. The water turned a disgusting, putrid brown.

They pulled the plug. Dirty water swirled down the drain. Once empty, Crow plugged the basin once more and turned the spigot. Three drops of water splashed into the washbasin before running dry. They stared, frozen. What were they supposed to do now? Their clothes were half-washed at best.

Karina said it was okay to ask for help. Loath as they were to bother the crew, this seemed like an *asking for help* kind of situation. They stepped out into the passageway.

Who could help with this? Their first thought was Mouse.

When Crow reached Mouse's door, they knocked, then reprimanded themself. What a silly thing to forget. Beside the door was a light switch, labeled in messy handwriting: *Knock*. Crow flicked the switch on, then back off. They heard some shuffling behind the door before it creaked open.

"Hey," Crow signed to Mouse. "I think the water tap is broken? I turned it on, and nothing came out."

"We're out of fresh water," Mouse replied. "I've already reloaded the desalinator. Give it a few hours to separate the salt from the seawater."

"Oh, okay. Sorry for bothering you." Crow moved to leave, but Mouse caught them by the arm, pulling their attention back.

"Good job against Jonah. How are you feeling?"

"Oh," Crow said, aloud, then signed, "Thanks. I'm tired and sore."

"It was super cool." Mouse's gaze shifted off to the side. Crow glanced over their shoulder to find Faye approaching with a smirk drawn across her face.

"And now," she snickered, both signing and speaking aloud, "you've cashed in your favor by borrowing Jonah's clothes."

"Uh, yeah. I needed to wash mine. I don't have any others."

"You know how many of us would kill to see him on his knees, scrubbing our clothes for us? Why didn't you have him do it? It's a pretty common post-spar favor, you know."

"I didn't want to inconvenience him. He's busy."

"Busy with what?" Faye asked. "Reading poetry and brooding in his cabin?"

Mouse snickered.

"I-I don't—" Crow stammered.

"I know, I know. It's okay. Once you get to know him, you'll realize he's like a stick of fish jerky. Salty and stiff on the outside, but soft on the inside."

"Your comparison sucks," Mouse signed with a roll of his eyes. "Fish jerky is unpleasant the whole way through."

"*Anyways,* give him a chance. He's curious about you, even though he acts like he isn't. If he tries anything, I'll kick his ass. It'll be good training—I want to beat him someday, like you did last night."

"You have a way to go," another voice, another pair of hands, cut into the conversation, "Last time you sparred him, you slipped on a puddle and almost fell overboard."

"Willow!" Faye screeched. Flustered by her girlfriend's comment, she dropped her hands, and Crow signed her exclamation for Mouse. "If you say a single word to Stranger, I'm disowning you. It's embarrassing!"

"I go by Crow, now," they interjected.

"Huh?"

"Crow." They fingerspelled the name for Mouse. *C-R-O-W.*

Mouse beamed with excitement, pride.

"Now." Crow rubbed their hands together. "What happened?"

"Willow, I swear to the gods above—"

Willow nudged Faye with her elbow. "It was the first round. She was doing pretty well, too. But a wave splashed over the deck, and Faye slipped and flopped over the railing. Jonah helped her before she fell overboard. He ended the spar and gave her a long, annoyed lecture about being aware of her surroundings."

Faye tackled Willow. The duo hit the floor with a *thud.* Willow squealed. Their horseplay didn't last long, though, as the telltale footfalls of their captain interrupted them. Faye and Willow froze mid-wrestle, staring up at Jonah from where they lay on the floor, tangled up with one another.

"Quit squabbling," Jonah grumbled. He nudged Faye with the toe of his boot. His attention drifted over to Crow. "Is your laundry done?"

"No," Crow muttered. Under Jonah's stare, they grew ashamed of taking this long. Jonah had been gracious enough to lend them his clothes, and here Crow was, wasting his time. "We're out of water."

Jonah nodded.

"I'm sorry," Crow added.

Another one of those peculiar, confused expressions crossed Jonah's face. "Get it done when you can."

Nyx and Ashe left in the afternoon. Their heading: eastward, to their home island of Blythe, much to Nyx's apparent chagrin. Despite her distaste for visiting her homeland, she and her sister parted with a cheerful goodbye and, courtesy of Faye, a barrel of ale for the trip.

Crow spent the day in the washroom, only stepping out when someone needed to use the latrine. As everyone retired to their cabins for the night, Crow hung their shirt and slacks to dry. They set out their boots on the washroom floor. Come morning, everything would be dry and ready to wear.

They flopped onto their hammock, glad to be off their feet. Even with the exhaustion, though, sleep eluded them. They tossed and turned, and when they did eventually drift off, their sleep was patchy at best. They'd hoped for blissful nothingness, but instead were faced with bizarre dreams about sea monsters, about Argonaut, about falling.

The dreams about falling were always the ones to wake them.

Crow rolled out of their hammock sometime in the dead of night. Stopping by the washroom, they changed into their half-dried clothes and made their way above deck. On their way out, they set Jonah's clothes outside his cabin door.

The fresh air soothed Crow's lungs, the humidity of daytime gone. Their muscles burned as they made their way up the mast. When they reached the crow's nest, they yawned and rubbed their eyes. Crow occupied their time by peering through the darkness, searching for the horizon.

They did not find it until sunrise.

12

"A thousand years is a long time, so expect most salvage to be decayed. As a general rule, do not bother salvaging unless it is made of the following materials: aluminum, steel, plastic, rubber, or glass. Some fabrics, if synthetic or plastic-infused, may have survived, but handle with great care. Everything will need refurbishment before sale."
—*A Salvager's Guide to Success: Vol. 1, Ch. 6*

26th Storm, Great Flood 1058

"I know we're short on cash," Karina said to Jonah. "But I think we should take Crow to a hub."

Jonah was drenched in sweat and wearing nothing more than a tank top and some loose pants. Slung over his shoulder was his training bag, fitted with a water flask and a towel he had shoved inside, leaving no room to cinch the bag shut. She found his dedication to exercise remarkable. Sailing was a tough enough job.

"I suppose," he agreed, to Karina's relief. "They can't be making a habit of borrowing my clothes."

A gentle breeze ruffled her hair, and she tucked a wayward strand behind her ear. A short span of silence descended between them, but it was not unwelcome.

"We could sail back to the Midnorthern hub," Jonah eventually said. "But I'm not eager to keep toeing the boundary of Anui."

"The Central hub." Another act of selfishness, wrapped around the guise of a kind gesture. "It's farther away, but it'd be safer, and... Well, Magnus said he bumped into my parents there."

"You *want* to find them?"

Karina balled a hand into a fist and did not reply. Jonah nodded. She was grateful for his sympathy. He hadn't had the best parentage situation growing up, either. He never knew his biological father, though he didn't seem interested in finding out who it was. Being adopted never bothered him.

Karina wished she didn't care about her parents' neglect.

"Central hub," he affirmed.

Karina eyed the compass—the current heading was dead south, so she turned the wheel until the *Vengeance* pointed southwest. It wouldn't take *too* long to reach the Central hub—two weeks tops, as they skirted the boundary between the Dead Zone and Østg.

Her gaze found Crow, who sat perched atop the mast as usual. Word about their new name had spread quickly, and Karina quite liked it. It suited them. Their wavy jet-black hair was not unlike the black of a crow's feathers.

A few seagulls gathered upon the crow's nest. She found it intriguing. Birds feared people. Did the birds see them as Crow, too?

"Should I still be worried about you tossing Crow overboard?" Karina blurted, unable to filter the thought out before it reached her mouth.

"They're a member of my crew," Jonah replied.

"What turned you around?"

"They... intrigue me."

"Did they intrigue you the day you swam back for them?"

"No."

"So, why..." she trailed off, but she didn't need to finish her sentence. For a while, all she heard were the waves crashing against the hull and the ship's gentle creaks and groans. Jonah worked his lower lip between his teeth for quite a while, his gaze distant. Karina gave him the time he needed to find his words.

"Sophie has always been my guiding light." His voice was small, the tone he reserved for private conversations. This side of him was rare. Karina cherished the moments when he let her past his emotional walls. "Well, not when you first found me, back when I was so *raw,* but before I lost her. She was good at stopping me from making poor decisions."

Karina didn't dare move a muscle, even if she wanted to wrap him up in a tight hug. For as long as she had known him, he'd been skittish about vulnerability. If anything made him uncomfortable or threatened, he put up those thick, impregnable walls again and would march off with a scowl.

"I mean, I'm...ugh. I hear her voice in the back of my head sometimes. I imagine her telling me off when I do something wrong. And I knew if she were still alive... If I didn't go back for Crow, she would have given me the silent treatment for a whole season."

"Sometimes you need a nudge, sure, but you have as strong a heart as she did."

Jonah contemplated this for some time, not quite convinced, though he nodded. Karina cast him a small smile, an encouraging one, as he disappeared down the ladder.

At the top of the hour, Crow descended from the mast. They looked exhausted, their posture slumped and their hair a mess, but even with the bags under their drooping eyes, they refused to rest. To quell their ceaseless anxiety, Jonah took to doing anything under the sun to keep them occupied. He had them scrape barnacles off the hull and count the *Vengeance's* food supplies. He had them secure all the rigging and examine every sail. Karina wished she could flag them down to chat, but helm duty pinned her to the quarterdeck, and Crow seldom crossed her path.

Mouse took over the helm at noon. She relayed the trajectory, then climbed down to prep lunch. Nobody stopped their work to eat, so Karina served oats in shell bowls and delivered them to everybody. Crow, however, found their place by the fire pit.

Karina joined them so they wouldn't feel so alone. And, though she'd never admit it aloud, so she wouldn't feel so alone, either. So long as she focused on someone else, she wasn't worrying about meeting her parents for the first time in eleven years.

"Something's on your mind," she said.

"Technically, nothing's on my mind," Crow replied. "It's empty. Foggy. It's not a pleasant feeling. I want to know who I am. Nothing can be done about it, I guess, but I'm frustrated."

"I'm sorry. It can't be easy."

"Something's on *your* mind," Crow pushed back, and Karina's eyes widened. She thought she was better at brushing her issues under the rug. "You're always helping your crew sort things out. Helping *me* sort things out. But you've never once mentioned your own—" They cut themself off and shrank back. "S-sorry. I shouldn't pry."

Karina made a mental note to work on building their confidence.

"No, it's okay," Karina replied. "You surprised me, that's all." Karina knew she shouldn't pile her issues on Crow, but they had asked.

Nobody ever asked her how she felt. She was always the one checking in on others. Having someone check in on her, in return, broke her down. *Practice what you preach,* she reminded herself. *Emotional honesty is as good for me as it is for everyone else.*

"My parents didn't raise me. They were merchants, too focused on their work to care for their own child. When I was fifteen, I gathered all the supplies I needed and ran away." She paused to gauge the small, sympathetic frown gracing Crow's face. "It's been a long time. I think I want to find them again, but I don't know if I want to punch them or make amends. I feel like I need to... I don't know, figure it out. In case I see them."

"It's okay to let things happen as they come," Crow said. "Forethought helps, but don't let yourself get so caught up in what *could be* that you forget to enjoy what *is.*"

"I suppose so."

"Also, I don't know the details, of course, and I don't expect them from you." Crow paused to poke at their oats, which they'd left untouched thus far. "But you're not obligated to forgive them because they're family. Heavens, they're *not* your family. Blood relation means nothing when there's no love."

"I suppose you're right," Karina mused. "Thanks, Crow. Are you sure there's nothing I can do to help you?"

"I doubt it."

Karina nodded, and the two of them finished their lunch in comfortable silence.

Two weeks crawled by. Karina spent most of her time reorganizing her ancient trinkets. She took everything out of her storage trunk and, one by one, decided what was worth keeping and what wasn't. A small pile of ancient tools, devices, and jewels she deemed worth selling sat on the floor in a crate. Willow stopped by somewhere along the way, and Karina took advantage of her presence.

"Do you think you could sell some of these when we stop?" she asked. "I know you hate cluttering your art stall, but we could use the extra funds, and I'm willing to part with some of my collection."

"I could," Willow replied. "A bigger table would cost extra, but it's not unaffordable. Are you sure, though?"

"I have to make space for newer finds," Karina said with a chuckle. "It does hurt to get rid of some of these—but... like, what is this?" She picked up an odd-looking tool from her *get-rid-of* crate. It consisted of a circular blade no bigger than her palm, affixed to a handle shaped for comfortable holding. Far too small to cut wood and too large to cut anything delicate, its use eluded her. Careful not to slice her skin, she spun the blade. Its axle, decayed from a thousand years undersea, did not allow the blade to spin far. "I bought it because I wanted to figure out what it was used for, but I don't think it's worth keeping."

"A lot of these things won't sell well. Think of it this way—the tool intrigued you, but it's not in high demand. People want salvaged furniture, pots and pans, sailing equipment. Practical things. The average consumer doesn't care much for oddities."

Karina chuckled, bashful. "I suppose you're right," she said. "Could you use any of this for your art?"

This piqued Willow's interest. "Making sculptures could be fun. I've never tried. Faye'll kill me, though, for taking up more space in our cabin."

"Take them. Whatever you don't want, we can dump back into the ocean."

Willow gathered Karina's crate and stood. With a smile, she lugged it out.

Crow and Jonah sparred again, but Karina didn't watch. Jonah won. According to Faye, Crow hadn't shaken their fear of him. Jonah had kicked them down, and they never got back up. Faye didn't give details, but she said it wasn't because of any injury.

Since then, Crow avoided Jonah whenever they could. When they couldn't avoid him outright, they didn't dare meet his gaze, ashamed.

The *Vengeance* docked at the Central hub on the fortieth of Storm. Central, unlike Midnorthern's coral and shell structure, was built of wood, thanks to its proximity to the tree-farming powerhouse Redwood Harbor. This was where Karina learned to pickpocket, at the tender age of eight.

Karina was the last to join the crew at the gangplank. As she approached, Jonah dropped a sack full of coins into Crow's hands. They flinched when it landed in their palm, then opened it and peered inside, a small frown on their face.

"Take this," Jonah said to Crow. "Use it to buy yourself some new clothes."

"Um," they stammered, "Wait—"

Jonah turned to the rest of the crew. "Be back by midday," he announced.

Faye carried the crate of Karina's sellable trinkets down the gangplank, and Willow followed, lugging a stack of paintings. Mouse tucked his pay into the pocket of his overalls and disappeared below deck, disinterested. Karina couldn't help but feel sad for the kid—a year or so ago, he told her he didn't like hubs. Nobody accommodated him. What would it take, she wondered, to make a hub more accessible?

"Wait, hang on!" Crow exclaimed, casting an anxious gaze out at the overcrowded tapestry of docks. "I don't know how this works."

Jonah sighed, exasperated. "Everything is marked with how much it costs."

"I can't read it."

He cursed. "Right. Karina, accompany Crow."

Karina was happy to. She led Crow down the gangplank and onto the hub. As she did, her curiosity got the better of her.

"You can't read?" she asked. "You're always reading Jonah's books."

"I can't read Midiri," Crow explained. "I can read Køveni, though."

Karina eyed Crow up and down. "Interesting," she said, her brow furrowed. No wonder Jonah was so intrigued. "Can you speak it, too?"

"Yes."

"You might be a scholar, then," Karina mused. "Or a scholar's apprentice. It's rare, but a few people have managed to decipher the language of the gods."

"Maybe."

Among the crowds and the narrow, unstable docks, Crow wrung their hands. To ease their nerves, perhaps their fear of slipping off the edge, Karina hooked her hand around the crook of their elbow.

Karina kept a keen eye out for any sign of her parents as they walked. Her heart pounded. She eyed every stall. How different would they look? Was Pop's hair gray now? Had Ma gotten the wrinkle reduction surgery she always raved about? Karina couldn't help but chuckle at the mental image of her Ma, skin on her face stretched taut like a canvas.

Karina was young when she ran away. Would they recognize her now? Or had they forgotten they had a child in the first place? Their business was their true child, after all.

Her parents weren't in the first row, nor the second, nor any of the corners between them. Karina was silly to think they'd be present now. They had moved on, headed to some other hub, gathering salvage as they sailed.

Karina tried not to let it bother her. Even now, when she sought them, they were absent. *Typical.*

Karina spotted a tailor at the end of the row. "Hey, look," she said, pointing toward the stall, and Crow's gaze followed her finger. It took up one of the larger available spots on the hub—in a U shape stood hangers showing off all varieties of clothing, from the simplest shirts to the most extravagant scarves. *This place is going to overcharge like hell,* she thought. *I don't see any other tailors around, though.*

Crow cast Karina a wary glance, then approached the stall with great caution.

"...Hi," Crow greeted the tailor, wringing their hands. "I need, um...a couple of shirts."

"What type?" the tailor asked, eyeing Crow up and down.

"Type?" Crow repeated. "Uh, I don't know."

"Something simple," Karina supplied, and Crow looked relieved she stepped in. "Variety helps—short-sleeved and long-sleeved. What color, Crow?"

"Light blue?"

Karina smiled, taking joy in learning the little details about Crow. Even without their memory, they had a preference for colors, activities they enjoyed, and an aggressive distaste for the god of the sea, Einari. Bits and pieces.

The salesman nodded. He approached Crow with a measuring tape, and they flinched as the man checked their height, the width of their slender shoulders, the length of their arms, and the circumference of their waist. Once he finished, he leafed through the clothes hanging on metal racks.

"How many?"

"One of each?" Crow tried.

Karina shook her head. "Two of each."

The tailor tugged two light blue button-up shirts and two short-sleeved shirts from their hangers and tossed them to Crow. Crow fumbled to catch them.

"Ya got coin?"

"Y-yessir," Crow said. "How much would it cost?"

"Three hundred glass."

Crow cast a glance at Karina.

"I'd pay three hundred *shell*," she muttered.

The shopkeeper scoffed. "Shell? For four shirts? I've got a business to run, lady!"

"One hundred glass," Karina offered. It was about the same amount of money as three hundred shell. Rephrasing it in terms of glass would lead to a more productive haggle.

"Lowest I'll take is fifty-five glass per shirt. Two hundred twenty, total. Take it or leave it."

"How about one hundred eighty?"

"Two-twenty."

"Two-ten?" she tried. *What a scam.*

The shopkeeper groaned. "Fine. Two-ten."

Crow fumbled with their pouch of coins. As they counted the money, a single shell coin fell between the slats of the pier. It sank into the ocean with a soft *plunk.*

"Can I show you a trick?" Karina offered. She lifted the coin bag from their hands. "First, hold it close to your body, okay? Thieves are everywhere. They won't hesitate to take advantage of you."

Crow nodded.

"Find the big ones—those are worth ten. It's faster, and all we need is twenty-one. Watch: one, two, three, four, five..." she counted out the coins, "...nineteen, twenty, twenty-one. Here you go, sir."

She handed the coins to the vendor. She was surprised Crow had enough coin to cover it all. Jonah gave them a generous first paycheck. The gesture was sweet.

"Thanks," Crow muttered. They took the near-empty coin bag from Karina and tucked it in their coat pocket. "I don't think I'll ever be as good as you are."

"It takes practice," Karina smiled, sympathetic. "When I was a kid, my parents would sit me behind their stall and have me practice counting coins. They wanted to keep me busy while they worked. But it's a good skill to learn. The faster you can do it, the less the chance a thief has to swoop in and steal from you."

"Have you been stolen from before?"

"Many times." *And I've stolen from others, too.*

Crow's attention drifted. She figured they didn't want to be lectured, but then they tensed. Their gaze locked onto a parallel dock. A thin strip of ocean separated them, enough for water to splash up and slick the surface.

"He's here," Crow gasped, grabbing tight onto Karina's arm. "He's here. He's here—"

"Crow? What do you mean?"

Karina turned to follow Crow's fearful gaze. She caught a glimpse of a tall, bearded man in a long black coat. His steel prosthetic hand glinted in the daylight. He strutted down the center of the adjacent aisle, minding his own business, but when he turned the corner, his cold gray eyes met hers, flitted to Crow, then widened.

"Argonaut," Karina hissed. There wasn't enough space to run. Not without pushing a few people overboard. She put herself between him and Crow as he approached. "Get lost."

"This is public territory," Argo shrugged. His feigned nonchalance sent a shiver down Karina's spine. "Now, I had stopped here to buy myself some gunpowder, as neither Northern nor Midnorthern could be bothered to stock any. How *pleasant* to find a familiar face among the crowd, hm?"

"I won't let you anywhere near them," Karina snapped. "They said you tortured them."

"Torture?" Argonaut scoffed. "What fanciful tales. Let's be civil. You must have questions about who you are, son. Come back to me, and I'll explain everything."

Crow stiffened. "Son?" they repeated with a frown. "But I remember you pulling me from the ocean."

"You slipped and fell overboard," Argonaut cooed. "I wasn't going to let my boy drown."

"Crow, ignore him," Karina said. "Let's get out of here."

"Crow?" Argo echoed, his voice thick with amusement.

"Yes," Crow whispered. They shrank back, and Karina wasn't sure she'd ever seen them look so small.

"Well, *Crow*," Argo said, dropping all pretense of cordiality. "I expect to see you at the *Godkiller* by sunset. If you don't show, I'll sink your newfound friends' pathetic little ship. After all, I know who you're sailing with, now."

He turned and vanished into the crowd.

Karina gripped Crow by the arm and led them back to the *Vengeance*. They stumbled behind her, struggling to keep up with her brisk pace. "I'm so sorry," she said, her gaze fixed ahead of her.

"Promise you won't go back there. Ignore his threat—we'll get sailing long before he can act on his word. Let's tell Jonah."

Crow did not reply as they weaved through the crowd.

"Hey, Crow?" Karina asked once across the *Vengeance's* gangplank. She placed both her hands firmly upon their shoulders. "You're loved here. You have a place in our family. Okay?"

"Y-yeah," Crow replied. "Thank you."

Karina let them walk below deck. Once they were gone, she stood by the gunwale and stared out at the crowds milling about the hub. She couldn't shake the feeling that this was her fault. If she hadn't been so eager to find her parents, they would have gone to a different hub.

And her parents weren't even here. What a waste.

Jonah emerged above deck with Mouse and stood with his arms folded. Faye and Willow crossed the gangplank together. They appeared to have sold a sizable portion of Karina's old trinkets, as well as a painting or two. They set their gear down and joined Jonah and Mouse. Karina joined them and opened her mouth, ready to inform Jonah of Argonaut's presence.

"I want to do a headcount before we set sail," Jonah called before she could get a word out, "Argonaut is docked at the north end—I would like to get out of here as soon as possible."

He knows, Karina thought as the crew lined up for roll call. *Good.*

"Where is Crow?" Jonah asked.

"Downstairs," Karina said. "In their cabin."

"Someone fetch them. I want to see everyone's face."

Mouse hurried below deck. The crew stood in silence. Faye fidgeted with the sleeves of her coat while Willow's gaze was trained on the horizon. When Mouse returned, Crow was not at his side.

"They weren't there," Mouse signed. "I checked the washroom, too. Nothing."

"Argonaut threatened Crow to return to his ship or he'd sink us," Karina gasped, "I told them not to listen."

Jonah's eyes widened. "You think Argonaut has them."

"He might. Gods, I—I thought they were safe downstairs. They must've snuck out."

He turned his gaze to the hub. "We would have seen them leave."

Willow whistled to gather Karina and Jonah's attention. "Mouse has something to say. Look at him."

Karina turned her gaze to the teenager. His mouth pressed into a tight frown. "Their window was open," Mouse signed. "They may have climbed around the hull."

Jonah cursed and kicked an errant nail lying on the deck. It flew in an arc over the gunwale and into the ocean.

13

"There were four at the beginning of time. Water, the king. Wilds, the advisor. Fire, the soldier. Sky, the fool."
—*The Book of the Tide*

40th Storm, Great Flood 1058

Crow nudged their way through the crowd. Hands tucked into their pockets, they kept their head down and their guard up. Karina said thieves were common at hubs, and Crow was both alone and vulnerable, even if they carried nothing of value. They had left their near-empty sack of coins in their cabin.

When they reached the *Godkiller's* long steel gangplank, an involuntary shudder racked their body. They cast a glance over their shoulder, back toward the *Vengeance.*

"Well, well." Argo's voice startled them. Too late to turn back now. "Look who made the right decision."

"I'm not boarding your ship," Crow called out, standing their ground with as much firmness as they could muster. Even still, they stuttered. "You...you said you wanted to see me—you never said I had to board. You'll tell me everything, a-and you'll tell it to me here."

"Don't be stubborn. It would be rude to turn down my hospitality."

"Hospitality?" Crow couldn't help but scoff, a little quirk they'd picked up from Jonah. "You threatened to sink an innocent ship."

"The *Vengeance* is not innocent," Argonaut said. "I won't speak to you until we're within a reasonable distance. So, if you want answers, I suggest you come aboard."

Crow's plan ended there. They had hoped to get what they needed from Argo without boarding the ship. Even standing in front of the gangplank gave them unwanted flashes of past experiences. *Needles. Chains. Steel. Pain.*

"Otherwise, I would advise you to hurry back to the *Vengeance*," Argonaut continued when Crow did not move. "So I can focus on shooting you and your pathetic new crew down."

Their instincts begged them to leave while they could, but if they ran, they would endanger the crew of the *Vengeance,* and they'd never learn who they were. Argonaut, loath as they were to admit, was their sole lead. Cautious, they stepped forward, hands shaking as they drew closer to the most dangerous man they knew.

"Good boy," Argo said with a smarmy grin. He placed his flesh hand upon Crow's shoulder and guided them onto the *Godkiller's* deck. The sleek steel surface was far less hospitable under their feet than the wood grain of the *Vengeance.*

Argo led them over to a small fold-out table. Two stiff steel chairs sat on either side, and atop the table was a white ceramic kettle and two mugs. Crow sat on the edge of the chair closest to the gangplank, poised to bolt.

"Would you like some tea?" Argo asked as he poured water into a cup and dropped a tea bag in.

"I'd rather we—"

"Please, I insist." Argo pushed the mug to Crow. He poured a second mug for himself. His tea bag had a different colored label.

"You promised you'd tell me."

"You're so tense, kid." Argo leaned back in his chair and took a long sip of his drink. "Relax."

Crow frowned. They scootched a tiny bit back onto the chair and picked up the teacup, the liquid within disturbed by their trembling hands. They took a sip. To their knowledge, they'd never had tea before, so they weren't sure what to expect, but it wasn't too terrible. Its warmth helped soothe their nerves. The roof of their mouth tingled. They drank some more.

"You like it? It's my favorite black tea blend. It's great with a dash of honey, if you'd like."

"Quit drawing this out," Crow said. "Tell me what you know. You promised."

"It's high time you came home, son."

"I'm not your son!" Crow stood. The chair, forced backwards, screeched against the metal deck. They stood too quick. A wave of dizziness hit them, and they stumbled. "Your story has holes. Knock it off."

"Fine. Listen, *boy*. You can run around and play pretend with those sailors who've got no clue where to even begin with you, but you'll always come running back to me."

"I have no reason to."

"Oh, but you do. Why are you here now?"

"Because you said you'd tell me who I was."

Argonaut had the gall to laugh, deep and hearty. He stood. "You poor, naïve child."

"I'm not a child."

"My apologies. How old *are* you, then?"

"Um..."

"Twenty-three? Twenty-four?" Argo circled around the table like a predator stalking its prey.

"I...I don't know."

Crow took a step backwards and tripped over their chair. Argonaut caught them by the arm before they could fall. Why were they so disoriented?

"I'll let you in on a little secret." Argo's long prosthetic fingers curled around their bicep. Crow wrenched free of his grasp and stumbled away. Their vision swam. "I have no reason to tell you anything. You knowing who you are will only serve to my detriment."

"But you *do* know." Their tongue was heavy. The tingling sensation spread down the back of their throat.

"Yes."

"Did you wipe my memory?"

"Heavens, no. To have that kind of power would be a dream come true."

Crow needed to get back to the *Vengeance*. The *Vengeance* was safe. They threw a punch, but it was sloppy and aimless. Black spots danced in their vision. Argonaut grabbed Crow's wrist and twisted their arm down, around, behind their back. Their shoulder lit up in hot agony. Crow kicked at Argonaut's legs, but the attempt was weak and ineffective. Their body refused to cooperate.

"Hey!" A deep, gruff voice cut through Crow's muffled hearing. They weren't sure they'd ever feel so relieved to hear the sheer rage in Jonah's voice. They blinked at the blurry forms at the top of the gangplank. Jonah, Karina, and Willow. "Get your hands off them!"

Argo laughed. So jovial. So wrong. He snaked his arm around Crow's neck, and they choked. Survival instinct cut through the growing haze and sharpened their awareness. They clawed at Argo's arm with renewed vigor.

Willow raised her rifle and trained it on Argonaut. Crow hoped she had steady aim.

"Put your weapons down," Argo snapped. Crow gasped as the pirate pressed the cold barrel of a pistol against the underside of their chin. *Where had it come from?* "All of you."

Karina dropped her long combat knife in a heartbeat. It clattered to the floor at her feet. Crow stared at it. The knife had a wavy blade, almost reminiscent of a sea monster's tentacle or a long, triangular flag in the wind. The shape was mesmerizing. If they kept staring at it, they could forget everything around them...

"You won't kill them," Jonah said. He hadn't dropped his sword. Willow, too, held her rifle firm.

"You think so?" Argo pressed the gun firmer against Crow's jaw. His arm tightened around their throat. Their constricted throat ached. They couldn't breathe—not even a tiny gasp of breath. Their vision darkened, blanketed by the threat of sweet, quiet unconsciousness.

"Why else would you be trying so damn hard to get your hands on them?"

Argonaut's finger danced upon the gun's trigger.

"Jonah," Karina warned. "Don't be reckless."

Jonah took a step forward. Two steps. Three steps. A gunshot ripped through the air.

But when Crow dared to open their eyes—when had they closed?—a dart poked out of Argonaut's bicep, pierced straight through the crisp linen of his button-up shirt. Argonaut's grip on Crow slackened. He collapsed, and Crow fell to their knees, too unsteady to stand upright.

Willow lowered her rifle.

"Good thinking," Jonah said. "How long will he be out for?"

"About two hours. Maybe an hour and a half, 'cuz he's so tall."

"Shoot him with another one."

Willow was more than happy to oblige.

Crow stared up at Jonah as he approached. He extended his hand. Crow didn't move.

"Come on." Jonah wrapped his fingers around Crow's wrist. Their mind was still reeling, still dizzy and disoriented. They flinched, squirmed, struggled. Jonah let go without much of a fight.

"Crow," he said, clearing his throat. "Uh. Look at me."

Crow couldn't bear to. Instead, they stared down at the steel underneath their palms. Their mind flashed to a much darker, scarier place, one with needles and anguish, where everything was far too fuzzy to remember...

"I—"

"You're fine." Instead of Jonah asking, he stated it as though it were a command. "Can you stand? We need to get out of here."

Crow nodded, even though they didn't think they could. Even now, they reminded themself, *don't be a nuisance.* They stood on shaky legs as Mouse steered the *Vengeance* beside the *Godkiller.* The wooden hull bumped against steel. The *Godkiller* rocked, and Crow fell back to their knees.

"I think 'm," Crow tried. They struggled to form words. "...allergic to tea."

"What?" Jonah stared at them with furrowed brows and a gnarled frown.

Crow pointed a shaky finger at the tea table. Karina rushed over to it. As she investigated, Crow lay face-first against the deck. For once, they found the cold metal against their cheek refreshing.

"Faye!" Karina called. "Come here! I need your help identifying something."

Faye tossed the gangplank between the *Godkiller* and the *Vengeance* and hurried across. She jogged over to Karina. The duo spoke in hushed tones Crow was too weary to make out.

Karina muttered, "Oh, Heavens."

"What?" Jonah barked.

"This is Blythian ashweed. He drugged Crow."

Drugged?

They struggled to keep up with the conversation as it progressed. Jonah said something. Faye replied. The voices melded into a big, mushy mess in Crow's brain. The muddy conversation came back into clarity when Jonah turned to Crow and snapped, *"Why the hell would you drink it?"*

"I'unno," Crow mumbled. "I didn't think—"

"Of course you didn't think," Jonah snarled. "It's a damn miracle you've got a brain in that skull of yours at all."

Faye slung her arm around them and helped them to their feet. Crow resigned to the discomfort of being touched. They slumped against her as she led them to the safety of the *Vengeance.*

"Willow," Jonah snapped. "Come with me."

"Jonah?" Faye called. Crow glanced over their shoulder. Jonah's blurry form stood at the steel trapdoor leading below deck, Willow at his side. "What are you doing? We need to go!"

"We won't be long," Jonah snapped back. He wrenched the trapdoor open and hopped in, disregarding the ladder. Willow followed him below.

The next thing Crow knew, they were on their hammock, alone.

14

40th Storm, Great Flood 1058

The bowels of the *Godkiller* were lit by the brightest artificial blue lights Jonah had ever had the misfortune of putting up with. Bluer than daylight and as bright as the sun itself, they were so intolerable that a headache pulsed against Jonah's skull. He much preferred the soft orange light of his beloved *Vengeance*. His hand hovered over the blade at his hip. The *Godkiller* was quiet. Where was Argonaut's crew? Some of them were walking the hub—but he couldn't expect *all* of them to be.

"Keep your guard up," he whispered to Willow. Her footsteps were soft. Had he not turned to look at her, he may have worried she wasn't there. "I'd like to figure out what he wanted from Crow."

Below deck, the whirring of the ship's engine was unbearable. The constant thrum grated on his nerves. A dreadnought like the *Godkiller* needed a damn lot of energy and moving parts to run. The unfortunate side effect of power was noise. Jonah was grateful his ship didn't have such loud machinery. He wasn't sure he'd be able to bear it.

"Hey," Willow whispered. "Over there."

A door toward the end of the passageway emitted a soft yellow glow. Against the fluorescents, Jonah had missed such a tiny detail.

He approached with caution and pushed the door open. Willow gasped.

This cabin was empty aside from two glass vats in the center. One was filled to the brim with liquid gold, which shimmered under the bright lights and cast gold reflections across the floor. The second was a quarter full.

"God's Blood," Willow muttered. She was not as devout as Karina, but she still paused at the threshold and muttered some bogus prayer. While she did, Jonah stepped inside.

Soph had always been enamored by the stories about God's Blood. A single vial held a lifetime of wealth. It could cure disease. It could heal wounds. It held an ethereal beauty unlike anything humanity had ever seen. That's what her favorite fables said, at least.

Unease coiled within Jonah. He still couldn't wrap his brain around the existence of gods—this must be fake. The man could get rich off people's beliefs. But if, on a slim chance, it *was* real, how often did Argonaut have to drain a god dry to collect this much? How had he stored it so it would not congeal?

Jonah popped his blade a knuckle's length from its hilt and ran his index finger across its exposed steel. The shallow cut beaded crimson as he approached the vats. Both had spigots on the side, and Jonah held his bleeding finger underneath one, turning the crank until a drop of gold splashed onto his finger. When he wiped the substance away, his cut was gone.

Shit.

His mind worked in overdrive to come up with a *practical* reason as to why his cut had vanished, but he came up dry. *Some sort of herbal serum,* he thought, but even then, the wound wouldn't have disappeared—it still would have taken a couple of days. *Or I didn't slice myself deep enough.*

He couldn't cut any deeper, though, lest he spiral back into his old self-harm habit. Already, the bitter sting of intentionally torn flesh taunted him.

Off to the side, against the leftmost bulkhead, stood a rack of empty vials. Jonah grabbed as many as he could carry. Six. Willow's gaze followed him, interest piqued, as he filled and corked each vial.

"Why would he want this much blood?" Willow asked, as though

Jonah would have any semblance of an answer for her. She paced a perimeter around the room, rifling through every drawer, every pile of paper. Whatever she sought, she seemed to come up dry.

Jonah tucked the vials into the inner pocket of his coat. He eyed the vats. He could ruin Argonaut's plan, whatever it may be, in one fell swoop. It would serve the man right for ruining Jonah's life in the wake of his grief. He drew his blade and slammed its hilt against the glass. Upon first impact, the glass did not budge. An alarm blared. *Shit.* On his second strike, thick webbed cracks crawled up the vat's surface. With his third, it shattered, and a massive wave of God's Blood poured to the floor. He did the same for the second tube. His clothes were drenched in gold. He tried not to think too much of it.

When the blood was nothing more than a pool on the floor, draining out the anti-flood system, which would eject the blood into the ocean, Jonah and Willow sprinted from the room.

"We need to find Argo's quarters," Willow gasped.

"Why?"

"He might have a journal or research notes—something pointing toward why he's collecting it!"

"No. We need to get out of here!"

Willow, instead of heading for the exit ladder, whirled around the corner and took to peeking through every doorway she passed. *What's the point of being captain,* he thought with some bemusement, *if nobody listens?*

Jonah caught Willow's arm. Loath as he was to humor her, Jonah gritted his teeth and said, "Follow me."

He'd spent his fair share of time aboard the *Godkiller.* He knew these passageways well enough, though Argonaut had reorganized a touch in the seven years since. His cabin, though, was in the exact same spot it always was, toward the stern.

In order to get there, they'd have to cross the most-manned cabins on the ship: the engine room, the bridge, and artillery. And with the alarms blaring as they were, the high screech grating at his eardrums, artillery was the biggest threat.

"Stay low," he whispered as they ducked around a corner. He

hunkered close to the bulkhead to his left. "Ready your gun."

The click of Willow loading her rifle cut through the sharp screech of the alarm.

As they passed the large, open doorway to the engine room, Jonah dared to peek inside. It was devoid of crew. He tensed.

The bridge was empty, too. *Shit, shit, shit.* He wished there had been at least one or two—he could have taken them out and eased the burden down the line. But, alas, it was all hands in artillery, the crew gathering their weapons in anticipation of the unseen threat.

"Look over there," Jonah whispered, pointing to a door past artillery. "Next to the support beam. Argonaut's cabin."

Willow nodded.

All hell broke loose before Jonah and Willow reached artillery. One pirate rushed out, two swords in hand, a second pirate in his wake. Not much longer, Jonah and Willow were dogged by pirates.

Jonah did not recognize a single face. Between when Karina first found him and now, Argonaut had replaced his crew in full. Piracy was a dangerous profession, and Argonaut had a nasty habit of throwing lives on the line to preserve his own.

Jonah pushed his body between the pirates and Willow. He hoped the action said enough. *I'll hold them off,* he would have said, if he wasn't so concerned about giving away their intentions. *Go.* As he parried a strike, Willow seemed to understand. She slipped away.

A pirate with long, scraggly brown hair raised his flintlock pistol and fired after her. He was the first to die by Jonah's sword. He drove the blade straight through the man's stomach.

Jonah hadn't taken a life since he worked with Argonaut. He had been raw and manipulable back then, and Argonaut had no problem employing him to kill. Merchants, innocent sailors, and pirates alike fell under his blade. All Argonaut had done was claim they were complicit in Sophie's murder.

He compartmentalized the thought and pressed on.

Keeping six pirates away from Willow as she sprinted for Argonaut's cabin was not an easy endeavor. He was a well-trained fighter and had, as Faye tended to put it, *the endurance of a god,* but he was no less mortal than any of the men around him. There was still a point when one drowned, and with each slash and jab, he grew ever closer. Sweat gathered around the neckline of his fitted gray shirt.

Another bullet slipped past Jonah's defense. Behind him, Willow screamed—and when he whirled around, the familiar terror of loss striking him, Willow clutched her leg. Her ankle was drenched in blood, which gushed from a wound in her calf. Everything around him dissolved away until only panic remained.

A pirate grabbed him, and he shattered.

He wasn't aware of himself when he whirled around, rage boiling to the surface. He was outside his own body as he stole a pirate's pistol and shot him down. He'd always hated fighting with guns. Guns made combat too easy. But now, the ease of killing was all he wanted, all he *craved.* The blaring of the alarms grew distant, replaced by a ringing in his ears. He wasn't sure of the details, because all he knew was rage— blinding, overwhelming. Jonah would be damned if he let Willow die the same way Sophie had, by a pirate's hand.

His senses filtered back one by one, long after six corpses dropped to the *Godkiller's* floor. Hearing came first. The alarm still blared. Next was touch. His face was wet. Had he been crying? His shaky hand found his cheek. When he lowered his hand, crimson coated his fingertips.

Rational thought came next. Argonaut kept a crew of ten. Where were the other four? Were they walking the hub? How long would it be until they arrived? How far away could one hear the *Godkiller's* alarm system?

Willow stood a few paces off to the side, a notebook clutched tight in her hands. Seeing Crow fear him was one thing, but Willow? Willow had never once feared him. She stood silent, stunned.

"Let's get out of here," he mumbled. As he cooled off, the shame crept in. He'd slaughtered all six of them. How much better was he than any other pirate? "I want to be long gone by the time Argonaut wakes."

"Jonah," Willow said, her voice steady. "We can't leave yet."

"The hell do you mean?" Jonah snapped, a bit too viciously. Willow flinched. "You're wounded. We're getting you back to the *Vengeance—*"

"I want to check the brig. A few more moments won't kill us. I'm okay, Jonah. Really. Hurts like a bitch, but I'll survive."

Jonah was too exhausted to argue. He let Willow drape her arm over his shoulders for support, and together, they hobbled their way down one more ladder.

Argonaut's brig was massive. Unlike the *Vengeance,* which employed a single cell, the *Godkiller's* brig spanned an entire deck. Each cell was state-of-the-art. Steel bars, all spaced at the perfect width to keep anyone from slipping through, not a dot of rust in sight.

"Hello?" Willow called, her voice soft and gentle, but she received no reply. She peered into each cell, one by one, as she limped along. "If the blood means anything, Argonaut has a god in his custody," she said. "We need to free him."

They found a cell toward the middle, which boasted broken chains and golden splatters all over the floor. In the corner sat a rickety IV drip filled with a familiar shade of violet. What had the dockworker said when Jonah sold the Monster Blood for a week on Farmstead? Monster Blood could somehow...kill a god? It hadn't mattered at the time, but something deep in his core nagged him. The evidence of gods' existence was stacking up.

"Monster Blood," he said, hesitant to acknowledge it. "How does it work?"

"You want to know?" Willow asked. Jonah didn't blame her for wanting clarification. Jonah had always brushed it off in the past.

"Yes."

"Legend says there's divinity in every fiber of a god's being," she said. "But in a mortal body, it's limited to the bloodstream. When Monster Blood comes in contact with God's Blood, it neutralizes divinity. Well, *neutralizes* is the wrong word. *Corrupts* is better. In small doses, like Argonaut must have been doing, I imagine the pain would be excruciating. But in a large enough dose, it can destroy divinity. When Monster Blood kills a god, they don't go to the Underworld like a mortal soul. They're gone forever."

Jonah didn't know what to say.

Willow eyed the bag of Monster Blood for quite some time, her eyes narrowed. "Let's get back to the *Vengeance.*"

Not eager to waste any more time, he hoisted Willow over his shoulder—much to her chagrin—and hauled her above deck. He ignored Argonaut's unconscious body upon the deck. If he were less selfish, he would have killed Argonaut, too, to spare the world from his piracy. But right now, all he cared about was getting his crewmate to safety.

The way he had lost control...it scared him.

The *Vengeance* sailed southward under Mouse's steady hand. Faye had settled the drugged Crow in their cabin, where they would sleep it off in solitude. Blythian ashweed wasn't too harmful in small doses—and judging by how full the mug of tea was, Jonah doubted Crow had taken much in. They'd be fine.

Willow was fine, too. Jonah hovered in the doorway while Faye patched up her wound. He had, after some convincing, spared a bit of God's Blood for her. Faye poured a few drops of radiant gold onto Willow's wound. The damaged flesh knit itself back together.

Glad as Jonah was to see Willow healed, he found himself rather horrified by the prospect of God's Blood being *real.*

Now, he sat across from Karina in his cabin. From his coat pocket, he produced the six vials of God's Blood. He tucked them into the safety of his desk drawer. The vials occupied the space right next to a slip of paper his ex-girlfriend, Priya, had given him some time back: the note was signed with a winky-face and a string of Køveni gibberish. A summons. *In case you ever want to chat.*

The sign-off wasn't flirtatious, it was playful. He doubted her enchantment even worked, anyways—but it was a tiny reminder that, in the wake of him coming out as gay, they were still allies.

Maybe I should read her incantation, he mused. *She might have answers.* He wasn't keen on it, though. While he had an amicable split with Priya, calling upon her was nothing short of awkward. He shut the drawer.

Karina slumped against Jonah's desk, her forehead braced upon her palm. *"Heavens Almighty.* What was he going to do with that blood? Nyx mentioned his sales, but that doesn't account for the sheer volume you saw."

Jonah handed her the notebook Willow had found. He hadn't looked inside yet. He was a little afraid to. "This might give us a clue."

Karina flipped through the notebook. Her hazel eyes darted left and right as she skimmed the pages. "It doesn't say much. Plunder records and sales receipts."

"Great," Jonah grumbled. "The whole endeavor was a waste."

"It doesn't look like Argonaut has sold much God's Blood—enough to make a reputation, to stoke his ego, but it's a mere fraction. And on another page," Karina flipped through, trying to find what she was looking for. When she did, she pushed it across the desk to Jonah. "He's secured a deal with a *big client.* There's mention of a ritual, but it's vague. I don't know what it entails—I didn't think God's Blood could be used for magical means, though I suppose I'm not surprised."

"It doesn't say any more?"

"No. He knew better than to detail things out, lest it fall into the wrong hands."

"Do you think he intended to...sacrifice Crow?" Jonah wondered.

Karina was quick to shake her head. "No."

"You sound so certain."

"Jonah, I think..." She frowned. "Never mind. You wouldn't believe me, anyways." She stood. Her gaze trailed down Jonah's form. "You should take a bath—you've got blood all over you."

Jonah nodded, and he sank into his seat as Karina disappeared from the room.

Gods, he thought. *Real, living gods.*

There was no other, more logical explanation.

15

"Einari is our lord! Our father! Our teacher! Rejoice in his mercy! Despite our sins, he has spared us: the worthy, the righteous!"
—Prayer #36 from the Book of the Tide

43rd Storm, Great Flood 1058

The cabin deck's lights flickered. Jonah sighed—he'd meant to replace the bulbs during the last hub stop. A faulty light fixture was the least of his worries, though, as he approached the last door in the passageway. His foot bumped a plate of lemon-seasoned cod, untouched since lunch.

Three days had passed since the encounter with Argonaut, and Crow had taken to locking themself away in their cabin. Faye and Willow had tried, on occasion, to speak with them, but were unsuccessful. Crow's behavior grew frustrating—he wanted to have a meeting with his whole crew about the findings. Crow was the only reason he hadn't done it yet.

Thrice, he rapped his knuckles against the door.

"Crow."

Jonah braced his forearm against the doorframe and leaned his weight into it. He paused. Waited. The only answer he received was the ship's creaks and groans, the lights' incessant buzz.

"Whatever Argonaut said, I... You're... Ugh." Jonah groaned. "You know what? I could give you the annoying *we're all here for you* speech you've heard a million times, but it won't solve any of your problems. It's not going to give you your memory back. It's not going to fix what happened on the *Godkiller*. Argonaut is nasty. He can claim he knows who you are, but it's a bluff."

Jonah allowed Crow the opportunity to respond if they wanted to. They didn't.

"So, what? You fell for his trap. You're not alone. I fell for one, too. He had me convinced I could take vengeance against the pirates who took my sister from me. All he needed in return was for me to work for him. Ridiculous, right? He *is* a pirate. The logic was faulty. But he has this weird *charm*. He tells you what you want to hear, and when you're vulnerable, you can't help but believe him. I made some awful decisions back then, and if it weren't for Karina, I wouldn't be here right now."

Jonah grimaced. He had worked hard to bury his past. The grief, even now, still pierced Jonah's heart like the knife that murdered Sophie Morgan.

"My point is," Jonah growled, "if you didn't know before, you know now. You can sit in your cabin and feel sorry for yourself. You can starve yourself until you wither away and die. Or, you can make the effort to figure out who you are. You're smart. You don't need someone like Argonaut to tell you jack shit."

Silence.

Jonah stood up straight. He was about to walk away when faint footsteps echoed behind the door. He waited a touch longer.

The door creaked open, slow and unsure.

Crow looked miserable. Their hair was unkempt, and deep bags lined their eyes. They stood with poor posture and wore one of Karina's blankets draped over their shoulders.

"...May I come in?" he asked, keeping his voice low. Crow stepped aside—it wasn't a verbal yes, but it wasn't a no, so Jonah stepped in. The first thing he did was prop open the small window. It didn't take a genius to know how much Crow enjoyed fresh air.

"Come here," Jonah said as he sat on the edge of Crow's hammock. Tentative, Crow sat beside him. The hammock rocked under their combined weight, and the rope flexed, forcing their shoulder to press against his. Jonah, keeping his movements slow and deliberate, pulled a fine-toothed seashell comb from his coat pocket and brushed it through Crow's messy black hair. Crow tensed at the contact, and Jonah hesitated—but in time they relaxed.

Jonah sat with Crow in silence. There was no expectation to talk. He combed out every knot and tangle in their hair. Their eyes drifted shut as Jonah worked.

He had a thousand questions rattling around in the back of his mind, but none of them Crow could answer. *Who are you? What's your real name? Why does Argonaut want you?* Crow was an odd little puzzle, bundled up into a small, anxious frame.

"What do you know about the gods?" he eventually asked. Maybe he could learn a thing or two. His comb found a snag toward the back. Using his fingers, he teased the wavy tangles loose.

"There's a core pantheon of four," Crow replied. Their voice was almost as hoarse as it had been the day they'd first met. "Einari holds the title of God King. The gods of the wilds, fire, and sky serve under him. But there's hundreds of others, too, lesser gods, like the god of indulgence or the goddess of luck, often overlooked, but no less important."

"You mentioned a distaste for Einari when we met up with the *Burning Maiden.*"

"He flooded Midir and left innocent people to suffer," Crow said. "A thousand years is far too long."

Jonah chuckled. "If I could empty the planet of all this damn water, bucket by bucket, I would."

"Hah. Good luck."

Jonah tucked the comb into his pocket. Combing their hair didn't fix the bags under their eyes or the stiffness of unwashed clothes, but they appeared to have brightened a touch. The hopelessness wasn't all-consuming anymore.

When Crow opened their eyes, Jonah realized how close they were. Something warm, deep in Jonah's core, bubbled to the surface. This was what he'd hoped to avoid by leaving Crow at Farmstead Isle. Affection.

He couldn't grow attached to another crewmate. Willow had gotten shot because of him. And Sophie—he hadn't protected her. Her blood was on his hands.

He stood. The farther he was from Crow, the better.

"Crew meeting in ten minutes," he grumbled, then he hurried to his cabin.

He needed to chart a route south before the meeting, so he could give his crew a proper directive, but he couldn't focus. His thoughts were too fixated on the gentle curve of Crow's jaw, the mop of wavy black hair that dared to fall in front of sincere blue eyes, and their slender, fidgety hands.

Jonah stared at the map, eyes glazed over. Focus did not come to him. He forced himself to his feet and gathered his crew. He'd chart the route later. Whatever.

He started with Faye and Willow. Their door was closed. Jonah groaned. The two women had an open policy, happy to take visitors, but when the door was shut like this...

Well, it meant Faye and Willow were getting *frisky.*

Jonah shuddered. He had no qualms, but he hated interrupting. It was awkward and uncomfortable for everyone involved. Gritting his teeth, he knocked. Loud.

"Uh, hang on!" Faye called out. Jonah could hear rustling from inside as they hurried to get themselves presentable. When the door opened, Faye's choppy dark brown hair was ruffled, and Willow wore one of Faye's shirts.

"Crew meeting," Jonah grumbled. "Grab Crow on your way up."

"Are they—"

"They're fine. Go get them."

Jonah stalked away.

Karina was already by the fire pit, so Jonah didn't bother looping her in—she'd figure it out. He instead joined Mouse at the helm.

"Still headed south?" he signed.

"Right on course," Mouse replied with confident hands. "We're headed toward the central Dead Zone."

"Good. Go ahead and slow us down."

"Yes, sir."

"Crew meeting by the fire pit."

Mouse nodded and set to work, engaging the appropriate mechanisms to ensure the *Vengeance* could sail steady on its own.

He waited beside the fire pit, staring out at the ocean. Sunlight reflected off the glistening waters below. The air was crisp and temperate. This was the clearest storm season he'd ever experienced. Sun season had long since lapsed—where was the rain?

When the rest of his crew arrived, Jonah turned to face them. "Argonaut had a revolting amount of God's Blood on his ship," he said. "Whoever the god is, he was nowhere to be found."

"I hope he's okay," Faye said. "Or, uh, she?"

"You know," Crow chimed in. Their voice, to Jonah's surprise, was peppy and bright. "The gods don't have genders. They reflect whatever the mortal folk depict. You could refer to Einari, for example, as *he* or *she* or *they* or *xe*, and it would all be accurate. Right now, he's *he,* but only because mortals perceive him as such."

"Since when were you an expert on the gods?"

"I don't know."

"Focus!" Jonah snapped. "I've been thinking about it, and I believe I made a mistake. I smashed Argonaut's blood supply. Watched it drain through his anti-flood system."

Faye raised her hand. "Why's it a mistake?"

"He's going to be desperate. He's going to try harder than ever to get the god back into his hands, and he's going to set a target on *us.* "

Ever since he met Karina, Jonah prided himself on not getting wrapped up in the latest pirate drama. Now, he sat at the center of Argonaut's attention again. The crew exchanged nervous glances.

"We need to be extra vigilant. I want everyone on lookout. If there's another ship on the horizon, I want to know about it. Buckle down on defense—I want the cannons prepped, and I want everyone to keep weapons on hand."

"What about the god?" Karina asked. Her gaze, for some reason, flitted over to Crow.

"We'll avoid the god, too," Jonah said. "If gods are real, then I have no doubt he can handle himself fine. He's a *god.* "

"I think we should find him," Mouse signed.

"We'd get ourselves killed." Jonah signed back with snappy hands. "We're already big enough a target as it stands. We'll keep moving south."

"And Argonaut's ritual?" Willow asked. "We have no clue what that entails, but it's probably bad news. If we can find him before he hires a new crew, we could have an advantage—"

"I don't want anything to do with Argonaut," Jonah growled. "Meeting adjourned."

He stomped off before he could let his crew get another word in.

"I don't understand them," Jonah grumbled, his gaze trained on the mast above, where Crow perched, feathery hair blowing in the breeze.

"Not everybody hates heights like you do," Karina teased. She knelt a few paces away, helping Mouse patch a hole in a tarp. "I once overheard them telling Faye they like to feel the wind."

"They can feel it fine from down here."

"The currents are stronger up high."

"Get back to work," Jonah grumbled. Karina shot him a smirk and signed a few things to Mouse—a translation of their conversation.

Crow perched atop the safety rail, disregarding the one implement designed to ensure occupants didn't plummet to their deaths. Jonah had half a heart to scold them when they returned to the deck later.

Iron handholds chilled Jonah's palms. He gazed at the rungs stretching upwards and recoiled. What the hell was he doing? Who did Crow think they were, luring Jonah to the place he hated most, like a siren's song? Curses! It angered him!

Still, Crow's mystery was alluring, and the more time he spent around them, the more he yearned to figure them out. They were such a fundamental part of Jonah's crew now, despite the resistance Jonah had initially put up, that he could seldom imagine a life in their absence.

"Woah! Jonah's climbing the mast!" Karina's voice was far below him. Jonah snapped from his thoughts and gasped.

"Why?" Faye replied.

"I don't get it, either."

Jonah glanced down. He had managed to climb to the mainsail yard—halfway between the ground and the crow's nest. Already, he was much too high for comfort. With a gasp, he clutched the handholds with all his might, his eyes blown wide.

Above, Crow sat with tall posture and a serene smile on their face. A tiny bird with gentle brown feathers, no bigger than Crow's palm, hopped along the railing beside them. Jonah wasn't sure he'd ever seen them so relaxed. Jonah pressed onward, rung by rung. He was far too stubborn to turn back. So long as he did not look down again, he would be fine. The mainsail blocked his view, so he could pretend he was still near the safety of the deck.

When he reached the top, he met Crow's inquisitive gaze. They hopped down from their perch at the edge and extended a hand. Jonah took it, his hand clammy against theirs. Crow's grip was firm as they helped him up.

The flooring beneath his feet was a minor reassurance.

"Are you okay?" Crow asked.

"Fine."

Crow hopped back onto the ledge, legs propped up on the rail as if such a precarious position were the easiest, most comfortable place in the world. Jonah stood to Crow's right. The little bird flew away, spooked by Jonah's presence. He gripped the safety rail until his knuckles turned ghost-white. Far from the ship's center of gravity, the sway magnified tenfold. The sensation almost made him seasick. He *never* got seasick.

"You don't like it up here," Crow observed. "So why come?"

"You're always up here."

"I like it."

"Aren't you worried you'll fall?"

"I've fallen from much higher before."

Jonah frowned. "Did it hurt?"

"Yeah. I remember hitting the ocean. You wouldn't think it, but falling into water *stings*."

"I'm surprised you were uninjured. I don't know all the science behind it—Mouse does—but the surface tension of water could wound someone. Kill, even. What happened? Do you remember?"

"No," Crow whispered. "But every time I think about it, it gets a smidge clearer. I remember how cold the water was. I would have drowned if Argonaut hadn't pulled me out."

"Hmm."

Crow's attention shifted. "It's a pretty view, don't you think?"

"Whatever."

"It almost makes me wish I didn't hate water so much."

"You're afraid of it." Like how Jonah feared heights.

"Yes, but it also angers me." Crow remembered nothing about themself, but they had some damn strong opinions about the god of the sea. They didn't seem eager to talk about it today. "The sun's going to set soon. You picked a great time to come up."

"I've seen thousands of sunsets. They're not special."

"I think it's breathtaking. The sky. Everything about it—the clouds, the sun, the moon, the stars. The way it could be blue, or orange, or pink..."

"It's alright."

"Despite how everybody except your crew seems to hate me, it's wonderful here."

"You speak as though you've never lived in Midir before."

"I must have, though. Where else would I have lived?"

He didn't reply. He didn't know what to say. The sun painted the sky a brilliant orange, which reflected upon the ocean's choppy surface, as it began its descent.

"I..." Crow sounded frustrated. "I don't remember anything about myself, about where I'm from, or anything about my surroundings. It all feels new to me."

Jonah had read plenty about amnesia since Crow's arrival, and even in the worst cases, patients still seemed to understand the rise and fall of the sun, the tiny islands dotting a world flooded by sea. Why didn't Crow?

"I was frustrated when I first found out you had no memory," Jonah admitted. "It was born of selfishness. I thought it to be an inconvenience. You were new and different, and I don't know how to handle things with grace. Karina's better at it. I have a set routine, I suppose, and when it gets disrupted, it stresses me out."

Crow's gaze drifted from the orange glow of the horizon over to Jonah. He dared to meet their eyes. The warm sunset light soaked into their hair and brightened their skin, giving them this ethereal glow. Jonah could have sworn there was a rim of gold around their pupils. *Central heterochromia,* it was called. A trick of the light, more likely, as the golden hour sun cast long beams across their skin.

"I get it. It's hard to know who to trust."

Jonah nodded. Crow yawned, raising a hand to cover their mouth as they did so.

"We should get down. I don't want you sleeping up here."

"I do it all the time," Crow stated, then paused, a tiny grin growing on their face. "*Oh,* I see. You need help getting down."

"I do not."

"Suuuure."

"I can get down fine on my own." Jonah approached the ladder, casting a quick glance up at the topsail. At least, the crow's nest wasn't all the way up *there.* He grabbed the iron handhold, ever-so-slow and cautious as he stepped out. "I don't want you to—"

His foot slipped. He grasped for the rungs and clung to them for dear life. His heart lurched.

"I could get you down to the deck faster if you wanted."

"The slow way is *fine,*" Jonah growled through gritted teeth. He lowered his foot to the next rung down, beginning his nervous descent. Climbing down was harder than climbing up, but he knew what the fast way entailed.

Crow grinned and saluted, then grabbed a rope belonging to the mainsail's rigging. They jumped. Jonah gasped, abject horror kicking in as Crow swung between ropes to the ground below.

Showoff.

Limbs shaking, he made his descent rung by rung. Gods, he'd made a mistake—he should never have climbed the mast. Relief washed over him as his boots kissed the deck. Crow lingered nearby, their eyes pinned on him, no doubt with the intent of making sure Jonah got down without incident. *Humiliating.*

When the sun disappeared, the crew disappeared, too. Crow,

however, remained. Jonah wondered how often they spent late nights alone above deck. They lay on their back in the middle of the deck, gazing up at the stars. Against his better judgment, Jonah sat beside them, hugging his knees. Soph had always loved to stargaze. Sitting beside Crow was a familiar comfort.

"You know, it's funny," Crow said when Jonah joined them, "I *know* I've seen the stars before. But I don't think I've ever seen them quite like this."

"You must be from an island," Jonah said. "The stars aren't as pretty there. Too much light from the houses—it's harder to see them all. The bright ones, if you're lucky."

"I don't want to be from an island."

"I know you don't."

They fell into silence. Crow stared upward, enraptured by the sky above. Jonah's eyes traced their jaw, the gentle smile on their pale face. His breaths came shallow and silent, as though any noise could disrupt the living painting that lay beside him, each brushstroke of Crow's form painted with the most masterful of intention. The gentle slope of their nose, their collarbone peeking through their new light blue shirt, top two buttons undone. This shirt fit them far better than the frumpy shirt they'd arrived in. It hugged them, tucked into their pants, accentuating their waist, and Jonah resisted with every fiber of his being the temptation of placing a hand upon their hip. No star could ever dream of being as radiant as Crow.

Jonah never once spared a glance at the sky.

16

"Let his wrath come. I am not afraid."
*—The Grand Catalogue of Last Words: Great Flood
Era. Death #0,000,000,001. Drowned.*
Note from Einari: "This wretched, foul-souled man...
he is the instigator, the crook who bled me dry. Make
sure he spends his eternity in Punishment, bearing the
weight of my wrath on his shoulders. Let him be the
face of humanity's sin."

44th Storm, Great Flood 1058

Crow dreamt they walked among the stars. Each footfall against a path of shimmering green and pink light echoed through a space existing both nowhere yet everywhere. The air around them was a dark midnight hue, deep violets and blacks that threatened to swallow them whole. The soft glow of the twinkling stars was their only respite from the reigning darkness.

Nothing was as expressive as the sky. The shimmering waves of an aurora, the wind, the thick clouds on a rainy day... The sky was vast, a symbol of freedom, vitality. It was male, it was female, it was neither, it was all. Crow's thoughts drifted over something fuzzy and vague, a memory they couldn't quite reach. A friend, speaking of the passion of a flame. But, their mind whispered, though flame was a wondrous thing, nothing could ever compare to the sky.

A beautiful white building stood proud in the distance, its stark marble demanding attention against the night sky. The temple looked similar to Farmstead Isle's, but taller, grander, as though the weaver of their dream had pinched the highest steeple between two fingers and stretched it upward. A deep, innate need to get to the building shot through Crow. They broke into a run.

The pathway narrowed, and Crow ran faster. No matter how hard or how fast they ran, the building did not grow nearer. The desperation built, pent up deep in Crow's gut, ready to explode. But when the walkway grew thinner than the sole of their own foot and they did nothing to slow their pace, they slipped.

And then they were falling, falling, *falling*.

When their back hit something far below, sending searing pain up their spine, their eyes shot open. They were far beneath the stars, confined to the *Vengeance's* deck.

Jonah was long gone. Crow didn't expect him to stay, but the emptiness beside them struck them as uncomfortable. They couldn't help but chuckle. Faye had been right. Jonah was odd, but he wasn't bad. He wasn't scary.

As Crow stood, their gaze drifted to the stars dotting the sky. They were so far away, and the distance left a lonesome feeling shrouding them. Crow reached their hand up and closed one eye. The tiny little specks danced atop their fingertips. If they reached high enough, could they touch one?

They couldn't. Discouraged, Crow retreated to their cabin, though they did not settle on their hammock. They sat cross-legged on the floor, bathed in silken moonlight, and gazed out their small, circular window.

"You look tired," Karina said, sidling up beside Crow at the fire pit. A set of matches lay ready for use on the iron fixture, but Crow had not lit the fire.

"I am."

"Have you eaten breakfast yet?"

"No, but I'm okay."

"Don't be ridiculous. I'll be right back—I'll grab some supplies." Karina hurried below deck.

Crow sat sideways on the bench, straddling it, staring at the horizon. They spotted a ship, a little speck where the sky met the sea. The morning sun glinted off its steel hull.

They didn't notice Karina's return until oil sizzled in the cooking pot. A small, contained fire burned below the pot, surrounded by an iron fixture designed to stop errant sparks from flying.

"There's a ship out there," Crow said. Karina turned away from the fire pit to take a look.

"It's far away," she replied, holding a hand to her brow, squinting against the morning sun. "Not flying any discernible flags—It's probably just a merchant."

Crow nodded. They stared at the fish simmering in the pot. Always fish. Karina chopped an onion and tossed it in. Onion seemed to be one of the few foods that lasted long enough in storage to be worth keeping aboard. Onion, potato, salted meat, oats, and citrus fruit, Karina had told them once.

"Jonah wants us all armed," Karina said. "Has he given you a weapon?"

"No."

Karina nodded. "We'll get you one after breakfast."

"Okay."

Karina flipped the fish. It sizzled in the pan.

"What's on your mind? We're here for you, you know. All of us. Jonah, too, even if he gives you shit about it."

"It's not important."

"Doubtful." Karina served the fish and onion onto a plate and held it out.

Crow took the plate. "...I know you all have been adamant I'm part of your family now, and I appreciate it, but...I still feel so alone."

They turned to look at the crew. Jonah chased Faye across the deck, angry. Faye laughed despite her frantic scramble to escape him, and off to the side, Willow stood with a hand to her mouth, stifling a giggle. A bucket sat by Willow's feet. Jonah's shirt was drenched. If they were in a better mood, they would have found it funny, too. *They're so tight-knit. But where do I fit in?*

Crow poked at their breakfast. They much preferred this over the bland oats Jonah made, but they didn't have much of an appetite. They took a tiny bite. "You've been through a lot. It's okay to feel a bit lost."

"Jonah thinks I'm from an island."

"I doubt it."

"You do?"

"I think I might know something about you. It's...well, would you be willing to humor me?"

"Um," Crow said. "Sure?"

"I'd like to prick your finger." She took their hand in hers. "It won't hurt. I promise."

She took Crow's hand and turned their palm toward the sky, tracing her fingers along the narrow scars lining their arm. They were somewhat sure Argonaut had given them those scars.

"When we first rescued you, I noticed someone had drawn your blood. I never came to a good conclusion as to why, and somewhere in the mess of everything, we all forgot about it. But I've had some time to think, and I wonder..."

She never got to finish her sentence. A cannonball sailed over the *Vengeance's* hull. A warning shot. The cannonball clipped the starboard gunwale. The ship shuddered. Jonah, across the deck, snapped to attention.

The ship, Crow thought. *Karina said it wasn't a threat. How am I supposed to know the difference?*

Faye hurried to the closest cannon and heaved it inboard, muscles straining as she rolled the weapon back as far as its rope fixtures would allow. She heaved the wormer off its stand and shoved it into the cannon's mouth. When she yanked it back out, its corkscrew-shaped tip pulled old ashes with it. She tossed the tool aside and grabbed another, a rod with cloth at the end, and shoved it into the cannon.

Karina gripped them by the wrist and pulled them toward the center of the deck, away from the front line. "Stay close to me, okay?"

"I can fight. All I need is a weapon." They eyed the training swords in a crate at the stern. They weren't ideal, but if they could get one, they wouldn't be defenseless.

"I know you can."

"What are you worried about, then?"

Karina did not reply.

On the opposing ship, Crow caught a glimpse of three crewmen. The captain stood at the bow, one hand up in the air. A call for peace. If these people were interested in a peaceful encounter, why would they fire upon the *Vengeance?*

"Faye, hold your fire," Jonah ordered.

"Yessir!" Faye heaved the cannonball into the gun's mouth. She pushed the cannon outboard and waited.

In tense silence, the crew waited. An uneasy stalemate settled as the ship pulled parallel to the *Vengeance.*

"Good mornin'!" a faux-cheerful voice called out. "Sorry 'bout the damage—nasty habit a' mine. Can't ever seem ta' land my warning shots right. Ha!"

Why would he say he was sorry if he wasn't sorry at all?

"Jack," Jonah snarled. "You're a bit far from home, aren't you? Shouldn't you still be in Anui, licking your wounds from the last time I kicked your ass?"

"Anui," Crow whispered.

"Pirate waters," Karina clarified.

"Køveni. Means *north*." The information was irrelevant. They weren't sure why they'd spoken. Karina nudged them a little farther behind her.

"Hospitable as always, Mr. Morgan." The pirate raised a hand to his brow, shielding his eyes from the sunlight.

"What do you want?" Jonah asked.

"Rumor's goin' around there's a god on the loose. 'Naut's got a pretty hefty price on 'is head."

"We don't have the god."

"Then ya won't mind me checkin' your crew real quick, will ya? Won't be much, don't gotta get messy. A li'l blood is all."

"Get lost."

"It's funny," Jack drawled, "how Argonaut put a price on 'im at all. A god is worth *so* much more than anythin' the ole man can dish out."

Jack reached into his belt pouch and pulled out a single bullet. Its hefty casing was painted violet.

"Ya see this?" he asked, a smarmy grin plastered on his scarred face. "This single bullet has enough Monster Blood in it to kill a god. One shot, and he's gone. Poof. Forever. This death ain't sendin' him back to the Heavens."

"Argo didn't put a reward on the god to get him back," Karina whispered in realization. "He did it to start a worldwide manhunt. Crow, we need to get you below deck."

"Why?"

Jack tucked the bullet back into his belt pouch while his crew lowered a gangplank.

"If you set one foot on my ship, I'm ending your miserable life," Jonah snarled. "You're outnumbered. You're picking a losing battle."

"Ah, with your first mate distracted, a teenager with raw noodles for arms, an' fresh meat who appears unarmed? A losing battle for you, indeed."

With a single gesture, the pirate captain authorized the boarding of the *Vengeance*. Faye, without waiting for Jonah's signal, fired her cannon. At such proximity, the cannonball slammed straight through the pirates' prow.

Two pirates sprinted across the gangplank. The burlier of the two, a hulking man clad in the fur of a skinned mountain goat, the endangered animal's horned head atop the man's head like a hood, grabbed Faye by the collar. She strained against his grip. Before she could grab the sword from her sheath, the pirate kicked her in the stomach, sending her tumbling across the wooden floor. Willow scrambled to her girlfriend's side.

Jack's other underling grabbed a barrel and threw it as far as he could into the chaos. It slammed into Jonah, sending splintered wood flying in every direction. Jonah skidded, his knees bent, arms up in front of his face. He teetered, but he did not lose his balance. Blood dripped down the slope of his forearms, seeping from long scrapes etched into his skin.

Jack loaded a standard bullet into his pistol. Still stationed on his own ship, he braced one foot against the gangplank and cocked the gun, searching for an easy target, a wicked grin plastered across his crooked face.

Willow helped Faye to her feet. A loud *pop* echoed through the air, and Mouse screamed in agony, a bullet lodged in his shoulder. Still, Karina's hand wrapped tight around their wrist, trying to pull them away from it all. Her effort was counterproductive and wasteful.

"The crew needs help," Crow snapped. They wrenched from her grip.

"Please, Crow, listen to me," Karina begged. "I can't tell you why now, not with pirates around, but you—*Get down!*"

Crow dove out of the way as the shell of a bomb slammed against the deck. The force of its explosion sent Karina flying in the opposite direction. Crow yelled as their head slammed upon the deck. Pain reverberated through their skull, pulsing with a loud, incessant thrum. Their ears rang. They squeezed their eyes shut and hoped it would pass.

Their face stung, sharp and bright. A chunk of shrapnel had caught them, leaving a long, diagonal wound from their cheek to the bridge of their nose. Without a weapon, they were useless. A fist was powerless against a gun.

Karina lay on the deck on the other side of the mainmast. Blood seeped from a wound in her side, which Mouse, despite his own injury, tried his best to patch up. Jonah and the goat fur-wearing pirate had their blades locked. Faye had the bomber pinned to the deck. Willow and Jack were in a stalemate, guns trained on each other, waiting to see who would dare shoot first.

Crow coughed. Their head spun. In their periphery, they spotted Karina's knife on the floor. With her incapacitated, Crow scooped it up and eyed its wavy blade. *I have a bad habit of stealing Karina's weapons.*

Jonah's opponent kicked him in the ribs. Jack fired his rifle. The bullet grazed Willow's cheek, a dangerous near-miss. Red, red, red. It was all so *red.*

As blood pooled at their chin, Karina stared up at them with wide, horrified eyes.

They squeezed the knife in their hand.

The man wearing the mountain goat fur grinned, wide and toothy. He sauntered toward Crow, cracking his knuckles. While he was too busy gloating over something Crow didn't feel in the loop on, they slammed the knife into his stomach. His large body fell out of Crow's line of sight, and their gaze found Jack's.

Jack slipped a hand into his bullet pouch.

Drip. Drip. Drip.

Crow glanced at the deck. A small puddle had formed at their feet, growing with each drop of blood dripping from their face. In the midday sunlight, it shimmered a beautiful, iridescent gold.

Jack loaded the violet-painted bullet into his gun, smirked, and fired.

Crow barely heard the pop of Jack's rifle over the pain that exploded in their stomach. They doubled over and screamed. White hot, acidic agony flowed through their veins, lighting every single nerve in their body aflame. They hit the deck, their body limp like a ragdoll. The world spun. They weren't sure which way was up. The brilliant aureate glow pooling beneath them turned the tainted yellow-brown of rust and decay.

The world around them faded into oblivion.

17

"And the mortal said to Blight, "You do not deserve your divinity!" and thrust the Monster Blood-coated blade into his heart..."
—The Book of Fire

44th Storm, Great Flood 1058

In a white marble hall, square in shape until it met a beautiful dome roof, four pristine marble chairs sat in a circle. In the center sat a pool of liquid silver contained within a basin of chiseled stone. Three bodies occupied the room. The easternmost seat sat empty.

"Look what you've done!" Elaine rose from her seat. Her stomach churned. She had not yet vomited today. For the sake of her dignity, she forced the nausea back. She combed her fingers through her short, wispy brown hair and tugged. Below her, the reflecting pool's surface was painted with the smoking barrel of the pirate's gun. "You've doomed them!"

"They needed to learn their lesson," replied the occupant of the northernmost seat. On any other day, sunlight would peer in through the windows above and illuminate Einari's blue skin and seafoam hair. There was no sunlight now, his face cast in shadow.

"What are we supposed to do now?" *Don't vomit, don't vomit, don't vomit...*

"All we can do is replace them."

Elaine shot Novika a pleading glance. Novika, a feminine figure with a small, unimposing frame and dark skin, neck draped with jewels and beads of green and brown, sat with their head down. Their frown told Elaine they disapproved of Einari's practice, but their silence took Einari's side.

"You should never have sent them down. We were supposed to vote! It was to be unanimous—I would have voted nay!" Elaine exclaimed.

"The circumstances required immediate action."

"Send me to Midir. I shall save them."

"No." Einari leaned back in his seat. "They needed to learn mortalkind has not changed. A shame, how this was the result."

"If you wished they learn from their supposed misstep, you should never have taken their memory. You banished them, vulnerable and afraid, and what? Expect them to take your side when it is all over?"

"They had a keen mind, save for their lack of grace. They would have come to their senses."

"Oh, they'd come to their senses, alright. They'd realize you have *failed* those who are faithful to you."

"Enough. This session is adjourned."

"Not until—"

"Begone!"

Elaine trudged toward the doors on the southern end of the hall. Novika hurried alongside her. After she breached the tall marble doors, away from Einari's judgment, she knelt. Thick, hot bile rose up her throat, and she let it loose over the edge of the aurora path. It fell into the nothingness below and ceased to exist.

Novika stood by but said nothing. Elaine was grateful.

"I'm going to make him pay," the goddess of fire growled. She wiped spit from her mouth. "And I'm not sure if I mean the mortal or Einari."

"Be careful," Novika warned her. "I doubt Einari will take such language kindly."

"I care not. Aeris is as good as dead." Elaine stood, turning to meet Novika's deep brown eyes. "Don't you find it strange?"

"What's strange?"

"Death has been vying for a seat on our council for as long as time itself. Does Einari not see him as a threat?"

"Death is far below us. He has the underworld to rule; he can stake no claim here."

"He could," Elaine whispered, "if there is an empty seat on the council."

Tangible realization settled on Novika's face. "Oh, Heavens! You're right!"

"Should we—"

"We've no time to bargain with Einari. Come with me."

Novika took Elaine by the arm and rushed her down the shimmering pathway, through the field of dying stars. Elaine struggled to keep pace.

"I shall send you down," Novika gasped as they ran. "But I cannot stall Einari for long. I will keep you down there for what the mortals denote as a fortnight. Any longer, and I will have no choice but to bring you back."

"I'll be quick. They need me *far* sooner than a fortnight."

The path ahead of them forked, circumventing the small lake of silver. Currently unutilized, it reflected the stars above, the purples and blues of the dying sky. This, like the pool in the Great Hall, was a window into the mortal realm.

"Lay within," Novika commanded, and Elaine waded in. Her robes soaked through and clung to her skin as she lay in the frigid shallows. "Envision a location below. It was I who sent Einari to Midir one thousand years ago, and it shall be I who sends you in kind."

Elaine closed her eyes as Novika recited the incantation. Their words blurred in Elaine's ears, growing distant and muffled, until everything around Elaine vanished, replaced with a gentle breeze and the chirping of birds.

Elaine opened her eyes. Such sounds had not graced her ears in three thousand years. She lay upon plush grass on a scenic hillside, surrounded by an array of yellow and white daffodils. The island of Blythe stood home to vibrant wildlife and smelled of both sweet nectar and volcanic ash.

Traveling between realms wasn't a smart thing to do while nauseous. She scrambled over to a nearby bush and retched.

"Mother, I'm not interested in permanent residence," a female voice floated atop the weak, sickly breeze. "I wasn't meant to be cooped up in the manor."

"Our constituents fear you've run off with pirates."

"They think every seafarer is a pirate. We have friends. Allies. It's a much freer life than that of a governor."

Elaine scrambled to stand straight and pooled all her energy into holding her nausea back. She smoothed out her long, flowy robes and wiped sweat from her olive skin. Over the hill appeared two women: one in her mid-twenties, and one twice that age. Both women boasted the same russet-brown skin and strong noses, but the youngest wore glasses, her dark hair straight and short, while the mother's was grayed and curly. Elaine was happy to see the family she'd blessed generations ago still thriving. The figureheads of Blythe had always been devout and faithful, and their loyalty reaped Elaine's reward.

The elder woman gasped, affronted, when she laid eyes upon Elaine. "Pardon me," she said as she marched toward her. "This is private property."

"I am aware," Elaine replied. "I apologize for the intrusion, but—"

"Get out of my courtyard at once."

"Please, ma'am, allow me to speak."

"I am not taking an audience at this time."

Elaine had not expected this family to be so standoffish toward her. She was a goddess! She was *their* goddess! They should be bowing at the very sight...!

"I do not have time for this. Do either of you carry a knife?"

"Don't change the subject," the woman snapped.

The younger stepped forward. From her belt pouch, she produced a small knife, laying it upon Elaine's palm.

"Phoenyx!" The mother gasped, as though her daughter had committed a grave sin.

"My name is Elaine," she said. "The goddess of fire. I blessed your lineage ten generations ago, and you'd *best* be grateful for it." She pricked her finger with the tip of the knife. Golden blood beaded to the surface. Elaine found the sting nostalgic. She had not felt pain since she'd ascended to godhood.

Most pain, at least. The other gods would never know how an eternity of backaches, cramps, and nausea felt. Such was her curse. She returned the knife to Phoenyx.

"Oh," Phoenyx's mother gasped, hands flying to her mouth. "I must apologize, Your Grace! What a rarity it is for our goddess to bless us with her presence...! Come, come inside! We've had a bountiful fruit harvest this year."

"I've no interest in being spoilt. Thank you for your hospitality, though a little overdue. What is your name?"

"Priscilla."

"What I need, Priscilla, is a boat and a guide, for I do not know this realm well. One of my own does not have much time left."

"I have a boat," Phoenyx offered. "My sister and I can get you anywhere you need."

Priscilla balked. "To run off with a divine is to throw yourself headfirst into danger! You could get yourself killed! Let us hire a—"

"It's a far better fate than sitting around and waiting for demise to come. I've sensed it, Mother. A disturbance. I will go, whether you like it or not."

Defeated, Priscilla's shoulders slumped. Her protective instinct as a mother couldn't reach farther than her adult daughter would accept. "...I understand. Make me proud, Phoenyx."

Phoenyx offered Priscilla a curt nod, then gestured for Elaine to follow her. She led the goddess out of the yard and to the grandiose docks at the western end of the island. They approached a little steel ship, a fraction of the surrounding ships' size.

"This is the *Burning Maiden,*" Phoenyx introduced. "The engine's in need of some minor repairs, but it's functional. The ship's smaller and lighter than most, and faster for it. My sister and I will be more than happy to take you where you need to go."

"Thank you."

Elaine crossed the gangplank with nervous caution. She braced a hand on her stomach. The rocking ship would do little to help her. She swallowed back bile.

"Ashe," Phoenyx called out to a young woman who, upon being called, poked her head out from the small inner cabin. "Sorry for the change in schedule, but Mistress Elaine needs our help."

"Elaine? You mean—"

"Her Grace, yes. I don't believe her to be the divine who has walked this realm as of late, though."

Ashe bowed before her.

"I arrived today," Elaine supplied.

"Let's get moving." Phoenyx hurried to the anchor and, with Ashe's help, heaved it out of the water. Elaine was impressed by the ebb and flow of the sisters' movements, like the reliable flicker of a flame, as though they'd done it a thousand times before.

"Tell me, Your Grace," Phoenyx continued, "What is the name of the vessel we're looking for?"

"I am unsure. It's a grand ship. It's wooden and propelled by sails, which I find rather unique. It has a crew of five—well, six, right now, including Aeris."

"The *Vengeance*," Ashe supplied. "We know it well."

Phoenyx gasped. "Let's get moving!"

Ashe untied the lines, and the *Burning Maiden* raced out to sea.

18

"I belong to you, my great king. Let your waters flood my lungs and carry me home."
—The Grand Catalogue of Last Words: Great Flood Era. Death #0,060,702,955. Drowned. This soul was sent to Paradise for his devotion.

44th Storm, Great Flood 1058

Jonah couldn't move.

He had seen his crew fall injured in combat countless times. He had patched up a huge, infected gash on Faye's back, he'd pried bullets and shrapnel from Karina and Willow and Mouse's bodies. Jonah had even tied his companions down to keep them from writhing as he cleaned and stitched their wounds.

But nothing—*nothing*—could compare to the shrill agony of Crow's screams.

Jonah couldn't tear his gaze away from the growing pool of gold. Its radiance faded, turning a sickly shade of rust brown, corrupted by the evil and malice that thrived in the blood of a monster. If Argonaut's stash of God's Blood wasn't enough to sway him, this was indisputable, tangible proof of gods' existence. And the *tangible proof* was dying before him.

The biggest of the pirate trio, Emir, hoisted Crow's soon-to-be corpse over his shoulder. He had his hand braced where Crow had stabbed him. He was pained. Weak. It wouldn't take much to topple him.

Karina surged in, clutching the gash in her flank with one hand, and punched Emir with so much force Jonah couldn't help but wince. The pirate yelled. He dropped Crow. Their limp body hit the floor with a dull thud.

Were they still breathing? Jonah couldn't tell.

Faye rushed to the cannon and fired into the ship's hull. The cannonball ripped through the ship's hull. Inside, the engine burst aflame.

"FIRE!" Jack shrieked. The trio retreated to quell the flames.

"May Elaine smite you in her fury!" Faye cursed as she kicked the pirates' gangplank into the ocean.

"Willow! Get us out of here!" Karina yelled. Willow, the closest to the quarterdeck, scrambled to the helm and cranked the wheel.

Jonah's chest squeezed. His surroundings were muffled by the pounding of his heart. He fixated on Crow's limp form upon the deck, and for the second time in Jonah's miserable life, he was powerless.

"Jonah!" Karina's voice snapped through the haze. "We need you!"

His limbs refused to cooperate. Karina placed her hands firmly upon his shoulders. Her blood smeared onto his coat.

"Focus. Come on. You can do it."

His crew was weary and wounded, but overall, they seemed alright. Aside from Crow, of course, who lay on their back as Faye worked to pry the poison bullet from their stomach. The work was gruesome. Faye's hands were covered in blood. With no other tools at her immediate disposal, she settled on using her fingers and Karina's knife.

"What are we going to do?" Karina's voice was small.

"Priya," Jonah choked out. "We call Priya."

Karina nodded.

Faye freed the bullet and tossed it aside. It clattered across the wooden deck. Jonah knelt beside Crow, scooping them into his arms. Their face screwed up in agony as he did. Jonah winced. Without a word, he hurried to his cabin. He laid them atop his cot. Blood soaked his sheets.

Blood soaked every damn thing Jonah touched.

In his desk drawer, by Jonah's stash of God's Blood, was the letter from his ex, Priya. Jonah fished it out and stared at the text. He read her incantation aloud, setting his skepticism aside in favor of his sheer desperation. *This had better work.*

The lights in his cabin flickered. A tension in the air shifted, then snapped. A low fog rolled into his cabin, one that could only be explained by a magical nature. Jonah turned, and before him stood a tall woman of Biqanti descent, dressed in a fine magenta dress and a black silk headwrap. The tall heels she wore accentuated Priya's already imposing natural height.

"It's about time you called me. When was the last time we got to catch up?"

"How the hell do you save a god from Monster Blood?" Jonah had no need to be so loud, not when she was right in front of him. Priya flinched. He couldn't bring himself to care.

"Pardon?"

"A god." He gestured over to Crow, limp and unmoving atop his cot. Their wound had not been stitched up yet. "How do you save a god from *dying?*"

Priya Bashar's eyes followed Jonah's gesture. "Oh, my."

She hurried over, the click of her heels deafening in the otherwise silent cabin. Kneeling beside the bed, she inspected Crow's wound, her brows furrowed.

"If his blood is this tainted, I fear there's not much we can do. He needs fresh blood. He won't survive without it."

Jonah cursed. He had drained all hope for Crow's survival from Argo's ship. What the hell was he supposed to do now?

The vials...! He had retrieved *some* blood before he smashed Argonaut's supply. It wasn't much. He'd never anticipated needing enough to rescue a god from utter ruin. He had grabbed enough to pay docking fees or heal a wounded *mortal* crewmate. Jonah rushed to his desk and rifled through his drawers. He presented the vials to Priya.

"This won't be enough. We need to dilute the corruption until his body can fight it off. This... This will prolong his death, at best."

Jonah slumped onto his desk chair, burying his head in his hands.

"There has to be something," Jonah begged. "Anything. You work the gods' magic. There must be a way."

"Do you have syringes?"

"Medkit."

"Go."

Jonah rushed out of his cabin. The medical kit hung mounted to the bulkhead at the bottom of the stairs. The others needed it too, but Jonah knew they would all insist he take the kit to Crow, so he tore the reed box off its peg. He hurried back into his cabin and tossed it to Priya.

She rummaged through the medkit until she found a syringe. Popping the cork off one of Jonah's vials, she drew up as much of the golden blood as she could. With the syringe prepped, she palpated Crow's arm until she found a vein—once she found one suitable enough, she pricked them with the needle and emptied the syringe into Crow's body.

The syringe was much too small to carry a whole vial worth of blood at once, so Priya retracted the needle and used it to draw up more blood. Back and forth, back and forth. She cleaned the needle with a rum-soaked cloth each time.

"Give me space," Priya said. "You're not helping by hovering, dear. Go get some fresh air. I'll get you if I need anything."

"You promise you'll do everything you can?"

"I promise. Now, get out."

Jonah forced himself away, casting her one final sidelong glance before his sore, unsteady feet carried him into Crow's cabin.

Crow didn't show signs of being an organized person. The spare clothes they had purchased at the hub hung haphazardly in the closet, one shirt threatening to fall off its hanger. Crow's hammock was unmade, rumpled sheets dangling off the side. Jonah had no doubt that if Crow owned more, this room would be a disaster.

So, in a feeble attempt to keep his anxieties at bay, he neatened Crow's clothes. He draped the bedsheets flat over their hammock. He brushed dust off the top of the near-empty shelf, occupied by a single book.

Jonah picked the book up, cradling its haggard, worn-down cover in his hands. He leafed through the pages, staring down at the beautiful script he could not decipher. If he believed more, he would have known from the start. Crow could speak Midiri fine—they even understood Mouse's language, which had taken the rest of the crew a long time to learn. Despite spoken and signed fluency, Crow could not read or write.

But a dead language was no problem. Køveni. The language of the gods.

And here Jonah was, thinking Crow must have been some island scholar. What a fool he was.

He couldn't contain his bemused snort when he stumbled across a page whose top corner was folded down. Would it have killed the guy to ask for a bookmark? Did they even know what a bookmark was?

Crow's inability to grasp basic concepts of life was another glaring clue Jonah had missed. There were so many little things that, amnesia aside, they didn't understand. So many things they'd never seen before. Eating and sleeping were high on the list—Crow couldn't take care of themself because they didn't know how. Presumably, they'd never had a mortal body before.

And *Argonaut.* Argonaut had been persistent in his pursuit of Crow. How could Jonah not have comprehended that their captivity and the scars and track marks on their forearms had a direct correlation?

Jonah shoved the book back onto its shelf. His frustration threatened to boil over. He strode out of Crow's cabin and tried his best to tune out the groans and whimpers seeping through his own cabin's door. He headed above deck. He paused at the top of the stairwell, like Crow did every time they emerged into the fresh air. Crow was an oddball, but even they had their patterns, and Jonah had already committed those patterns to memory. Another crossed his mind: Crow's reverence for the sky. Was it possible they, a god without their memory, yearned for the Heavens above?

"I wonder what kind of god they are." Willow's voice was quiet but carried across the deck, given how silent the space was otherwise. The crew had gathered at the fire pit, tending to one another's wounds.

Her attempt at easing the tension as she poked Mouse with a suture needle did no good. Jonah joined his crew, sitting on a bench and staring out at the sea. He furrowed his brow and picked at his nails. The only solace to his nagging nerves was that his crew had found more medical supplies. If his memory served, Mouse kept a few extras in his cabin in case of emergency.

"They probably aren't a major god. I don't think the Big Four

would allow someone important to have their memory wiped, right?"
Willow continued.

She received no response.

Jonah was more than aware of his crewmates' eyes on him. He did
not acknowledge any of them. He couldn't.

"How are they?" Karina dared to ask.

"Priya Bashar is here," was Jonah's response. The answer was not
substantive. He glanced up toward the mast, as if by some stroke of luck
he'd find Crow up there, wind blowing through their hair, carefree and
happy. His lip quivered. He forced his gaze away and buried his head
in his hands.

Thirty minutes after Priya kicked Jonah from his cabin, she
emerged with a flat, resigned expression. Jonah leapt to his feet and
faced her, eyes wide and, dare say, hopeful.

"Are they okay?" Faye was the first to ask. Jonah cast a fleeting
glance in her direction—she was a mess, her short, choppy hair slicked
to her forehead with sweat. Her hand was clasped tight in Willow's.

"No."

"What the hell were you doing all this time, then?" Jonah snapped.

"Communing with the gods," Priya said. "Praying to any I could. I
went ahead and administered some, but not all, of the blood you gave
me. I don't know if it'll make a difference, but I'd ration it. For now, I
convinced Shav, goddess of time, to put him in stasis."

"Them," Jonah muttered. Priya nodded.

"He—uh, they won't bleed out, but they won't improve. It's not
ideal, but...you need to be prepared to lose them."

"We *can't* lose them."

"The best I could do was buy you time. I did everything I could.
Come." Priya gestured for him to follow.

She led Jonah down the staircase and into his cabin, though she
opted to linger in the doorway as Jonah stepped inside. Upon his cot,
tucked under cotton blankets, was the god, who laid still and silent.
Jonah found the stillness unnerving. If he hadn't been as observant, they
might have looked as though they were sleeping. Jonah, however, was
nothing if not attentive.

"They're not breathing."

"They don't need to," Priya replied. "In their stasis, not even a moment has passed. If they're breathing, it means time is no longer frozen."

Jonah couldn't tear his eyes away. Here in his cot lay a being as old as time itself, wearing a body that appeared only a few years younger than Jonah's twenty-nine. He had never seen such innocence before. Brand new to the realm and devoid of all memory, Crow had nothing to ground them. They'd been tossed around, abused, and mistreated by everyone they encountered.

Including him. He gritted his teeth.

"Get them out of my cabin," he snapped. Priya had the audacity to shrug.

"Moving them will compromise the stasis."

"Where the hell am I supposed to sleep, then?"

"Not my problem."

Jonah tightened his jaw. How long would Crow be out for? How long until there was a corpse of a god in his cot?

"Take this," Priya said as she stole a sheet of paper off Jonah's desk and scrawled something on it. "Read this incantation aloud when you're ready to wake them up. Remember, once you do, you won't have much time before the Monster Blood kills them. Minutes. It's been a miracle they've survived this long—you'd better have a damn good reason to wake them."

"Wait—" Jonah began, glancing down at the words on the paper.

But when he looked up, Priya was gone.

"I don't know how the hell to pronounce this," he muttered, finishing his thought even though nobody was present to hear it. He tucked the paper in his pocket, rolled his sleeves to his elbows, then marched out of his cabin.

Three uneasy days passed. Jonah refused to acknowledge Crow.

Without a cot, Jonah opted to forgo sleep. He avoided his cabin at all costs. When he did catch a nap, he did so above deck.

Faye seemed fed up with his misery, because she roped him into a discussion with Mouse about the crew's next steps.

"Do you think mortal blood would hurt them?" Mouse signed.

"Hell if I know," Jonah replied from where he sat atop Mouse's desk. He yawned.

"If the Monster Blood hurts them, then mortal blood should, in theory, be neutral, right? It shouldn't taint their blood; it should stabilize it." Mouse's hands were shaky, and his face was sullen as he signed. He didn't seem confident in his theory.

"Couldn't it also harm their godhood?" Faye asked. "Giving a god mortal blood could... make them mortal? Or, at least, dilute their divinity. I think anything aside from God's Blood would be risky."

"It's a possibility." Mouse paused to write some notes on his chalkboard. His handwriting was messy. Messier, even, than Jonah's. He turned back to the captain. "Jonah, could you spare a few drops of the blood you took from Argonaut? I'd like to run a few tests."

"No. Crow needs it."

"I don't need much. Please? Crow needs the blood, but we need a more permanent solution."

"You're an engineer, not a chemist."

"If mortal blood *did* make them mortal, would it be such a bad thing?" Faye asked, countering her own argument. Jonah cast a glance at her—she was smart to consider every possible scenario. "It would keep them alive."

"They're a god," Mouse signed. "There's something they're responsible for controlling. Mortality would be as dangerous as death."

Jonah slid off the desk and strode out of the room. He couldn't stand to be part of this conversation anymore.

He lingered in the passageway for some time, not sure what to do with himself. He eyed Karina's door. He wanted to figure this out on his own, truth be told. Karina shouldn't have to shoulder the role of *Captain's Therapist.* The job was a grueling one. But her insight was valuable, and she was the only person on the crew he allowed himself to be vulnerable with.

He knocked. Karina shuffled around inside. While he waited, he combed his fingers through his hair. Soph used to scritch her fingers across the top of his scalp whenever he grew anxious. Ever since her death, he mimicked the gesture.

"I can't do this," the words spilled out of Jonah's mouth when Karina opened the door. She ushered him inside. Jonah did not take off his boots, and Karina didn't say anything about it as he stepped onto the rug.

"Can't do what, exactly?" She sat down on the edge of her cot, elbows resting on her knees. She leaned forward, a clear sign he had her attention. He wished she would rearrange her knickknacks or something instead of watching him.

"They're a *god,* Karina! What the hell?" He raked his nails across his scalp. Combing his fingers through his hair no longer reflected Soph's soothing touch, but rather, something far more aggressive. He took handfuls of ginger and tugged until the nerves in his head burned. "I don't want a damn thing to do with them. I want them gone!"

"Don't lie to yourself."

"I hate them."

"You don't," she urged. "Sit down, take a minute to cool off. I'll brew you some tea, okay?"

Jonah nodded but did not sit as Karina retrieved her dented electric kettle. When she first purchased it at a hub, Jonah had thought her to have lost control of her hoarding tendencies. Most ancient electronics were too rotted and broken down for use. The kettle had been no exception, but she and Mouse had figured out how to get it working again.

"What kind of tea do you want?" She asked as she emptied her drinking flask into it. She plugged it into the single outlet by her door, flipped the switch, and left it to heat up.

"Black."

Karina fished through her desk drawers, plucking out two tea bags. "Sit."

Jonah did not.

"Jonah," she said. "Please. Let yourself relax. It'll help, I promise."

"How the hell am I supposed to relax?" Jonah shouted. "Everything's going to shit! I told you we shouldn't have let Crow on board! They've caused us misery after misery. And look where trusting *us* got *them!*"

Steam billowed from the kettle. "Jonah," Karina said.

"If we'd left them on Farmstead—"

"If we had left them on Farmstead Isle, someone else would have found them and exploited them. We did the right thing by taking them in. *You* did the right thing."

The kettle's beep was tinny and pathetic, its sound board damaged beyond repair. Karina poured hot water into a glass mug, followed by both tea bags and a single scoop of sugar. Good, she remembered he liked it strong. She pressed it into Jonah's hands.

"Sit. I don't want you to spill tea on my rug."

Reluctantly, Jonah sank onto the beanbag chair. He didn't like the thing. It was ugly and uncomfortable. Though it *was,* he had to admit, an interesting find, even if he gave Karina shit for buying it. According to Karina, the salvager had found it deeper than sunlight could reach. There was something in the story about an ancient high-rise apartment complex, though Jonah couldn't quite remember the details.

Focusing on the kettle and the chair helped settle him.

"You haven't been sleeping," Karina said.

"I have work to do."

"You don't want to have nightmares."

"What the hell makes you think so?"

"It's okay," Karina offered him a sad smile. "I've been having them. I think we all have."

"I don't want anything to do with Crow," he admitted. "It's not about nightmares. It's about *them* in my cot. Things were easier when they were some random sailor. They're—I can't do this. I'm not strong enough, Karina."

His voice broke. He chewed on his lip. The urge to hurt himself nagged at the back of his mind. He could pull his knife from its sheath and...

He buried those thoughts as deep as he could. If nothing else, he was too stubborn to relapse after five years.

"You're stronger than you know. You're not the man you were when I first met you. Remember how far you've come."

"I don't want to see them ever again."

"That's not true."

Jonah took a sip of his tea. It was a little too sweet. He stared at his boots and counted the scuffs on the toes. "I've been nothing but a thorn in Crow's side since we met."

"And yet, they still trusted you. They wanted to spar *you.* They opened up to *you* when Argonaut threatened them."

Karina emptied her kettle into a second mug. She tossed a tea bag in, and the water turned a deep raspberry color.

"I... Karina, I..." Jonah's hands trembled, so he set his mug on the floor at his feet and hoped the ship wouldn't rock enough to spill his tea. "I can't watch them die. I—Soph—It still hurts. I can't do it again."

Karina knelt. Hazel eyes searched his face. Jonah avoided her gaze.

"You won't," she said. "We'll figure something out. I won't let us lose them, okay? We'll find a way."

"Okay," he said, though he didn't feel convinced.

"Now, drink your tea, then go wash your hair. You're all grimy. Get some sleep, too. We all need to be at our best right now. You'll feel better, I promise."

Jonah picked his mug up and drank in silence. Karina left him to cool off, opting to water her collection of potted plants. When he finished his tea, he slipped out of Karina's cabin without a word. He approached his door. Inside, Crow lay frozen in time, a dying breath caught in their lungs and poisoned blood in their veins. He braced his palms against the door and cast a glance down the passageway. The cabin at the end of the row haunted him.

Was anyone who slept there destined to die? Soph? Crow?

With a grimace, Jonah stepped in. His cabin was dark, the thick blinds stopping any sunlight from seeping through his window. Jonah made his way to the lamp drilled into his desk and flicked it on. Its dim light illuminated the room enough for Jonah to find his way without tripping or stubbing his toe. He dumped his boots on the floor, grabbed a fresh set of clothes, then headed back out into the passageway, to the washroom.

All the while, he did not glance once at his cot.

He drew a bath. The water came out sort-of warm. The water heater was finicky. Always had been. Jonah considered himself lucky to even have one at all.

He climbed into the washbasin and lathered his hair with soap. He sat for a while, letting suds drip from his hair down his cheeks. After the water had long since gone tepid, he rinsed his hair and heaved himself out of the basin. He held a thousand weights upon his shoulders. The weight of a god's life was a lot to carry.

Once he was dry and dressed, he stumbled back to his cabin. Only then did he dare turn his gaze to Crow. Despite every fiber of his being begging him to sleep, Jonah filled a syringe with a ration of blood. He sat on the edge of the cot beside Crow's time-frozen form, poked the syringe into a vein, and administered the dose. Not bothering to gather blankets or even a pillow, Jonah lay on the floor in front of his desk, his eyelids heavy.

Through the night, he dreamt of gunshots and knife wounds. Crimson blood and long ginger hair. Radiant golden blood and vibrant blue eyes.

19

44th Storm, Great Flood 1058

Elaine sat at the bow as the *Burning Maiden* rocketed westward. Face resting upon her chin, she stared out at the flat, endless horizon.

"You seem bothered, Your Grace." Phoenyx's voice was gentle, but she startled Elaine anyhow. Elaine turned to regard the woman. Her brown skin and brown hair were characteristic of Blythe's inhabitants, and yet, despite her averageness, Elaine couldn't help but find her pretty.

"Three thousand years ago was the last time I walked the mortal realm," she said.

"Before you ascended."

"I have always found the Great Flood to be heartbreaking. The islands are tiny, but from above, at least I can see them. From a mortal's eyes, everything feels so desolate. Oh, what a miracle your kind has persevered so long."

"It's thanks to Aeris. We wouldn't have survived the altitude. The air would have been too thin for us to thrive."

"Aeris," Elaine repeated. Her gaze drifted toward the sky, watching one wispy cloud dissipate in the air. "Indeed. I am relieved to hear at least one mortal still respects them."

"It would do mortalkind well to respect *all* gods," Phoenyx said, rolling her pale yellow eyes. Elaine remembered when she had first blessed the Calloway family ten generations ago, through which their eyes turned a fiery red. Now, fragments of her blessing remained.

"Tell me about modern mortalkind," Elaine said, turning around and leaning against the *Burning Maiden's* steel rail. Her cream and red robes had a low back, leaving her spine and shoulder blades bare against the steel rail, which chilled her skin. She winced. Pricking her thumb on a loose steel cable, she brought forth enough divinity to heat the metal. "Your quality of life, your culture."

Phoenyx jerked her hand from the rail and shook it off, inspecting the scald mark on her palm. "Everything is patchwork. We make do with whatever we can find. It's not the best life, but we're stubborn. We salvage, we build, we adapt. Those who are brave enough can find a living diving for scrap. Others turn their backs on their own kind and find lives as pirates."

"Pirates," Elaine echoed.

"There's pirates, seafarers, land folk," Ashe chimed in from where she stood at the stern, hands on the tiller, "Or some variation."

"And the difference between 'pirates' and 'seafarers' is…"

"The pirates harm others to reach their goals; the seafarers are…everyone else. The land folk call us all *sea slugs*." Ashe paused to peek at the compass in her hand. "If I'm being honest, there's something fun about being a slug *and* second heiress of Blythe."

"Is there nobody to stop these pirates?"

"No," Phoenyx said. "Enforcement is a luxury only islanders can afford. Enforcers only care to protect the wealthy and the privileged."

Some things did not change, no matter the era.

A flock of seagulls flew overhead, and Elaine couldn't help but gasp. Their pristine white feathers reflected the sunlight, and their caws filled the air with life.

"Odd of them to be flying west," Phoenyx muttered. "They're heading straight for the Dead Zone. What are they doing?"

"Follow them," Elaine said.

"Pardon, Your Grace?"

"Aeris has been enamored with seagulls as of late. One of the most resilient birds since the flood. I'm willing to wager they sense Aeris's suffering. The flock may lead us to the *Vengeance.*"

Ashe pulled the tiller, and the *Burning Maiden* turned northwest. Once she set the new heading, she fiddled with the motor. When the motor did not respond as Ashe had seemed to hope, she slammed her fist upon it twice, and it kicked into gear with a whirr.

The *Burning Maiden* pursued the flock of gulls. Elaine stared at the horizon. A few little boats drifted in the distance, though none of them matched the ship Elaine sought. *Hang in there, Aeris.* How long would it take to find them? Elaine found reassurance in the sky's continued life. Clouds floated with the breeze, the sun and moon still danced their daily waltz around Midir. Aeris, despite all odds, had managed to hang onto life for this long.

Another pang of nausea hit her, and this one she could not choke back. She leaned over the railing and vomited into the ocean.

"Your Grace?" Phoenyx asked. "Are you alright?"

"Fine."

"No shame in being seasick," Ashe said. "We've all been there. Let us know if you need anything."

"Thank you." Elaine was relieved Ashe thought it to be seasickness. She ruffled her robes and hoped they hid the truth well enough. They didn't. She was silly to think they could.

"It's not seasickness," Phoenyx said, and Elaine's relief melted. "Haven't you *read* the Book of Fire?"

"Of course I've read it. You ask as if Mother hadn't drilled every verse into our brains."

"She's pregnant, Ashe."

Elaine grimaced. She loathed the word. Annoyance swirled amid her nausea. "I am *not* pregnant."

"You're not?" Phoenyx asked with a contemplative frown. Her eyes flicked down to Elaine's stomach, then back up. The swell caught the drapes of her robes. "But the Book of Fire says you conceived before you ascended, Your Grace."

"I did, yes."

"So, there's a baby."

It wasn't a baby, it was an underdeveloped curse. *Baby* was a word said with love. Elaine held nothing but contempt for the damn thing. "There is a fetus, yes."

"So..."

"I implore *you* to carry a fetus for three thousand years. You will find pregnancy implies an end. But there is no end. You'll carry the fetus for three thousand more years, and three thousand after that. An eternity of morning sickness and backaches. An eternal reminder of your lover's gruesome death. You can never escape it. I'm not pregnant, Miss Calloway. I'm...something else."

"As Blythian natives say: you are with Mt. Azhir," Ashe said. "Like our dormant volcano, you, too, have magma flowing through you. Most dormant volcanoes erupt one day. But, while the implication is eruption, many never erupt again."

That was far more palatable. Elaine turned her attention back to the choppy ocean, disinterested in furthering the conversation. A flicker in the water below caught her eye. A long, slender silhouette passed underneath the vessel. It swam perpendicular to the *Burning Maiden*, its deep blue scales catching a glint of light filtering through the shallows.

The sea monster's body bumped against the *Burning Maiden*. The ship rocked, and Elaine caught herself on the rail and clung for dear life.

"What was that?" Ashe gasped.

"I've attracted a monster," Elaine replied, gritting her teeth. *Curse my luck!*

"Your Grace, get away from the edge!"

"I know," Elaine groaned. On wobbly legs, she stumbled away from the gunwale. She hunkered beside the trapdoor leading below deck.

"The *Burning Maiden* isn't strong enough to withstand a monster attack," Phoenyx whispered. "We'll be at the bottom of the ocean in minutes."

"I thought monsters showed up in times of crisis to usher *mortals* into premature deaths," Ashe had a nervous waver in her voice, low both in pitch and volume. "Why would they seek a god?"

"It's not a lie, but it's not the whole truth, either. Death has been vying for a seat on the council for as long as he's existed. His monsters are an extension of such desire. A dead Big Four god would give him the chance to seize it. Thus, they hunger for gods." She craned her neck and sat up straight. Where had it gone?

"Stay down, Your Grace."

Elaine crouched low once more. If they were lucky, the beast would not deem the *Burning Maiden* the source of the divine vomit.

"Ashe," Phoenyx said, "Go get your gun. No sudden movements."

"I don't know if shooting will—"

"Go."

Phoenyx took Ashe's place at the tiller. Her posture was tense, her jaw set, as Ashe crept toward the trapdoor. Elaine held it open for her. She caught a glimpse of the narrow passageway below as Ashe descended. The space looked rather uncomfortable. The *Burning Maiden* boasted a single lower deck, whose cramped bulkheads left little room for lodging and storage. A few steel crates sat tucked toward the bow, and two cots with pale yellow sheets, bordering beige, sat divided only by a brown curtain for privacy.

Phoenyx and Ashe preferred *this* over a life on land?

Ashe returned, an old pistol in hand. The gun was no doubt dated from before the flood. One of many items salvaged from the life before.

"I'm going to try and speed us out of here," Phoenyx said after Ashe returned.

"Not a good idea," Ashe countered. "There's no way we'd be able to outsail the serpent. Look how streamlined it is—it was built for speed."

Elaine dared to peer over the edge. Indeed, the beast had a long, sleek body and massive fins to propel it through the ocean. What the *Burning Maiden* lacked in strength, it made up for in speed, but outrunning a monster was a tall order. Elaine met Ashe's gaze and gave her a curt nod.

Brown eyes, Elaine noted. *My blessing ended at Phoenyx.*

"It'll work," Phoenyx insisted. "It has to. What other options do we have?"

"Not many," Ashe combed her fingers through her long, rich brown hair. "Let's do it. You focus on the motor, I'll steer."

"Elaine steers," Phoenyx cut in, "Ashe, you're our gunner—if anything goes wrong, I can't have you distracted at the tiller."

"I don't know how," Elaine said as Phoenyx waved her over. The monster slammed once again upon the *Burning Maiden*. Elaine fell, and when she couldn't find the balance to get back upon her feet, she crawled the rest of the way to the tiller.

"Hold it fast," Phoenyx instructed as Elaine took the tiller within her clammy hands. "Keep us straight."

Elaine nodded. Phoenyx cranked the motor's speed dial. The *Burning Maiden* hastened.

"Is this as fast as we can go?" Ashe asked. She aimed her pistol toward the monster, but her finger remained off the trigger.

"I think so," Phoenyx said, frustrated.

The monster swam in the *Burning Maiden's* wake. It bobbed and weaved, following the ship's pace with an ease akin to a light jog. They weren't going to outrun it, and soon enough, it would strike. What other options were there?

Elaine pushed the tiller away from her as hard as she could, and the ship jerked as it turned to its starboard. Everybody, including Elaine, gasped.

"What are you doing!?" Ashe shouted as she scrambled to find purchase on whatever could hold her steady. She ended up grabbing Phoenyx.

"Trying to shake it off!" Elaine yelled back. "I thought if we sailed in an erratic pattern—"

"With all due respect, you'll launch us all off the ship and into the beast's mouth, Your Grace!"

"We need a new plan," Phoenyx cut in. The sea monster's ugly face breached the surface, and it snapped its teeth at the crew.

"There's no time for planning!" Ashe snapped, cocking her pistol. Phoenyx, beside her, gasped.

"Ashe, no—!"

Ashe pulled the trigger, firing a bullet straight through the sea monster's throat. Violet blood sprayed across the deck. Elaine abandoned the tiller and dove toward the bow in hopes of avoiding the onslaught. She tumbled across the small deck. Monster Blood splattered down her back, sizzling against her olive skin. Frantic, Elaine grabbed a dirty rag and wiped it off. The monster dove back below the water.

"Are you okay, Your Grace?" Ashe asked.

"Peachy," Elaine grumbled.

"It won't be down for long. Stay sharp."

"It won't be? I shot it in the *throat*. It's gotta be as good as dead."

"It's a monster, Ashe. One lucky shot isn't going to take it down. It's *going* to resurface, and it's going to be furious."

"I'll get back to steering," Elaine muttered.

"I don't trust you to steer anymore, Your Grace," Ashe chuckled. "Best let us do it."

Phoenyx took the tiller. "There's not much I can do with the motor to get us going any faster. Elaine, keep an eye out, okay? If you see any sign of it, I want to know."

Elaine nodded. She peered into the water. From the bow, she could see well over both the port and starboard railings. The stern was a blind spot, but Phoenyx and Ashe were both positioned there.

Elaine caught a glimpse of its long, streamlined body in the depths under the bow. "It's below us. Prowling. It's far too deep to get a good shot at it."

"How many bullets do you have, Ashe?" Phoenyx asked.

Ashe fished through the bullet pouch affixed to her belt. "I forgot to restock back home. Wasn't expecting to turn around so soon—I've got five."

"Our harpoon gun?"

"Loaded and operational."

"Get below deck and fire as soon as the monster is in range."

Ashe disappeared below, though she left the trapdoor below deck wide open—no doubt for ease of communication. Elaine frowned at the water below, watching the serpent twist and writhe, pained. A shot to the throat was no pleasant injury, regardless of species. Though its gills were lower on its body, there must be some major blood vessels in its throat.

"Ashe!" Elaine called out. "Cover me!"

Elaine ducked under the rail and plunged her hand into the ocean. The blood caked on her skin dissipated into the water. Between it and her residual vomit, her divine energy spread enough in the ocean's current to call upon her power.

"Are you *trying* to get your hand bitten off?" Phoenyx gasped.

Elaine ignored her. She focused on the water around her fingers. Willing another Domain to do her bidding was no easy feat, but so long as she conjured enough heat, she could make it work. Below, Elaine caught a glimpse of the monster's violet eyes, which eyed its easy prey.

Boil, Elaine urged the water below the *Burning Maiden.* The serpent swam toward the surface, its murky, refracted form growing clearer the closer it got. Her latent mortal instinct screamed at her to pull her hand away. She ignored it.

The ocean's current rendered her task difficult. New water filtered in at a constant rate, cooling the temperature as Elaine fought to raise it. If she had been in the Heavens, all she would have needed to do was snap her fingers. Not in the mortal realm, though. Here she was beholden to a cage of flesh and bone. She dug her fingernail into the little wound and freed more blood.

Heat pooled around her hand. Water within a tight perimeter around the *Burning Maiden* bubbled, not a rolling boil but a simmer. She wondered, *will it be enough to cook the beast?* From below, the harpoon gun's deep, heavy metallic *boom* startled Elaine. The harpoon skewered straight through the sea monster's belly, sending clouds of deep violet billowing in the ocean water and rendering it murky.

Traces of Monster Blood in the ocean stung her hand. Elaine pulled her hand out and wiped it on her robes with a wince. Squinting through the bloody murk, she watched the sea monster flail.

"What's happening?" Phoenyx dared to ask.

The beast stilled. Before long, its corpse sank into the murky depths, gone from sight.

"It's dead," Elaine replied as Ashe ascended the ladder.

Phoenyx relaxed. "I'm slowing up on the motor. Otherwise, we'll wear the thing out long before we reach the *Vengeance.*"

"We lost the birds," Elaine muttered.

"It's okay. We'll keep our northwest heading. We'll find them."

For the good of all mortalkind, Elaine hoped so.

20

52nd Storm, Great Flood 1058

A flock of seagulls perched on the gunwale. Karina stared at them. Three times, she had shooed them away, but no creature was so stubborn as a seagull. Each time, they fluttered away only to settle elsewhere on the *Vengeance.* Pesky birds. All those things did was make noise and shit all over the deck.

Four more seagulls landed. They settled near the helm. Karina groaned and grabbed the broom.

Even after a week, the crew had yet to find a viable solution. Night and day, Mouse struggled to figure something out. No adequate substitute for God's Blood existed. Divinity was irreplicable. The crew's spirits remained grim, and guilt weighed on Karina's conscience. If only she'd approached Crow about the topic sooner...

Mouse stumbled above deck, and the seagulls cawed and flapped their wings, alarmed. He took only a few steps before he collapsed.

Karina dropped the broom. She grabbed a rag and rushed over, wetting it from the water in her flask. She pressed it to his forehead, wiping away the thick sheen of sweat that lingered on his skin.

She sat him up and held out her flask. He took it, gracious, and sipped. Karina noted the deep bags under the kid's eyes, the way his hands shook with such a simple exertion as holding a flask to his lips.

"I think you should take lookout for the rest of the day," she signed.

Mouse frowned and furrowed his brow. "I can't waste my time like that. I need to—"

"You've done everything you can, Mouse. You can't think straight if you're not well-rested."

"I don't want to rest."

Karina sighed. Mouse was a smart kid, but he was still a kid. He experienced the same stubbornness as any other teenager. He, in many regards, was not dissimilar to how Karina was at his age.

Taking on the role of *big sister* had its ebbs and flows, and today was one of those days she couldn't be so gentle.

"Too bad," she signed. She took Mouse by the wrist and helped him to the bow, sitting him down atop a crate full of sailing tools. Once he was settled, she slipped away. Best to leave him alone.

Mouse sat there for two hours before Karina checked on him again. He sat with slumped posture, his gaze focused down the length of the bowsprit. Karina wouldn't be surprised if he were examining all the knots of rope securing the jib sails, making notes of which ones he needed to fix once he was allowed to get up and move again. But when she approached, his gaze looked distant, empty. She tapped his shoulder, and he flinched, startled. She offered him a reassuring smile, though it was empty and fake. How could she reassure him when their crewmate was dying?

"I hate feeling so powerless," Mouse admitted to Karina with trembling fingers.

"We all do."

"Jonah got after me earlier for trying to sneak God's Blood from his cabin."

"I'm not surprised."

"How am I supposed to find a solution if I have nothing to work with? He's mad at me for *trying*. He's so afraid of harming Crow, he's not letting me do my job. I'm afraid, too, but—"

"He's struggling a lot right now," Karina said. "He's coping. Be patient with him, okay? His brashness is a result of his grief. Crow is frozen in time—we won't hurt them by taking a bit longer. We don't have to rush."

"I thought he moved on from his sister's death."

"It's a trauma response," Karina explained, her signs slow, grim. "It's happening again, and all that terror came rushing back."

Mouse nodded.

"Go get some sleep. I'll take over on lookout."

"Okay."

"And I mean *sleep,*" Karina pressed, her signs firm and resolute. "If I catch you trying to work, I'm strapping you to your cot."

Mouse rolled his eyes, a small smile gracing his face.

Lookout was uneventful. Merchant ships and other families sailed by on occasion, affable enough to offer Karina and the crew a wave hello as they passed. When evening fell, Faye took cooking duty. In an attempt at damage control, Willow helped her. Willow scrambled to grab the fish from the cooking pot as it billowed black smoke. She didn't need to hear their conversation to know Willow chided Faye for not paying close enough attention.

Neither Mouse nor Jonah came to dinner. Karina typically loved the opportunity for a *girls' night,* but ever since the pirate attack, the energy aboard the ship had been solemn. They ate in silence.

After dinner, Karina took two plates to the cabin deck. When she opened Mouse's door, she was pleased to see him curled up atop his cot, fast asleep. She left the overcooked fish atop his worktable and snuck out. She visited Jonah's cabin next. She tried the knob, but it jiggled and did not turn. *Locked.* She knocked, and when Jonah did not answer, she left the food on the floor.

Another day passed. Karina floated through the motions. She scrubbed the remnants of blood from the deck, both divine and mortal. Mouse hadn't made any more progress on his research. Unless the crew found fresh God's Blood, an impossible feat knowing Jonah had obliterated Argonaut's reserves, Crow would die.

Time crawled on. Another day, another task, another dinner.

"Has anyone seen Jonah lately?" Faye asked through a mouthful of salmon.

Karina frowned. It wasn't uncommon for Jonah to be rather reclusive, but he at least showed up for meals. A few days had passed since she'd last seen him.

"No," Willow replied. Mouse, seated beside Willow, shook his head.

"I'll bring him dinner," Faye offered. She stood and gathered a slice of bread and a cut of salmon onto a shell plate. She squeezed past her girlfriend and Mouse and headed below.

It did not take long for Faye to return. The plate was still in her hand.

"He didn't open the door." She set the plate by the fire. "He told me to get lost."

Starving and depriving himself of sleep wasn't going to do him any favors, but it was up to him to make the right decisions. If he wanted to suffer, he could. If he sought her, she'd help, but she had long since learned to mind her own business. Jonah was twenty-nine years old. Karina wasn't going to spoon-feed him and sing him a lullaby.

She stared out at the ocean. Dusk had fallen, and silhouetted by the fading light was a ship. Karina gasped and sat up straight. In the moody dusk, she feared the prospect of more pirates.

"Someone's approaching!" she exclaimed. Beside her, Willow peered through her spyglass.

"It's the *Burning Maiden*."

Karina turned to Mouse and signed, "Send up a distress flare."

Mouse scrambled to the quarterdeck and sifted through the crate of flares. He lit a fuse, and the flare exploded upwards, a large plume of deep red smoke billowing upwards into the sky, glowing in the darkness of night.

Mouse climbed down from the helm as everyone awaited a response.

"They won't be able to help us," Faye muttered. "How could they?"

From the *Burning Maiden* came a cobalt blue flare. *Acknowledged.*

"Ready the gangplank," Karina commanded.

Mouse and Willow heaved the gangplank into position, ready to drop it when their allies arrived. Karina sprinted to the supply closet and pulled a lantern off its hook. Its bulb was dying—a flame lantern would have been far more efficient. However, it shed enough light to see faces. Good enough.

The *Burning Maiden* joined the *Vengeance*. Willow and Mouse lowered the gangplank, and Ashe, on the other side, tied it down. Nyx hurried aboard, Ashe a few paces behind. A third, unfamiliar face followed the Calloway sisters. She was tall and resolute, her wispy light brown hair framing her fair, rounded face.

"New crewmate?" Karina asked, trying to break the silence with a tense smile.

"Temporary," Nyx replied. "Let's not waste time. We know about Stranger."

"Crow," Willow piped in.

"Wha—" Karina stammered. "How do you—"

"Mistress Elaine has descended upon us from the Heavens to aid them."

Elaine offered the crew a polite bow. *Elaine,* slayer of Blight, goddess of fire! Karina was awestruck to be in her presence. She knelt before the goddess with a gasp, a hand over her heart.

"You may rise," Elaine said, and Karina stood. "Take me to them."

"Okay." Karina's mind reeled. "Yeah, let's go."

Mouse, Ashe, and Elaine followed Karina below deck, the rest remaining above. Karina was grateful for it. Too many bodies would only cause more problems. A solemn silence descended upon them as they walked. When they reached Jonah's door, Karina pulled a bobby pin from her hair and picked the lock. *I should get a copy of Jonah's key,* she thought. *In case he decides to lock himself away again.*

The lock clicked. Karina turned the knob and pushed the door. It opened an inch before catching. "Shit," she cursed, "the chain."

Mouse ran down the passageway to his own cabin. She hadn't thought to sign her frustration, and Mouse had never been the greatest at reading lips, but that did not mean by any standard that he was unaware. He must've had a solution. She took a step back. He returned with a chain cutter, snapped through the chain, then tucked the tool into a loop on his belt. Mouse nudged the door open with his foot. Jonah, who knelt on the floor beside his cot, stared. His eyes were wide, startled.

While Crow seemed well tended to, Jonah boasted the exact opposite: strings of oily ginger hair fell in front of his eyes. His clothes were wrinkled and carried the stench of a garment unwashed. In his weakened state, having not eaten or slept in days, Ashe swooped in and pulled him away with little difficulty. He struggled in her grip.

"Elaine is here," Ashe told Jonah. Her words didn't settle him. He hadn't put two and two together. Elaine was a common mortal name.

"They're in stasis," Elaine observed. Karina interpreted her words for Mouse. "It's a miracle, indeed. Which of you was blessed by Shav?"

"None of us," Karina replied. "Jonah's ex was blessed by some other god, who allows her to borrow power from anyone who will listen."

"Irina," Elaine mused, "the messenger goddess."

"The name sounds familiar."

Elaine turned her attention to Crow. "In order for this to work, their blood needs to flow. We should prepare as much as we can beforehand."

Mouse sprinted out of the room, tripping over his own feet in his rush to gather supplies. When he returned, he dumped his handful of syringes and plastic blood bags onto Jonah's desk.

"May I see your arm, Your Grace?" Mouse signed. He pointed to the chair, and Elaine sat, presenting her arm. Karina opened her mouth to translate his signs, but Elaine seemed to understand him. She held out her arm. Did the gods have an inherent knowledge of all languages? They must—they created Midiri, Avetic, Biqanti, and Sonallan, including their corresponding sign languages. If Karina remembered from her readings, the only thing the gods did *not* create was the written word. Such was a mortal invention. Crow's inability to read Midiri, then, made sense.

If Karina weren't so exhausted and stressed, she would have found it fascinating.

Mouse pulled his fluffy blond hair into a ponytail and got to work. He swabbed the crook of Elaine's arm with a wet cloth, then, as the water dried, he put on some tight gloves and poked at her arm until he found a suitable vein.

"This may sting," Mouse signed. "You can look away if you want."

He attached the catheter, then pricked her with the needle. Elaine gagged.

"Would you like some ginger tea?" Karina asked as golden blood flowed. "It helps soothe nausea."

In her youth, Karina had read the Book of Fire cover to cover, as with the other Books. She knew every detail of Elaine's story. *She conceived the baby before she ascended,* Karina reminded herself, racking her brain for relevant details. *When she ascended, the baby did, too. She's stuck like this for eternity, the baby unable to grow, unable to be born, unable to miscarry.*

"No, thank you," Elaine said, though she clutched her stomach and leaned her head back. "I don't like tea."

"Water, then?"

Elaine nodded. Karina hurried out of the room and retrieved a flask of water. When she returned, Elaine sipped from it with a small, grateful smile. Content that Elaine was settled, Karina looked to Jonah. He sat slumped, his gaze glued on Elaine's blood bag.

When the bag was full, Mouse retracted the needle and pressed a wad of gauze against the puncture site. He gestured for Elaine to press it down, and she did.

"This will be a good start," he signed. "In theory, this should be enough to get Crow stable. Then, if you're up for it, we can draw more."

"I can do it," Elaine said, though she looked ill. Because her arms were occupied, she did not sign, so Karina translated for Mouse. "Take more. We don't have much time."

"What do you mean?" Karina asked, brow furrowed.

"I can feel it. The pull. Einari may have discovered I'm here. Do not heed my wellbeing, a simple death such as this would return me to the heavens."

"It feels inhumane," Karina muttered. "If you insist, Your Grace."

Mouse prepped Elaine's opposite arm, found the vein, and punctured it with a fresh needle.

"Let us know if you need anything," Karina said.

"I'll be fine."

"You said we'll have to take them out of stasis." Karina's gaze drifted from Elaine over to Crow. "Once we get their blood flowing again, we'll be pressed for time."

Once Mouse had Elaine's blood flowing again, he hurried over to Crow. He swapped out the needle for a clean one. Rolling up Crow's sleeve, he wiped down their arm in the same manner as he had with Elaine, using a cloth dampened by water in his drinking flask. He punctured the vein in one swift jab and squeezed the catheter between his fingers to stop the blood flow.

"How do we wake them?" Karina asked.

"There's—" Jonah choked. "I have a counter spell."

Jonah fished through his pockets until he found a sheet of paper. Karina took it from his shaking hands and unfolded it.

"Crow would know how to read it," Jonah muttered, "But they're..."

"Give it to me," Elaine cut in. She held out her hand, and Karina pressed the paper into her palm. She took a second to read it, then glanced up. "Are you all ready?"

Mouse tensed, prepared to stop squeezing the catheter when Crow's stasis lifted. The cabin fell silent. If *anything* went wrong...

Karina nodded at Elaine.

"*Shav ejeví Ø davøl,*" she began. Køveni had a beautiful, melodic lilt. Karina considered it a small blessing to have the opportunity to hear the ancient, lost language spoken right in front of her. "*Suhíþ íen cinua. Suhíþ fea silmítha Aeris.*"

Karina's heart lurched. *Aeris.*

A tension in the air snapped as the stasis lifted. Crow's body lurched. They coughed and choked. Mouse slid his deft fingers down the catheter's length, pushing the blood, urging it to flow.

Jonah trembled. The wounds of his sister's loss ran deep. Karina knelt beside him and leaned her head against his shoulder, hoping he would find the weight soothing. His tension did not settle, though, as blood flowed into Crow's veins.

Ashe kept busy by removing the second blood bag from Elaine's arm. She patched up the goddess with tender care.

Crow's fingers twitched. Karina sat up straight.

"It's working," Karina whispered, breaking the tense silence. Their face was no longer screwed up in agony. Karina had not realized how much her stress had sapped her energy until now, as relief washed over her and a daze settled like a warm blanket over her soul.

Elaine pulled her chair a little closer to the cot.

"Oh, thank the Heavens." She leaned forward, taking Crow's hand in hers. The gesture was intrinsically mortal, but Elaine was mortal once. Some mannerisms never went away, even after thousands of years.

Crow's eyes fluttered open. They blinked once, twice. Karina's heart soared at the sight.

"Aeris. Gí kisiven sevai."

Crow hummed. Their voice was small, weak, and fragile. It was a pathetic sound, but even still, Jonah perked up. His amber eyes shimmered, wet with hope, perhaps desperation.

"Ilinoé." Crow rasped. *"Eren Ø je kali."*

For some reason, Elaine cast a fleeting glance over her shoulder at Jonah.

"I'm afraid I'm out of time," Elaine admitted. "I can feel the pull grow stronger. It won't be long until I cannot resist it anymore."

"Wait!" Karina cried, "But we have so many questions! Will Crow get their memory back?"

"No. Einari will not allow it, no matter how hard I've fought." Elaine's body was shimmering with an ethereal, heavenly light. "I'm sorry."

"What will become of you?"

"I am unsure."

Karina did not understand why Elaine wasn't nervous. Would Einari punish her? Maybe the relief of rescuing Crow overshadowed any fear of facing Einari. It was hard to say—Elaine was one of the Big Four. Karina supposed she'd fare fine.

Elaine's attention turned to Jonah as her body faded. *"Crow,"* she said with a smile, putting an emphasis on their mortal-given name, "adores you."

Karina blinked, and Elaine was gone.

21

"There is nothing more beautiful and profound than repentance."
—*The Book of the Tide*

54th Storm, Great Flood 1058

Rise, fall. Rise, fall.

The *Vengeance* bobbed in tandem with the pulse of Crow's heart. Such a gentle lull brought Jonah into a tired daze. After many sleepless nights, he found himself somewhat at ease.

He knelt beside his cot, tracing with his eyes Crow's slack face, down the slope of their neck. If Jonah were to pull back the sheets draped over their shoulders, he'd see the fresh, neat bandages hugging tight around their torso. However, Jonah couldn't bear the thought of acknowledging their wound, so the sheets remained as they were, and he avoided looking at his wastebin in the corner, piled high with yellowed gauze.

Karina, Mouse, and Ashe had stepped out an hour ago. Nobody had said a word, but he could see it in their eyes as they cast glances at him—*let's give Jonah some privacy.* The full crews of the *Vengeance* and the *Burning Maiden* were now above deck. Nyx, Willow, and Faye no doubt had questions. Jonah hoped Karina had enough answers.

I should join them, the captain in him supplied. His muscles refused to comply. He couldn't tear himself away from the thrum of Crow's vitals. *What if something happens and I'm not here? What if I look away, and they die?*

Should he keep a stock of Crow's blood in case of emergency? The thought left him grimacing. What would differentiate him from Argonaut? Crow had spent so long struggling against a man who stole their blood, and for what? For someone else, someone they thought they could trust, to do the same?

A knock at the door startled Jonah from his thoughts.

"Come in," he heard himself say. His voice sounded far away.

Faye opened the door and stepped inside. "Will they be alright?"

"I think so."

"Nyx and Ashe are going to stay a few days, so if there's any emergencies, they can help."

"Let's hope there aren't any emergencies."

"Get some sleep tonight, yeah? We need you, Captain."

Faye slipped out of the cabin.

When Jonah turned back to Crow, he found himself staring into those beautiful blue irises, pupils rimmed with gold. Jonah remembered the first time he'd noticed such a detail, atop the mast, high above the safety of the deck. Another obvious clue he'd neglected. Another chance to have saved Crow long before danger could come.

Crow's eyelids drooped, then blinked back open in a pitiful attempt at staying awake. They looked how Jonah felt—but how could Jonah compare the suffering of a god to his own petty exhaustion? How dare he try to relate his self-inflicted lack of sleep to the anguish of a poison bullet wound? *Selfish. Pathetic.*

"How are you feeling?" Jonah asked, keeping his voice low.

"Onasi þídes," Crow muttered.

"I don't know what you're saying."

"Onasi þídes."

"Crow. In Midiri."

Crow let out a soft, weak groan, squeezing their eyes shut. It was hard to tell if it was borne of pain or frustration.

"What is my name?" Jonah asked.

"Ilinoé."

"No."

"Sevej Ilinoé."

"Jonah," he spoke slow and deliberate. "Jonah."

"J..." Crow started. "Jo...nah."

"Good. Now, try again. How are you feeling?"

"Onasi..." Crow said. "Ghh...ev—everything."

"Everything?"

He did not receive a reply. Crow's eyes drifted shut.

What did they mean by *everything*? He dug for meaning. Crow's speech was slow and weak. They had an easier time in their native tongue, but Jonah could not translate.

Everything, everything...

Everything hurts.

Jonah flopped into his usual seat at the fire pit at sunrise. His body was sluggish and heavy. He had, after tearing his eyes away from Crow, spent the night with his nose buried in Argonaut's notebook. Jonah searched every letter for clues about his ritual. Jonah knew a few of Argonaut's codes, courtesy of having worked with him, but he didn't see any patterns he recognized.

There were patterns present, though. At the bottom corner of each page sat a random number. Jonah had, at first, thought it to be an invoice number or a sum total of whatever wealth he'd denoted on the page. But no, the numbers were too small to be sums, nor invoice numbers. They sat between one and forty. Some repeated. Did each number correspond with a letter of an alphabet? They did not align with Midiri or Avetic—those alphabets produced nothing but gibberish. Jonah wasn't yet fluent in Sonallan, but that didn't appear correct, either.

By sunrise, Jonah had given up.

Now, the warmth of the fire soothed his tired soul. Beside him, Mouse stoked the fire, getting ready to cook breakfast. Jonah yawned. His consciousness drifted in and out, fuzzy and unfocused. He half-dreamt of starry skies and temples tall enough to pierce the clouds, overrun by moss and vines, left unattended and submerged under rising tides.

"Jonah," a voice snapped him from his daze. "Go downstairs and rest."

His entire crew, plus Phoenyx and Ashe, were now gathered around the fire pit. If he was being honest, he wasn't sure who had spoken.

"No, no," Jonah grumbled, "I'm fine."

"I agree with Jonah, honestly," Faye chimed in. "We can put him back in his cabin and tell him to rest, but we all know he'll go right back to acting like some storybook damsel, draped over the bed of her dashing prince."

Jonah shot her a sharp glare. He sat up straight and rubbed his eyes, determined to cut through the sleepiness weighing him down.

"If you don't mind me asking," Mouse signed, Karina interpreting for Phoenyx and Ashe. "Did Elaine tell you anything about Crow?"

"I'm sure she left out quite a few details," Nyx explained. "But she told us she'd tried and failed to get Einari to relinquish their memory. Einari seemed to believe their punishment of mortality and voided memory was just."

"What were they being punished for?"

"Speaking out. They requested Einari lower the level of the ocean."

"Wow," Karina muttered.

"I suppose such a drastic punishment is... not unexpected, given how he and Aeris have historically never gotten along."

"Aeris," Jonah echoed. He recognized the name. Sophie had mentioned it before. The god of the sky, core member of the Big Four. The Fool, people called them. The Storm God.

The god of the sky's Domain extended farther than storms, and even though it was Einari's fault for mortal struggle, Aeris was a scapegoat for people's frustration. Jonah never understood the logic. Why were storms such an issue when they watered crops and washed away toxins while the ocean choked out the landmasses? The answer was infuriating in its simplicity: Einari mandated it. He had placed those words into the Book of the Tide, and mortals, gullible as they were, believed it.

A crow landed on the gunwale and cawed.

Jonah slept on the floor in front of his desk, through the entire day and long into the night.

When his eyes blinked open, his cabin was dark. Sitting up, he stretched his aching limbs. The stars and the moon illuminated the world outside his window, no clouds in sight to obstruct them. As his gaze turned across his cabin, he spotted his empty cot.

Jonah scrambled to his feet in alarm.

"Crow?" he whispered, not wanting his voice to carry through the passageway and awaken his crew. "Uh...Aeris?"

The name rolled strangely off his tongue. He wasn't sure he liked it.

He hurried out into the passageway. A quick glance revealed the door at the end was ajar, the cabin empty. Had Karina decided to look after them while Jonah slept? Before he could sneak toward her cabin, a noise tugged his attention upwards. Faint, uneven footsteps above deck.

Jonah scrambled upstairs. When he breached the doors, he spotted Crow stumbling across the length of the deck. They were almost to the mast, their intention clear.

Jonah broke into a run. "Crow!"

Each step Crow took was pained and stiff, their body struggling to keep upright. They clutched their wound. Jonah caught up and stood between them and the mast. Crow reached out, and instead of finding the ladder rung, their hand found Jonah's chest. Their touch was firm, fingers splayed. The warmth of their palm ignited something in Jonah. His heart thrummed against his ribcage. He knew what this feeling was. He tried his best to shove it deep down.

"You can't go up there," he said. "You'll hurt yourself."

"I..." Crow rasped. They tried to push Jonah out of the way. "I can..."

"You can't," Jonah said, his voice firm and commanding. "You're in no shape to climb." He placed his hands on Crow's waist to support them as they teetered. Their knees buckled, and they slumped against him. Jonah gasped, firming his grip as he took on Crow's full weight.

"Come on," he whispered. "Let's get you back to bed."

"No," Crow slurred, though they did not put up a fight as Jonah guided them toward the stairwell. "*Ø gepiel,* I need..."

Fresh air. Out here, Crow could feel the wind. The deck was a treacherous place, though, its hardwood paneling and open vulnerability a looming threat of further injury. Should a monster find them, they'd be dead in an instant. Or a band of pirates with ill intent, roaming much too far from northern seas...

Crow seemed somewhat revitalized, however. The longer they spent out here, the straighter they stood, the brighter their eyes shone. Was it worth the risk?

No.

Jonah guided them below and settled them in his cot. His delicate fingers trailed up their arm as he tucked his sheets around them.

Their tiny burst of energy faded in an instant.

22

54th Storm, Great Flood 1058

Crow awoke before sunrise, tangled in Jonah's sheets. They were alone on the cot—Jonah slept on the floor by his desk, no pillows or blankets to soften the wood floor. Wasn't he uncomfortable? If Crow scooted over, there would be ample space for Jonah to lay with them. They couldn't blame him, though. In the aftermath of a bullet wound that spewed gold, Jonah was right to be wary.

The wound in their stomach throbbed as they peeled themself off Jonah's cot and tiptoed toward the door. Best not to wake him. If the dark bags under Jonah's eyes said anything at all about his current state, he needed to rest. Besides, they had no energy to translate their thoughts into Midiri. If Jonah were to wake, he'd expect Crow to communicate in a language he could understand.

Crow slipped out of the captain's cabin and pulled the door shut with a tiny, soft *click*. They limped up the stairs, gripping the railing for support. One of the nails popped loose, and the handrail lurched. Crow gasped, gripping it tighter to save themself from faceplanting onto the stairs. They steadied themself, then pulled their weight off the fixture before they could snap it clean off the wall. Jonah would *not* be happy if that happened.

When they breached the upper deck, they paused at the top of the stairs, happy to let the fresh air soothe their aching body. With the sun not yet up, the humidity of daytime had yet to set in, leaving the air a pleasant kind of warm.

Climbing the mast hurt like hell. Each rung was agony incarnate, ripping at the seams of their stitches, threatening to tear their wound open. Halfway up, black spots danced in their vision, but they pushed onward. The desire for fresh air overshadowed the pain of climbing.

Crow spent three hours atop the mast. The wind rustling their hair and clothes rejuvenated them. The darkness of night waned, and for now, they were *okay.* No pain, no exhaustion.

They returned to the deck as the sun threatened to rise—best to climb down before anyone snapped at them for being reckless—and took their place at the bow.

Ashe was the first to stir. She emerged from the *Burning Maiden* and crossed the gangplank at first light. Crow didn't blame her for the way she faltered when her eyes caught theirs. How did one approach a god?

"Good morning, Your Grace," she said as she joined them. Her long, thick brown hair fell loose over her freckled brown shoulders. She hadn't bothered to tie it back this morning. She wore a tank top whose thin straps accentuated the broadness of her shoulders, and Crow wondered if she kept her hair down to obscure them.

"You don't have to call me that," Crow muttered. "I don't want to be treated any different."

"I get it," Ashe said. "It's not the same at all, but when I first told my mother I was trans, she got all weird about it. She didn't understand. It took a lot of coaxing from Nyx for her to start calling me Ashe, but... even when she did, she said it with such awkwardness I didn't feel at home."

"I'm sorry."

"She came around. I guess I want you to know I can relate, in a way. It's not like I became a whole other person by being a girl, y'know? I'm still me. Like how you're not a whole other person because you're a god."

"I could be a whole other person. I don't know."

"You won't be. Even if you get your memory back, your time here has shaped you. Who you turn out to be, Aeris, matters more than who you used to be."

Crow looked at Ashe. The name didn't stir anything within them.

They wished it did.

"…Please call me Crow."

"Sure thing."

"You shouldn't be on your feet," Jonah's deep voice snapped Crow's attention away from Ashe. "You need to rest."

"I needed to get some fresh air," Crow replied. "I climbed the mast this morning. I'm feeling pretty good now."

"You climbed the mast!?" Jonah groaned. He reached for the top button of Crow's shirt. "Let me see."

Crow allowed him. They didn't know much about the culture they lived in, but it seemed such an intimate gesture, something Crow could have done themself. Jonah's careful fingers undid each button, revealing the blood-soaked bandages underneath. Jonah grimaced and peeled back the bandages. Underneath, a couple of stitches had broken.

"You're being foolish, Crow," Jonah said. "You're making things worse."

Crow couldn't help but adore how Jonah had no qualms about calling a god foolish. While uncertainty raged around them, Jonah stood as a bastion of normalcy.

"I'm fine," Crow said. "The fresh air helps me, and—"

"If you're going to be a little shit about it," Jonah snapped. Crow flinched under his frustration. Jonah stopped fussing with Crow's bandages. "Fine."

"Wait, Jonah—"

"That's *Captain* to you."

Jonah marched away. Crow wanted to call out, but their words died in their throat as he disappeared back below deck. They slumped against the gunwale.

"Let me see those stitches," Ashe said. "I can fix them for you."

"…Thanks."

Ashe hurried to retrieve her medkit. When she returned, she urged Crow to sit. They leaned back against the gunwale as she redid three of their stitches.

The needle spiked their anxiety. They flinched whenever it drew close to their skin. *It's not a syringe,* they tried to rationalize, but even still, their heart raced. They couldn't bring themself to look away.

"What's up with Jonah?" Crow couldn't help but ask, trying to quell one anxiety by babbling about another. "It's like, one minute he's my friend, and the next thing I know, he hates me. I don't get it."

"You're not alone," Ashe supplied. "He's not the easiest guy to understand."

"Oh."

"In my time knowing him, though, I've learned he tends to push away the people he cares about. He thinks if he doesn't *care,* then he won't have to deal with the anguish of loss. He lost his family long before I ever knew him. To my understanding, his adoptive father's death bothers him less because he'd seen it coming—he'd had time to prepare. But he lost his sister in the blink of an eye, and in a far more violent manner, and he never figured out how to cope." Ashe paused. "And now you've shown up, and he's afraid, because he cares more for you than he's willing to admit."

Jonah was adopted? They found themself thinking. *Who were his real parents?*

"He wants you to take it easy," Ashe shrugged. "We all do. And you're not, which he finds annoying."

"I don't want to rest. I'm tired of resting."

"I would be, too, if I were you. Come sit at the fire pit, at least?"

Crow nodded. They followed Ashe to the fire pit and sat in Jonah's usual spot. Ashe lit a fire with some flint, and Crow leaned back in their seat, trying their best to relax.

Jonah ignored Crow all day long. By the evening, Jonah's avoidant nature grated on Crow's nerves. Was Jonah always this petty?

Crow waited until they knew Jonah was in his cabin, then knocked on his door. He grunted out a *"Come in,"* thinking it was Karina or Faye or whoever. Crow pushed through the door and made eye contact with Jonah for a mere second before he grimaced and turned away. He hunched in his seat and pretended to look busy as Crow took a seat on the stool across the desk. He dipped his pen in ink and didn't write anything. He poked at the page a couple times. Squinted at it. Ink dripped off the nib, leaving splotches on the paper in front of him.

"I'm sorry," Crow said.

Jonah did not reply. Crow's instinct was to fill the silence. Jonah could pretend he wasn't listening all he wanted. Crow didn't care.

"In Køveni, you would say *kiri*. Or, to convey the sentiment a little stronger, *je kiri*. An apology laced with sorrow. The word *je* emphasizes whichever word it precedes. I guess there isn't anything comparable in Midiri, huh? Just *sorry.*"

Jonah wrote a word and drew a circle around the word. He wrote something else beneath it, and circled it, too. Twice. It was hard to tell from this angle, their view obstructed by a stack of books, but they wondered if Jonah had made note of those Køveni words. He seemed interested in languages—teaching him new words was a way to get on his good side. Crow filed the knowledge away in the back of their mind.

"I didn't mean to be dismissive," Crow rambled. Jonah's silence was unbearable. "I don't want people to see me as vulnerable and pathetic as I feel. Karina always gives me these... these *looks,* like I'm something to be pitied."

Crow stood. Their wound stung.

"I'll get out of your hair. I guess I'll see if Ashe and Nyx would be willing to give me a ride to some island in the middle of who-knows-where, like you'd wanted when we first met." There was no venom in their voice, only resignation. They paused and stared at Jonah. *Please look at me. I don't care if you yell at me. Yelling would be better than this.*

But Jonah appeared as though he could be made of stone. He sat still, staring at his papers. Whatever he was feeling, he was doing a damn good job of hiding it.

Crow made their way above deck. Karina had laid out a large, colorful woven blanket near the foremast. In the center of the blanket sat her kettle, full of hot water, and a bowl of oranges. She sat with Nyx, Ashe, and Faye. Crow joined them. Karina scootched over to make space.

"Aeris," Nyx greeted. Crow still wasn't sure they liked the name. "Elaine told me about you, Your Grace. I'm humbled to be in your presence."

"Elaine," Crow chose the goddess of fire's name to repeat aloud. "She's..."

"My patron goddess," Nyx said, "And a close friend of yours."

Crow nodded.

"She said Einari is holding your memories captive. You're being punished for making a request of the God King to lower the sea level."

"Even without my memory, I still think I'm right," Crow grumbled. They stared out at the horizon, dotted by the ships sailing in the distance.

They leaned back, bracing their hands behind them. The whole ordeal left them feeling aloof. Here Phoenyx was, telling them their true name, their true identity, and Crow was...blank. Should they be angry? Sad? Happy? Nervous?

"I, um..." Crow turned their gaze to the visitors from the *Burning Maiden*. "I wanted to ask a favor, if it's okay."

"Of course," Ashe said.

"Would you be willing to give me a ride somewhere? It doesn't matter where, I guess. Drop me off on some island and leave me—"

"What?" Faye cut in. "Why?"

"I'll bring you all trouble, right?" Crow laughed, but there was a sadness to it. "I wouldn't want to harm you all. I...I think I want to find Argo again. If you drop me off somewhere, I could get a boat of my own."

"Why, though?" Faye asked. "Argo hasn't done anything other than exploit you, Your Grace. What do you want from him? There are other ways for us to move forward. There are libraries and temples on every island, full of holy texts you could read."

"Are they written in Køveni?"

"No. Midiri."

"Then, they're useless to me," Crow said. "Argonaut has been collecting my blood. He has a divine motive, and I think my way home might lay with him."

"I thought he wanted to get rich."

"No, there's something else. His ritual, remember? I need to figure out what it means. I'm in a better position to face him, since I now know who—er, *what* I am."

"Did Jonah put you up to this?" Karina asked. "Oh, he's so hard-headed sometimes..."

"What? No!" Crow exclaimed. "I mean, sure, he's been ignoring me, but I made this decision myself."

"We're not letting you deal with this alone," Karina said. "You're part of our family. We'll take you back into Anui. Together."

As night fell and everyone retreated to their cabins for the night, Crow remained above deck, leaning their forearms against the gunwale at the bow. A long day of refusing to rest had left their body aching and their energy drained. They could still feel the acidic tang of the Monster Blood remnants in their system. Their body had been working overtime to fight it off.

Even though the exhaustion threatened them, Crow made their way to the starboard hull, near the stern, where the dinghy was hitched. Their muscles and their wound ached as they heaved the spare life vests off it, keeping one for themself. They peeked into the rations box—it was filled to the brim with dried meats and nuts. Deeming it good enough, they closed it once more and tucked it back underneath the seat.

The oar leaned against the gunwale, and as they turned to grab it, they caught another presence in their periphery. They whirled around, startled.

Karina stood a few paces away, her arms folded across her chest, her expression flat, unamused. "Where do you think you're going?"

23

"On the seventy-first of Sun, in the year Great Flood 01, one hundred days after its beginning, merciful Einari ceased the flood's rise. The generous king could have drowned everything, but he was gracious and kind, offering mountaintops for mortalkind to dwell upon..."
—Book of the Tide

57th Storm, Great Flood 1058

Karina was almost remorseful for having spooked Crow. *Almost.* They stood before her, one hand gripping the oar, the other braced over their wound. They didn't answer her, but they didn't need to. Karina knew.

"I heard you, you know," she said. "You're not as stealthy as you thought you were."

"S-sorry," they croaked.

"You're not in trouble, okay? I get it. You have a lot on your shoulders. But you're wounded, Crow, and you're not as well-armed as you think you are. Argonaut will still chew you up and spit you out. If you even reach him. The ocean is cruel. You won't get far in a dinghy."

"It's not your responsibility to look after me."

"No, it's not," she echoed. "But I can speak for the whole crew when I say we still *want* to."

Crow's hand slipped off the oar. Balance against the gunwale upset, the oar clattered to the deck. Their pale fingers tightened around the wound in their stomach.

"Come sit with me," she said. She nodded toward the fire pit. Crow glanced over their shoulder at the dinghy, contemplative, then hobbled behind Karina.

She helped them sit. They seemed adamant about hiding their pain, but the stiffness of their posture spoke volumes. *Pushing your pain down won't help you heal,* she wanted to say—but now was not the time nor the place. For now, she took her seat on the bench adjacent to theirs, close enough for comfort, but far enough away as to not impose.

"Can I tell you a story?" she asked. She held their gaze until they nodded, the tiny movement nigh-imperceptible under the moonlight.

When Karina was six years old, her parents stopped taking care of her.

Once they taught her to read, Ma and Pop pushed a pile of books into her hands and focused on their job. They expected Karina to feed herself, keep herself occupied, protect herself. While her parents spent hours, days, weeks selling junk at whatever hub they could, Karina had those same hours, days, and weeks to wander the hubs or sit around on her ship, alone. She had no friends other than the mussels latched onto the floating docks. This was a lonely way to grow up.

At age ten, she learned to pickpocket, and by the time she was thirteen, she'd mastered the skill. Ma and Pop never knew what she spent her time doing or how she earned money to survive. She wasn't allowed to touch their money. That was *business money,* they insisted. They loved their business far more than they loved their own child.

Karina was willing to wager the sole reason Ma and Pop even noticed when she ran away was because she'd stolen a sizeable chunk of *business money* to buy a small boat. Otherwise, she doubted they felt her absence.

She was fifteen when she left.

Sailing brought a different sort of loneliness. At hubs, there were other people around. People to steal from, people to walk past and brush shoulders against, people to talk to and learn from. But out on the ocean, there was nobody but herself.

Loneliness was an endless cycle, one she was born into, one she would never escape. She sailed like this for four years, until, five weeks after her nineteenth birthday, she found Jonah.

Jonah was a damaged young man. He carried with him all the pain and baggage of a boy who, too, had no family. He owned nothing more than a big, empty ship and a broken heart.

The day she met him, he had gunned down two merchant vessels. Karina knew neither ship belonged to Ma and Pop, but she wished one of them had. From his mast he flew the flag of Argonaut the Lawless, its black and white pattern depicting a dismembered hand, radius and ulna protruding from tattered flesh. Karina remembered staring down the barrel of his cannon, thinking she'd face a merciful death, given how her heart ached with empty resentment she could never shake, how her tiny boat fell apart at the seams. Had she not been looking closely enough, Jonah would have shot her down. But she spotted the muddied eyeliner staining his cheeks in long streaks, and anguish burned in those amber eyes. He knew a similar pain.

"You don't have to be a pirate," she called. She chose her words with precision, as these could be his redemption or the sanction of her death. "There are other ways to express your anger. I'm angry, too. There's a lot in this world to be angry about."

His hesitation at the cannon told her everything she needed to know.

"You fly the Pirate King's flag, but killing isn't in your heart. What does your heart want?"

He did not reply. He stared, conflicted.

Three pirate ships lingered nearby. They anchored north of Aurora Isle, and Karina wondered if they were lurking, waiting for this boy, aged twenty-two, to finish whatever crime they'd ordered him to commit.

"*My* heart," Karina said, "wants to not be so alone. Are you lonely?"

"That's none of your business," he replied. From her tiny boat, she stared up at where his mangled, choppy, self-cut ginger hair poked over the gunwale.

"You look like you could use some company. Can I come up?"

The boy stared at her for a little while longer, his brow furrowed, then he disappeared from Karina's view. Karina frowned. Had he left? Should *she* leave?

He came back and dropped a rope ladder down the side of his ship. With no other way to anchor, she tied the ladder's ends to the little boat, then climbed. As she made her way up, she caught the neat, precise writing on the side of the ship. *Vengeance,* this ship was called. Some other name, a previous name, had been shaved off.

"My name is Karina," she said when she reached the *Vengeance's* deck. "What's yours?"

The boy had an intense stare. A dark stare. A distrustful stare. He had since dried the tear streaks off his face, but his lip still quivered. Karina offered him a warm smile.

"Jonah," he whispered.

"Jonah," Karina repeated. "Your name is not well-suited for piracy. You deserve a gentler life."

Jonah stared at the floor. One strand of choppy bangs was far longer than the others and fell in front of his face. Another strand toward the back stood straight up. His hair looked like he'd cut it in the midst of a mental breakdown. Karina wondered if he'd let her trim it.

"Those ships you sank," Karina said. "They were merchants. Why did you sink them?"

"They were complicit in her murder."

She didn't press who the '*her'* was. "Merchants?"

"Argonaut said so," Jonah justified. His voice wavered. "He told me they helped kill her. They deserved to die."

Karina eyed him up and down. His trembling hands, the way he cast glances over his shoulder at the looming pirate ships. Karina could see the fear in his eyes. She wondered if he feared getting caught speaking with her.

"Can I sail with you?" Karina asked. "We can leave those pirates."

"I can't," Jonah whispered. "I have to get revenge. Argonaut says he knows what I need to do."

"I think he's lying," Karina said. "Who killed her?"

"Pirates."

"Why would Argonaut want to turn against his own?" She pushed her luck. Jonah could send her away, and she'd be on her own again, or he could kill her, but at least she would have planted the seed of questioning. "And why would he then tell you to work *with* pirates to take down *merchant* ships?"

"The merchants were involved."

"How?"

"They—They—Argonaut said they were."

"And you took him at his word? You didn't press for details?"

"Stop it. Stop!" he snarled, balling a hand in his fist. He threw a punch, and Karina dodged. His anger made him sloppy.

Karina couldn't remember the details of what followed. The fight was a blur. Karina knew how to steal, how to pick locks and pockets, but she did not know much about combat. She had witnessed plenty of fights at the hubs, but seldom did she need to throw a punch of her own. She tried her best, but by the end her face and arms were blanketed with bruises. She stood with one hand braced on her knee and the other stifling the blood oozing from her nose. Jonah stood in front of her, staring her down. His gaze was softer, now, something of realization.

"Let me sail with you," Karina said. Jonah would be *interesting* company, but he was company, nonetheless. "I think we can help each other."

Jonah, to her surprise, accepted.

When the *Vengeance* sailed off, three pirate ships had gone up in flames. Jonah and Karina stood shoulder to shoulder as they sailed away, and for the first time in her life, Karina didn't feel quite so alone.

"Why are you telling me this?" Crow asked. They fidgeted with the hem of their shirt.

"Being alone isn't the boon you think it is," she said. "It's harder to get by. Especially when you're at your most vulnerable. Like I was. Like Jonah was. Jonah—you have to understand, Crow, Jonah's been troubled since the day I met him. But together, we built ourselves into far better people than we would have been, had we never met."

"I think I understand."

"Stay with us, Crow. You're not ready to face Argonaut, but we can help you get there. I have no doubt you'll find a way to help us, too."

Crow didn't respond right away. Karina allowed them the silence they needed. *Aeris,* Karina thought. *They're so small. It's so easy to forget they're the god of the sky.*

"Okay," Crow said. The stars, far above them, twinkled. "I'll stay."

Karina smiled. "Then let's get to bed, okay?" She stood and extended a hand to Crow. Crow took it, and she helped them to their feet. "You've had a long day. You could use some rest."

Crow yawned, and Karina was thankful they nodded. She led them downstairs, not taking her eyes off them until they were in their cabin.

24

59th Storm, Great Flood 1058

Jonah was well aware he was being dramatic. But Crow was so... so *infuriating!* How could they brush their injury off like nothing was wrong? How could they pay no heed to it? They could have died, and here they were, climbing the mast and refusing to rest, as if their near-death meant nothing.

But it sure as hell meant a lot to Jonah.

As he trudged above deck, ready to bid farewell to Nyx and Ashe, his heart clenched. Would Crow leave the *Vengeance* like they said they would? He wasn't so sure he could bear the thought. Funny, wasn't it? How, at the beginning of the season, all he'd wanted was to be rid of them, and now, here he was, wishing they wouldn't go?

The crew gathered at the bow and waved the *Burning Maiden* off. Relief washed over him when Crow did not cross the gangplank, and he felt embarrassed by it. They lingered, elbows braced on the gunwale, wispy black hair falling in front of their face. Though they stood watch as the *Burning Maiden* departed, their gaze looked distant. Thoughtful.

When the rest of the crew dissipated, Crow remained, and so did Jonah. He stood a few paces back, out of Crow's eyeline. Though it would be easy to keep being petty, he couldn't bring himself to step away. The fragment of Sophie in the back of his mind urged him not to. *Silence won't fix anything,* she would say.

Sophie always seemed to win. He joined Crow at the gunwale. Without thinking, he reached out and brushed the strand of hair away from their eyes. Whatever turbulent thoughts swirled behind those eyes vanished, and their gaze snapped to him.

"How's your wound?" he asked.

"Fine."

A pang of frustration shot through him. "You almost died!" he snapped. "How are you this indifferent?"

"What's the point?" Crow asked, sharp and cold. "It was terrifying, okay? Yes, I almost died. And yeah, it hurts. But what's the point in dwelling? What good does it do? Am I supposed to wallow in my own misery over what could have happened? Unlike you, Jonah, I want to move *forward.*"

Jonah winced. Their words stung. His fingers twitched. If someone had said this a few years ago, he would have punched them in the jaw for the insult. Now, however, he was a mature enough man to know Crow was right.

"I'm not mad at you," he mumbled. "I get it."

"Sorry. I shouldn't have snapped. Karina told me—"

Jonah wasn't eager to let them finish their sentence. "I know the feeling. Like you need to do everything alone. It's better, don't you think? Nobody gets hurt because of you."

Crow nodded.

"If there's one thing I've learned in my life, you should never feel the need to endure your pain alone. That road leads to more suffering. You can thank Karina for teaching me."

The pesky strand of wavy raven hair fell back into Crow's face. It bugged Jonah, so he brushed it aside again. His hand lingered against Crow's cheek, soft like an infant's, unmarred by the cruelty of the world around them. What a silly comparison to make. Cruelty was all Crow had seen of Midir.

Crow chuckled. "She told me the same thing."

Jonah brushed his thumb along their cheekbone. Their face was warm with life. Crow's heart was still beating.

"I should..." he struggled to get the words to roll off his tongue. "I should apologize. I haven't been kind to you."

Crow cast him a small smile. "It's okay."

"No, it's not," he pressed. "This is something I still need to work on. Owning up to mistakes is a skill that needs practice."

"I appreciate it. That's what I admire about you, Jonah, you know? You work to make things right."

Jonah's hand slipped from Crow's cheek, falling back to his side. He turned away from them, facing the endless ocean beyond. "You shouldn't admire me. You're a god. I'm a wreck."

Crow chuckled. They nudged Jonah with their shoulder. "I'm a wreck, too."

He couldn't quite conceal the smirk threatening his lips. He nudged Crow back. They laughed, then pushed back from the gunwale. They took two steps before Jonah figured out where they were headed.

"Crow."

Crow cast a glance over their shoulder.

"No climbing the mast."

"What? Why?"

The frustration dared to boil over once more. One sharp snap and he'd undo all the progress he'd made. He drew a long, slow breath and closed his eyes.

"Because," he said, "you need to let yourself heal. If you keep screwing your stitches up, you'll be in for far worse than a sore wound."

Crow deflated. "But—"

"That's an order."

"Fine," they grumbled, then rerouted, ambling not toward the mainmast, but instead the fire pit. They joined Faye and Mouse there.

One by one, Jonah pulled his crew aside and instructed them to, under no circumstances, allow Crow to climb the mast. He knew, after all, the moment he took his eye off them, they'd try.

And try, they did.

Not long after Jonah retreated to his cabin, Willow's voice carried through the floorboards. "No climbing," she barked. And then, in the evening, Karina did the same. Despite his frustration, he couldn't help but chuckle.

Classic Crow.

25

"Must I become a goddess?" Elaine asked. "Is there nobody better for the job? I am sinful and broken."
The Fool handed her the knife. "I know of no soul better suited than yours."
- The Book of Fire

59th Storm, Great Flood 1058

"How was it," Einari asked, "to taste mortalhood after so long?"

Elaine, knelt on the Great Hall's cool marble flooring, knew he was not asking of a kind heart. He wasn't asking about her vacation to Midir. There was something dark and angry behind his deep, rich voice. Elaine was not incapable of reading between the lines, but she played aloof anyhow.

"It was nice," she said, schooling her tone into something pleasant, amicable. "A kind reminder of who I used to be. I miss the mortal realm. I wish you would give us the freedom to visit more often."

"You risk your life. Mortalkind is cruel. I'm looking out for my kin."

"With all due respect, not everyone will endure the same trauma as you."

"Look at Aeris. How are they faring, now?"

"They're doing quite well, I hear," Elaine toyed, meeting Einari's steely gaze. She rose. At her full height, she stood a touch taller than him.

"You put your life in the hands of the mortals," he drawled, "for the Fool."

"My life has always been in the hands of mortalkind," she argued. "Before my ascension *and* after. We are servants of our creation."

"Our creation is servant to *us.*" Einari turned from her, facing the marble arches which glittered under perpetual starlight. "We stray from our topic."

Elaine frowned, displeased he'd seen through her distraction.

"You went to Midir against explicit orders to remain here," he said, holding his arms behind his back, poised and proper. Elaine stared at the back of his head. Today, his long seafoam hair was tied back, forming a waterfall, which rushed down before dissipating into gentle mist at the nape of his neck. Once it left his scalp, like when vomit left Elaine's mouth, it ceased to exist.

"I did," Elaine replied, seeing no reason to lie.

"And you rescued Aeris, against said orders."

"I did."

Einari turned to face her again. His expression was flat, unamused, frigid, like the ocean in winter. "We are at a crossroads, Elaine. I hope, when it all boils down, you'll be standing on the *correct* side. Your loyalty will be rewarded, but continued defiance warrants consequences. I respect you, Elaine. You'd be best suited to keep my respect intact."

Without a word, Elaine turned. She made it halfway to the Great Hall's grand doors when Einari spoke again.

"You know," he said. His voice was chilling, saccharine. "You should not strain yourself so much. It might harm your baby, hm?"

Elaine balled her hands into fists and stomped out. She refused to gratify Einari with a response. The gall of men! To think they can place themselves in a station above her! The one good man she'd ever known was her beloved Isaac, the man who died in raging flame, the man whose *leech* sat lodged in her belly.

It is not a baby. I am not pregnant. Magma boils within me but will never erupt. I am a dormant volcano. I am with Mt. Azhir.

Elaine burst into Novika's garden. "Blessed be!"

Novika, knelt in the dirt and surrounded by blue and yellow flowers, glanced up from their work, startled. "Mind the clovers, please. You always manage to burn them."

Elaine chuckled. "My apologies. Your garden looks beautiful, by the way. Your ivy has grown!"

"Ah, thank you." Novika blushed as they stood and wiped dirt off their knees. "What brings you here? I'm relieved to see you're no longer glued to the reflecting pool—and in such high spirits, no less."

"I have grand news. Aeris is healing. The Monster Blood is gone from their system—if they were to die now, they would walk right past Judgment and find their way back here."

"A relief." Novika paused. "The Great Hall is much too quiet in their absence."

Elaine nodded, solemn. The Heavens would suffer without end if Aeris were lost to the pantheon. It was bad enough knowing Aeris was trapped, devoid of memory, in the realm below. In the wake of Elaine's ascension, Aeris had come to be her closest friend. Losing them would be as devastating as the day her betrothed died.

"Would you be willing to help me retrieve their memories?"

"What? No! I will not go behind Einari's back any longer. He was upset enough as it stood."

Elaine groaned. "It's not fair. You send me down to save their life, and what do I get? A slap on the wrist. Aeris said a few harmless words, and they were banished."

"It's cruel, but who are we to undermine our king?"

"We're gods, Novika! We can do whatever in damnation we please!" Elaine rubbed her temples. "I understand. You don't want to damage your friendship. Sorry for disturbing you."

"...How is Aeris faring?"

"Well enough." Elaine couldn't help but worry. Aeris was kind and gentle—and yet, Einari had conditioned the mortals to detest them. *As if anybody could survive without the sky,* Elaine thought. *As if plants could grow without the sun, as if fire could burn without oxygen, as if the seas do not respond to the moon.*

There had to be a reason behind why Aeris was the scapegoat, but it evaded Elaine's grasp. How? She was a goddess. Shouldn't she be all-knowing?

Elaine glanced down to find a few of Novika's precious clovers had charred beneath her boots. She winced and hoped Novika wouldn't notice. They did. Their eyes flicked down to Elaine's feet, and they sighed.

"If you won't come with me, would you at least be willing to distract Einari for a little while?"

"Fine," Novika muttered, brushing a hand through their long, beaded braids. "I'll distract him. But don't expect any more favors. I wish to keep my friendship with Einari *intact.*"

"Thank you. I am in your debt."

"Indeed, you are."

Novika invited Einari to their chamber to share tea harvested straight from their garden. Elaine never understood the appeal—tea was a bitter and unappetizing drink. She hadn't even enjoyed it when she was mortal, three thousand years ago. Nonetheless, this was the perfect time to snoop—they would be occupied for some time.

Elaine snuck down the long, starlit path. Around her stood tall, ornate archways which seemed to lead nowhere, if not for the swirling portals framed by each set of marble columns. She hesitated outside Einari's archway. Should Einari learn she had trespassed his chamber, his wrath would have no end. She needed to get in, find Aeris's memories, and get out before they finished their tea.

As Elaine crossed the threshold of the archway, the world around her shifted into a large, opulent space filled with shallow pools of water, whose ripples cast beautiful light patterns upon the tile walls. A set of stairs led to a dais, upon which sat an uncomfortable-looking shell chair. The room was so pristine, Elaine wondered whether Einari even used it.

Elaine hurried up the stairs and onto the dais in search of a secret door, a storage unit, a closet... anything. Where did Einari keep Aeris's memories? She inspected tiles on the wall, ran her fingers along patterns and cracks...

Nothing.

Was this it? Einari's chamber was empty, pristine, non-incriminating. Had he stored something as crucial as Aeris's memories somewhere else, where intruders like Elaine would never find them?

She turned, ready to trudge out of Einari's chamber. A shimmer caught her eye. A beam of reflected light hit an odd crack in the marble wall, accentuating lines of deep shadow that formed a square outline. A small, concealed door.

Elaine heaved it open, revealing a staircase. She hurried down.

Deep in the bowels of Einari's chamber was a library, full of dusty old books Elaine had never seen before. A few little spiders Novika had created to care for her gardens had somehow found their homes here. Their webs spread across bookshelves.

Why not use the library near the Great Hall? she wondered. *What is he hiding here?*

These texts were old and ratty, far older than most books, mortal or divine. She scanned the titles. They were old versions of religious texts, dating from long, long ago. Not too long after the creation of life itself.

She carried on. There was no time to waste. The corridor led her to a workroom, whose far wall was lined with hundreds of glass compartments. Each square a different color, the wall appeared a giant quilt of stained glass—but behind the colored panes, something flickered. The three compartments in the center caught Elaine's eye, bigger than the others, their glass green, red, and blue. The blue one was packed to the brim with what appeared to be wispy smoke, which danced and twirled within its container. Aeris's memories.

But why were there so many others here, too? The red- and green-labeled compartments also contained a few memories. The same could be said for every minor deity in the realm. She reached out, her fingertips ghosting against the glass of Aeris's...

"I believe you've spent long enough down here."

Einari's voice startled Elaine. She whirled around to face the king with a sharp gasp. *Heavens,* she cursed, *I was much too slow.*

"Einari!" she exclaimed. She let slip a nervous laugh. "I'm sorry, I didn't mean to snoop. I was, um, looking for you. I couldn't find you anywhere, so I thought I'd check your chamber."

Einari's stare was flat, unconvinced.

"You have our memories, too," she whispered. "You didn't take only from Aeris."

"Minor affairs. Nothing to concern yourself with."

"I think it is very much *something to concern myself with,*" Elaine argued. "You have violated us all."

"I have been patient with you, Elaine, but your loyalty to Aeris has proven rather problematic. Do you want to be responsible for our pantheon's downfall?" Einari pinched the bridge of his nose. "Oh, I hoped you would come around..."

"Come around!?" Elaine shouted. "You have done *nothing* but disrespect and devalue Aeris—nay, all of us! Did you think I'd take sides with you after this?"

"Don't leap to conclusions. Aeris cares too much for the mortals and not enough for their own ilk. For the good of the pantheon, they need to be disposed of."

"I want to know what you're hiding." Picking a fight on Einari's turf was a dangerous game. Water and fire did not mix in fire's favor. "I want to know what you took from *me,* what you took from *Aeris,* from *Novika.* What would your friend think if they found out you were hiding something from them? We're supposed to be a unit, the four of us. A team!"

Heat blossomed in her palms, begging to be released. She lunged toward Einari, nails digging against her palm as she thrust her fist forward. Flame erupted around her hand, and Einari rolled his eyes and stepped aside. With a frustrated growl, she tried again and again, her punches laced with red-hot flame. Each time, he dodged with the grace and fluidity of water itself.

"Don't bother," Einari snarled. He grabbed her arm mid-punch. Water bubbled around her fist, shackling her. "If you knew what was good for you, for *all of us,* you'd do what you're told. *Behave.*"

"Aeris never behaved," Elaine snarled, trying to pull her hand free. "And neither will I!"

"...Unfortunate." Einari mused. "I cannot kill you in the Heavens, but I could send you back down to the mortals, where you may perish at the hands of Death's servants."

"You never wanted them to learn their lesson," Elaine muttered, her brow furrowed. "You wanted them dead!"

"You must understand," he said, his voice cool and level. He released his grip on her, but the water swirling around her fists remained. She took a few steps back, and he let her. "Their mere existence is a threat."

"A threat!? To *what*, your pride?"

"To the integrity of our pantheon! I'm trying to protect you! All of us! They won't stop at Blight's death. Which god is the next to die by their hands?"

"Blight died," Elaine snarled, "by *my* hand!"

"Aeris sanctioned it!"

Elaine darted for the wall. As Einari moved to grab her, Elaine slammed her elbow into one of the compartments. Glass shattered, and the few memories residing within dissipated into the air.

Green. The color of the plants that thrived upon what little land remained available to mortalkind. Elaine knew she wasn't going to make it out of this, but now Novika, goddess of the wilds, knew what Einari had worked hard to keep hidden.

Sorry, Nov, Elaine thought. *You wanted to preserve your friendship, and I've doomed it.*

Rage wrinkled Einari's features. Elaine's attention snapped to Aeris's capsule. Millennia of memories flitted around in their casing, yearning to be freed. Elaine punched at the glass. As her fist nicked the capsule, Einari grabbed her and threw her to the ground. Tendrils of water wrapped around her torso, her arms, her legs.

Come on, Einari, she thought, *turn it to ice.* She could melt through ice. But her bonds did not freeze.

"Sending you to your doom would be too merciful," Einari growled. "I ought to put you in a friend's hands."

"Let me go!"

Einari turned away and lifted his hands in the air, palms upwards.

"Come up from the shadows, deepest divine," he chanted. *"Come to me, father of end."*

Dread welled within Elaine. Sigils etched into the marble flooring, unnoticed until now, glowed a deep, eerie violet. They took up the entire floor, concentric circles of dreadful runes and symbols. Elaine gasped as the center of the circle opened into an inky void. It swirled, angry, unforgiving.

Out of the portal rose a massive, imposing frame draped in deep black robes. He was not quite human, something demonic, monstrous. Big, wretched black horns protruded from his head, curling like a ram's, and Elaine shuddered under his piercing violet-eyed gaze. This was the godly incarnation of pure, unbridled malice, of rot and loss. This was Death.

"I apologize for calling you at such an hour," Einari smiled, as though pleasantries meant anything. "I'd like to ask a favor of you."

"A favor?" a deep, hollow, soulless voice replied. Horror dripped down Elaine's spine. "What will I receive in return?"

"Miss Elaine has been misbehaving," Einari cooed. "I wish for you to punish her. In return...might I offer you the seat on the council I promised? You can take Elaine's place—I've no need for her anymore."

"NO!" Elaine screamed.

Aeris was the one who had pushed the most against Death's presence on the council. Mortal life was a fickle thing, and Aeris had always fought, first and foremost, to protect it. *'He will take control, and what will ensue?'* Aeris had once said. *'Nothing short of calamity upon the mortals. Famine, illness, death. His sole priority is collecting souls.'*

Einari handed her off to Death. Hopelessness flooded her.

Her gaze fell upon the wall lined with all those glass compartments. Hundreds upon hundreds, all containing some secret Elaine may never know. But the one in the center, the fullest of them all, was cracked.

26

"'My Domain is a vast one,' Death decreed to the council. 'All I wish for is a few servants to aid me in such a daunting task.' And the Big Four allowed him such emissaries."
—The Book of Death

60th Storm, Great Flood 1058

The ocean churned. The *Vengeance* sailed at the mercy of the water's fury, its desperation. With each wave battering its surface, the ship rocked and lurched. By Jonah's count, this had started at three in the morning, when a wave slammed the hull hard enough to send him tumbling from his cot. Startled awake, he hurried above deck, expecting a terrible storm—and a *god of the sky* downstairs to get after. He was met, however, with still air and a dark, starry sky dotted with the occasional wispy cloud.

Jonah rushed to the helm. At night, the crew allowed their ship to drift unguided upon the ocean. Mouse's stabilizer, a rudder designed to sense and counter the ocean's currents, kept the *Vengeance* from drifting too far—but the system was of little use in the throes of this angered sea. Jonah disengaged the stabilizer mechanism and took the helm. His arms burned as he fought to keep the ship steady. Sweat poured down his brow.

An hour later, Faye rushed above deck. "What's up with the ocean?"

Jonah didn't reply. His jaw was as tight as his grip upon the wheel. Something knocked against the hull. The *Vengeance* lurched. Faye fell to one knee with a grunt and remained on her knees until the ship settled.

"What hit us?" Jonah snapped.

Faye hurried to the starboard gunwale. Before she could peer into the ocean, a long, webbed dorsal fin breached the surface, massive enough to tower over the *Vengeance's* hull. Faye gasped, scrambling away from the edge. Jonah stared, eyes wide, mouth agape. The fin was gruesome and scaly, a shade of gray-violet visible under the dim, dying bulbs on the *Vengeance's* quarterdeck.

"Holy shit," he muttered.

"There's another one not too far off the bow," Faye reported, her voice wavering. "I can see it from here. What should we do?"

Jonah squeezed his eyes shut to steady his nerves. The monsters weren't aggressive yet—maybe he could keep it that way. "Don't engage. Get below deck. Wake Willow and Mouse."

"Your orders?"

"Willow will come aid me. I want Mouse to make sure that under *no* circumstances should Crow be allowed up here. You, get some rest. I want you taking helm at sunrise."

Jonah didn't know much about monsters. He'd never cared to learn. Would they recognize Crow? *Aeris?* He wasn't eager to find out.

"Yessir!" Faye saluted, then scrambled down the ladder to the main deck. Jonah caught a glimpse of her tripping over her own feet as she scrambled out of sight.

Jonah wrenched the wheel to avoid crashing into the monster keen on getting in his way. His biceps burned. If he knew how to pray—if he *cared* about praying—perhaps he would have prayed that the monsters find another ship to harass. But prayer was a waste of time and offered no tangible result.

Willow hurried out from below deck. She still wore her black sleep bonnet, her locs tucked inside it. She made no move to take it off.

"I want you on lookout," Jonah barked. "If you see *anything,* I want to know about it. Monsters, islands, weather, whatever."

Willow nodded and hurried to the bow. She planted one foot on a storage crate and hoisted her rifle up, peering through its scope. "There's so many of them!"

"Give me a headcount!"

"Five? I think?"

Jonah cursed. Back when they'd first found Crow, the crew couldn't handle even one monster. How the hell were they supposed to deal with five? "Do not, under any circumstances, fire your weapon. Got it?"

"Yes, sir!"

"If we find a lull, load the cannons. I want them standing by. Last resort, self-defense."

A lull came half an hour later. The seas calmed long enough for Willow to scramble over to the cannons. She wasn't as skilled at loading them as Faye was, nor was she as strong. She managed to load four cannons—two on port, two on starboard—before the ocean grew inhospitable once more. As a wave crashed against the *Vengeance's* hull, Willow stumbled to her perch at the bow.

Every few minutes, she shifted her position. She ran a perimeter around the deck, making sure no monster dared lay fin, tooth, or tentacle upon her home. Her face was schooled into something of a snarl, jaw tense, her round nose wrinkled at the bridge. If Jonah were a monster, he'd turn tail and run.

He remembered the day he rescued her. The *Vengeance* had sailed past a nasty shipwreck. Chunks of steel and wood alike jutted from the water, the bulk of the ship long since sunk beneath the merciless waves. Karina spotted her, huddled on a small rock jutting out of the ocean. She was shaky and thin, back then, with tears rolling down her cheeks.

Her crew hadn't made it.

Now, she'd found a new crew to call a family, and Jonah knew she would be damned if she did not protect her new kinsmen with her life.

The night dragged on. Jonah struggled against the helm and wished his resident god of the sky would make it morning already.

When Jonah caught a glimpse of the sun breaching the horizon, he heaved a heavy groan of relief. Willow had yelled out a curt *"Sunrise!"* not long ago—now, orange sunlight nudged the darkness away. He considered the *Vengeance's* survival until dawn a success.

His biceps and back ached from the strain it took to steer. Faye returned at first light, and he waved her to the helm. Once she took over, he shook off his sore arms and made his way below deck to retrieve his first mate.

"I want you to take over leadership," Jonah said. He leaned against the doorframe as Karina stepped out of her cabin. "If you need me for anything, I'll be in my cabin. Keep rotating helmsmen. I spent three hours there, and I'm beat. Nobody works at the helm for more than one hour. Maximum."

"Our heading?"

"Same as it's been. North."

"Going toward Anui is a terrible idea right now."

"Turning around won't be easy. The best we can do is continue our path, though..." Jonah frowned, thoughtful. "A detour may not be a bad idea. If we can manage it."

"You'd better be getting rest," Karina drawled, her hazel eyes narrowed. "I'm not going to let you work yourself into the ground."

"Yeah, yeah." He planned on disregarding her advice. Karina knew this, too, and she gave him a stern frown. She disappeared upstairs without another word, though.

Jonah wasn't alone in the passageway for long.

The door at the end of the passageway flew open, Crow, whose brows furrowed and whose eyes shone, livid. They wore a determined, displeased frown—they would have looked a bit more intimidating if they didn't wobble with each step, struggling against the *Vengeance's* rough sway. Mouse scrambled behind them.

Jonah folded his arms across his chest and stared them down as they approached. He took a wide stance in the middle of the passageway to block Crow's path. Mouse's nervous posture, upon seeing Jonah, relaxed.

"Why can't I go up there?" Crow asked, gesticulating with a firmness fit for their frustration. "I want to help!"

Crow pushed past, and Jonah grabbed them by the arm. Under the barrage of angry waves, the *Vengeance* rocked toward the port side, and Jonah utilized the unstable floor to his advantage. Crow stumbled, and Jonah pushed their back against the bulkhead beside Karina's door. They let out a small groan.

"*Aeris,*" Jonah snapped. "Look at me."

They met his gaze. Their stare was stubborn, intense.

"What are you?" He asked. He pinned them by their biceps, his grip firm, unrelenting.

"A member of your crew," Crow replied with a cocky grin. The cunning bastard knew what Jonah was asking.

"You're a god," Jonah drawled. "And out there are countless monsters. If they see you, it's over. You understand, yes? You will die. *We all* will die."

Crow deflated. "...Yeah."

"You got lucky with the bullet. Elaine risked everything for you. I doubt she'll be able to do it again." Jonah pulled back. He released Crow and turned to Mouse. "Get upstairs," Jonah signed. "See if Karina needs anything."

Mouse nodded and jogged off.

"You want to help?" he asked Crow.

"Yes."

"Then come with me. We're going to chart our path forward."

Crow rubbed their forehead as though they had a headache. They sat across from Jonah at his desk, elbows against its hardwood surface. The two of them gazed down at one of Jonah's many maps, scrawled with old annotations that were meaningless now.

"What if we went to an island?" Crow asked. "What's the closest one to us right now? This one?" They pointed at Avet, which lay at a similar latitude the *Vengeance* sailed on—it would have been a good guess, if not for the fact that Avet was half a globe away. Sailing there would take weeks, if not an entire season, to reach.

"Look. We're right here." Jonah placed a shell coin atop the map, a touch southwest of the Eastern hub.

"Oh. So..." Crow paused. They furrowed their brow, stumped. There wasn't any one island more optimal—Emelle and New Kovi were closest, but both would take days to reach. They pressed a finger against Emelle. "This one?"

"It's easier said than done," replied Jonah. "Everyone's going to be fighting to get ashore right now. Ports will be jam-packed, and I'm willing to wager prices have skyrocketed. We don't have the money to—"

"Money," Crow scoffed. "You have a *god* on your ship."

Jonah eyed Crow. He was about to object when Crow grimaced. They put their head in their hands, massaging their temples, their eyes screwed shut. Jonah waited for their pain to subside.

Crow opened their eyes.

"Are you okay?" Jonah asked.

"Fine," Crow bit. "Look, my blood is worth a fortune, right? I can pay the docking fee."

"I don't want to fall into a pattern."

"What pattern?"

"Exploiting you for your blood."

"I don't mind."

Jonah shook his head. "You're not a commodity, you're a person. We're not bleeding you out. Captain's orders."

"Well, technically—"

"Don't *technically* me. You may be a god, but this is my ship. My ship, my rules."

Crow flinched. The volume of his voice had not helped their headache. As captain, he'd grown adept at snapping. If it were closer to the beginning of the season, Crow's flinch would have been borne of fear. Now, though, if it weren't for the headache, Jonah was certain Crow would have snapped back.

Deciding it best to leave them be, Jonah stood. "I'll go check in on the crew. Stay below deck. *Please.*"

"Shouldn't you be resting too?" Curse them for seeing straight through him.

Instead of answering, Jonah swept out of the room.

27

60th Storm, Great Flood 1058

Every step Crow took was a burden. Their headache pulsed in tandem with their heart. Their knees felt jellylike. They had made it halfway through the passageway—twenty more steps and they'd reach the safety of their cabin. To keep their attention away from the pounding in their skull, they counted each step they took. *One. Two. Three. Four. Five.*

The *Vengeance* rocked, and their legs gave out. When their knees collided with the hardwood, everything went dark.

An ornate marble temple shone under ethereal light, nothing like the grit, grime, and mildew blanketing the mortal realm. This, in contrast, was effortlessly pristine. Everything about the temple was without flaw, as if this place had been created rather than built.

They walked up the iridescent walkway, gold-banded sandals clicking with each step. Their airy, sky-blue robes billowed behind them as they climbed a short stretch of stairs. In the shimmering pathway, they caught their reflection. They didn't look the way they thought they would. Their hair was a brilliant shock of white, like a puffy cloud atop their head, and their eyes were every color the sky could be, somehow, all at once.

Near the entrance of this temple stood someone else, someone familiar, a woman whose cream and red robes draped over her slender frame, except around the slope of her stomach. A pang of guilt shot through Aeris for allowing the woman to ascend while with child, a god of nothing she would never be free from.

There had been no other option at the time. They had done what was necessary.

"Einari's furious with you," Elaine said, "because you showed up late to our last meeting."

"Yeah, yeah. Don't remind me."

Aeris strode into the Great Hall and sat in the easternmost chair. They leaned forward, elbows resting on their knees, and gazed into the reflecting pool.

"Interested in making a bet?"

Elaine sat in the seat to their right. She eyed Aeris with piqued curiosity.

"See this boat here?" Aeris pointed at a tiny steel ship sailing across the vast, never-ending ocean of Midir. The glossy silver reflecting pool rippled under their finger. "I'm willing to wager, by the time it passes this island here, Einari will have come stomping in to give me a piece of his mind."

"This isn't something we should play games over," Elaine said, watching the tiny boat sail across the water.

"It'll be fun!" Aeris insisted with a cheeky grin. "If I'm right, you have to steal some flowers from Novika for me. Bluebells. Lilies."

"Are you serious? They'll be furious if I touch their garden." Elaine grumbled. "Fine. And if I win?"

"Whatever you want. C'mon, it'll be fun!"

"Anything?"

"Anything."

"Help me figure out how to get rid of the fetus."

"Deal."

The two gods sat forward in their thrones as this little boat made its way northward. After a while, the boat took an unexpected turn east. Not long after, though, the boat turned northward once more, having rerouted around what appeared to be the floating wreckage of a sunken ship.

The minor delay ensured that, as the nose of the boat dared to cross the latitudinal degree upon which the island sat, Einari had ample time to show his face. He stepped into the Great Hall, his shadow looming over them both.

"Elaine," Einari said with a sickening, sweet voice. "Would you mind stepping outside?"

Aeris shot Elaine a grin that had 'you owe me' written all over it.

When Crow awoke, they were face-down on the floor. A gentle hand pressed against their shoulder and rolled them onto their side, revealing the concerned face of the *Vengeance's* engineer. Mouse's long, shaggy blond hair fell in front of his face.

Ah, right—they were far below their true home.

Mouse helped Crow to their feet and accompanied them to their cabin. Crow kept keen attention on each step they took, lest they lose their balance again. Their headache disappeared, leaving them in a shaky, unstable, but unharmed state. Their mind reeled.

What they'd seen—was it a memory? It was so tangible, as if they could still feel the reflecting pool's cool surface between their fingers.

"What happened?" Mouse asked, concern laden in his stiff fingers.

"Not sure," Crow lied. Their hands shook. "Seasickness, I guess."

Mouse nodded, though he hesitated before he slipped away. Crow closed the door, sat on the floor in front of their hammock, and held their face in their hands.

They clung to the memory for dear life. But... why *that* memory? Its incidental nature solidified one thing: Einari had not returned a memory out of the kindness of his heart. To Einari, Aeris was an errant toddler in need of punishing. And if one little memory held any weight, then this wasn't a one-time occurrence.

Excitement above deck about an hour later drew Crow out from their cabin. As they stepped out into the afternoon air, an acrid stench hit their nose. They hurried over to where the crew stood at the bow.

In the near distance, a massive plume of smoke billowed over a tiny village gracing the hillsides of Emelle.

"Change course," Jonah ordered. "We're not docking."

"What!?" Crow exclaimed. "There are people out there! We could help them!"

"I won't risk burning my ship."

"And *I* won't let innocent lives come to harm. I want to help."

"How, pray tell?"

They met Jonah's gaze. "I'm a god. I'll figure it out."

Somewhere deep inside of them was divine power waiting to be unlocked. What better way to figure out how to wield it? If they wanted to face Argonaut, they needed more skills than sailing and swordplay. They approached the dinghy and propped one foot atop the gunwale.

"You don't have to come along," they said. "But I have a duty to these people. Their prayers are going unanswered."

"Crow—" Karina started.

They cranked the dinghy to sea level, then climbed atop the gunwale. "Don't try to stop me. I'm tired of being kept on a leash."

A sea monster's fin breached the water not far from the *Vengeance*. A hand met Crow's elbow. Crow knew those hands. The grip was firm, fingers calloused. Jonah. They turned to face him, prepared for his inevitable attempt at hauling them below deck. They would be a prisoner again, in a different, less conventional way. But Jonah's eyes were warm like the sun above, soft with understanding. Jonah did not say a single word. He offered Crow a knowing nod, then released their elbow. A silent acceptance.

Crow peered at the island. Flames danced across the thatched rooftops dotting the once-grand mountaintop, now eroded by wind and sea. Tiny silhouettes of islanders crowded the shoreline, forced from their homes. Crow hopped off the ledge and into the dinghy.

The gray ocean raged against Crow's oars. Their arms burned. As they drew closer, the smoke grew thicker. Still, they rowed, despite the way their lungs ached and their head felt fuzzy.

A sea monster surfaced. It had a massive, gaping maw and three rows of sharp ivory teeth. Long, tendril-like limbs surfaced and wrapped around the stern. The dinghy sank under the added weight. Thick, globby drool dripped from its mouth, eager for an easy meal. Frantic, Crow rifled around the dinghy, looking for something, anything they could use to defend themself—they found, beside the ration box, a paring knife. With a quick jab, Crow drove the knife into the sea monster's flesh, and it recoiled.

Crow rowed faster, harder. Choppy waves threatened to overtake the dinghy. The sea monster pursued them. If they weren't careful, they'd sink into the ocean, where they would be defenseless and unrescuable.

The ocean grew angrier the closer Crow got to island—waves slammed against the shoreline, threatening to encroach farther upon the land. A sharp, searing pain ripped through their shoulder, their muscles unable to keep pace.

They weren't strong enough.

A wave knocked the dinghy off balance. Before Crow could recover, another wave overtook them, and the dinghy capsized. Crow plummeted into the ocean's swirling depths. They struggled against the current and tumbled at the ocean's mercy. They caught a flash of the monster's fangs in the murky, sandy depths. They flailed.

A wave slammed them upon the rocky shore. They scrambled onto solid land, coughing and gasping. They stood and brushed sand off their clothes.

A thousand years ago, this island had been a jagged mountaintop. Now it boasted rolling, grassy hills. The buildings Crow could see from shore were all ruined, and the farmland and trees were scorched, blackened with soot.

Townsfolk had fled their burning homes and found refuge by the water. Some were brave—or desperate—enough to dive into the ocean to escape the heat and smog. Did they know a sea monster prowled nearby? How long until it snatched someone into its jaws?

All eyes were glued on them, hawkish and incredulous.

"Um..." Crow stammered. "Hi."

Nobody dared speak, but their faces said it all. Even amid the flames threatening their lives, these islanders still had room in their hearts to hold disdain for seafolk.

"My name is—" Crow froze. What *was* their name? Was it Crow, or was it Aeris? How could they use a name they hardly knew? A name they were unworthy of? They expelled the thought from their mind. They couldn't afford to doubt themself. "My name is Aeris. I'm here to help."

Crow made their way up the beach. They wrestled past islanders who intended to stop them—hands grabbed them, trying to push them into the dinghy, which had found its way to shore upside-down, to send them back to sea. Crow slipped around them, jabbing their elbow into the islanders' ribs when they needed to. They weren't fond of doing so. *Violence begets violence.*

They found a worn path lined by dense bushes, not yet aflame but awaiting their doom. The islanders stopped putting up a fight. *If the sea slug wants to walk to their death, why stop them?* Did they not recognize the name Aeris? Did they not realize their aid came in the form of a god? Or did they not care?

The town gracing this island was a humble one, built of thatched reeds, stone, and imported timber. The buildings of stone—temples—were scorched but otherwise unharmed. Murals of the sea lined stonework walls. One such mural depicted Einari, standing tall over the town, wearing a beautiful crown woven in delicate, glowing silver. The crown of the God King. The mural made Crow feel insignificant under Einari's authority.

Despite the ocean's wrath, these folks—like most others in Midir—revered Einari.

Crow choked, the thick, unrelenting smoke scalding their lungs. They stood in the center of town by a brick well long since dried out, its water exhausted to douse the flames. Crow cast their gaze to the sky, gray and muddled by the billowing plumes of smoke.

What could they do to help these people? They were useless to mortalkind. They deserved to be cast aside, neglected, like the tall temple at the southernmost part of town, so tall it pierced the sky, but succumbed to rot and decay. Was it, at one point, a temple dedicated to them? Abandoned because these people thought worshipping Aeris was not a worthwhile venture? Why? Because they created a few storms here and there?

Now would be a fantastic time to conjure one of those detested storms.

Crow covered their mouth with their sleeve to filter out the sour air. Rain could put out the fires, it could wash away the soot, clear out the smoke. How could they summon rain? It had to be possible, even on the mortal realm. That was their whole *thing,* after all. A god was supposed to have complete control over their Domain. What was the extent of their divine power? And how could they get in touch with it?

Their first step, they supposed, was to get in touch with themself.

Aeris closed their eyes. Yes, Aeris was their name. It was distant, locked away with their memories, but it was inextricably theirs. For the first time, they allowed themself to believe it.

Exhaling, slow and controlled, they reached a hand toward the sky, fingers splayed. When they had sparred Jonah, their excitement had created a storm. The sky had always, to some degree, been tied to their subconscious. But how could they pull it forth? How could they turn control *conscious?*

"Work with me," they whispered to the sky above them. They couldn't survive in the blistering heat and dense smoke for long. If they couldn't figure this out soon, everyone on this island would perish, and so would Aeris. To an extent. They'd walk up the stairwell to the Heavens, toward the answers to every question, toward their missing memories. But would it be worth destroying these mortal lives? Never.

They turned their thoughts to the stars, which they gazed upon many times from the *Vengeance's* deck. They thought of the mast, sail billowing in the breeze, and they thought of the freedom it all brought. Birds, clouds, every single hue from blue to orange to gold—there were so many things about the sky Crow found beautiful. But beauty wasn't enough. Respect wasn't enough.

They were a god—they needed to *command* it.

When Crow first met the crew of the *Burning Maiden,* Nyx demonstrated her blessing by pricking her thumb. Right—their body was mortal. They needed to work with mortal constraints.

Aeris carried no weaponry, having dropped the dinghy's paring knife somewhere before they reached shore, so they scanned their surroundings. The well they stood by had a metal roof, the only sharp item in sight. They reached for the corrugated steel sheets and, in one quick jerk, sliced their arm upon its edge. They grimaced as blood gushed down their wrist. They may have cut too deep, but they needed enough blood to conjure a whole storm. A simple prick of a finger wouldn't suffice.

When they thrust their hand into the air once more, blood flew from their fingertips and into the air above. Golden droplets caught the firelight and glowed.

"Come to me!" They yelled at the sky. Dark clouds swirled overhead. Aeris curled their hand into a fist. Thunder rumbled in the distance. When they threw their hand down, a massive torrent of rain followed, soaking them to the bone.

They couldn't help but watch in wonder as the downpour doused the raging flames. Cool rainwater rolled down the slope of their face. As the fires simmered into smoke, Aeris raised their hand, out of curiosity, to stop the swirling storm. But storms were wily things, alive in their own right, and once they'd brought it into being, Aeris found they could not stop it.

Aeris fell to their knees as a wave of lightheadedness hit them. Their life force was already limited in the wake of their bullet wound, and they had not sacrificed an insignificant amount to conjure the storm. Jonah would not be pleased. Aeris chuckled. Even now, their thoughts still managed to drift back to him.

For now, all they could do was kneel in the mud and bask in the storm, listening to the pattering of rain against rooftops and stone walkways. Despite the exhaustion, despite the thick smoke and the churning seas, Aeris smiled.

28

"No god is more worthless than the god of the sky. To find salvation, thou shalt cast Aeris aside. Do not kneel for the Fool; kneel for your king."
—*The Book of the Tide*

60th Storm, Great Flood 1058

Neither Karina nor Jonah could tear their eyes away as they watched the gathering storm. Deep, menacing, angry gray clouds swirled above the island of Emelle.

Karina spent her life worshipping the gods. In her parents' absence, she had delved into all four holy texts with devout vigor. But to see an act of divinity with her own eyes? This wasn't anything like Nyx's blessing. This was far grander. Crow, nothing more than a tiny speck in the distance—with so much raw power packed into such a small, unimposing frame—had done this.

A small pang of guilt settled in her stomach. The Book of the Tide taught her that Aeris was an ignorable figure, and she was ashamed to have fallen for Einari's words. She had never heard of a Book of the Sky—did such a book even exist? Karina got the sinking feeling that if there ever was one, it was long gone. Lost in the flood? But even surviving texts from the Era of Prosperity spoke nothing of a Book of the Sky.

The torrent came. The *Vengeance* sat outside of the storm's range, so Karina and Jonah were at a perfect vantage point to watch as the flames simmered into steam.

Jonah didn't authorize the crew to dock until long after the fires had gone out. When the rain subsided to a trickle half an hour later, Faye maneuvered the *Vengeance* toward Emelle. The hull scraped against the pier. Anti-seafarer engineering. Narrow spaces between piers kept the big ships out at sea, limiting the number of visitors.

Crow greeted the crew when Willow lowered the gangplank. They waved, their arm bloodied, an excited grin plastered on their face. Karina dropped the anchor and secured the mooring lines.

"Did you see me?" Crow exclaimed, a bright grin on their face.

"Yeah, yeah," Jonah grumbled as he descended the gangplank. When Crow's stance wavered, Jonah was quick to catch them, his attention turning to the gash on their wrist.

"Oh, don't act so unimpressed."

"The hell happened to your arm?"

"Had to do it. It's okay."

While Jonah fussed over Crow's wound, wrapping it with the roll of gauze he always kept in his pocket, Karina turned her attention to the dockworker. She was a tall, portly woman dressed in a fine silk blouse charred from the fires. She folded her arms across her chest and waited, with feigned patience, for the crew to pay her.

"What's the fee?" Karina asked.

"Eight hundred glass," the woman replied.

"Eight hundred?" Jonah exclaimed. "For this shithole?"

"You see those waters?" The woman's pretense of patience faded into the annoyance characteristic of dockworkers. "Everyone's looking to take refuge, and in case you haven't noticed, we're short on resources."

"Even after our crewmate rescued your entire village?" Karina asked.

"The storm would've come anyway."

Ah. Pragmatic, atheist. Once upon a time, Jonah would have responded the same way, making leaps to explain the logic behind divinity. This woman was one of the rare few skeptics in a world of devotion. Expecting every single soul to devote themselves to the gods was silly, but Karina couldn't help but wonder. If the skeptics converted, would Einari rescind the flood?

Please be understanding, Your Grace, she prayed. *We love you. Most of us do. But to ask it of everyone? At such a rate, we may never see continents again.*

"I got it covered," Crow said. Jonah's jaw tensed.

"Crow, I told you, *no*," Jonah snapped. The bridge of his nose was wrinkled, his brows furrowed.

"She needs to see it," Crow replied. "Ma'am, do you have a jar?"

"The hell do you need a jar for?" The dockworker spat. "Piss in the ocean, slug."

"I wasn't going to—ugh. Fine." Crow held out their bleeding arm and peeled back the bandages Jonah had set. The dockworker froze, watching with a look of shock and horror as liquid gold dripped from Crow's veins and onto the dock floor. Crow maintained eye contact with the woman as the precious commodity stained the rusted steel at their feet.

"There," Crow said with a cold finality. "Your payment. You can scrape it off the floor." Crow turned and marched off, leaving the rest of the crew to hurry after them.

"Crow," Karina chided when she caught up. "Don't you think you were being a bit harsh?" *They need to take fewer notes from Jonah.*

The god of the sky shrugged.

Most islanders treated seafolk with flat-out aggression. In a sense, Karina understood the sentiment. If an island *wasn't* inaccessible on some level, it would grow overcrowded. Karina wished she was surprised the islanders treated Crow with the same disdain as any of their mortal companions. If the giant mural of Einari in the center of town said anything, his teachings ran deep.

Even if they had saved the island, Aeris was still the Fool.

"Hey, check this out!" Faye exclaimed. She ran over to the inn and pulled a sheet of paper from its tack upon the wall. "Emelle's annual ocean festival," she read as the crew approached. "It says: *'All are welcome to honor His Grace through prayer and song. Indulge in delicious food, refreshing drinks, and entertainment.'* It's three days away!"

"No." Jonah was quick to cut in. "There's no way they'll host it, not with all the damage. They have higher priorities."

"You'd be surprised," Karina said. "They may not end up with what they advertised, but faith is stronger than wildfire."

"Um," Crow eyed the paper in Faye's hands.

"Yes?" Jonah prompted.

"What's a festival?"

"A big community gathering," Mouse signed. "Islandfolk culture. They're held to gain divine favor. I'd wager if you had your memory, you'd know what a festival is."

Jonah groaned. "We're not going. Don't get any ideas. I want to get off this island as soon as possible. You have work to do, *Aeris*."

Crow deflated. "C'mon, Jo!"

"Don't call me that."

"JoJo."

"I will drag you all the way back to the ship, then throw you overboard."

"Joseph."

"That's not even—" Jonah dragged his hands down his face.

Karina snickered. Their bickering was endearing. She could see the affection in Jonah's soft eyes and in his settled posture. She wondered if Jonah considered Crow to be anything more than a crewmate, a friend.

"I don't know how long I'll be around." Crow fixed Jonah with as pathetic a stare as they could muster. "Would you deprive me of the chance to see what mortal life is like?"

"Oh, no, you don't," Jonah growled. "Don't you dare give me that look. They're worshipping *Einari*, Crow. You hate Einari."

"But it's still a festival." Crow's blue eyes glittered, and they wore a tiny, quivering pout. A strand of hair fell between their eyes, black curls following the ridge of their nose. Jonah groaned and tore his gaze away, his face flushed pink, and opted to glare at a tiny, scorched tree in the distance.

"I... suppose it would make sense," he grumbled, "to let you experience what this world has to offer."

Crow cheered, snapping out of their act in an instant. "You won't regret this, I promise!"

"I'm pretty sure I will."

Karina smiled as the crew walked into the inn. She lingered in the back of the group, beside Willow, as Jonah paid for two rooms. Crow tried, she noted, to offer their blood—they unwrapped the dressing again—but Jonah nudged them aside, adamant they *not* use their blood to pay.

Jonah could act as gruff as he wanted, but Karina saw straight through him.

29

*"Don't let go of me, okay? Don't let go. I've got you.
We're going to be fine. Einari will save us."*
*—The Grand Catalogue of Last Words: Great Flood
Era. Death #4,977,064,698. Drowned.*

62nd Storm, Great Flood 1058

True to Karina's word, the festival went on despite the fires. Colorful strings of light lined the town square, blues, greens, and yellows cast across the otherwise drab stonework roads. Someone had taken the time to set up long, charred banners, and a small market spanned the main road, the stalls, tents, and crowds reminiscent of hub structure.

Despite Jonah's distaste for such festivity, he wound up in the thick of it. Crow had an iron grip on his wrist as they dragged him through the crowd.

People stared. This wasn't out of the ordinary. Jonah and his crew were seafolk at an islander event, wearing cheap, practical clothes which would never hold a candle to the elegance of islander fashion. Islanders kept their distance, wary to interact with the god of the sky—the god Einari's texts taught mortalkind to despise. Jonah was grateful for the extra space. Even now, as he stood with Crow at the front of a food cart's line, people stood back a few steps.

"Oh, Heavens," Crow crooned as they leaned against the cart. The baker looked agitated. "Everything here looks so good! Can I, hmm..."

"You're holding up the line," Jonah whispered in Crow's ear.

"Okay. Okay. Wait, I think I got it now. I'll get the... um, wait, but that one looks good, too..."

"The fruit tart," Jonah cut in. "I think you'll like that one."

The baker packaged up a tart piled up with vibrant, ripe fruits and berries settled in a bed of cream and pressed it into Crow's hands. As a thank-you for rescuing the village, the mayor had decreed that Crow may get whatever they desire free of charge. Jonah was grateful he could save some money. He herded Crow away from the cart, noting the way the baker's shoulders slumped with relief.

"Crow," Jonah said. "Not that I care, but you're not making a good impression." Gods were supposed to be poised and regal. Crow was anything but.

Crow wasn't listening, their attention fixated on something across the street: hand-sewn stuffed animals, hung by twine. Most were sea creatures—dolphins, jellyfish, whales—but there were a few land animals, and one bird. There was no stopping Crow as they bolted across the street.

Jonah hurried after them.

Not too long after Jonah had won the beady-eyed parrot plush for Crow in a game of darts, he walked to the ship to drop off the armful of miscellaneous trinkets Crow had amassed. Could he have stopped at the inn? Sure. But he may as well save the extra trip. Make departure easier.

Jonah couldn't help his fond amusement as he set the parrot on Crow's shelf, next to a book Crow had stolen and not yet returned. This book was a Midiri book on birds. They'd taken it to look at the pictures. Whether Crow knew it or not, it was open to a page with a gorgeous illustration of a raven. The image emphasized the bird's sleek black feathers and cunning personality. In its beak, it held a shell coin.

Crow loved birds, and birds loved Crow. Even now, a seagull sat perched atop the rounded windowsill, pecking at the glass.

The silent, solitary ship soothed Jonah, but he did not linger. He arranged the handful of other knickknacks he'd wrestled from Crow on the next shelf down, then strode back out into the open air.

Even though Jonah had instructed them to *stand still and wait,* Crow had wandered off. He spotted them at a table—if it could even be called such, as it was a mere slab of flat stone lying upon the dirt. Faye, Willow, Mouse, and Crow all crowded around it.

On his way over, Jonah bought a mug of ale for an obscene ten glass. He'd almost been tempted to fetch Crow, so they could get him the drink for no cost—but they looked invested in their conversation.

Based on the signing, he could see from this distance that they were telling the crew all about how they'd conjured the storm. It would be a shame to interrupt. He sucked it up and paid.

Jonah squeezed between Mouse and Faye. He knelt at the table, knees sinking in the dirt, still damp from Crow's rain three days prior. He eyed the tall, narrow glass in Crow's hand. He couldn't identify the drink, but it was light in color and half-gone.

Willow and Faye's drinks were empty, and not long after Jonah joined the group, Willow hurried off to get a refill.

"Jonah!" Crow exclaimed. They slid their glass across the table. "You should try this!"

"What is it?"

"Lemonade. Did you know people make juice from fruit?"

"It's common." Jonah couldn't help but chuckle. Amnesia aside, Jonah had no doubt there were countless aspects of mortal culture unnoticed by gods.

"The guy at the drink cart said it was supposed to be, like, *hard?* I dunno, it looks pretty liquidy to me."

Jonah picked up the glass and sloshed the drink around in it. He narrowed his eyes and glared at Faye. "You let them have alcohol?"

He wasn't confident that letting a god get drunk was a great idea. Crow didn't understand what alcohol was. They would find out the hard way.

Faye shrugged. "They're old enough."

"Is all lemonade spicy?" Crow asked.

"Spicy?" Mouse repeated, his face screwed up in confusion as he signed.

"*Y'know,*" Crow seemed to strain to find the right words, "It's got this, this...spice to it."

"Let me try."

"Mouse," Jonah signed. "You're fifteen. Don't drink it."

"I just want to see what they mean."

Jonah slapped a hand to his face. Control slipped from his grasp. Mouse snatched the drink from Jonah's hands. The boy had at least *some* common sense, as he took the tiniest of sips before passing the

214

drink back to Crow.

"It's carbonation," Mouse signed.

"No, the guy said it's lemonade."

Faye chuckled. "If this is what Crow's like when they're tipsy, I can't wait to see what they're like when—"

"Don't encourage this," Jonah spat.

Willow came back with two new drinks, Karina following her. She passed one to Faye, who took it with a gracious smile. There was no space left at the makeshift table, so Karina knelt on the stone road to the side. She didn't look pleased about sitting on the ground, but in the islanders' haste to set up the festival after the disaster, they seemed to have forgotten chairs.

"Keep an eye on Crow," Jonah leaned over and whispered to his first mate. "Faye is trying to get them drunk."

"Come on, Faye. Behave."

Faye snickered. She pulled a deck of cards from her pocket and dealt everybody a hand. She could have at least prefaced with, '*Anyone want to play?*' Oh, well. Jonah picked up his cards and looked at them. An average hand. Nothing spectacular.

"What're we playing?" Karina asked, trying to scoot a little closer to the crowded table.

"What do you want to play?" Faye asked.

Jonah groaned. "You don't even know what you're dealing for?"

"I figured six per person was enough to do whatever." Faye dealt cards for herself, then placed the remaining deck in the center of the table. "Death's Gambit?"

"Too complicated," Willow said. "What about Ajiya?"

"I don't have Avetic cards on hand."

"We can't make do with these?"

"No." Faye paused to take a sip of her drink. It was a deep cherry red, but it did not look like wine. Islander drinks were difficult to identify, but if Jonah were to wager a guess, it had some mixture of liquor and fruit juice. "Siege?"

"Siege would be easy enough to teach Crow," Karina chimed in.

Jonah thought Siege to be a boring game. He wasn't interested in playing, but Faye had dealt him a hand. *Whatever.* He set up his own strategy as Karina explained the game to Crow.

In Siege, players built a ship by laying cards on the table. One card for the bow, one for the stern, one for the engine, and one for the cannons. The cannon card sat face-up, but the rest remained face-down. Three defense, one offense. The two left over were maintenance cards.

The objective of the game was to be the last ship standing. When it came to the player's turn, they chose which person, and which part of the ship, they wanted to attack. If the cannon card was higher in value than the ship card, the ship would be damaged. Too much damage, and the ship would sink.

Jonah set up for defense. He laid his highest cards upside-down on the table. A king for the bow, an eight for the stern, and a six for the engine. Then, he laid out a three for the cannons.

Crow looked like they were having a tough time. They stared at their cards. Crow couldn't read Midiri markings—an easy thing to forget when they spent their spare time reading from Jonah's library of Køveni books.

They placed a two face-up on the table. Not much worse than Jonah's cannon card, but they lacked strategy. Crow's ship would be the first to sink. That was probably for the best.

The game dragged on longer than Jonah expected, thanks to the sheer volume of players. The whole crew seldom played games together like this. Willow was the first to sink, and while Jonah never managed to cause any real damage, his higher fortification helped him last a little longer. He sank third, one turn after Karina.

Crow held out for a rather impressive amount of time, because by pure chance they'd managed to put an ace down for their stern. Their attention was distant, though, their gaze pinned on the musicians in the middle of the street, dressed in gaudy outfits and playing an energetic tune. Karina had to nudge them whenever it was their turn to play. Their attacks were weak and worthless until Karina suggested they upgrade their cannon, at which point they replaced their two with a five and landed a shot on Mouse's engine.

Jonah was bored. Crow looked bored, too. Or, at least, lost.

216

Faye spent both her repair cards to upgrade her cannons, which she then used to gun down Crow's bow and engine. Faye and Mouse remained to battle it out.

Jonah slammed the rest of his drink, stood, and extended a hand to Crow. They took it without hesitation. Jonah helped them to their feet. "Let's go dance," he whispered.

The alcohol must have loosened him up—but it hadn't been long since he'd bought the drink. Regardless of what he blamed the fluttering of his heart on, he led Crow toward the crowd gathered in the street.

Jonah was no dancer, but by virtue of being mortal, he had leagues more experience than Crow. The responsibility fell on Jonah to take the lead. He stood in front of Crow and, with great hesitation, placed his hands on their waist. He stood stiff for far too long, eyeing the others who danced in the streets. Nobody stuck to any one style of dance. People swayed, hopped, and waltzed. Children chased each other around, weaving between the adults' bodies. Some danced alone, some in pairs.

Crow rooted their hands on Jonah's shoulders and pushed him to take a step backwards. They whirled him around in a circle with a laugh. "You're thinking too much. Quit thinking."

He stumbled along with Crow as they twisted and turned. The clumsy dance was humiliating. It had no rhythm or form. But the more he danced, the less he overthought and overcalculated. He kept his gaze locked on Crow's pale face. Their cheeks were flushed, a gentle yellowish dusting over their soft skin. On any other, the color would look sickly. On Crow, it looked natural.

Jonah stepped on Crow's toe and tripped. Crow caught him before he could faceplant on the stone paving. Jonah couldn't help but laugh as he righted himself. When was the last time he was this carefree? This happy? Not since he lost Sophie. Not even since his adoptive father died of cancer, two years prior to Sophie's death. Crow lifted all the tension from his shoulders and set it aside.

The warmth scared him. Attachment did not come easily, but Crow was something special.

Their divinity was more than the blood running through their veins—it was the gentle puffs of breath against Jonah's neck. It was the way their thumb brushed over his shoulder, their touch feather-light. It was their soft hum, trying and failing to follow along with the music. Sophie sat waiting for him in Paradise, but the notion of eternal bliss paled in comparison to Crow.

Crow stared with such wonder in those blue eyes. They blinked once, twice, then leaned their head against Jonah's collarbone.

"You done?" Jonah whispered.

"Feelin' kinda dizzy." Crow hadn't had much to drink, but their tolerance was low, and the effects had caught up.

"Alcohol will do that to you."

"Alcohol," Crow repeated.

"An alcoholic drink can make you feel warm and fuzzy, in moderation. But if you drink too much, your body doesn't know how to handle it."

"Oh."

"Let's sit."

Jonah guided Crow away from the music and the crowd. As he sat beside Karina, he tried his best to ignore the gentle smile gracing his first mate's round face. He scoffed at her as he sat beside Crow.

Everyone was a different kind of drunk. Faye got a little too reckless, Karina was excitable and friendly, and Willow always got lovey. Crow, though, seemed tired. Jonah wondered how much stemmed from sheer inexperience. He dug through Willow's satchel until he found her water flask. He held it up, then gestured to Crow. Willow nodded. He passed the flask to Crow, and they took a sip.

"Do you think the flowers are okay?" Crow asked. Their voice was soft, wistful.

"What?" Jonah asked.

"The flowers," Crow repeated, as if it were obvious as to what they meant. "I don't know if Elaine's been watering them since I've been gone."

"I'm sure your flowers are fine," Willow said. She offered Crow a gentle smile, which seemed to reassure them well enough. They leaned against Jonah.

Faye gathered up her cards and stood. "I'm heading off to bed. You coming, Wils?"

"Sure." Willow nodded and stood. Faye extended her hand, and Willow took it.

"Put a sock on the doorknob," Karina said. "Don't forget I'm sharing a room with you. Or should I plan to sleep on the *Vengeance?*"

"Don't worry," Faye laughed. "We'll behave."

They walked off. Mouse called it a night not long after, leaving him, Crow, and Karina at the table. Crow slumped against Jonah's shoulder, their eyes shut, and Jonah couldn't tell if they were asleep or not.

"You're out late," Karina said, breaking the silence between them. "I'm surprised. Thought you'd be the first one in for the night."

"The festival's not so bad," Jonah grumbled. Feathery black hair tickled his cheek.

"You had a nice time tonight."

"I suppose I did." He turned his gaze up at the stars. The world around him had grown dark. The tiniest sliver of moon lingered in the night sky.

"Hang onto this, okay? You deserve it."

Jonah nodded. He looked back down at Crow. They looked peaceful. "You awake?"

Crow offered no response.

Jonah scooped Crow up into his arms and stood. "I'd best get them to bed," he muttered, offering Karina a parting glance before he carried the sleeping god to the inn.

Jonah awoke long before the sun rose. He opted to sit sideways on the stiff padded bench shoved in the dormer, feet up and back braced against the wall as he gazed out the scratched window. The window faced south—not a great view of the sunrise, but Jonah watched the sky anyways as it grew lighter and bluer.

A soft groan tore his attention from the window. Crow sat up and combed their fingers through their hair. "My head hurts."

"Not surprised."

"I'm going to get some fresh air."

"Sure."

Crow stepped out of the room, leaving Jonah alone in the room aside from Mouse, who was still fast asleep, face-down on the couch. He did not move from his spot at the window until Karina knocked on the door. She dragged him to the farmer's market.

The market was pitiful. Emelle's farmers suffered from a shortage of crops thanks to the fire. The meager quantity—and quality—meant Jonah would have to cough up more money per purchase. After all the spending from the prior night, between the whole crew's food, drinks, and the lodging from the past few days, they were running short on cash.

"Have you seen Crow?" Karina asked as she picked up an apple and examined it. The apple was black with bruises and mud. She set it down with a grimace.

"Not since they stepped out this morning."

"Should we go find them?"

"Let them do what they want. We don't need to keep tabs on them."

"I'm worried," Karina admitted as she inspected a small straw box of charred, dingy-looking strawberries. "They said something kind of weird last night."

"Weird?"

"The thing about the flowers." Karina set the strawberries in her burlap bag, deciding they were decent enough to purchase. Maybe they'd be fine after a rinse. "I think they may have remembered something. Something they're not telling us."

Jonah sighed.

"Do they not trust us? Did we do something wrong?"

"They'll tell us when they're ready," he said. "It's their memory, not ours. They have no obligation to tell us anything."

By noon, Crow returned, lugging the dinghy along with them. Mouse helped them hitch it to the hull, then the *Vengeance* left port. A small group of villagers gathered on the docks to see them off. They had big smiles on their faces, though they were not cordial. These folks were happy to see the crew gone. So devoted to Einari, they would never dare consider Aeris.

A shame, Jonah thought as he stood at the bow beside Crow. His knuckles brushed against their hand. He intertwined his fingers with theirs.

If he was Aeris's only worshipper, so be it.

30

"A deceased soul must first go through Judgment. There, last words are collected, and the soul is sent to one of three circles: Paradise, Purgatory, or Punishment."
—The Book of Death

60th Storm, Great Flood 1058

The circle of Punishment was dreary, gray, and dank. Here, Elaine was neither human nor goddess, but rather a soul laid bare.

Death was cunning—Elaine would give him credit where credit was due. Once the goddess of fire was at his mercy, he caged her in a tiny room full of frigid water. With no connection to her Domain, she grew weak. A god's divinity—their life force—was inextricably tied to one's Domain. Without divinity, what was a god but a powerless sack of flesh?

The fetus squirmed, unhappy. *Leave me alone,* she thought. *Wretched creature.*

The Underworld had a knack for magnifying sensation. In the cold and the silence, Elaine was far too aware of her body. In the fetus's every movement, memories of her betrothed's corpse accosted her. Twisted, mangled, burnt. The fetus was her grief, coiled up in the pit of her stomach, an amalgamation of everything she hated about herself.

"It is the magma within me," she muttered. Ever since Ashe Calloway gave her the term, it had become something of a mantra. *"I am a volcano. I am with Mt. Azhir."*

Elaine wasn't sure how long she knelt in the frigid water, hands shackled, a chain keeping her tethered to the floor. Ice crawled up the shackles and bit her wrists. Her hands, chained below the water, could not produce any flame.

Closing her eyes, she willed her hands to produce heat. Flame was futile, but she could warm the water, as she had done while fighting the sea monster with Phoenyx and Ashe. Freezing water turned tepid.

Tepid water turned to something comfortable.

Such a simple task ate away at her weakened divinity and left her woozy, but now she could think things through with a clearer head. She siphoned some divinity from the fetus. It squirmed, displeased.

Elaine knew of only one means of escape. She had walked the Underworld's caverns before, back when she was mortal. The path to Midir involved a winding labyrinth full of monsters. She wasn't so sure she had the luck to make it through again.

Elaine channeled heat into the shackles. They turned red-hot and singed her wrists. The water around her boiled. With a quick jerk, the shackles broke. She snapped to her feet and rushed to the door. Elaine wasn't sure how to pick the lock, but she hunched over and fiddled with it until the knob clicked.

Beginner's luck, she supposed.

She straightened and made to turn the knob. Before she could, the door swung open. Water spilled out of the room. She stiffened.

Not beginner's luck. Her luck couldn't have been any worse. In front of Elaine loomed Death, who leered at her with a stiff, displeased snarl.

"Uh—" Elaine winced. What would Aeris do? They had always been proficient in talking themself out of trouble. "Nice weather today, yes?"

She offered Death a strained smile. Her feigned innocence did not get her far.

"I hoped we could be civil," Death's eerie, hollow voice floated into the chamber. "I thought disconnecting you from your Domain would be punishment enough. My benevolence aside, you see fit to attempt escape."

"I will not roll over."

"I respect your Domain. We're not too different, you know. You bring many deceased souls to me. I'd like to come to an agreement, of sorts," Death said. "You do as I tell you, and I'll let you stay here without pain. Einari wished for me to punish you, but I'm willing to put aside our differences. If you don't oblige, however, there shall be consequences."

Familiar nausea resurfaced. *Please, not now.* "What kind of agreement is that?"

He grabbed her by the shoulders and shoved her to the floor. With a snap of his long, gnarled fingers, the broken shackles reformed and mended around Elaine's wrists. The violent movement left Elaine gagging at Death's feet. Vomit slipped past her lips before she could stop it. The taste of bile lingered on her tongue.

Death laughed, the sound hollow and scathing. Of *course* he would take joy in her illness. He regarded her as she convulsed, fighting back nausea. He may have stared deeper, too, past her flesh and at the little soul beneath, the godling with no Domain.

"I've always been fascinated by you," Death said, though it was no compliment. "A scrappy girl who couldn't fit in her armor because she couldn't wait until marriage, hm? What did your village think of it? They viewed such behavior as sinful. We gods don't care, but mortals have always obsessed over the concept of *sinful relations.*"

Elaine bit her tongue and said nothing.

"Their deaths were slow and miserable. Blight made sure of it."

The ancient god of fire, the god she had slain, had been ruthless. "Stop."

"Isaac, hm? Wasn't he the father of your child? His soul is in Paradise, I'll have you know."

"Stop," Elaine begged, a little more forceful.

"Let's get started, then." He snapped his fingers, and the pool of vomit vanished. He produced a small mirror from somewhere underneath his thick, draping black robes and placed it on the floor in front of Elaine. He forced her head down, and she peered into it. Her own reflection shifted into a reflection of the mortal realm. "See this pathetic island here?" he continued, pointing a clawed finger at the single major island in the *Erith* region. "I want you to burn it to the ground."

"No!" Elaine gasped. "Flame may kill when misused, but I will never do something with such cruel intention—"

"I was hoping you would deny me." Death's cold tone sent a shiver down Elaine's spine. "Let's have some fun instead, then, shall we?"

Death circled around her. With the shackles and chains as tight as they were, she couldn't turn to watch him. His shadow loomed upon her from behind.

A stiff *crack* snapped through the air. White-hot pain flared across her back. She howled.

"This whip," Death purred, "is laced with Monster Blood. Makes it so much more painful, don't you think?"

Crack!

Elaine bit back a scream. The whip's barbed end dug through the fabric of her gown and into her back, and the Monster Blood burned her skin like the aftertaste of bile burnt her throat. A third lash struck her spine. Her body trembled. Shackled as tight as she was, there was no hope of getting away.

Three more. She'd endure endless torture if it meant keeping agency over her decisions.

Death paused, offering her some reprieve. Elaine took the blessed silence to regain her bearings.

The next lash burned far more than before. Black spots danced in her vision. She squeezed her hands into fists, digging her nails against her palms in a fruitless attempt to mitigate the agony.

Death had not paused to show her mercy. He had paused to coat the whip with more Monster Blood.

"Stop!" Elaine screamed, her voice hoarse and desperate. "Stop, please!"

Death listened. He strutted around to her front, taking a knee before her. He took her chin between his thumb and forefinger and tilted her gaze up to meet him.

"You want me to stop? All this could have been avoided, you know. Burn the island."

"Why?" Her voice was weak.

"It would be enjoyable to have a few more deceased souls to torment."

"You are nothing but cruel."

"Do you want me to whip you again?"

"No! Don't!"

"Then burn the island."

She didn't want to hurt innocent people, but her whole body ached. She could keep enduring the agony until it destroyed her, or...

In the mirror, she spotted a familiar ship. The *Vengeance*. Aeris was near. They could save these people. The plan seemed logical enough, one to spare her from torture while sparing innocent lives. So, defeated, she focused on the island, and she let it burn.

Death, pleased, stalked out of the room without another word. Elaine stared at the mirror.

Please notice the island. Please save these people.

Aeris answered her plea. Death would come back to beat her when he learned the fire did not bring many souls to the afterlife, but for now, she relaxed as best she could.

31

"Einari's blood touched the girl's skin, and her wound disappeared. The only evidence was the stain of crimson on her clothes."
—The Book of the Tide

63rd Storm, Great Flood 1058

If Crow were to make a list of their most frequent hangout spots aboard the *Vengeance,* the top three would be the crow's nest, the fire pit, and Jonah's cabin.

They perched atop the stool at Jonah's desk, heels on the seat, knees tucked close to their chest. In front of them sat Argonaut's notebook, which Jonah had been studying with some intensity as of late.

"Not sure I can help much," Crow said. The notes were written in Midiri. This, however, didn't seem to concern Jonah.

"At the bottom of each page," Jonah said, "there's a number."

Crow flipped through a few pages. Some of the markings seemed familiar—they'd seen a few of these numbers on Faye's playing cards, though they weren't sure which marking was which number.

"I'm damn sure it's a code, because they're not page numbers. But I've combined them with corresponding letters from every major language on Midir, and all I've come up with is gibberish."

"Is it scrambled? Or are the numbers backwards? Last letter is one, and so on?"

"You think I haven't already tried? There's one language I haven't yet tried, and it has no translation resources. *Your* language, Crow. Køveni. So, I'll tell you each number, you align it with the letters of your alphabet, and we'll see if it forms anything."

"Argonaut wouldn't know Køveni."

"If he's planning a divine ritual, he may be in contact with someone who does."

Crow nodded. They passed Argonaut's notebook to Jonah. Dipping one of Jonah's pens into the ink pot, Crow poised to write on a spare sheet of parchment. "Give me the numbers."

Jonah read them off. One by one, Crow counted through the Køveni alphabet and wrote the corresponding letter. At the end, they were left with one word.

"Morgan."

"My last name," Jonah mumbled. Crow eyed the crease between his brows, the heaviness in his shoulders.

"Jonah—"

"I need space to think this through. You're dismissed."

Crow hopped off the stool and left him alone.

The air outside was far too humid and stagnant to bear, so Crow retreated to their cabin. The space was more lived-in now. Their desk, otherwise unused, was piled with pastries and sweets from the festival. The parrot plush sat on the shelf, which had accumulated a couple more books, all stolen from Jonah. Crow kept forgetting to return them.

Unlike Jonah's shelves, Crow's books lay wherever there was space. No matter how often Jonah came in and organized—and he did so rather often—things did not stay orderly for long. Crow's belongings always ended up strewn about the shelf, wherever there was space around the vase in the middle...

Wait, what?

Slow, almost cautious, Crow approached the shelf. The vase was tall and sunshine-yellow, handmade out of gentle and delicate porcelain. Sitting against the shelf's back wall and sandwiched between a few books, the vase was somewhat secure—but if the *Vengeance* swayed the wrong way, it could topple off the shelf and shatter. They brushed their fingers against the flowers' velvety yellow petals.

Where had they come from?

Beside the vase was a note. Crow picked it up. Without missing a beat, they walked out of their cabin and a few doors down, then knocked.

"Crow!" Karina exclaimed when she opened the door. She looked surprised to see them.

"Uh, hi." They fidgeted with the paper in their hands.

"You got my note."

"Oh. You wrote this?"

"Here, come in." Karina ushered Crow inside. They kicked their boots off before stepping onto her pink plush rug.

"Y'know," Crow rambled, "Einari, Novika, Blight, and I created the modern *spoken* language, but mortalkind developed a writing system on their own. Pictures turned into symbols, and symbols turned into letters. There was...a point, I suppose, when it no longer was legible to me."

"Blight," Karina mused. "The god of fire before Elaine. What was he like?"

"I can't remember," Crow said.

"Here—I'll read my note to you." Karina took the parchment. *"You said you were worried about your flowers, so I thought I'd get you some as a reminder of your home. Take good care of them. From, Karina."*

Crow frowned. Had they spoken of their memory? Their recollection of the festival's later hours was hazy.

"Thanks," Crow whispered, taking the note back. They shoved it in their sweat-sticky shirt pocket.

"Are you okay?" she asked. "I hope they didn't upset you."

"No, no, I just... Why?"

"I thought it would be a nice gesture. I found some at the market before we left Emelle's shores. I can take them off your hands if you don't want them."

"No, I—I want them. They're nice. I feel... I..."

"You don't know how you feel," Karina inferred.

"No."

"Do you want to talk about it?"

"I'm frustrated. It's the only memory I have. I made a bet over something trivial, and Elaine lost, so I made her steal flowers from Novika's chamber for me. I don't—I don't know why it had to be this memory, why I can't recall any others. It's almost worse than having none at all."

Karina pulled them into a hug. Crow sat and let her. "I know there's nothing I can do to get your memories back, but I'm always here for you, okay?"

"Thank you, Karina." Crow peeled away from her. They lay back on the rug, letting its pink fluff swallow them whole. Karina eyed them with amusement. She had plenty of furniture—the orange beanbag chair, a table with seats, her cot—but whenever Crow visited, they preferred the rug. It was cozy.

"Hey," Crow said after a stretch of silence. "Where'd your sword come from, anyway? The one above the door." They fixed their gaze on it. It hung with its sheath in the shape of an X. The mount was made of bamboo and lined with rich black velvet. An expensive setup.

"I stole it from my mother," Karina replied. "She was worse than my father. After I turned six, she never looked at me again. She was going to sell this for a fortune—wouldn't stop talking about how much money she'd earn. 'We'll be set for life,' she'd say. So, I stole it right out from under her when I ran away. One last act of defiance."

"I..." Crow hesitated. "I'm sorry. For using it."

"It's okay. You didn't have a weapon."

"I still don't have one."

"You don't?" Karina frowned, incredulous. "Jonah never gave you one?"

"No. I'm sure he considers it an incentive to keep me out of trouble."

"Okay, that won't do." Karina stood, and Crow propped themself up with their elbows to watch. She pulled a stool over and stood atop it, retrieving the sword and its sheath from its mount. "Your safety is our utmost priority, but fights are inevitable."

"I can't take this," Crow argued as Karina pressed the blade into their hands. "This is—this is important to you. It's wrong."

"Take it."

"You're not doing this because I'm a god, are you? I won't accept it. I'm not the type."

"I'm not. I'm giving it to you because you're family."

They eyed the sword. It brought back memories of a sea monster, back when everything was hazy and foreign. The blade was sharp and spotless, and the sheath was beautiful, decorated with vibrant red hand-painted roses.

"It's yours," she urged.

"I'll take good care of it."

Karina smiled. Crow carried the blade back to their cabin, hugging it, sheathed, tight to their chest.

Crow stood at the bow as the *Vengeance* crossed into Anui waters. The blade Karina gave them sat holstered to their hip. In the distance stood the silhouette of the Midnorthern hub, which, Jonah had told them, served as one of the two strongest markers of the Anui boundary. Not too far from the Midnorthern hub was Farmstead Isle. The other marker.

Pirate territory didn't look any different. It wasn't foggy or ominous or dark. Sure, the air was chillier to the north, but it was nowhere near the biting cold of the glacier patch where Crow had first fallen. The water was calm, the skies were blue, and nothing seemed out of place.

They unsheathed the blade a fraction and sliced their thumb upon its blade. With their blood drawn, they willed a breeze to urge the *Vengeance* forward. It didn't seem to work. Had they not drawn enough blood? Had they not put enough intention into it?

Dark, slow footsteps approached from behind, and Crow didn't need to turn to know who had approached. They pressed their thumb firmly against their forefinger to stem the bleeding. They'd try again later, when Jonah wasn't around to chew them out for drawing blood again. He fell in place beside them. Crow couldn't help but eye the constellations in the freckles upon his cheeks, his nose, his neck. Strands of ginger hair kissed his cheekbones, framing his angular face. It was getting a tad long—the top's length didn't matter as much, but the tight shave around the back and sides of his skull was starting to grow in.

"Did you know Farmstead was so close to pirate territory?" Crow asked, tearing their gaze from Jonah. Ships sailed in the far distance. Were they pirates on the prowl? Or merchants?

"I did," Jonah admitted.

"You wanted to leave me there anyways."

"I'm... a selfish creature. I had no idea how important you were. None of us did."

"If I'd known back then, I don't think you would have been too inclined to believe me."

Jonah let out an amused huff. "I suppose I wouldn't have."

Crow held no grudge. They dared to lean against Jonah, their shoulder pressing against his. Something about this man made them feel warm. Cozy. They smiled.

The crew sat around the fire pit, which sat unlit, the iron fixtures cold.

"Should we disguise ourselves?" Mouse asked. "Pretend we're pirates, then ambush him?"

"Argonaut knows my ship too well," Jonah replied, both signed and aloud, his voice low. "It's not like we can transmute the *Vengeance* into steel."

"Why do you have a wooden ship, anyways?" Crow blurted. This wasn't the time or place to ask, but they'd been curious. "Seems like most other ships out here are metal."

"It belonged to my adoptive father. Whoever his great-great-grandparents were, they were rich enough to afford it. Steel is more accessible."

"I haven't seen many steel refineries around."

"There's a few in Blythe. Mining island." Jonah sat straighter and rolled his shoulders. "Crow, focus. We're getting off topic."

"Sorry."

"I think we *should* be recognizable," Karina offered. "Let's lean into it. If a pirate sees us, they'll know we've got Crow, and they'll take us straight to Argo."

Faye grimaced. "Or they'll kill us and harvest Crow of all their blood."

Crow shivered. They thought back to those fuzzy early memories, locked up in a steel cell, dosed with enough Monster Blood to keep them disoriented and weak, but not so much as to taint Crow's blood.

"Crow, are you sure you want to follow through with this?" Willow asked, sensing Crow's apprehension. "There's always the chance we could find some other way to get you home. Elaine could come back."

"I can't sit around and wait for someone to come get me. The likelihood is slim." Crow stood. "So, we push on."

Crow sat at Jonah's desk at sunset, feet propped up on its sleek hardwood surface. After the meeting, Jonah had taken to working with Mouse on routine maintenance. Crow wondered what that entailed. Was it difficult, maintaining a ship? Crow performed their fair share of tasks, but their work was a small chunk of it. They cleaned, they learned to cook—they rather enjoyed cooking, though they weren't great at it—but they took lookout more often than anything else. Most other responsibilities were a mystery.

Jonah made his presence known half an hour later. He nudged his way into the cabin and fixed Crow with a flat stare. He did not appear surprised, nor put off, by Crow's presence.

"Feet off my desk," Jonah grumbled.

Crow shot him a toothy grin. They did not move. Jonah shed his coat and tossed it into his hamper. Crow couldn't help but eye the muscles in his biceps, his shoulders, evident even through the thin fabric of his dark gray tee.

"The quiet before a hurricane," Crow mumbled, "It's always the worst part, don't you think? You know it's coming, but all you can do is brace."

Jonah said nothing. He wasn't ignoring Crow—he just didn't have anything to say. Crow had Jonah's idiosyncrasies memorized. He didn't speak unless there was something worth saying.

"Do you think," they continued, "there's any way we can convince Argonaut to change his mind?"

Jonah shot Crow an odd look. "You're too naïve, Crow," he said. "He's not the type to be swayed by a compelling conversation. He'll get what he wants, or he'll die trying."

Worth a shot, I suppose, Crow thought.

"The way you feel about Einari," Jonah said as he leaned his hip against the desk's lip. With one hand, he pushed their feet off the desk. Crow settled their feet firmly upon the floor. "It's the same way I feel about Argonaut. He's unshakable. I know you don't want to believe it, but some mortals *are* evil."

"You're not evil," Crow said. "Despite everything Karina said you've lived through."

"I'm also not Argonaut."

Crow had no counterpoint.

The following day, Crow took up residence at the bow instead of the crow's nest. They climbed as far down the length of the bowsprit as they dared. This perch was precarious, for if they fell, they would plummet into the unforgiving ocean. They could feel the wind here, though, nice and strong. And, as a bonus, the frustration with which Jonah looked at them an hour later was amusing. Jonah would no doubt pull them aside later and chew them out for taking unnecessary risks.

"Pirate ship," Willow called out at some point along the way. "Southeast. Heading our way!"

"Is it the *Godkiller?*" Jonah asked. He hurried to the gunwale where Willow stood.

"Doesn't look like it." Willow paused. "Name at the bow says *Duplicity.*"

"Can we outrun it?"

"Doubtful. Look at how fast it's moving. It's got a powerful engine."

"Crow can give us wind," Jonah mused. He turned and met Crow's gaze. "Crow!"

"I'll try!" Crow called. They sliced their finger on their sword and waved their hand through the air. The result was a gentle, refreshing breeze which did nothing to move the ship. They deepened their cut and tried again—they didn't have a perfect grasp on how much blood to draw. This seemed to help. A stiff wind pushed the *Vengeance* faster. It would, at least, buy the crew time to prepare.

Faye primed and loaded every cannon. Willow and Mouse battened down the hatches and secured anything loose or hazardous. Barrels, tools, errant ropes. When the pirates neared the *Vengeance* in ten minutes' time, they made their presence known in the form of a cannonball, which slammed into the hull. The impact rattled the ship. Crow gripped the bowsprit for dear life—they managed to catch themself, arms and legs wrapped around the bowsprit, limbs tangled in the rope securing the triangular forward sails. Their heart lurched as they eyed the churning, uninviting water.

Crow clambered off the bowsprit and sprinted to the impact site. These pirates hadn't graced the *Vengeance* with a warning shot.

A member of *Duplicity's* crew dropped a gangplank so heavy it crushed the *Vengeance's* deck. Two pirates, one female and one male, stood at the top of the gangplank, dressed in matching green waistcoats. Which one was captain? Was it possible *both* were captains?

Behind the captains, the crew gathered. Crow didn't need to count bodies to know the crew of the *Vengeance* was outnumbered.

Jonah stood at the base of the gangplank, arms folded across his chest.

"The *Vengeance!* What a delight!" the green-clad woman exclaimed. Her eyes darted off to the side, to where the *Vengeance's* name was written upon the hull in deep black paint. With a wave of her black-gloved hand, she offered a single order, "Subdue, don't kill."

The pirates rushed across the gangplank. Crow drew their sword and stood with bent knees, ready. They'd subdued a sea monster fifty times their size, but that was one single opponent. A full crew of big, burly pirates was far different, and Crow struggled against the waves of bodies. They ducked and weaved between fists and swords.

If these pirates managed to draw Crow's blood, they'd be a target. No doubt these pirates knew there was a god aboard, but did they know *who?* Crow's anonymity would be their key to victory. They focused on self-preservation.

Crow did, however, cast frequent glances around, keeping tabs on their crewmates. Karina, Jonah, and Faye were seasoned fighters. Jonah took on three pirates at once, his form flawless, though how long would it be before he grew tired? Even a man with inhuman stamina had his limits. Karina and Faye handled a more modest single opponent each.

With the deck swamped with pirates, there wasn't any distance Willow could find, no perch to settle in and snipe from. The pirates overwhelmed her. Mouse was scrawny and small, better suited for engineering than combat. All he had was a thick steel one-and-a-half-inch spanner he'd pulled from his tool belt, not much longer than Karina's knife but far heavier. It would deal some good damage, but Mouse's small stature made him a target. They weaved their way toward him.

A tall, muscular woman intercepted Crow, and they realized their smallness made them a target, too. Crow met her blade and strained against every strike. Their muscles burned. Their shoulder, still sharp and achy from rowing to Emelle, made its displeasure known.

The pirate kicked Crow in the chest, and the next thing they knew, their back slammed against the deck. They wheezed, all the air escaping their lungs. Crow scrambled to their feet, but before they could reorient themself, a fist slammed into their cheek. They stumbled, clutching their face as pain rattled their skull. The woman gave Crow no time to recover from the blow. She punched Crow in the ribs, and something in their body snapped.

Crow doubled over, and their vision blurred. When they looked up, they caught a metallic glint under the sunlight. She wore brass rings around each finger. No wonder it hurt so much.

They were too slow to dodge the next punch. The pirate wailed on them. This was nothing like a spar, no natural give-and-take. *Jonah was right.* Another fist slammed into their face. *Pirates are ruthless.*

Brass-reinforced fingers tore into their cheekbone, leaving sharp, digging agony and wetness in their wake. Proof of their divinity gushed down their face and pooled at their jaw.

"This one!" the woman yelled. "This one's the god!"

Crow gripped their sword's hilt with both hands, hoping to use the pirate's distraction to their advantage. They swung, pained and clumsy, and their opponent stepped aside with idle disinterest. She slammed her fist into Crow's temple. Their vision swam. They stumbled, and before they could regain their wits, she grabbed them by the throat. They gagged. Their head throbbed. Squeezing their eyes shut helped mitigate the dizziness.

Karina or Faye, they weren't sure who, shrieked *"CROW!"* as the pirate shoved them to the floor. Their face smushed against the deck, smearing golden blood into the wood grain. The pirate released their neck in favor of pinning them by the shoulders. They gasped for air.

"Should we kill the god?" someone asked. Oh, Heavens, they hated this part. *A bullet in their stomach. Pain. The rot of Monster Blood tearing them apart from the inside out.*

"No," a male voice ordered. If they opened their eyes, they would have seen the male captain somewhere nearby, but the prospect of doing so seemed horrible right now. "Keep it alive."

It.

Crow was happy to adapt to however people referred to them. Crow was *he, she, they,* and sometimes none of those, too. But *it* felt a bit demeaning.

Karina grunted, and a soft thunk followed. Had the pirates subdued her, too? What about the rest of the crew? Crow dared to peek, and sunlight assaulted their vision. Too bright. Their headache spiked, sharp like a knife to their skull. They tapped into the blood dripping down their cheek and urged a big, puffy cloud to float in front of the sun. Once it did, they blinked once, twice, three times. Their vision was blurry, and the world around them tilted on its axis. Every member of the *Vengeance's* crew knelt with their backs to the mast.

"A nice catch, dont'cha think, Thaddeus?" the female captain asked. "The more pathetic the crew, the easier to force 'em into submission."

Pathetic, something in the back of their achy mind repeated. The voice didn't sound like their own. This voice was deeper, richer, full of malice. *Worthless, good-for-nothing Fool.*

The male captain—Thaddeus—laughed. "Would you like to do the honors, Ramona?" Thaddeus asked. He handed her a violet-tipped knife. *No, no, no!*

Ramona took the knife and strode over to Crow. "Don't worry," she cooed. "This won't end ya. This is insurance. Don't want a god actin' up, after all." She pressed the knife to their wrist and sliced it open, parallel to the other scars lining their skin. The Monster Blood on the blade mixed into their bloodstream. The acidic tang bit their flesh.

"We seek Argonaut the Lawless," Jonah said with a tone as smooth and level as he could manage. "Take us to him, and we'll make it worth your while."

"Lucky for you lot," Thaddeus replied, "Argonaut is looking for you, too."

The pirate who had pinned Crow down released them. They considered trying to get up. But even if they wanted to, they were in too much agony to move.

32

64th Storm, Great Flood 1058

Jonah picked at the cable binding his wrists as a pirate sailed his ship northwest alongside *Duplicity*. He glared, teeth bared in a rather animalistic manner, at the pirate whose greasy hands marred his helm. *Get your hands off my ship.* The cable's fraying steel sliced into his hands, and blood oozed down his fingers. If he broke free, the pirates would subdue him before he could get the upper hand. That wasn't going to stop him from trying.

Drip. Drip. Drip. The blood on his hands rendered the cable slippery. Jonah could feel Karina's gaze on him, and when he ignored her, she nudged him with her shoulder.

Annoyed, Jonah looked to his first mate. She stared him down in silence, her expression steady. She held his attention with a calm firmness, which did nothing to ease his nerves. How could she be calm? There was *no goddamn reason* to be calm. He wrenched his hands. He needed to break free.

Settle down, Karina's steady gaze told him. He would never know if that was the message she wanted to convey, but it's what he read in her expression. *You won't do us any good if you panic.*

Jonah was somewhat sure the knot had loosened, but it could have been his imagination. The cable still chafed his wrists. He worked at the knot no matter how much it dug into his raw, bloodied palms, no matter how many fingernails he destroyed in the process.

A pirate kneed him in the jaw. He spat blood onto the floor in front of him. The inside of his cheek stung, and the bright, metallic taste of iron flooded his mouth.

"Sit still," his assailant snapped. When Jonah jerked against his bonds once more, she kicked him in the stomach.

Karina never broke her steady stare, even as one pirate stalked behind Jonah and tightened his bonds. His fingers tingled. Soon, they'd be numb.

He could almost hear Karina say something like, *Do you want to get yourself killed?*

I'd rather die than sit idle, he would say, in return.

The crew is fine. Sit still, let these pirates take us to Argonaut, and we'll figure something out then.

My crew is NOT fine! He imagined himself snapping. He bared his teeth, and still her firm demeanor did not waver. *Crow's not moving. What if—*

This isn't about Crow, is it? This is about Sophie. She died right in front of you. Pirates plunged a knife into her heart.

Don't you dare.

You did nothing to save her. All you did was watch her die.

Stop.

You need to put aside your terror in the face of loss. Sophie died ages ago. Crow is a different person.

Jonah was fully aware this conversation was one he made up in his head. They were words Karina had not spoken and would never speak. He tore his attention away from Karina, training his gaze instead on the deck's wood grain beneath his knees.

At sundown, Jonah caught sight of the *Godkiller.* The massive steel dreadnought sent a chill down his spine. He cast a sideways glance at Crow. The trace amounts of Monster Blood in their veins, mixed with a deep, gross yellow bruise on their temple, kept them pliant. What would come of them when Thaddeus and Ramona hauled them to Argonaut's mercy?

The pirate at the helm steered the *Vengeance* parallel to the *Godkiller,* and Thaddeus hauled Crow to their unsteady feet. He shoved them across the gangplank. When Crow reached the *Godkiller,* Ramona forced Jonah and his crew to their feet. She nudged them across the gangplank, a gun pressed to Mouse's spine.

Jonah would be happy to never see this damned ship again. *Godkiller.* The name had never struck fear into Jonah's heart until now. There had been no reason to fear such a name. He had never believed the gods to be real.

Ramona forced Jonah and his crew to their knees once more, then joined Thaddeus, Argonaut, and Crow.

"My deepest gratitude," Argonaut said, thick with feigned cordiality. "You've done well to return the god to me."

"As for our payment?" Ramona replied, her hands on her hips.

"Ah, of course." Argonaut reached into the inner pocket of his long black coat. He fished for coins from a concealed satchel.

Pirates were annoying. So much bureaucracy for a group of cruel, intractable folk.

Argonaut, it seemed, had the same mindset, because instead of a sack of coin, he whipped out a pistol. With two sharp pops, he shot Thaddeus and Ramona in the head, and their bodies slumped to the deck before Jonah could blink.

"You," Argonaut barked at the remaining pirates, whose hands hovered over their weapons, more than eager to jump into a fight. "Lest you want to meet their fate, I suggest you leave the *Vengeance* here and get gone. The ship's a beaut—it'll sell well."

A pirate on Thaddeus and Ramona's crew drew his gun. Argonaut shot him down without hesitation. As the pirate's body toppled overboard, the rest of the crew ran for the *Duplicity.* Jonah scoffed. Argonaut had always taught him running equated to cowardice. He knew better, now, but something in the back of his mind still nudged him. *Cowards.*

One of Argonaut's newly hired crewmates hauled Thaddeus and Ramona's corpses overboard. They hit the water with an insignificant splash. Jonah was glad to see them gone. The matching green getup annoyed him.

"I'd like to thank you for saving me the hassle of sailing south," Argonaut said, turning his gaze to Jonah and his crew. He eyed Crow for quite some time, and the Monster Blood-dazed god tried their best to glare. Jonah respected the effort, though it made them look trapped and cornered rather than threatening. Crow's balance wavered, and with one swift nudge, Argonaut pushed them to their knees. "I was going to come find you lot, but now I don't need to worry 'bout expending the energy. It costs thousands of glass, you know, to take this ship from Anui to the Suhin-Erith."

"Cut the chatter," Jonah snapped. His bruised jaw throbbed as he spoke. "What do you want us for? What do you want *me* for?"

"You? Ha! So self-centered."

"You wrote about a servant," Crow cut in.

"I was wondering where my logbook went," Argonaut mused. "You have a million other things to worry about, and a mere servant has garnered your attention? Einari wants you dead."

"Dead?" Crow repeated. "He wanted me punished."

"He wants you *dead,* boy. And I must say, I agree—you're a nuisance."

"What does he have to gain?"

"I'm happy to tell you, given you're not long for this world. You die, someone else takes your place. The new god of the sky steps aside, becomes a lesser Domain, and Death takes his place on the council. It *happens* that Death has already chosen his champion."

Jonah couldn't wrap his brain around what he meant. The politics of gods were far beyond his comprehension—what did it matter, who was on this so-called council?

"Now," Argonaut drawled, "I can get on with this damned thing. You—" he pointed to the closest of his crew. "Fetch the knife, a brush, and the blood."

"Blood," Jonah repeated. "I destroyed your supply!"

He slipped free of the cable binding. He shook his hands off, urging feeling to return to his fingertips.

Argonaut seemed unbothered by Jonah's freedom. He laughed, jovial, borderline maniacal. "Oh, quite the contrary! Did you think I didn't have a failsafe? Did you think those drains led to the ocean? No, they drained straight to my backup reserves. I didn't lose a damn drop. You've always been a foolish man, Jonah, and never a smart one."

Shit. He reached to untie Karina. He wasn't discreet enough. One of Argonaut's crew grabbed him before his fingers could brush the cable around Karina's wrists, forcing him away. The pirate shoved Jonah facedown against the deck and pinned him there. His cheek squished against frigid steel.

The other pirate returned. In one hand, the man held a knife and a brush. In the other, he lugged a dolly loaded with a large vat, full to the brim with Crow's blood. Argonaut opened the vat and dipped the brush inside.

Jonah couldn't see his crew—in his current position, pinned by the pirate whose fingernails dug into his bloodied wrists, he could only see Crow and Argonaut. He knew, though, his crew was in no better shape than he was. Mouse was unconscious. Faye had a nasty gash in her thigh and was no doubt woozy from blood loss, and Willow wasn't faring much better. Karina could do something, should she break free from her bonds. The pirates knew this, too. A gun clicked, followed by Karina's soft grunt.

Using Crow's blood, Argonaut painted a large circle upon the deck. Inside it, he drew a tapestry of interweaving lines. The radiant gold sparkled upon the deck under the hot sun. Before him lay a sigil drawn in divine blood. It was beautiful, in a rather horrifying sense.

When Argonaut used up every last drop in his stash—an entire swath of the deck turned gold, decorated with swirling lines and incomprehensible patterns—he sliced open Crow's skin and bled them enough to finish the sigils. Then, he dosed Crow with a small injection of Monster Blood.

"Crow," Jonah whispered. "Call a storm. I don't know what *this* is, but you have to stop it. You could wash it all away."

"I can't," Crow grunted back. Their body was tense, their voice thick with agony. "There's 'nuff blood to use, but I can't—not like this."

Did Monster Blood also inhibit a god's ability to call upon their divine power?

"Release Jonah," Argonaut commanded, and the pirate obeyed. Jonah sat up and glanced at his crew. When Karina fought against her bonds, the pirate holding her at gunpoint fired a warning shot over her shoulder. She flinched, then stilled.

Argonaut dragged Jonah to his feet and forward, through the lines of gold. Jonah was surprised the runes did not smear as he stumbled along. Was it divine intervention? Or had the blood dried that quickly? He pressed Jonah's bloodied palm firmly against the deck in the center of the rune. His crimson blood joined the beautiful gold, a gruesome handprint between meticulous lines and letters.

Argonaut released him, and Jonah scrambled back to his crew. "Why the hell do you need me?"

Argonaut did not gratify him with a response.

"I call to you, Death," Argonaut exclaimed, throwing his hands into the air with a reverence akin to a priest. "Bring her to me! Bind her to my mortal soul!"

The shadows at Argonaut's feet swirled and morphed into something far more physical. Jonah's shadow, too, and Crow's and Karina's and the rest of his crew's. These borrowed shadows coalesced into a tangible human form, solid and three-dimensional. Jonah watched, horrified, as they weaved together into flesh and bone, the female form pitch-black, obscured, as though she was a black hole. No light could enter. No light could escape.

When the shadows slithered back to their respective owners and sunlight fell upon the servant, what remained was...

"No," he wheezed, turning his petrified gaze to Argonaut. "No, not her."

In front of him stood a young woman with warm brown eyes and long, straight ginger hair, which fell like a curtain down her back. She wore a jumpsuit as deep black as the shadows that built her. *Wrong. This was wrong.*

Her face was as gentle as the day she died.

"Soph," he choked. Sophie was to be Argonaut's servant. Sophie was bound to this horrible, disgusting man. Sophie was supposed to be dead! *But,* something gruesome in the back of his mind reminded him, *Argonaut called upon Death.*

Jonah stood, slow and shaky. His long-dead twin sister surged in and pulled him into a constricting hug.

Her skin was cold.

"I don't understand," he rasped. He chewed at the inside of his lip to keep himself from breaking down. "You... How—"

"You'll love this!" Sophie cheered. She pulled away from the hug, opting instead to hold Jonah at arm's length, her frigid hands planted on his biceps. "We play a bigger mythological role than I could have ever imagined! Jonah, we *are* our own folktale!"

"I don't understand," he said again. He couldn't manage much else.

Jonah never thought he'd see Sophie's smile again. He'd committed it to his memory many years ago. Yet here it was, right in front of him.

"I'd say you wouldn't *believe* what happened, but rumor has it you've been running around with a god, huh? Look at you! You used to scoff at me!"

Jonah's mouth was dry and scratchy. "I..."

While her body was cold and there was something fundamentally different about her, her enthusiasm had never faded. While Jonah was speechless, Sophie had no qualms about filling the silence. "When I woke up in the Underworld, at first I was like, *oh no, Jonah's going to be all alone out there.* Y'know? And I missed you. I missed you a lot. You missed me, right?"

"More than you could ever know," Jonah whispered.

Sophie relaxed. A small chuckle slipped past her lips. "Look at you. You were such a string bean! You look so strong now!"

"I... Yeah."

"Well, anyways. So, funny story! I wasn't ushered along with the other souls, which was weird, y'know? Like, what about me was any different than anyone else? But instead of waiting in line at Judgment, one of Death's constructs led me to his personal chamber. And I was thinking, *what did I do to deserve this level of punishment?* Because I totally expected I was gonna be punished for something. Why else would I have a personal audience with Death? Anyways, I went to his chamber, and he told me who our biological father is."

Jonah had never cared about his lineage. His adoptive father was enough for him—he was a good man, kind and gentle, but at the same time, hardened by a life out at sea. He had raised Jonah and Sophie well, and that was all that mattered.

"Our father," she said, a wide grin plastered on her face, "is Death!"

Jonah stared at her.

"We're godlings!"

"Correction," Argonaut chimed in with a grin. "You're *monsters.*"

33

"Jonah... please, keep fighting, okay? I'll see you again someday. Promise me you'll do good things."
—The Grand Catalogue of Last Words: Great Flood Era. Death #7,900,525,731. The daughter of Death sustained a knife to the back, which pierced her left lung.

64th Storm, Great Flood 1058

"Jonah," a voice floated in the back of his mind—a familiar voice, Soph's voice, light and excitable. Jonah had never understood where she got all her energy from. "Do you think we'll ever see a real monster?"

"Don't be ridiculous," Jonah remembered telling her, a year and a half before she died. "Monsters don't exist."

He remembered the way the wooden flooring creaked as the ship swayed, covered in old rugs in a futile attempt to liven up the space. The ship, once the Charlotte—named the Vengeance after Sophie died—carried a bland manner of decoration, courtesy of his father. The cabin in which this conversation had taken place was familiar. This cabin was now cluttered with Jonah's ancient texts and pastry crumbs and shed strands of wavy black hair. Back then, though, it was Sophie's.

"Come on! You have to admit it's interesting," Sophie said as she combed a wide-toothed comb through Jonah's tangled hair, parting it straight down the middle, as he liked to style it. The twins sat cross-legged on the floor. "There are ancient tales all over the world! All from different cultures! They all have the same depictions of monsters. There's no way a worldwide phenomenon could be made up."

"Folktales get passed around. It's not unreasonable."

"I want to see a monster someday," Sophie declared. "I'm sure they're beautiful creatures. I'd love to do some proper research on them."

In Jonah's experience, monsters were not beautiful. From the moment he saw the first one, not long after Crow's rescue from the unforgiving ocean, he'd yearned to tell Sophie how scaly, slimy, and gross they were. Disgusting. Revolting.

By extension, then, how disgusting and revolting *he* was.

Jonah's chest tightened. He turned his gaze from Sophie over to Crow. Their eyes were dim, and their tight frown said something of confusion, unsurety. He couldn't bear either of their gazes.

"My blood is red," Jonah muttered, staring down at his bloodied hands. "I'm mortal. I've always been mortal. It can't be *true—*"

"You think I would lie to you?" The hurt in Sophie's tone tore shreds into Jonah's heart.

"I don't know!" His hands fell back to his side. "How am I supposed to know what the hell to believe!? You could be some…some farce created by Argonaut's sick, twisted fantasy, all to make me and my crew suffer."

"I make you suffer?"

"YES!" Jonah's patience snapped. The ache in his chest, the pounding of his heart, the anguish, the rage, the hurt: it all culminated here. "You've done *nothing* but cause me suffering since the day you died! I grieved for eight years! And for what? For you to drop back in as though death was an inconvenience? To uproot the life I've built for myself and expect me to accept it as truth?"

"I can prove it to you." Sophie took Jonah's hand. "I can prove everything I've said was true. You'll love this, Jonah."

Sophie did not wait for confirmation. She reached for Jonah's belt and pulled the sword from its sheath, only far enough to expose a sliver of its blade. She sliced her thumb on it. A tiny bead of violet formed atop her freckled skin. Jonah choked. It was one thing to fight a proper monster—a wild, violet-blooded beast—but to see it flowing through his sister's veins? Sickening.

She pressed her thumb against one of the cuts on Jonah's hand. Jonah watched in abject horror as the tainted, vile purple hue crawled up his hand and overtook the crimson. Panicked, Jonah shook his hand off, desperate to get the blood off him. When he looked at his hand again, he found he had no luck. Violet seeped past his torn flesh and into his veins.

Jonah expected it to hurt. He remembered all too well Crow's raw, agonized screams. And yet, it worked its way through Jonah's body and mutated without even a sting, as if his body had been reminded of its true nature.

This whole time, Argonaut had kept this up his sleeve. How long had he known? Since he got his hands on Sophie? Did he know after Sophie's death, taking Jonah under his wing to weaponize his monstrous grief and anger?

Or did he know *before* Sophie died? Did he target her with intent? Was he the catalyst?

"Come with me," Sophie urged. "Argonaut says he can help us. We can be together again."

"And what does he want in return? What unspeakable deeds have you bound yourself to, Sophie?"

"He's going to ascend," she said, a gleeful grin on her face. "We get rid of Aeris, Argonaut takes his place as the god of the sky. Argonaut becomes a lesser god, and Death takes his spot on the council. Isn't it so cool? We'll be a part of something huge! And for our help, Death will let us reign over Paradise!"

"No," Crow gasped, horror-struck.

"Jonah, please. Come with us."

Jonah was at a complete loss. His hands shook.

Crow was on their guard, and they had every right to be. Jonah was vile, unworthy of a god's friendship or admiration. He glanced down at the violet oozing from his cuts, mixing with the leftover crimson dried upon his shaking fingers. Unable to come up with any sort of response, Jonah broke down. He did nothing to conceal the fat tears rolling down his cheeks. He hiccupped between sobs. He felt as though he were drowning.

"You don't like it," Sophie whispered, sad and discouraged. "Jonah, we're *special.*"

"This isn't what I wanted," Jonah's voice cracked under the weight of his anguish. "I don't want to be special. I want to live my life, Soph.

With—with a family and a crew I can rely on. I never asked to be tangled up with gods or monsters or anything. I don't want this. *I don't want this!*"

What did Karina think? He looked at his crew. She'd managed to school her expression into something so flat, unreadable. Mouse was still unconscious, and Jonah wasn't looking forward to explaining the situation later. Faye and Willow, battle-weary as they were, were horrified. But Karina? She looked so steady. Whatever she was feeling, she did an excellent job of burying it.

"Jonah, you're our family." Karina's voice wavered. "You know this."

Did he deserve to be, though?

Crow's steely gaze was fixed on Jonah. A puffy little cloud floated in the distance. Jonah expected thunder. Dark, swirling, angry clouds.

"Crow," Jonah croaked. "I don't want to hurt you."

"But what will you do for Sophie?" they asked, a hint of fear in their voice.

...What *would* he do for Sophie? He couldn't go back to Argonaut. He'd spent a year suffering at the pirate's side, and he did not want a repeat of the lowest point in his life. The anger, the fear, the grief, the killing. But the thought of turning his back on his sister was far too much to bear.

Argonaut seemed more than happy to stand back and watch. A smirk tugged at his bearded face, no doubt enjoying seeing Jonah fall apart. He almost wished Argonaut would step in and strike him down. Put an end to it all. Get it over with. Jonah's continued existence wouldn't help him—so why stall?

As long as Jonah knew him, Argonaut was blunt and wasted no time. But Jonah also knew Argonaut was more than happy to torture.

This... This was torture.

Argonaut lifted his flesh hand and snapped his fingers twice. "Wrap it up, girl," he snapped. "We have work to do."

"Yessir," Sophie affirmed, and Jonah shuddered. Argonaut was not worthy of the title *sir*.

Sophie approached Crow with a lax posture and a small smile.

250

Crow tracked her every movement. Despite her friendly disposition, her intentions weren't quite so kind. She grabbed their throat and pulled them to their feet, her firm grip constricting their trachea. Crow choked.

"Sophie," Jonah gasped, wide-eyed. "What are you doing?"

"Don't worry, Jonah! I'm going to help fix everything!"

Idealistic as always.

"Don't take their life, Soph. It's...it's not something you can come back from. Once you kill, it haunts you. You can't. You can't, there are other ways."

"No, there aren't, silly! Aeris is like a blight. Have you ever heard of a blight, Jonah? Not as in the old god, *Blight.* Lowercase-b blight. It's a type of disease plants can get. The leaves wither away and die. To treat it, you have to remove the infected parts."

"This isn't right," Jonah begged. "Don't make me choose."

Crow thrashed in her grasp. Sophie squeezed Crow's throat a little tighter. Her grip was strong. Not quite human. Crow pawed at her hand.

Sophie looked at Jonah, genuine confusion written upon her face. "...You don't have to choose," she said, her brow furrowed, as though she thought it obvious. "There's no choice to make. Aeris takes up space and gives nothing in return. I miss you, Jonah. Stay with me."

She didn't understand. She *couldn't* understand.

Jonah's fist slammed into Sophie's jaw. Guilt tore away at Jonah's innards. Never in his life had he thought he'd hit his beloved sister. Sophie shouted, raw and pained, and she released Crow from her grip. Crow gasped, sharp and desperate for air.

When Sophie straightened, her face was screwed up with anguish. Hurt. Betrayal. Tears welled in the corners of her eyes. Misery looked horrible on her. She snatched Crow's sword off the deck—Karina's decorative blade—and swung. Jonah was grateful she'd never learned the art of combat. She lacked form. She gave away her intentions.

Jonah's first instinct was the incorrect one. He thrust his bare hand upwards and intercepted the blade.

Steel slammed into his palm, slicing through his already torn-up flesh, possibly even the tendons and bone underneath. Blood gushed from the wound, and Jonah howled. Hot agony flared through his body, radiating from his hand, down through his wrist, his shoulder. Nonetheless, his fingers squeezed the blade, knowing full well he may end up losing function in his hand.

He could have dodged in the time it took for her to swing the blade, but a large fraction of him believed he deserved the pain. He'd told Crow never to do this, but Crow was special, worth protecting. Jonah, with his awakened monsterhood, was not.

The inky violet dripping down his wrist did not look like his blood. If he pretended, he could imagine he'd been in combat with some *other* monster, one whose blood still stained his hand. It was a fantasy he could not sustain for long. Blood dripped down the length of the blade.

Sophie gasped. She dropped the sword, eyes wide, as though she only now realized what she had done, and Jonah let it clatter to the ground.

"I don't want to fight you, Soph," Jonah said. His wounded hand twitched. "But I can't let you do this."

"Jonah, *please.* Come with me. I've missed you so much. I miss the—do you remember when we used to stand out on the deck and catch lightning bugs together?"

Lightning bugs might not exist if Aeris dies, Jonah thought. *Argonaut wants the glory of godhood. He'd neglect his Domain.* "My crew is more of a family than Death will ever be."

"What about me? Am I less important than a failure of a god?"

"I don't believe Aeris to be a failure."

"Has he ever contributed anything? Not even to the Heavens, but to *you?* He's not worth your time. Would you choose him over me?"

"They." Jonah knew Crow didn't care much about how people referred to them, but he couldn't help but correct Sophie nonetheless. "They are a victim of abuse from a system they helped create."

When Sophie didn't say anything, Jonah pressed onward.

"After you died, Argonaut exploited my grief. I murdered innocent people, Soph. I knew no better. He told me to kill people he claimed were complicit in your murder. He said he would help me avenge you. I didn't realize how messed up it was until Karina found me. He's not the man you want to strike a deal with, because you always lose."

"This is different. This is so much bigger!"

"I don't give a damn. I may not know Aeris's full story, but I'm not willing to perpetuate injustice. So long as you're working with Argonaut," Jonah growled, "you are not my ally."

Jonah whirled around and stalked over to his crew. Turning his back on Sophie was a risk, but he needed to untie Karina. He knelt beside her and picked at the knot. If he could at least free her, she could untie Willow and Faye, and she could tend to Mouse. So long as he kept himself distracted from the consequences of turning away from his sister, he wouldn't wallow in his misery.

"Argonaut, give me your gun," Sophie said, her voice shaky with malice. "We need to put the god down now. If we don't, Jonah will never come home."

Jonah stiffened. His attention shot over to Crow. They looked stronger, their eyes in sharper focus as their body fought the Monster Blood coursing through their veins. It wouldn't be long, Jonah estimated, before they'd have the strength to smite every damn pirate on this ship.

He knew it was wishful thinking. Crow wasn't the type.

"Don't be foolish, girl!" Argonaut snapped. "We don't have all the components for the ascension rites yet—kill Aeris too soon, and you'll never be granted reign over Paradise."

A rather horrid idea struck Jonah. Terrible, monstrous, irredeemable.

He rose to his feet, leaving Karina's bonds half-untied. The knots were loose enough—she could finish the job. With one quick jerk, Jonah hauled Crow to their feet, a touch rougher than necessary.

Jonah drew his sword and, with a quick swipe, coated its blade with the deep violet blood gushing from his palm. He pressed the blade tight to Crow's throat, their back firm against his chest. Argonaut and Sophie wanted Crow dead, but they didn't want them dead *yet*. This was a weak point. A crack in their armor.

Crow gasped. Despite their fear, they leaned back against Jonah, the back of their skull pressing against his shoulder.

"You're going to let us leave," he snarled at Argonaut, "or else you'll never get your goddamned *Paradise.*"

"Jonah!" Sophie exclaimed. "Wait! I thought you said—"

Though Sophie's reaction was one of desperation, Argonaut waved his hand. "Let them go," he commanded his crew. The pirates backed off as Karina finished untying the cable around her wrists. She made quick work of Faye, Willow, and Mouse's bonds, hoisted Mouse into her arms, and ran for the *Vengeance.* Faye and Willow hobbled after her.

Step by step, Jonah made his way toward the gunwale. He kept his body facing Sophie and Argonaut—he didn't trust them to keep their word. He would have trusted Sophie eight years ago, but now? She was a different person, now. Jonah was, too.

"If you fire on us," he continued, "if you try to sink us, I'll slit the god's throat."

"We can't let them get away!" Sophie raised her stolen sword. Jonah eyed its ornate hilt, decorated with pressed flowers encased in resin and gold leaf. Though he had no doubt Sophie would appreciate the artistry, it did not belong in her hands.

"Drop the sword," Jonah snapped.

Sophie hesitated. Her grip on the hilt tightened. In return, Jonah pressed his sword firmer against Crow's throat. Crow tensed. Their bright blue eyes were wide, terrified. Monster Blood seared the tender flesh of their throat. How much better was he from Argonaut, now? But, loath as Jonah was to admit it, Crow's life was the best weapon at his disposal.

Sophie dropped the sword. "Think of Paradise, Jonah," she whispered. "Think of *us.* Don't sacrifice us."

Jonah scooped up Crow's sword and slotted it back into its hilt at their hip, where it belonged. He nudged Crow across the gangplank, and even once both stood firm on the *Vengeance,* he did not release them. He walked them to the stern and removed his blood-coated blade from their throat to nudge them up the ladder to the quarterdeck.

"Go," Jonah snapped.

"Jonah—"

"That's an order."

Crow, shaky, obeyed. Jonah followed after them. He herded them to the sternmost gunwale and pressed his sword to their throat again.

"I have to make sure they don't follow us," he whispered against Crow's skin. He loosened his grip—there was no need to press the sword so tight now. There was a yellowed mark on their neck from where the Monster Blood had ravaged their skin. "I'm sorry."

"I understand," Crow whispered back.

When the *Godkiller* was a speck on the horizon, Jonah released them. "You can go."

Crow met his eyes and nodded once, firm, resolute. They slipped away, rubbing at their throat, and stumbled below deck. Jonah leaned against the gunwale.

Violet blood dripped from his hand and rolled down the hull into the water below. Jonah put his head down upon his arms and sobbed.

Karina joined him. Her silent presence steadied him. *It's important to cry,* he remembered her saying four or five years ago. *Don't hold it back. You're not weak for it.*

After Jonah's torrent of emotions leveled out, she said, "I'll get the first aid kit."

"No. I'll take care of it myself."

She nodded. He was grateful she understood. He didn't want anyone looking at his disgusting blood, a reminder he was unworthy of the compassion his crew gave him. A monster.

"I don't agree with your method," Karina said, "but thank you. For getting us out of there."

Jonah did not reply. He didn't deserve to be thanked. He stood there for a while longer, watching blood stain the hull of his beloved ship. Scrubbing it clean would be a pain. Right now, he was too numb to care.

His crew's eyes were glued on him as he peeled away from the rail. He trudged toward the thick doors leading below. He heaved them open, his exhausted body straining against their otherwise manageable weight. Blood stained the doors now, too. Disgusting violet infected everything he touched. It was a disease. A curse.

Gripping the handrail with his less-injured hand, he staggered down the stairs. His vision swam, his knees threatened to give in. The combined physical and emotional toll was far too much to bear. He tripped over the last step and stumbled, crashing into the bulkhead across from the stairwell. He was grateful his cabin door was within arm's reach.

Jonah expected to be greeted by an empty cabin. Instead, he found Crow, who sat at Jonah's desk. They regarded him in silence. The first-aid kit sat on the desk, and Crow rummaged through it. They pulled out a suture needle, but no thread.

Crow jerked their head, a silent gesture for Jonah to come sit down. With great hesitation, Jonah complied. In any other circumstance, Jonah would have put up a fight over Crow sitting in his chair. Now, though, he slumped onto the stool in dazed silence.

Crow cracked open a bottle of vodka and doused an old rag with it. They held out their hand, palm up.

"I'll hurt you," Jonah whispered. When Crow didn't respond, Jonah stared down at Crow's hand, regarding their silent invitation. What right did he have to place in Crow's hand a substance capable of killing them? After he'd held a sword to their throat?

Crow's offer spoke volumes. They didn't care if it hurt them. Jonah laid his hand atop Crow's. His knuckles brushed their palm. His hand was drenched in blood, but Crow's touch was warm and steady. They tensed as his blood stung their divine flesh, but they did not pull back.

Crow pressed the rag upon Jonah's palm, and he sucked in a sharp breath as the alcohol bit at his raw, tattered skin. As they blotted at the wound, cleaning it of its grime and excess blood, Jonah tore his eyes away. His gaze wandered to his desk—atop it was one of Jonah's many medical texts. The book was written in Midiri, but thanks to the copious illustrations and diagrams, Crow seemed to have figured out what to do. Crow had it flipped open to a page on how to clean an open wound.

What hurt the most wasn't the alcohol sting, but the gentleness with which Crow handled him. Their touches were feather-light against Jonah's sensitive skin. He didn't deserve it.

Crow drew back. They set the stained rag atop the desk and

inspected their work. Jonah peeked at his hand—all the blood coating his fingers was gone, leaving nothing but the long gash and the scrapes from the cable. Seeming satisfied, Crow picked up the suture needle and, letting go of Jonah's hand, sliced its sharp tip across the wound on their wrist, which hadn't gotten much chance to heal. Blood dripped from the wound and worked its way down the slope of their arm.

"Don't—" Jonah's voice caught in his throat as Crow took his hand again, holding it steady. They held their bloodied arm above the wound and allowed radiant gold to drip and meld with sickly violet. Jonah didn't deserve it, he didn't deserve it, he didn't—

The first drop hit his palm. Then, a second, a third. Jonah's wound was long, deep, and gruesome, but with each drop of God's Blood, the muscles and tendons knitted themselves back together. His hand tingled. Jonah wasn't sure how long he sat there for, watching, mesmerized.

Crow paused halfway through and wiped Jonah's hand clean again. Their fingers brushed Jonah's wound, and they hissed and jerked their hand back as if they'd been burnt. But, undeterred, Crow returned to their work, wincing and gritting their teeth as Jonah's blood hurt such delicate fingers. When they finished, they tossed the rag aside once more and resumed the slow process of squeezing their blood into his wound.

"I wasn't sure this would work," Crow muttered. "It wouldn't have worked on a true monster. You've still got enough mortal in your system. It's taking a lot more blood than usual, but it's okay."

Jonah found that somewhat reassuring.

"Did you ever know your mother?"

"No. I was told she died during childbirth."

Crow pulled some bandages out of the first-aid kit. They couldn't quite get the wound to heal. A sliver of raw flesh remained, a fraction of the original injury. It oozed beads of violet. Crow wrapped it up. Once the bandages were tucked into place, Crow pressed their lips atop the treated wound. Jonah's heart caught in his chest.

"You're not a monster," they whispered.

"Helping me... It hurt you. My blood—"

"I don't give a damn about your blood. By definition, sure, a monster is a being created by Death. But there's a difference. A true monster seeks out the harm of others for its own benefit. It has no compassion, no soul. You have more compassion and soul than I've ever seen in a living being. Even when you threatened me earlier, it was to protect me. I'm grateful. Your soul is warm, *Ilinoé*." Crow stood. "I'll leave you alone."

"Wait," Jonah gasped. "What does *Ilinoé* mean?"

Crow smiled. "Sunshine."

They wrapped up their own wound, then packed up the first aid kit. Everything went back into their proper places except for the suture needle, which Crow had tucked into their pocket. Then, they were gone.

34

"Every realm offers a god a different perspective on power and vulnerability. In the Heavens, they wield great power and feel no pain. In Midir, a god feels the pain of mortalkind. And in the Underworld, a god does not feel the pain of flesh, but rather, kalpides: pain of the soul."
—*How to Kill a God by Anonymous*

64th Storm, Great Flood 1058

Death slammed open the door to Elaine's frigid cell. Elaine expected him to abuse and belittle her, but instead, he stooped to unlock her shackles. Before Elaine could leap to her feet, he grabbed her wrist, his clawed, ashy hand digging in where the cuffs had been.

He forced Elaine to stand. This was the first time she'd stretched her legs in what felt like millennia—her knees were stiff and achy in a way so mortal, distant yet familiar. Death gave her no time to stretch as he pulled her out of the cell and down the Underworld's murky, cavernous maze. She stumbled behind him.

If I can get away from him, I could find my way out of here. She gave her arm an experimental tug. Death cast an unamused glare over his shoulder.

"Where are we going?" Elaine couldn't help but ask.

Death did not answer. Elaine trudged behind him through the interweaving caverns, tripping over errant stalagmites she couldn't quite see. The only thing breaking the silence was her own footsteps. Not even Death's footfalls made a sound.

They reached a set of slate-gray double doors, thrice Elaine's height and decorated with ornate bas-relief carvings of demons and monsters. Death graced her with his hollow voice. "You have a fighting spirit," he said, though he did not sound impressed. "Killing Blight was no easy feat.”

“Um, thank you?”

“I’m looking forward to testing you.”

Death pushed the doors open, revealing a massive, octagonal arena. It was packed to the brim with deceased souls and gods alike, all vying for entertainment. A gentle murmur filled the air, no longer stifled by those thick, heavy doors. Elaine gasped.

“Go on, give us a good show.” A malicious grin drew across Death’s gaunt face. He pushed Elaine, sending her stumbling through the door and into the arena’s sandy pitch. “Let’s see what you’re capable of, goddess of fire.”

The doors slammed shut. Designed to swing inwards, with no handles in sight, these doors were inoperable from the inside. A perfect cage. Elaine slammed her fist on the door once, twice, before slumping in defeat. She had nowhere to go but forward.

She trudged across the arena’s sandy floor toward the center. Bright light accosted her. She squinted and shielded her eyes with her hand, and a wave of nausea rolled over her. She squinted through the light, hoping to catch a glimpse of the stands circling the arena one story above, but her eyes struggled to adjust. The crowd’s murmurs turned to hoots and howls, riled-up and eager to watch another poor soul be tortured in the pit. The sound alone told her she was to entertain a grand audience today.

“Demons and deities!” A voice boomed from some unknown source. The jeering crowd settled down. She didn’t recognize the flamboyant voice. It belonged to some minor Underworld god—a god of pride, gambling, or sadistic pleasure. Elaine didn’t care. The host, whoever they were, didn’t deserve the attention they garnered.

Elaine’s eyes adjusted to the light. She could make out a few of the bigger shapes, like the grandstand at the western end of the stadium, opposite the entryway. On it, she spotted three figures. Death’s horned silhouette was clear as day, the second was too small to make out, and... she squinted at the third form.

Einari.

“Tonight, you’re in for a real treat!” The host boomed with glee.

"You all know her name: the killer of Blight, the human turned divine! We're *blessed* to see her here in the flesh, it's the goddess of fire, *ELAINE!"*

The crowd roared.

"We all know she can kill a god, so I don't know about you folks, but I'm eager to skip right to the nastiest of our opponents, hm? Let's see how she fares against the *sokaívi!"*

A metallic screech from behind Elaine forced her attention away from the stand. She whirled around. A metal grate in the wall, rusty gray-brown in hue, struggled its way open. Behind the grate stood a hulking beast, lion-like in its build, but taller and slimmer, like a hound. Drool dripped from its jowls and matted its mane. Elaine could see its ribs—the handlers kept the beast hungry for a more entertaining show.

With no weapons and dwindling divine energy, thanks to the frigid confines that sapped her, she was defenseless. The fight was not fair. She did not have long before the *sokaívi* was free—she needed to prepare. She threaded the skirt of her robes around her legs and tied it into a messy knot. At least she could move easier.

The *sokaívi* prowled from its cell. Its hungry gaze locked on Elaine. Elaine shivered as she met its cold black eyes. The beast crouched. Through its thin, wiry obsidian fur, its muscles flexed.

It pounced.

Elaine dove. She tumbled to the floor, kicking up a cloud of sand in her wake. She scrambled to stand, regaining her bearings as best she could before the beast struck again. Sharp claws raked through the fabric and flesh at her collarbone. Gold oozed from the wound. The crowd chittered and jeered from the stands above.

She ran for the edge of the arena in hopes of putting distance between herself and the *sokaívi.* Her toes dug up sand with each step, particles finding their way inside her boots. The beast gave chase. Four-legged creatures were designed to be deft runners. It caught up as she reached the outer rim. It loomed over her, thick strands of drool dripping from its maw and onto her head and shoulders.

Monster saliva, Elaine thought, her lip curling up in disgust. She wiped a glob off her cheek. It sizzled against her skin. *Gross.*

The beast opened its maw. Elaine ducked out of the way as it snapped at her. The beast's snout slammed into the arena wall where her head had once been. In the time the *sokaívi* needed to regain its bearings, Elaine backed away, taking advantage of the lull to appraise the beast.

Long, sharp spines ran down its back. They flexed as its muscles tensed, as the *sokaívi* backed away from the wall and shook itself off. They were thick and sturdy, and it would no doubt be painful if one were to run her through.

It faced her, and with a snarl, it broke into a run. Massive paws thundered across the ground. This beast would kill her. She knew it. The audience knew it. The *sokaívi* crossed the short span of sand between it and her. When it neared, Elaine grabbed its mane and swung upon its back.

The beast thrashed and ran across the arena. Elaine gripped its mane tight, fighting to keep steady upon its back. She released its mane with her left hand, keeping her grip firm with her right, and reached for one of its spines. The beast took a sharp turn and skidded to a stop. Her hand grasped air, and her momentum sent her flying. She tumbled through the sand.

Elaine lost track of the *sokaívi.* She whipped her head around. The *sokaívi* took a wide loop around the arena, building up its speed, which it then directed toward Elaine.

She had a small reserve of divine energy at her disposal. If she got lucky, she could wound the beast with her flame. For the shot to count, she needed to identify the most vulnerable spot on the beast's wiry body. She could land a blow upon its underbelly. If she scorched it, she could put the beast out of commission for long enough to land a few meaningful strikes. Or she could wound one of its legs, so it could no longer run...

When the *sokaívi* was upon her, she dropped to the ground. The loose sand would be her advantage, even if it scraped her skin something fierce. She slid underneath the creature as it ran. Balling her hand into a fist, she thrust it upwards, summoning a plume of flame. The *sokaívi* squealed, high-pitched and pained.

Once she was clear of the beast and smoke billowed in the air, Elaine struggled to her feet. The creature's dark, thin fur was charred and smoking, but it stood, seething with fury. She had failed.

Elaine could feel it in her soul. She had a scant fragment of her divinity left. Her strength, wasted.

This is it, she thought as the beast snarled at her. *I'm gone for good.*

The *sokaívi* lunged, slicing a long gash from her temple down to her chin. It pinned her to the sand with its massive paws. Its weight crushed her. A few of her bones cracked under the pressure. Sharp, vicious teeth sank down into Elaine's shoulder, and she screamed.

She choked as fang bore through muscle, as the monster's venom—not quite Monster Blood, but nasty anyhow—seeped into her bloodstream. Spit, venom, and blood pooled in the sand beneath her. Her vision blurred. The fetus writhed, anguished, as venom seeped from Elaine's bloodstream to its own. Would she be rid of the thing?

Not before she died, too.

Underneath her palm, a pathetic little sprout with a few soft leaves grew through her fingertips. Elaine brushed over the leaf with her thumb, leaving a faint scorched path in its wake. Despite everything, Elaine couldn't help but smile with a certain fondness for the times Novika scolded her for charring the plants in their chamber.

This stirred her into a sense of heightened awareness, despite the beast gnawing at her body. As her gaze traveled to the grandstand, she spotted the small, unimposing figure in the grandstand and understood.

Novika. Novika was here, urging her to finish the fight. With the meager last bit of her divine energy, Elaine thrust her hand up toward the beast's face and blasted the wretched thing with a puff of fire. The *sokaívi* wailed and reeled back, off Elaine, stumbling away from her. Its eyes were screwed shut. The flame had blinded it.

Her body ached, but she forced herself up and limped toward the *sokaívi*, which had collapsed to the ground. It licked its paw, Elaine noted, before bringing the wet paw to its eyes, trying to soothe the burn. Here was an animal, tortured and abused, forced to fight for entertainment.

It's not an animal, Elaine had to remind herself as she brushed a hand down its flank. *It's a monster. It was designed for destruction. It deserves no sympathy. Should it live, it will go on to torture another soul.*

She tore one of the spines from the monster's back. It was long and gray-violet, wider at the base than at its sharp tip, lightweight but solid. The *sokaívi's* tall, rounded ears flicked in her direction. It snarled and clicked at her. It swiped its paw, but without sight it couldn't aim, and it struck nothing but air and sand.

Elaine poised the spine above its neck. She squeezed it with both hands, then plunged it into soft flesh. Violet blood spewed from the wound. Elaine knew she should have been more worried as the Monster Blood mixed with her own blood, already venom-stricken, already weak. But she didn't worry. She sank to the sandy floor, relieved the *sokaívi* was dead.

A pair of hands wrapped around her from behind. She couldn't tell who it was, but it wasn't Death's skeletal hands—they were soft, tender, gentle against her battle-torn body. These hands lifted her from the sand, and when she looked up, she was gazing into Novika's warm bronze eyes.

Elaine succumbed to unconsciousness.

35

"My daughter! Please, save my daughter!"
—The Grand Catalogue of Last Words: Great Flood
Era. Death #2,001,627,183. Drowned.

64th Storm, Great Flood 1058

A glistening waterfall splashed into a crystal lake. Made up of and surrounded by all four of the purest elements, it stood as the embodiment of purity. Its warmth came from the lava bed beneath, and earthen minerals enriched the waters. The still, glassy surface reflected the stars above. Sky, wilds, water, and fire: these energies imbued the waterfall and its lakebed with spiritual power.

Elaine lay in the rejuvenating waters. Her robes billowed around her, weightless, drifting like seaweed. The soaked fabric clung to her skin and accentuated the fetus. She stared at it. The curve of her stomach was far past the point of being concealable, as if the universe wanted to taunt her for eternity.

The waters soothed her ever-present nausea, and the fetus was unbothersome and still. Had it died from the monster's toxins? Could she be free of her hatred toward her own body?

The fetus nudged her, and her hope deflated. *You're a fighter, huh,* she thought. *Like me.*

Elaine lay in silence, aware of Novika's presence beside her. The goddess of the wilds sat with their legs folded, gazing into the pool in front of them.

"Where's Einari?" she rasped.

"You're awake," Novika said. "Einari is still in the Underworld. I closed our portal behind us. I anticipate he won't linger there long."

Elaine sat up. She willed the water warmer with her rejuvenated divinity and splashed some upon her face.

"How are you faring? Einari invited me to see a show, but I... I hadn't expected the show to be *you.*"

"I'm much better, thank you."

"It was the least I could do." Novika smiled. "And how is the—"

"We mustn't dawdle." She cut them off before they could say the word *baby.* She didn't want to hear it. "Tell me, Novika. What do you remember?"

"You knew I remembered something." Novika's gaze was inquisitive. They looked as though they were trying their hardest to put on an act of calm. Something raged behind the sheen of her deep brown skin.

"I found the memories. I'd expected Aeris's, but Einari has stolen from every one of us. Even the smallest of deities. I couldn't free more than one person's memories, so I chose yours."

"And not Aeris?"

"I wanted to. But I was doomed, and if I could pick one person to remember *something,* I knew it had to be you. You had the most power to do something. Anything."

"No wonder," Novika muttered, awestruck by something Elaine was not privy to. "He had to alter *everybody's* memory to get away with such an egregious deed."

"What did he do?" Elaine pressed. Despite her lethargy, she was antsy to get moving. She stood. Novika followed suit.

"Einari is not our true king," Novika stated with a matter-of-factness that left Elaine's legs feeling weak. "He stole the throne."

Elaine's hands flew to her mouth. How could it be? If the title of God King did not belong to him, then whose was it?

"We need to spread word, but nobody will believe us," Novika continued. "Einari has everyone wrapped around his finger."

"We don't need to *tell* anybody. Come."

Elaine led Novika along the aurora path. Before the stairwell to the Great Hall sat the Big Four's personal chambers. Novika's was the only archway showing signs of life, verdant ivy growing up and around its marble structure. Across the path sat Elaine's archway, framed by two unlit sconces. Adjacent to Elaine's was Aeris's, left dim and dull since the day Einari cast them out. Elaine missed the puffy clouds, the rains dampening the ground at the entry.

Elaine turned to the fourth archway, no more than rubble on the path. Shattered, unusable.

"When did this happen?" Elaine rasped.

"Not long after he sent you Below. He's been acting odd. He knows I remember, Elaine, but he acts as though he doesn't."

"I freed your memories right in front of him."

"Yet he invited me to the show. Despite everything...does he still cherish our friendship? Or was it a charade this whole time?"

"I can't say. But we need to find a way in—everybody's memories are hidden in there."

"How can we?"

"Does he have a secondary entry point? I do. Aeris does." Elaine nudged the rubble with her foot. "We can either try to rebuild this, or we can look for another way in."

Elaine wasn't sure she could piece the archway back together. Even if she managed it, it did not guarantee the revival of Einari's portal. Opening a new portal wasn't so easy—the owner of the chamber had to be present and willing.

"I do not wish to rebuild," Novika said, echoing Elaine's thoughts. "He wouldn't destroy his archway if he didn't have another way in. He never told me where it may be, but I think I know."

"Lead the way."

Elaine followed Novika down the path to a little pocket in space that housed a large crystal lake. It wasn't dissimilar to the pool by the waterfall, but it lacked the elements of sky and fire.

"Einari spends time here when he's upset." Novika gestured toward a long, flat rock jutting into the lake. "I gave him this to sit upon. I thought he'd appreciate a place to rest and think."

"You think this might have another way in?"

"I can't imagine it being anywhere else. Underwater, I'd imagine."

Elaine climbed upon one of the rocks and walked to the edge. She peered at the water. A massive, dark, looming shadow flickered under the waves. She flinched.

"Something's in there," she gasped. "A monster. What is a monster doing in the Heavens?"

Novika edged closer to the shoreline. "I don't see it."

"There." Elaine pointed toward the dark shape twisting and turning in the depths. From above the surface, all she could discern was a shadow, inky against the crystal blue water. If one weren't looking closely, the shape could be mistaken for a plant or a rock.

Neither plants nor rocks moved like this, though, circling like a predator.

"Oh," Novika gasped.

"If his portal is down there, my flame won't be of much use. Can you handle defense?"

"I can try."

Elaine knelt and leaned over the rock's brittle edge. She plunged her head underwater, her gaze trailing down the lakebed's steep, sandy slope, finding a blue-violet portal at its deepest. It sat nestled against a rocky cliff face, shrouded by fronds of underwater foliage.

The sea monster prowling below had large flipper-like fins and a long, protruding neck. Its beady-eyed gaze found her. It bared its long, needlelike fangs.

Elaine pulled her head out of the water. "It's down there. The portal."

"And the monster?"

"It knows we're here."

"So, there's no way to sneak around it."

"Do you think we can distract it?"

"What could distract a monster?" Novika kicked a pebble into the water. It hit the surface with a gentle *plunk* and sank into the sand below. Some critter in the shallows skittered away, disturbed.

"Then we push on and hope for the best." Elaine waited as Novika climbed upon the rock outcropping. "Are you ready?"

"I hope so," replied Novika. "I have to be."

She nodded and dove headfirst into the lake. Novika dove in behind her, and Elaine pointed at the portal in the cliff face. Novika nodded, and the goddesses swam.

The monster spotted Elaine and Novika when they were a quarter of the way down. Nerves spiked in Elaine's chest as it swam toward them, fierce and unforgiving. Her Domain was of no use underwater—she channeled some heat into her hands. If she needed to, she could burn the thing with a touch. She hoped she wouldn't get close enough to resort to that.

Novika waved their hand, and long vines of aquatic plants slithered up from the lakebed, providing cover. *Smart.*

Elaine's latent mortal instinct nagged at her. If she did not hurry, she'd have to resurface for air, and all her progress to this point would have been for naught. She'd been a goddess for three thousand years, but mortality was a hard habit to break. So easy it was, to forget she did not need to breathe.

The sea monster ripped through the shroud of foliage. The water around Elaine's hands simmered, and Elaine caught it by the snout, divine heat scalding the monster's scaly face. As it wrenched away, its hind fin slammed Elaine into a jagged rock. If pain existed in the Heavens, she would have been in a world of agony as the sea monster surged in, eager to sanction her demise.

Below, Novika waved their hand, and the rock behind Elaine crumbled. She scrambled deeper. Her stomach cramped, and the fetus made itself known. A kick, a wriggle, an ache. That was the only pain she felt in the Heavens. No burning muscles, no throbbing wounds.

Novika reached the portal first. Elaine was not far behind. They tumbled into Einari's chamber. Relief washed over Elaine.

Novika peered around. "What are we looking for?"

"Follow me." Elaine strode to the hidden trapdoor and popped it open. She led Novika into the secret study below.

Novika gasped as they laid eyes on Einari's library. "What is all this?" They brushed their hand across the spines of all these old, lost books. They answered their own question. "All the books he redacted from the mortal realm. Everything stating he was not king."

The titles dated back to the time of creation, long before Einari ever stole the throne. These religious documents and histories remained in their unaltered form. Novika pulled the last existing copy of the Book of the Sky from its home and brushed away some dust. They gazed down at it, studying its worn leather cover, before placing it back upon the shelf.

"I'm surprised Einari didn't destroy them," Elaine said.

"He respects our history. I—"

Novika cut themself off as they stepped into the workroom. Elaine gave them the silence they needed to take it all in. They stared at the hundreds of compartments lining the back wall, forming a quilt of stained glass, each pane colored corresponding to the god whose memories it housed.

"This is horrible. Unbelievable." Novika approached the single shattered compartment, tracing their finger over the jagged green glass. "This one's mine?"

All Elaine could do was nod.

"And this one..."

They drifted down the line, a few compartments over, so full it could burst, decorated with a long, gnarly crack. The crack had grown, but the glass still held strong.

Aeris's memories crowded and pushed against the weak point. If left untouched, it would be but a matter of time before the glass shattered.

"I remember the way Einari strapped me down and tampered with my mind," Novika admitted. "What can we do to stop such power? How did he even learn this magic?"

"He worked Underworld magic when he banished me. He allied with Death."

Novika's hand balled into a tight fist. "He was supposed to be my best friend."

"Maybe he still can be. Maybe he can learn." Elaine wasn't convinced, but if it would help Novika...

"I want him to," Novika said, their voice broken, "but I don't think so."

Novika sobbed. Heartbreak was a familiar feeling. Elaine had known the feeling well in her mortal life, three thousand years ago. She remembered the anguish of loss. Flashes of her betrothed's corpse crossed her mind. Charred, lifeless.

Everybody handled grief in different ways. Novika's turned to anger, and their fist swung before Elaine could get a comforting word out. Their strike slammed against the damaged glass encasing Aeris's memories. The glass exploded. They shattered Elaine's next.

Wispy smoke poured from the glass and floated toward Elaine. When it found her body, entering through her chest, her heart, Elaine stumbled. The room spun. But she, too, remembered.

Elaine braced against the wall behind her as her mind swam. Aeris used to wear a radiant crown, woven of raw divinity itself. She remembered the day Einari forced her to forget. She remembered the way he made Aeris small and worthless. One day, the rightful God King, the next day, nobody.

Memories stolen from the fetus, too, flashed before her eyes, though the fetus did not have much to remember. A dark, warm home, a gentle embrace of soft, gold-blooded flesh. This home boasted safety, nestled in a cozy blanket of amniotic fluid. Little fingers grasped around nothing, legs stretched and retracted. A tiny heart pattered under thin, translucent flesh. This was a part of her. An extension of her own body.

Awareness came back in waves. In front of her, Novika's blurry frame rampaged. They grabbed a stepladder from where it sat by a bookcase and hurled it at the wall with a scream. Though Elaine's hearing was muffled, she registered the sharp shattering of glass, Novika's ragged, panting, rage-fueled screams. Memories dissipated into the air, finding their way to their owners.

She brushed her hand over her stomach, daring to acknowledge the wretched creature inside her. *I am a volcano, and it is the lava inside me. I am with Mt. Azhir.*

When Elaine's vision cleared and she could support her full weight, Novika was laughing. Something manic glinted in their eyes as they grabbed the chair by Einari's work desk and hurled it at the wall. They threw books and furniture, anything they could get their hands on, until every memory was free from its confines. A mosaic of shattered glass blanketed the floor.

Novika's laughter devolved back into sobs. They fell to their knees, their face buried in their hands. "How dare he?" they gasped. "I trusted him."

"I know," Elaine whispered, sinking to her knees beside Novika. She wrapped her hand around Novika's shoulder and pulled them close, their head against Elaine's collarbone.

Novika shuddered. "I always forgave him when he made poor decisions. I thought he deserved forgiveness. But—does he deserve it? After he manipulated and abused *everyone?*"

"I don't think he does."

"He was my friend," Novika said again. Their voice broke.

Elaine held them tight. She wasn't sure how much time passed before Novika sat up straight.

Novika's dark skin was stained with tears. "Let's..." they cast a glance over her shoulder at the carnage she had wrought upon Einari's study. "Let's get out of here."

"Yes. Let's."

36

"Don't you think the god of the sky gets treated like crap? Why are we taught to hate him? Why are we taught to hate anyone?"
—*The Grand Catalogue of Last Words: Great Flood Era. Death #6,825,027,402. Drowned. This soul was sent to Punishment for heresy.*

67th Storm, Great Flood 1058

"Have you ever seen lightning at night?" Crow asked, their voice wistful as they leaned against the gunwale and stared out into the distant nighttime sky. Karina stood beside them.

A few tense days had slid by. The news had torn Jonah apart. What was he supposed to do, knowing he was a *monster?* It called into question his entire identity, his self-worth, his pride. She could see him now, in her periphery, slumped in his usual seat at the fire pit. The gentle orange glow illuminated the sharp angles of his face.

Tonight was the first night Jonah had appeared above deck since the crew met Sophie. He was so ashamed, he spent his days hiding away. When he emerged above deck an hour ago, Karina had made him tea, which sat in its mug on the bench to his side, untouched. The residual heat of the dying fire kept his drink lukewarm.

Karina turned her gaze back to Crow, who had one elbow propped against the gunwale, forehead leaning upon their hand. "It's common this time of year."

"It's beautiful, isn't it? The way it lights up the whole sky for a split second." They snapped their fingers, and far in the distance, a bolt of lightning struck the surface of the ocean. Their palm glinted, wet with the sheen of spilt blood. "I've never seen it from this angle before. Gives me a new appreciation for this world, seeing it how you do."

"What does it look like from your point of view?"

"I see it from above. I see the way it illuminates clouds. It's fun, sitting and watching a storm sweep across Midir, swirling and shifting..."

"You remember?" Karina asked. She tucked a strand of hair behind her ear for the third time in the past five minutes. The wind betrayed the unease Crow hid.

"Hmm," Crow hummed. "I suppose I do."

They seemed distant.

"Are you okay?" A loaded question.

Crow stared at the distant storm, watching it pass. Another humid breeze ruffled Karina's hair, undoing the adjustment she'd made. The stretch of silence would have been pleasant if it hadn't carried the weight of a question unanswered.

"Not really."

"How so?"

"My head. My brain is trying to grasp memories it can't access. And it keeps getting worse. I wish it would *happen.*"

"It hurts you." Karina inched closer to Crow, her shoulder brushing theirs, and hoped they'd find the gesture reassuring. "To remember."

"Yeah."

"You should get some rest."

"I can't sleep like this," Crow replied. "The fresh air helps a little."

"I get it," she said, even though she *didn't.* She'd had her fair share of long nights, nights spent ill, nights where she couldn't sleep no matter how hard she tried. She'd had plenty of headaches and stresses, but she would never know the strain of a god void of memory. Having one's life upended wasn't easy—and Crow had lived for millennia. "Do you want company?"

"You don't need to stay up for me."

"I'm happy to."

"Get some rest, Karina." Crow nudged her with their shoulder and cast her a weak smile. "At least one of us should be functional."

She nodded. "I'll leave you alone, then. Come get me if you need anything, okay?"

"Yeah."

"And Crow?" Karina kept her voice soft, tender. She waited for

Crow to meet her gaze before she continued. "Don't forget, we all love you."

"Yeah."

Karina walked down the deck. A soft rumble of thunder followed—Crow had gone back to watching the storm.

She paused by the fire pit. Jonah met her eyes, and Karina wondered if he would call her over, let her in. But he broke his gaze not long later, turning his body away. He did not want her company either.

She slept, at a maximum, two hours.

When Karina emerged in the morning, rubbing her tired eyes, Crow was gone. Jonah joined her after she had settled at the fire pit. She hadn't expected him to show his face in the morning light, under which he could be *perceived.* She was glad he did. He sat in his usual spot on the edge of the port-facing bench.

"Hot cocoa?" she offered. Cocoa was a rare treat, but she'd managed to stock up during the *Vengeance's* last hub visit. She saved it for when someone needed a boost.

"Sure."

Karina smiled. She walked over to the supply closet and filled a small pot with water. The trickle from the spigot was slow and thin. Having running water was a luxury Karina never dared take for granted, but it was hard not to grow impatient on occasion. Today, though, she had all the patience in the world.

She carried the pot to the fire pit, lit the fire with a match, and hung it from the iron fixture stretched over the flame.

"We're running low on matches," Karina said to fill the silence. Jonah hated small talk. Karina had learned, in her time knowing him, to talk about actionable topics.

"We're running low on a lot of things," Jonah mumbled. He glanced at the pot. "You don't have to do this."

It would be a while before the water heated enough to be pleasant to drink, but Karina went ahead and poured her cocoa powder and sugar in, mixing it all together with an old wooden spoon. She bumped her wrist against the pot's metal casing and gritted her teeth as it singed her arm.

"You said you wanted it."

"I..." his voice came out quiet, shaky. "I do."

"Then accept it," Karina pushed, pointing the spoon at Jonah. A few droplets of the cool, partially mixed drink landed on Jonah's cheek. He wiped it away with the back of his hand.

"But—"

"Don't try me, mister. You deserve nice things. You deserve to be happy."

Jonah's amber eyes fell to his steel-toed leather boots. His brow creased, his mouth turned down, his eyes glazed, he looked like he was enduring a lifetime of heartache.

"You're wasting your supplies on someone like me."

"No, I'm not."

Karina dunked the spoon into the water and stirred. Bubbles floated to the surface, a gentle simmer. She pulled the pot from the fire before it could boil.

"Have you seen Crow today?" she asked.

"No," he said. "It's for the best."

Karina's heart sank as she poured cocoa into the mug and pushed it into Jonah's hands. He stared at the drink. Karina would kick him if he let the cocoa go to waste.

Karina let her eyes wander as Jonah took a sip. Faye was out, now, helping Mouse with whatever project the boy had taken on. Always working, Mouse was. Always innovating.

Her gaze trailed upward, to the crow's nest. "Oh, my," Karina gasped. "There they are. They look miserable."

Karina couldn't quite make out the details at such a distance, but Crow's posture said it all. They stood slumped against the safety railing, arms tangled in the rail bars in a feeble attempt to keep them from falling right over the edge.

"Why?" Jonah asked. Karina fought to conceal a small smile. Crow had a nasty habit of piquing Jonah's interest, no matter the circumstance.

"They complained of feeling ill. Nasty headache, they said."

"What the hell are they doing up there, then?"

"The wind helps. Something about being closer to their Domain."

Jonah stood and set his cocoa down. In his eyes, Karina caught the fiery glint of the captain she knew.

"CROW!" Jonah shouted. Across the deck, Faye looked up from their project, startled, and Mouse, seeing Faye's distraction, followed suit. But Crow, far above, did not respond.

A modicum of relief washed over Karina when Crow peeled away from the edge. They seemed to have decided it was high time they returned to deck. They made it down a couple rungs before their grip slipped. They plummeted toward the deck.

Crow did not once flail.

Thousands of horrific scenarios crossed Karina's mind as she leapt from her seat. Crow could hit the deck headfirst. They could crash through the deck in its entirety, splintering the wood, falling into whichever cabin sat below. The splintered wood might impale them, golden blood spewing out of their mangled body. Or, maybe the deck would hold firm, and the *Vengeance's* crew would have to watch as their body crunched against the surface—

Jonah surged forward. His steel-toed boots slammed against the surface of the deck with each frenzied step. There was a palpable terror, desperation, in his eyes. Sweat beaded at his brow, catching the glint of morning sunlight.

One more step and Jonah's form coalesced into shadows, not dissimilar to how Sophie had materialized on Argonaut's deck. If Karina had blinked, she would have missed it, as Jonah reappeared beneath Crow in time to catch them.

He stumbled, disoriented, then sank to his knees, holding Crow close to his chest.

"Are they okay?" Karina dared ask as she knelt beside Jonah. Mouse joined Karina's side.

"I don't know."

"Yo!" Faye hollered as she ran over. "Dude! Did you guys see that?"

"See... what?" Jonah asked.

"Oh, man, it was so cool! You were, like, running, and I didn't think you were going to make it in time—but then, *whoosh,* you reappeared right under them—"

"Faye," Karina said, trying to be as gentle as she could. "Not now."

Faye paused and regarded the situation, then nodded.

"I thought I blacked out." Jonah turned his gaze up at Karina and Faye. "I... what?"

"You're blessed," Karina cooed. "Something must have awakened in you, Jonah."

"It's no blessing." His voice was grim. He stared at his bandaged hand. The half-healed wound split open, violet blood staining the gauze. He must have channeled some form of latent power without realizing. "This is nothing like Nyx's flame. It's a curse."

Jonah stood and carried Crow downstairs, abandoning his mug of cocoa by the fire.

37

"This book has been something of a passion project of mine, cobbled together using journal entries of my crewmates and interviews with Aeris. It is high time Aeris take back what they lost."

—A True History of Midir Theology: The New Book of the Sky, written year Reconstruction 02, by Faye Montoya

67th Storm, Great Flood 1058

At the beginning of time itself, four newborn gods created Midir.

They fought over what this world should look like. One wanted sprawling seas. One wanted lush landmasses. One wanted unrelenting heat. And one insisted it was all for naught if this fledgling world did not have a sky to blanket it all. Insults led to water crashing against shorelines, daring to intercede on the large landmasses. Shouts turned to plumes of fiery lava exploding from the tallest of mountains. Arguments turned into storms, which swirled through the skies and pelted the seas.

When they stopped bickering long enough to take notice, the four gods fell in love with their creation. Midir was messy, chaotic, and incidental, but chaos was what gave it character.

The gods created animals to roam Midir, starting with tiny, rudimentary organisms, but moving to fish, then land-dwelling animals, then flying creatures. These beings came into existence and went extinct. With life came death. A new god was born. One who resided far below the living realm and herded deceased souls into the afterlife.

Only then did the gods create a domineering species. Humans. They had opposable thumbs and large, problem-solving brains. They were smart, adaptable, creative. Even still, humankind struggled. The earliest humans did not know how to best navigate their environment. Many died of disease or infection. The most fascinating thing, though, was how these creatures learned to survive—no, flourish—over

"

generations. They discovered fire and learned to cook. They perfected the art of hunting and foraging. They painted cave walls using pigments made from berries. They told stories with the language the gods had given them, Køveni, the same language the gods themselves spoke. 1,500 years later, the gods developed a few new languages, ones better suited for human tongues: Biqanti, Avetic, Sonallan, and the lingua franca, Midiri.

Humans developed weapons, tools, medicine. They developed distinct cultures. These cultures fought, stole, subjugated, and ravaged. They developed rudimentary governments, which rose and fell. Tribes, kingdoms, colonies, empires. Most importantly, these intelligent beings learned of their creators' existence. They worshipped the gods with reverence, gave them names.

Aeris. Einari. Blight. Novika.

These were the original four. And at the very top of it all, adorned with a crown, silver in color and woven from pure divinity, sat Aeris.

Somewhere among the thousands upon thousands of years of development, Blight grew bored. He burnt villages and erupted long-dormant volcanoes for entertainment, despite the protests of his fellow gods. Aeris feared human extinction.

A human woman, devout to the gods but displeased by Blight's actions, prayed for help. Aeris named her their champion and assigned her a task: travel through the treacherous depths of the Underworld, and gather blood from the monsters residing there.

Nobody expected her to survive her journey. Aeris took great glee in her triumph.

Blight visited the mortal realm to teach the girl a lesson. Such was his demise. The mortal subdued him. Aeris led her through a ritual, at the end of which she coated a ceremonial knife with Monster Blood and stabbed Blight in the heart.

The god of fire existed no more.

The mortal, named Elaine, ascended to godhood at the age of twenty-three. The rush of divinity through her veins halted both her aging and her unborn child's. Elaine took Blight's place as the goddess of fire, and the developing infant took no Domain at all. The first ever god of nothing. This caused Elaine great suffering, but there wasn't much Aeris could do. Not on the day of her ascension, and not after. Aeris pitied her, but her ascension—and her child's—was for the good of Midir.

Humankind's recovery from Blight's terror was slow. Faith in the new goddess was tentative, but from the fires and destruction rose new farmland, new tools, new ways of life, and new devotion.

The following two thousand years comprised the Era of Prosperity. Aeris enjoyed this era. Mortalkind invented lightbulbs and vehicles that no longer needed to be pulled by animals. Cities grew and buildings pierced the skies. Midir was vibrant, even in the dead of night.

But despite Aeris's temperate rule, another god yearned for power. Einari.

Aeris remembered the day they lost the title of God King. Einari had asked for help with something in his chamber. The request, in hindsight, was rather vague. Aeris, unassuming, was happy to lend a hand, none the wiser.

Einari led Aeris into a back room, one they hadn't ever known existed. Einari had instructed them to sit upon a chair, then channeled some strange, foreign magic. Underworld magic. Aeris stood, affronted. Einari, cunning as he was, anticipated Aeris's distrust and wasted no time using his magic to pin them down, long tendrils of shadow and darkness restraining them.

Then, Einari reached into Aeris's mind and stole every memory pertaining to their status as God King. They didn't have any time to question Einari. It all happened too fast.

They remembered *not* remembering.

Nobody remembered. The gods jeered at Aeris. Any input they offered was cast aside and disparaged, only for someone else to speak the same thought and be applauded. And in the Mortal Realm, things didn't fare too much better for Aeris. With a snap of his fingers, Einari replaced old religious texts with new ones, ones where Einari was and had always been the king.

Mortalkind forgot, too.

A new normal descended. Einari ruled with a stricter temperament.

He encouraged mortals to worship him with unwavering devotion, and they did. Amazing, how pliable mortals were.

To praise the Midiri folk for their devotion, Einari graced the mortal realm with his presence. His blue skin turned tan, sun-kissed, and his long seafoam hair turned black. With piercing blue eyes, golden jewelry, and ornate robes draped over his body, there was no doubt this man was a god.

Not long passed before mortalkind realized a god could be utilized for personal gain.

It all started with a little girl.

Einari rescued her from a collapsing building. She and Einari were both injured as he shielded her from falling rubble, but Einari's golden blood mixed with the girl's, and her wounds sealed up. The girl told her family. Her family told their friends. Rumor escalated at an exponential rate, and it didn't take long for the entire world to hear.

Einari said, after the fact, he wished he had let the girl die.

Humankind was hellbent on trying to get their hands on God's Blood. People begged, threatened, and attacked Einari. As desperation built, so did market price. While many wanted God's Blood for wholesome purposes—curing a loved one, saving a wounded animal, among others—many lashed out at Einari so they could sell his blood for profit.

Aeris hunched over the reflecting pool, watching Einari hurry down a near-empty street, pursued by a man wielding a pistol. Bullets shattered nearby windows, damaged property. One bullet struck him in the back and pierced his lungs. Einari collapsed, and his pursuer siphoned as much blood as possible into the plastic bottles strapped to his belt. The man did not leave until there was no blood left in Einari's corpse.

When Einari's soul returned to the Heavens, he was irate. Over the next hundred mortal days, angry oceans threatened the landmasses. The water level crept higher, forcing millions of mortals from their homes to seek shelter at a higher elevation.

A vast majority of mortalkind died by drowning. Death was happy to welcome their souls into the Underworld. Those who did not die were forced to kill to make space on what little land was left. Aeris begged Einari to stop, to have compassion, but it was Novika who managed to convince him to cease before he drowned the entire world and decimated Novika's Domain.

Only the tallest mountaintops remained.

The human population, along with most animals, were nigh-extinct. And yet, they still worshipped Einari. Now, out of fear.

Over time, jagged mountaintops eroded into gentle hills, and Aeris—after a substantial fight with Einari—adjusted the density of the atmosphere to allow these people to thrive.

To host the regrowing population, many people dove undersea and salvaged steel to build boats. Most islands farmed lumber, but the industry was an unreliable one. Trees took years to grow, and they provided the oxygen mortals needed, and thus could not be felled indiscriminately. For a while, everyone worked together toward the same goal: survival. Humankind, though, had always been volatile. As the population regrew, the richest of the mortals pushed poor folk off the islands via high fees and taxes. The poor scraped by on the seas.

The catalyst for Aeris's downfall happened so fast nobody on the council could stop it.

The Big Four gathered in the Great Hall, each occupying one of the seats circling the reflecting pool. Here, Einari pitched the idea of introducing Death to the council. Novika was the first to speak out against their friend's idea. "He will cause nothing but trouble," Novika had said, which Elaine seconded.

"Death has no place here," Elaine said. "His Domain is not pure. Not like ocean, fire, wilds, and sky are."

"Do you not consider death to be a pure element?" Einari countered. "One cannot have life without it."

"His Domain is the Underworld—he needs to be present there to ensure his realm functions the way it's supposed to."

"The consensus is negative, Einari," Novika urged. "It's best we drop it."

Einari narrowed his eyes, displeased. "Fine. Meeting adjourned."

"Wait!" Aeris exclaimed. They jumped up from their seat. "There's something else we need to discuss."

Einari groaned. "Get on with it."

"The mortal realm has been flooded for one thousand years. I'd like to bring forth a vote for you to lower the sea level. It's cruel to have punished them for this long."

"I will do no such thing," Einari snapped. "Mortalkind is unworthy. Let them die."

"After they have worshipped us? Your anger is not worth the lives lost! What kind of king are you, if you do not protect those you rule?"

Einari stood. "You have no right to question my authority."

"I have every right! As a member of this council, I don't believe what you're doing is fair. I'm as authorized as Novika or Elaine!"

"Your authority will have to be remedied, then. You will be removed from the council, effective immediately."

"What!?" Elaine cried out. "You can't!"

"How about this: after the passing of one mortal day, we shall reconvene and vote. You are all dismissed."

The vote, whose results had to be unanimous to pass, never took place.

At a time which, in the mortal realm, would be considered the dead of night, Einari grabbed Aeris and dragged them into the same room where Einari extracted their first memory. Aeris kicked and fought. Once they arrived in the hidden chamber, he threw Aeris to the floor.

"I'm *so sorry* to do this, but you must learn your lesson. The mortals do not deserve a life of comfort when they've done nothing but exploit us. You shall see."

Einari was not sorry at all.

He conjured the same magic he'd used once before. He reached into Aeris's mind and plucked every last memory from within. Their mind wiped clean, Einari opened a portal to the Mortal Realm and shoved them through it.

The next thing Aeris knew, they were falling through a gap in the clouds and hurtling toward the ocean below. A single steel ship drifted in the near distance.

Hitting the ocean was the most painful thing they'd ever

experienced. Pain was mortal, and as such, was their first sensation in this new world. It was a miracle they survived the fall. Miracles were, of course, a commonplace occurrence for gods. Aeris had survived the fall because Einari wanted them to. After all, dying would send them back to the Heavens prematurely.

"Do you think they can hear us?"

There was a pause.

"Crow?"

Their head hurt.

"Crow, come back to us, we're worried sick."

Their head *hurt.*

Aeris's eyes snapped open with a jolt. They gasped as though they'd emerged from underwater. They coughed and sputtered. Their lungs ached. They stared up at the surprised faces of Mouse, Karina, and Faye, all huddled around the cot they lay in. Shaky, Aeris attempted to push themself up. Their mortal body was weak, unreliable.

Karina placed a hand upon their shoulder and urged them to lie back down, speaking words which sounded muffled and distant to their frazzled brain.

Cognizance came back slowly. They lay in Jonah's cabin, bundled up in cedar-scented bedsheets. Funny, how it was always Jonah's cabin, and never their own, when they woke up injured.

They closed their eyes and lay a while longer. The cotton in their ears faded, and the world around them came back to higher clarity. Only after they could make out the footsteps of another occupant in the room did they open their eyes again.

When Aeris found the strength, they sat up. Karina placed her hand upon their back and handed them a flask of water. Mouse hurried out, and when he returned, he held a plate of food. Roasted fish and bread. Aeris couldn't help but chuckle. Such mortal needs. They signed a *thank-you* as they took the plate.

Einari had hated being mortal. He spoke of nothing but misery and held nothing but contempt. But Aeris had grown fond of mortality. The pains and the joys alike were what made life worth living. Aeris loved eating, drinking, sleeping, bathing. They loved wrestling with their crewmates and looking at Willow's art. They loved the feeling of getting splinters from rough wood, no matter how much it hurt. They loved watching the sun rise and set, the feeling of the wind, the glimmer of stars far above.

Aeris had learned so much in such a short span of time. They lived immersed in the struggles mortalkind faced.

These people were not evil. They were desperate.

38

68th Storm, Great Flood 1058

When Aeris next awoke, their mouth was dry as bone. They let out a tiny groan and stretched their stiff legs. Their toes brushed against something warm. A strand of ginger hair tickled their nose.

There was something primal in them, something mortal, begging Aeris to remain here with Jonah. There wasn't a care in the world: two bodies, two souls, tangled together. In the grander scheme of things, they were insignificant, like tiny, distant stars in a vast night sky. More than anything else, Aeris wished they could be small. They wished they could be *Crow*. If only it were so easy. If only they weren't now held down by the crushing weight of memory.

Aeris sat up. Their muscles were sore, jellylike. They swung their legs off the edge of the cot, bare feet touching down on the floor. Beside them, Jonah grumbled in his sleep. Long, muscular arms snaked around Aeris's torso, trying to pull them back in.

Look at you, Aeris thought with a smile, gazing down at Jonah's slack face, void of all the tension he held in his waking hours. *You big softie.*

Aeris slipped out of the cot and put on their socks and boots. They snuck out of Jonah's cabin.

The *Vengeance* rocked at Einari's mercy. Like the ship, all Aeris had been for thousands of years was a pawn, a toy, under Einari's cruel,

"

unforgiving hand. All this time, they'd been complicit—all of the gods had. Aeris, Novika, Elaine, and every single minor god. Aeris was furious they'd let this go on for so long.

I didn't know, they justified. How could they have fixed a problem they weren't aware existed?

A sharp breeze announced their presence as they stepped out into the open air above deck. Karina, Faye, and Willow were milling about. Aeris didn't take the time to catalogue what they were doing.

There's no excuse, another part of them argued back. *Einari did nothing to conceal his distaste for me. If I'd investigated a little deeper...*

The sun was too bright. They sliced their finger on the suture needle they'd tucked into their pocket, and dark clouds rolled in. When the rain came, the crewmates scattered across the deck looked up from their work to offer Aeris a disgruntled glare. Their glares didn't last long, though. Their displeasure washed away with the rain as one by one, it dawned on the crewmates that *Crow* was on their feet, *Crow* was okay.

Karina hurried over with a relieved smile. "How are you feeling?" she asked. "We were worried sick, you know."

Aeris didn't know how they were feeling, so they didn't answer. They took to standing at the bow. They leaned their elbows against the rail and muttered to themself in Køveni. The crew's stares bore into the back of Aeris's skull, and they tried their best to ignore it. The crew meant well. They were all worried.

Aeris speaking out against the flood had been the final straw, the last in a long chain of events. Einari wasn't trying to teach Aeris a lesson, as they'd learnt from Argonaut. No, Einari wanted Aeris dead, gone, out of the equation. And right now, Einari was unchecked and teeming with the same power that had killed Blight.

Aeris needed to get back to the Heavens.

They turned to face the crew. Mouse and Jonah had joined at some point. Aeris wasn't quite sure when. It didn't matter.

"I need one of you to kill me," they announced. Their statement was simple and matter-of-fact, but the crew looked appalled. Jonah, in particular, appeared stricken with abject horror at the prospect of Aeris's request.

"What?" Karina found her voice first. "Crow, no!"

"Please, you need to trust me."

"We're not killing you!"

"There's no other way!" Aeris shouted. "The quickest way to the Heavens from Midir is through mortal death! If you won't do it, I'll do it myself."

Aeris turned their gaze toward the vast waterscape surrounding the *Vengeance.* Drowning would be a miserable way to die. Risky, too, with the ocean teeming with monsters. They would run the risk of their death being made permanent, or worse, a monster taking its wrath out on the remaining crew.

If not by drowning, then by knife or gun. Their hand floated over the hilt of the sword strapped to their hip.

"Nobody is killing anybody," Jonah growled. "Pull yourself together."

"Right now," Aeris said, slow, deliberate. "Einari is up there, amassing power, making decrees that will destroy us. And so long as I'm *living*, I am *useless*, do you understand? There's nothing I can do in this body to save the realm I worked so hard to build!"

"We can help you," Karina said, taking a step toward Aeris. She took their trembling hand. "But we need a fuller understanding."

"There's no time." They pulled their hand from Karina's and turned to face the ocean. They drew their blade. They'd wake up in Judgment soon.

They did not make it far. A strong hand gripped their shoulder and turned them around. Before they could react, they were pulled into a tight hug. The vivid red of Jonah's coat filled their vision. Their heart softened.

Jonah gave them permission to stop being Aeris and start being *Crow* again.

"There are other ways," Jonah muttered into their ear. He *was* right—if they were at their full power, they could have conjured a portal, but they couldn't easily perform such a feat whilst locked in a mortal body. Not without bleeding themself to death first. "When Elaine visited, back when she rescued you from the bullet wound, she was...

retrieved by an external force. Einari."

"Einari conditioned every single one of them to hate me. Nobody's going to try to bring me back."

They now knew what worth they were supposed to have. But if nobody else remembered they were the rightful God King, then they would still be the Fool, and nobody would take their claims of kinghood to heart.

"Then we'll figure something out." Jonah took a step back. "I'm guessing you got some of your memories back?"

"All of them." Crow's posture slumped. "Thousands upon thousands of years. It's a lot to sort through."

"I can't begin to understand what it must feel like," Karina said. "But when you're ready, we're here for you."

Crow nodded.

In the passing days, the crew gave Crow the space they needed to sort themself out. They spent most of their time on the crow's nest, staring up at the troubled gray clouds above.

At some point along the way, they filled their friends in on their newfound memories. Those worth sharing, at least. They did not mention their kinghood. They danced around the issue as much as they could. The crew caught on to their flightiness but seemed to know better than to press for sensitive information, so the glaring detail slid under the rug, untouched.

"I can't get through to Elaine," Crow admitted. They sat on the floor with Jonah in the middle of their cabin. "Nor Novika. They're not answering my prayers. I... I hope they're okay."

"Is there a chance they're not?" Jonah asked.

"There's always a chance. I hate being so cut off from everything."

"Try a lesser god," he suggested. "One who doesn't get prayed to as much. They might hear you. Like, I don't know, a god of...grass?"

Crow couldn't help but snicker. Jonah's lack of theological

knowledge was endearing.

"There's a nymph of the forests," Crow muttered. "She works under Novika. Ever since the flood, her Domain dwindled to the few lumber farming islands. Her name is Víchí. She's...functionally dead. She receives scant mortal prayer. But she still exists, she lives in the Heavens and waits for the day she can rebuild her influence."

"Do you need space? To pray?"

"Yes, please."

Jonah disappeared from the cabin. Crow spent the next hour and a half praying, but they received no response. They couldn't help but wonder if their prayers were reaching the Heavens at all.

Could a god pray to another god?

39

"Do you think it's possible Einari is not the God King?"
—The Grand Catalogue of Last Words: Great Flood Era. Death #2,977,913,700. Drowned. This soul was sent to Punishment for heresy.

73rd Storm, Great Flood 1058

Below deck was too stuffy. Above deck was too watery. They were tired of seeing the ocean everywhere they turned. Crow considered Einari's intentions: what could he gain from kinghood? Power, of course, as if being a cardinal member of the Big Four wasn't already enough. Was there more, though? Something Crow wasn't privy to?

Leadership was slippery. Someday, Einari would lose his footing. His Domain would overpower all life on this beautiful planet, until only water, decayed bones on the sea floor, and a damn lot of fish remained. If Death found his seat on the council, such a fate would be assured. But what would he accomplish, aside from hate-fueled retribution for sins a thousand years old?

His intentions would not improve the pantheon. They would not improve Midir.

Somewhere along the way, the *Vengeance* docked at the Midnorthern hub. Karina had decreed they needed to stop for supplies. Rope. Tinder and matches. Food. Whale oil. New bulbs for the cabin deck lights. Medical supplies. Crow wasn't paying much attention as Karina rattled off the list to the crew. Everyone was gathered by the gangplank, but Crow hung back. They didn't plan to disembark. They had things to do, like *fret* and *worry*.

"Crow, are you paying attention?" Karina asked, and Crow's head snapped up from where they'd spent the entirety of the meeting analyzing the floorboards. Their neck ached.

"No," Crow said. There was no point in lying.

Karina's mouth turned to a frustrated frown. She opened her mouth, no doubt considering chastising them for not listening, then paused. Her face morphed into something of sympathy.

"It's okay," she said. "Your ship is encumbered."

"The *Vengeance* isn't my ship."

"It's an expression, silly," Karina stifled a giggle. "It means you've got a lot on your mind."

"Oh."

"Okay." Karina clapped her hands together. The sharp sound jolted Crow. "Everyone, pair up and go look for your assigned supplies. Crow, you need a serious pick-me-up. You're coming with me."

"I shouldn't."

"You *are*. What else are you going to do? Pace around like Jonah?"

Jonah scoffed.

Teasing the captain should have lifted Crow's spirits. They quite enjoyed poking fun at him. But everything was so dull now. So devoid of life. How could they find joy with the knowledge they now possessed?

"Come on!" Karina urged. She took Crow by the wrist and urged them along.

Faye and Willow were already halfway down the gangplank. With Karina taking Crow to be her partner, that left Jonah and Mouse buddied up. The combination, Crow mused, was a match made in Paradise. They'd be the most efficient pair in the crew.

"Jonah, you're in charge of looking for food."

"I thought you were," Jonah grumbled.

"Change of plan. Promise me you'll make sure the food isn't rotting before you buy it, okay?"

"That was *one time*, Karina."

Karina herded Crow down the gangplank and onto the hub. Crow had to admit, the change of scenery was refreshing.

"We're going to treat you to something nice, okay?" Though Karina posed it as a question, Crow could tell in her tone that there was no room for argument.

"Sure."

"With more enthusiasm!"

"Yeah."

They trudged beside Karina as she led them through the market, pointing out all the little knickknacks in each of the stalls. Jewelry, books, plants, handcrafted trinkets. None of them interested Crow.

"Hey, look at this!" Karina called, and she crossed the dock, dodging around other hubgoers. A few people glared at her for cutting in front of their path.

Crow joined Karina and eyed the item in her hand: a long, sleek tube, built of steel and painted black. "A spyglass?"

"A telescope! You can use it to look at the stars. I'm buying it for you," Karina announced with such finality, Crow couldn't bring themself to decline. She passed a few shell coins to the shopkeeper, then tucked the telescope and tripod into the burlap bag she carried over her shoulder. It was an awkward fit.

They carried on.

Something caught Crow's eye from a young man who made hand-sculpted clay jewelry. A necklace, boasting a delicate carving of the sun. They observed the craftsmanship and iconography. Triangular rays emitted from the sun, and inlaid in the center was a glittery little topaz.

"I knew you'd find something you'd like," Karina said with warm affection. "I'll buy this for you, too."

"No, I—" Crow stared down at the necklace in their hands, laced with a braided twine chain. "I'll buy it myself. How much does the sign say?"

"Ten shell."

In front of the craftsman sat a locked box with a slit at the top. Crow deposited the money into the box. The man smiled at Crow. Crow offered him a shaky smile back as they tucked the necklace into their pocket and stepped away.

"Feeling any better?" Karina asked as they rounded the corner. Ahead, Crow spotted Jonah and Mouse. They stood in the middle of a wider platform, chatting with a young woman in a magenta dress and a silk headwrap. She was unfamiliar to Crow, but Jonah chatted with her as though she were a friend.

"I...think so."

"Retail therapy," Karina said. "It works, you know. Helps you get your mind off things."

"I suppose." Crow adjusted the collar of their shirt. "You would have adored the Era of Prosperity. They had malls so tall they pierced the sky. Everything was bright and colorful, even at night. Lots of little trinkets and things to collect."

"How long ago?"

"A smidge more than a thousand years. It preceded the flood."

"I'd love for you to tell me all about it. I—oh! Jonah and Mouse are up there! And Priya, too. Want to go say hello?"

"Sure."

Crow couldn't help but feel apprehensive as they approached. Their mortal instinct told them new people equated to trouble. Jonah wasn't one to gab with people he didn't like, though. Priya was, therefore, trustworthy, but it was hard not to let the anxiety creep in. Crow walked behind Karina to conceal themself from the new face.

"Ah!" Priya exclaimed as she met Crow's eyes. "You managed to save your god, huh? It's a pleasure to meet you, Your Grace."

Priya bowed before Crow. Being revered on such a personal level felt odd. Crow was accustomed to devotion, yes. Such was the nature of mortalkind. But to be bowed before rather than be prayed to? To witness devotion on the mortal plane, standing on the same ground as those who revered them?

"Um," Crow stammered, "You knew about me?"

"Of course," Priya rolled her eyes. "Jonah won't shut his yap about you."

"He..."

"Crow, Crow, Crow. I wish I were joking."

"Enough," Jonah grumbled. He rubbed his cheeks, as if it would do anything to quell the flush. "Crow, you've met Priya. Sort of. A better way to put it: Priya's met you."

"You were dying," Priya piped in. "I got Shav's help, put you in stasis. Jonah says Elaine came to give you her blood."

"I..." Crow paused. "Wait, you can commune with the gods?"

"Indeed. Blessed by Irina." *The messenger goddess.*

"You can help me!" Crow lit up. Hope wasn't all lost. "I'm trying to get in contact with Víchí."

"Why her?"

"She won't be swamped with prayer. I need to get home. Someone has to be able to open a portal for me, right? I need to know what's going on. I'm cut off from it all."

"I see." Priya hummed, thoughtful. "I'll help you."

Relief washed over Crow. "Thank you."

The *Vengeance* spent two days docked at the Midnorthern hub. Beside them was the *Sapphire*: a small vessel, but not insignificant. Crow paced and fretted, and Jonah allowed them to, no matter how much the rest of the crew complained about the disturbance.

Somewhere along the way, Crow perched upon the crow's nest, sitting atop the safety railing and staring down at the hub below. They observed the little specks of people, trying to pick out a singular person and track them. With the crowds, it was nigh-impossible, but it kept Crow occupied.

As Crow was considering descending, they turned to find themself face-to-face with Jonah. Crow stared, puzzled.

"You're afraid of heights."

"The things you make me do..." Jonah grumbled, bashful.

"Are we allowed to be here?" Crow asked. "Is there a time limit on docking at a hub? Fees to pay?"

"Merchants dock for weeks at a time. We'll be fine. There's always a risk of raiders, but it's nothing we can't handle."

Jonah settled cross-legged in the center of the crow's nest, his back against the mast. Crow hopped off the rail to join him. They much preferred their previous perch, but they knew better than to stress Jonah out any further. Besides, if they weren't close to Jonah, they wouldn't be able to drape themself across his lap, would they?

Jonah grunted when Crow flopped down on top of him. "I like my personal space, you know."

"I like your personal space, too."

Jonah grumbled some sort of protest, but he also buried his nose in Crow's soft, curly black hair, so Crow counted it as a win.

"Did you find anything in the market?" he asked, his voice low. Crow could feel the rumble of his chest. "With Karina?"

"I did. Well, Karina bought me a telescope. I'll try it out tonight. But I found..."

Crow rifled through their coat pockets until they produced the necklace. They held it up for Jonah to look at, then clasped it around his neck. It fell below his collarbone. Crow paused to admire their handiwork.

Ilinoé.

"Why do you keep equating me to the sun?" Jonah asked, a confused frown creasing his features. Crow found it amusing. "I feel like I'm more... I don't know, I'm..."

"I know what happened with Argonaut shook you, Jonah, but you shine brighter than you realize." They didn't mention Sophie. They didn't need to.

Jonah shook his head. "I'm a monster."

"Your blood does not define you. Your heart does."

"The heart pumps blood."

"Don't—wait—quit trying to mess me up!" Crow squeaked. "You know what I mean!"

"I'm just saying."

"Doofus," Crow jabbed their pointer finger into Jonah's chest. "Dweeb."

Jonah chuckled.

Later, Crow set up their telescope on the quarterdeck and spent the whole night watching the stars.

Priya boarded the *Vengeance* on Tuesday. When Crow spotted her, they dropped the cannonball they'd been lugging—eliciting a yelp of surprise from Willow—and ran to the gangplank to greet her. Karina ushered them over to the fire pit. Priya, Crow, and Karina sat, and when Jonah joined, he remained standing, leaned against the gunwale, arms folded across his chest.

"Communing with a forgotten god is not easy," Priya said, wiping a bead of sweat from her brow. "Pretty sure my ship'll reek of patchouli until dew season."

"Any luck?" Crow pushed.

"Víchí doesn't know how to open a portal to bring you back. Even if they did, they wouldn't have enough power."

Crow's heart sank. Even Priya's help amounted to nothing. They were lost, powerless, frustrated.

"They told me, though," Priya continued, "to tell *Their Highness* the entire Heavens is in chaos. Every god is up in arms. Whether that is in your favor or not remains to be seen, but every god remembers their true king."

"True king?" Jonah repeated. "You mean Einari isn't...?"

"No. He stole the throne."

"If Einari isn't the true king, then who is?"

Crow had hoped to avoid telling their crew, their family. They didn't want to cause anyone additional stress. They turned away, unable to bear Jonah's reaction.

"I am," Crow whispered so quietly, their voice was almost lost to the breeze. Jonah's gaze bore into the back of their head.

"You..." Jonah started. He paused. "You?"

"Yes."

"Hell," Jonah groaned, and Crow dared to peek. His face was buried in his hands. "The God King, on *my* ship. I'm going to rot in the Underworld someday."

Crow let a laugh escape. "Don't be dramatic."

"I'm not being dramatic!" Jonah exclaimed. "It's *perfectly reasonable* to have a crisis over every shitty thing I've done to the most powerful damn entity in the universe."

"You're not going to rot."

"Priya," Karina cut in. "Is there any other way to get to the Heavens?"

"Trust me, if I knew, I would have gone up there myself long ago," Priya said.

"What about the other gods? If we got through to Víchí, we could get through to Novika or Elaine. They could open one for you."

"If it took two days for Priya to get through to Víchí, it'll take even longer to get through to the Big Four goddesses," Crow said. "The chances are too slim. Besides..." they trailed off. Their posture wilted.

"Besides, what?" Jonah prompted.

"Do you think they've forgotten about me?" Their voice was small.

"Forgotten about you? No. You're unforgettable."

"Ha," Crow chuckled, but it was halfhearted. "I appreciate the sentiment, but you know it's not true. It's happened before, and... I guess I wouldn't be surprised if, in the calamity of it all, I was left behind."

"Crow..."

"And if I'm not left behind, will I be accepted? Nobody's going to throw thousands of years of conditioning away. I'm a joke."

"So, what can we do?" Karina asked. "If we can't get you to the Heavens."

"I can still make a difference. I can do *something*."

"Which is...?"

"We go back to Argonaut. We stop his ascension," Crow said, sitting up straight and looking Karina dead in the eye, "and we take him out of the equation."

"Kill him?" Karina asked, her voice wavering.

"If he kills *me,* he'll take my place and pave the way for Death's rise to the council. There's too much at stake, and I don't trust Argonaut with the sky."

"You're taking a damn big risk," Jonah grumbled. "Taking your life straight to him won't solve anything—it'll give him the opportunity to fulfil his goals. Your life is his biggest barrier. Preserve it."

"I can't sit idly by. I refuse."

Karina came to their rescue. "We'll fight by your side, Crow. Always. *Right,* Jonah?"

Jonah scoffed at the glare Karina shot him, but still, he acquiesced. "I don't think it's a good idea, but...yes."

"Well," Priya said, hands on her hips, "I'm no fighter. I'll be making my leave."

"Thanks for your help," Crow called after her as she made her way to the gangplank. Before she crossed, she offered Crow a small, courteous bow. Then, she was gone.

"Are you going to be alright?" Crow asked Jonah. They sat on the edge of their hammock, watching as Jonah reorganized the books on their shelf: books they'd borrowed and never returned, which grew disorganized and scattered mere days after Jonah last neatened them.

Jonah paused. His grip around the book he was holding tightened.

"You'll have to face your sister again," Crow added. "I know it hurt you to see her. You can't keep shoving those feelings down."

Jonah stared at the book's brown, worn-out cover. His eyes glistened, threatening tears, his face screwed up into something pained.

"I'll be fine," he whispered. Crow didn't believe him.

40

"What is the difference between sea and sky? They are both blue. They are both vast. But one suffocates all life, while the other we would not survive without. I care not if this sends me to Punishment, but I am devout in my love for Aeris. Einari cannot take my faith from me like he's taken my home."
—The Grand Catalogue of Last Words: Great Flood Era. Death #0,000,000,861. Drowned. This soul was sent to Punishment for heresy.

75th Storm, Great Flood 1058

Jonah toyed with the necklace draped around his neck. He hadn't taken it off since Crow gave it to him three days ago. Perhaps he would choke on the twine in his sleep someday, but he didn't dare remove it. The weight against his chest proved to be a calming force, one that halted his anxieties enough to render him somewhat functional.

Crow, too, was anxious. No wonder. They had more going on than Jonah could have ever imagined. The nervous energy spread. Mouse confessed to dreaming that the cannons clogged mid-fight, leaving the ship defenseless. He handled his anxiety by repairing every cannon on the ship. Thrice. Meanwhile, Willow worried about supply rations, even though the crew had restocked at the hub, and Karina plotted out every possible course of action once engaged in combat with Argonaut.

Jonah was trying real damn hard to hold himself together, but the prospect of seeing Sophie was unbearable. The necklace was a minor comfort.

The *God King*. He was still wrapping his mind around the news. A god's offering to a mortal, full of the same reverence accompanying a mortal's offerings to a god. Crow loved everything around them with such devotion that Jonah worried he'd drown.

But Crow was not the ocean.

Crow was the sky. They were expansive and infinite. They were the clouds and sun and snow, they were the orange sunset to the deep black night, and every single hue between. They were beautiful, timeless, awe-inspiring. Crow had created everything a mortal needed to be alive. Oxygen. Rain. Sunlight. Jonah would not drown in Crow's tempest, but he very well may suffocate.

He was okay with that.

Crow scrambled down the mast when they spotted Argonaut's *Godkiller.* They leapt and swung down the ropes, much to Jonah's ever-constant displeasure, and today, as they landed, they tripped over their feet.

"The *Godkiller,*" Crow threw their finger out toward the bow. "North-northeast."

Jonah glanced out to sea, eyeing the *Godkiller*—and the puny island in the near distance. The *Godkiller's* bow pointed toward the island, foamy white water churning in the ship's wake.

"He may need to restock at that island," Jonah said to his crew, who had all gathered around, awaiting orders. "If he's short on supplies, we'll have an advantage. Mouse," Jonah turned to the engineer, then signed, "you're on navigation. Full speed ahead. Sail us between Argonaut and the island. I want to block him from the pier."

Mouse nodded and hurried to the helm.

"Everyone else," he snapped, "prepare for combat. I want all the port-side cannons primed and ready to go. I want the gangplank on standby. I want all nonessential items to be tied down or stowed. *Go!*"

The crew scattered. Faye, Willow, Crow, and Karina set to work. Faye primed the four port-side cannons. Karina hauled the gangplank from starboard to port, placing it in an accessible but unobtrusive spot against the gunwale. Willow and Crow set to work organizing the deck. They tucked stray cleaning supplies into the supply closet, strapped down every barrel and tool, and secured the lines.

The *Vengeance* was not a stealthy vessel. If Argonaut noticed their approach, however, he did nothing to prepare. The *Godkiller* remained on its course toward the island. The margin grew slimmer.

The *Vengeance* pulled in front of the dock before the *Godkiller* could get there, but the *Godkiller* did not slow.

"Anchor down!" Jonah yelled.

"No way!" Karina snapped back. "He'll run right into us!"

"I know."

"Jonah—"

"Anchor us down, Karina! He's calling our bluff. It's either us or innocent lives." He glanced back at the docks to the *Vengeance's* starboard side. The *Godkiller* was massive and heavy—there was no chance of it slowing in time, even if Argonaut had wanted to.

Karina heaved the anchor into the ocean. This close to the island, the water was shallow enough for the anchor to make purchase. It caught in the reef below, and the *Vengeance* stilled.

Now, all the crew could do was brace.

"Jonah," Crow 's voice turned Jonah's focus away from the *Godkiller*. "Whatever happens today..."

"Don't say another word. I won't let you."

Crow pulled Jonah into a tight hug. Their hair tickled his nose. Crow's small stature made it easy to nestle against him, their cheek pressed against his collarbone. They said nothing. Jonah was grateful for it. He didn't want some grand goodbye speech or a profession of feelings. Crow would be fine. Jonah would be fine. His crew would be fine.

"*Incoming!*" Faye shrieked. "He's not even *trying* to slow down!"

"Fire a warning shot. Everyone, get to the helm!" Jonah barked, pulling away from his embrace with Crow. Faye aimed the cannon off the *Godkiller's* port side bow. She lit the fuse. Willow, Karina, and Mouse scrambled to the quarterdeck.

With a concussive *BOOM,* the cannonball sailed past the *Godkiller* and splashed into the water below. The two figures who stood upon the deck—Argonaut and Sophie—flinched.

Faye loaded the cannon, then primed, aimed, and fired a second cannonball. This one slammed into the *Godkiller's* hull, leaving a deep, gnarly dent in the steel. Then, she too scrambled for the relative safety of higher ground. Jonah followed.

But halfway between the helm and the projected point of collision, he stopped and turned around. Crow had not moved. They stood in the center of the deck, staring down the *Godkiller's* bow.

"Crow!" Jonah snapped. "Come on!"

Sharp blue eyes met Jonah's gaze. "Go." Their voice was soft, carried on the same wind that ruffled their curly black hair.

"Don't risk your damn life like this!"

"I'm a god," Crow smiled, a combination of affection and a healthy dose of adrenaline. "I can handle it."

You're a god, Jonah thought, *but don't forget, that's the Godkiller.*

Crow waved him to safety, and despite everything in his body begging him to grab them while he could, he ran to the helm. He heaved himself up the ladder and joined his crew at the sternmost edge.

"What are they doing!?" Karina gasped, her eyes glued on Crow on the deck below.

"I don't know."

"They're going to get themself killed!"

Jonah straightened his posture. "I trust them."

Nobody was prepared for the moment the *Godkiller* slammed into the *Vengeance.* The impact sent the crew stumbling. The gunwale stopped anyone from toppling over the edge, but Jonah figured his back would bruise something fierce as he crashed against it. Wood splintered in all directions, the *Godkiller's* reinforced steel far too strong for Jonah's beloved ship to bear. Beside him, Faye hunched over on her knees, a thick splinter lodged in her shoulder.

"Is the dinghy still intact?" Jonah gasped.

Willow peered over the starboard edge. "Yessir."

"Good." He turned to Mouse and signed, "Get everyone to the docks."

Mouse helped Faye down to the main deck, mere inches above sea level. Willow hurried behind them. Karina lingered at Jonah's side—Jonah nudged her. "Go," he urged.

"What about you?"

"Crow can't swim."

With a curt nod, Karina scrambled down the ladder and joined the crew at the dinghy. Mouse disengaged it from the ship, and the crew made their way to safety.

Crow, on the deck below, had found a sturdy stance, which did them little good as the *Vengeance's* wooden deck splintered. Golden blood dripped down their bicep. They, too, must have been hurt by the splintering wood.

"Argonaut!" Crow shouted as the *Godkiller* came to a halt. They threw out their arm in front of them, and their fingertips brushed the *Godkiller's* hull. Any closer, and Crow would have been crushed. Jonah winced.

"How brave of you," Argonaut jeered from atop his ship. "You think you have the power to stop me? You're nothing more than a fly beneath my boot."

"Bold words to say to the God King."

"You're a weak, pathetic mortal, cast away because nobody wants you. How does it feel to fade away into oblivion, Aeris? How does it feel for a king to be forgotten? You will die, and I will rise to give Death the council. This is the beginning of a new era."

"You can't even fathom what you're getting yourself into!" Crow spat. "Do you think Death wants to see your deal through to the end? He'll throw you by the wayside the moment you give him the council seat. This path will not offer you glory."

The *Vengeance* had sunk enough, now, to coat the main deck in a thin layer of water, which soaked Crow to the ankle. Jonah's beloved ship, the ship he'd grown up on, was sinking fast. Soon, all the memories attached to this vessel would lie on the sea floor. Jonah's feet slid. He struggled to keep his footing as the *Vengeance* tipped. Crow, not far from the impact site, was doomed to lose their balance and fall into the water soon.

The scaly head of a sea monster breached the surface. Jonah jolted as a tentacle gripped the *Vengeance's* bowsprit. The appendage's weight jerked the whole ship downward. On the island behind him, people panicked, fleeing farther inland. As workers on the docks pushed and shoved, a few fell off and into the water. Those who fell were in a frenzy to pull themselves back up—even more so when the monster snapped one unfortunate man into its jaws.

"Why don't you come up here?" Argonaut asked. "We can settle this face-to-face."

Sophie dropped a ladder. *Don't take the bait,* Jonah wanted to call out to Crow. But they were far beyond his command. They were the God King.

Crow hurried up the ladder. Jonah said nothing. Jonah *was* nothing.

The helm became a tiny island in the ocean. It wouldn't be much longer, by Jonah's estimate, until there was no solid floor beneath his feet at all. Alone on the *Vengeance,* Jonah would have to swim to shore, with nothing but the sea monster to keep him company.

Argonaut nudged Sophie's arm and pointed toward the *Vengeance.* Sophie dove off the *Godkiller* and hit the ocean with a splash.

He wasn't ready to confront her.

Jonah wasn't sure he'd ever seen Sophie so adept at swimming. Sure, she'd always loved swimming as a kid, but she swam with the clumsiness of any mortal human being. Now, she tore through the water like it was nothing at all.

Sophie climbed onto what was left of the *Vengeance's* helm. She wrung out her shirt. The black shirt and off-green slacks, Jonah thought, were combat-practical but not Sophie's style. She'd always loved flowy dresses and colorful blouses. The militaristic look did not suit her. This Sophie was so... so *different* from the girl Jonah had once known.

She had a broadsword strapped across her back and a pistol sheathed at her hip. Sophie shouldn't be a fighter. This was wrong.

"Argonaut says I have to kill you," Sophie's voice was quiet. "For not joining us."

"You don't have to. You're not his puppet, Soph."

"I'm bound to him," she said. "I can't be any farther than half a ship's distance away from him. You left us. You left *me!*"

"I had to. Sophie, I—you sail a path I can't follow."

Sophie's jaw tensed. "Fine," she said, her voice flat.

Sophie drew her sword and charged. *The gun would have been a more efficient weapon,* Jonah thought. *But she's not looking for efficiency.* Jonah drew his blade and parried her strike, and as he did, his stomach flipped, a hot searing unsteadiness flooding his core. His throat felt thick, tight, choked. He had tried so damn hard to quell this anxiety, only for it to make its resurgence here.

"Did you ever care about me at all?" Sophie screamed as she threw another sloppy strike.

"Of course I did!" Jonah swerved to dodge another strike. "I love you, Soph!"

"Then what's the problem!?" Tears streamed down her face. Jonah hated when she cried. "Death has given us a chance! We could *be something,* Jonah! Something bigger than…than *this!*"

"What you want us to be is not what Death wants us to be." Sophie's foot caught his ankle, and he tripped. He fell to his knees with a splash. The *Vengeance* would not be afloat much longer now that water was gathering over the last remaining surface. The doors against the wall to the quarterdeck, leading below, snapped off their hinges, allowing water to flood inside and weigh the ship down. He stood and stomped on the deck. They couldn't fight if they were swimming. *Sink, sink!* "He wants to use us as weaponry. Are you a weapon, Sophie?"

"It's a means to an end. We're going to be important. We're going to mean something." Sophie grabbed Jonah by the collar of his shirt. Jonah could have maneuvered out of this grip with ease if this had been anyone else. But with Soph, all he could do was stand there and take it. "Come home with me, Jonah. It'll be okay. I can get Death to rebuild the *Vengeance.* It could be like I'd never died. Like Aeris never ruined your life."

"They didn't—"

"You'll have a home, and…and…a family! You won't have to worry about whether you can feed everyone. There'll be no fighting. The Underworld isn't all misery and torture, Jonah. All souls go there. We'll rule Paradise."

Sophie released his lapel and pulled him into a hug. He couldn't bring himself to lift his arms and hug her back. His limbs felt as though they were made of lead, weighing him down, weighing his ship down as it sank.

"Give me your word," Sophie begged. "Stay with me. I don't want to hurt you. Argonaut will help us."

"Argonaut promised to help me before. He's a liar and a crook."

"This time it will be different. Argonaut will pave the way for Death, and we can find our new home. Death said he'll build us a Domain. It'd be so cool, Jonah. We'll be—well, not quite gods, but we could be something else, something unique. You and me. Son and daughter of Death. Your crew can go on without you, but I don't think I can."

Sophie pulled back and sheathed her sword. She took Jonah's hand in her own. Her skin was icy. Alive as she seemed, her flesh never quite shook the chill of death.

"I don't..." Jonah couldn't think straight. "I don't want to join Argonaut, nor Death. If it were you and me, no other variables, no *Paradise* nonsense—"

"Means to an end, Jonah. It'll be the two of us soon enough. No Argonaut, no Death. I promise. We can catch up. I'm sure you have a lot of stories to tell!"

He knew he shouldn't. Like a sailor lured in by the tempting call of a siren, this path was a dark, dangerous one. But even with the sun-shaped necklace around Jonah's neck, Crow was a blinding star, and Jonah was a black hole. They were, by nature, incompatible. Sophie, though... Sophie was his sister. Sophie was *home.*

"What do I have to do?" Jonah whispered. He dropped his sword and leaned against Sophie as the helm sank farther into the ocean. He wished Sophie's skin was warmer.

"How do you feel about killing a god?"

41

"To sacrifice is to love."
—The Grand Catalogue of Last Words: Great Flood Era. Death #0,000,014,946. Shot in the head. At the gates of Judgment, she stated: "I would have taken a bullet for her any day."

75th Storm, Great Flood 1058

What was it worth, to kill one to be with another? To betray for the sake of loyalty? This wasn't a choice Jonah ever fathomed he'd have to make. They were both so special, so bright, so innocent.

Though, were either Sophie or Crow innocent?

If someone had asked Jonah a few weeks ago, he would have said Sophie was. She had bright eyes and an optimistic disposition. Despite this, she'd never gotten the chance to become someone, to leave her mark on history. She was twenty-one when she died.

He presumed her death had ended her. Her death had been her beginning. *Pirates,* Jonah remembered. *He gripped her hand as he ran. Confined to the ship's perimeter, escape was futile. Still, though, he ran, hoping to get below deck and hide. Someone snatched Sophie before his hand could brush the door, and when he whirled around, there was a knife lodged in her back. Her body, bloodied and still, grew pale as crimson stained the wood at Jonah's feet.*

The pirates had slaughtered Sophie to awaken the monster side of her, to turn her—and Jonah—into a weapon for Argonaut's gain.

Sophie stood before him as though nothing had changed, as if death were a mere obstacle she had cleared. She was not the innocent girl Jonah remembered her to be. She hungered, now, like Argonaut, like Death, for something more than she could have. Even still, her proposition beckoned his weak, torn heart.

If he had to choose, maybe he'd choose Soph.

And Crow... They were a god. No god was capable of innocence. The two terms couldn't be any more opposite. Every god, no matter how benevolent, was responsible in some manner for mortal suffering. Jonah knew Crow would agree. But those glassy blue eyes, so full of wonder over every joy and pain the mortal realm offered... They held a different sort of innocence.

Crow was far more important, in the scheme of the universe, than Soph could ever be. They'd left their mark on Midir, and there were plenty more they still needed to make. Without Crow, would Einari and Death take over and choke out mortality for good? Would Jonah doom his own species by taking his sister's side?

So, would he choose Crow?

His crew yelled from the dock. Perhaps they wanted him to get to safety. Perhaps they wanted him to put up more of a fight. Jonah's legs were jellylike and weak under Sophie's gaze. The thought of being with Sophie again after so long, versus the prospect of losing Crow, was too much to bear.

Not Aeris. Never Aeris. *Crow.*

The image of Sophie's bloodied corpse never left him after all these years. Unmoving. Lifeless. A chill ran down his spine. He imagined Crow in her place, their golden blood the same vile shade of brown it had turned the night they were shot by the Monster Blood bullet. Poisoned, corroded, gone forever.

"Come with me, Jonah," Sophie urged.

"I-I don't—"

Sophie did not conceal the annoyed groan that slipped past her lips. "I'll give you some time to think it over. But until then, we'll be fighting on opposite sides."

"I'm not your enemy," Jonah choked out as Sophie dove back into the ocean and swam for the *Godkiller.*

The *Vengeance* succumbed to the ocean. The current pulled Jonah under, and he fought his way to the surface before the ocean could claim him, too. He struggled to keep afloat in the biting cold water.

Would the sea monster prowling below attack him? Or would it see him as kin, as it did with Sophie? If Jonah had gone with Sophie, it would have seen him as family, too. But right now, the beast saw more *mortal* than *monster*. It surged toward him, and he swam.

Jonah gasped for air between strokes. He kicked the water with fervor. His muscles cramped. His lungs ached. He choked on ocean water. When he reached the harbor, he caught a glimpse of a massive open maw, filled with three rows of razor-sharp teeth. He scrambled at the pier, but the steel was slippery and unforgiving. He couldn't find purchase.

A hand grabbed his forearm and helped him atop the dock before the monster's jaws snapped shut. A tooth tore through his pant leg and raked down his flesh. It managed to leave a long, gnarly gash, but the monster caught nothing but water and seaweed in its mouth.

"What the hell happened?" Karina gasped as Jonah coughed up water. "You shut down! What did she say to you? Are you okay?"

"We—we need to get to the *Godkiller*." His voice came out raspy.

"How? The *Vengeance* is gone. Our dinghy isn't going to hold against the sea monster."

"We have to try." Jonah eyed the dinghy, which sat atop the sandy shore along the base of the pier. "We can't abandon—" *Sophie. Crow.* He wasn't sure whose name mattered more. Both swirled in his head and threatened to meld into one.

"I'll go fetch the dinghy. Jonah, patch up your leg."

As Karina hurried down the pier, he turned his reluctant gaze to his right leg. Deep violet oozed from the gash, dripping its way down the side of the dock and into the water below.

Would my blood deter the serpent? Jonah wondered. He doubted it.

Focusing on his crew was easy. So long as he worked to keep his family safe, he didn't have room to worry about Sophie's offer or Crow's goals. He focused on Mouse's trembling frame, hunched over, his eyes wide with terror. He was so small, so young, with pale skin and ratty blond hair he refused to trim. He wasn't built for this.

"You can stay on the island," Jonah signed. "None of us will think any less of you."

"I'm not going to stand by while everyone else risks their lives,"

Mouse signed back, resolute and stubborn despite the way his hands shook.

Brave kid.

Karina rowed toward them. Her teeth were gritted, and her grip was tight upon the oars. Jonah could see fear in the way her eyes darted around, trying to catch a glimpse of the sea beast below. She pulled up beside the crew. "Get on," she urged.

Faye boarded first. She pulled the bloodstained fabric off her wound, balled it up, and lobbed it into the ocean as far from the dinghy as she could. Her blood permeated the water, and the serpent rushed to capture what it expected to be its next meal.

"Good thinking," Willow said as she squeezed between Faye and Karina. Mouse boarded next, taking a seat in the frontmost row, his back to the *Godkiller.* Jonah sat at his side.

The dinghy had two oars. Karina took one, and Faye insisted on taking the other, despite her injured shoulder. Eager to speed things up, Jonah nudged Mouse and pointed toward a few loose steel slats on the dock. Mouse wrestled two from their bolts. He passed one to Jonah. It was awkward to hold.

"*Pull!*" Jonah snapped, and all at once the four crewmates rowed. Mouse had his gaze fixed on Jonah's lips, awaiting the next command. *"Pull!"*

Willow, crammed in the center, looked around and fidgeted with the bottom hem of her tank top. She had nothing to do.

"Willow, take lookout," Jonah ordered. Willow sat up straight. "*Pull!*"

"There," Willow pointed in the direction Faye had thrown her bloodied rag, "Monster's coming back toward us."

"*Pull!*"

"There's no way we'll make it," Faye gasped as a tentacle breached the water.

She was right. Jonah stood. He set his makeshift oar down.

"What are you doing?" Karina snapped, "Don't you dare try to—"

"I'm going to distract the monster," Jonah cut her off, making it clear with the sharp, gruff edge to his voice: he would not accept argument. "It'll buy you enough time to get to the *Godkiller.*"

"Jonah, no!"

Jonah stood at the edge of the dinghy, one foot propped up on the rim. When he dove, Karina screamed his name again, but her voice was lost, muffled by the water.

He wouldn't survive this. Death was a better fate than what awaited him aboard the *Godkiller.* If he died here, he'd never have to make the choice between Sophie and Crow. Jonah swam through the sea monster's field of vision. When those bulging eyes turned from the dinghy, Jonah rushed through the water, his heading aimed somewhere away from his crew, away from the *Godkiller,* away from Sophie and Crow, away from the burden of decision sitting on his shoulders.

When he turned his head for air, his crew screamed, sobbed, begged him to come back to safety. But Jonah did not stop. He couldn't stop. Not now.

The water here was murky, dark. Even still, wide jaws and sharp teeth pierced the darkness, ready to swallow him whole.

Jonah slipped away from the monster's gaping maw and swung around its side. He breached the surface long enough to take another gulp of air, then dove back down and straddled the monster's neck. He gripped its massive blue-green horns.

Its slitted yellow eyes surveyed its surroundings, unsure of why its prey had vanished. From underwater, Jonah spotted the dinghy floating along the ocean's surface—his crew was close to the *Godkiller.*

The serpent noticed Jonah's presence atop it. It flailed its slippery body, and all Jonah could do was cling to the beast. His lungs begged him for air. He knew he'd take an instinctive breath soon, inhale a mouthful of water, and drown.

Jonah heaved downwards on the serpent's horns, forcing its head to turn toward the surface. They breached. Jonah gasped for air.

The monster thrashed until Jonah's grip, weakened by the water slicking the horns' surface, gave out. It threw Jonah into the air. He flailed. There was nothing around to grab, and the *Godkiller* was too far away. This would be his end.

For the first time, he considered prayer. Consideration was as far as he got.

Praying was a waste of time. Even in the wake of every divine event he'd witnessed, he still held this sentiment. The only god he would ever consider was Crow—but Crow was far too occupied, tangled up with Argonaut and Sophie aboard the *Godkiller.* Jonah doubted they could hear prayers on the mortal plane, anyhow.

When he hit the apex of his upward momentum, he caught sight of his crew climbing, one by one, using a makeshift grapple of old rope and steel, up the side of the *Godkiller.*

Good, Jonah thought as he fell. The sea monster opened its mouth, ready to catch its prey. *They made it.*

Sharp teeth pierced through Jonah's thigh. He screamed.

Through the haze of pain, Jonah understood enough about anatomy to know his chances of survival were slim. There was an artery in the thigh. The femur was the strongest bone in the body, and if it broke, it could prove fatal. Even if he somehow got away, he would die of infection or disease. More probable, though, was the prospect of decaying in stomach acid.

The calculation kept his mind away from the excruciating pain.

The serpent shook him like a ragdoll. Crow's blurry form stood at the *Godkiller's* bow. His head felt fuzzy. As his vision blackened, he hoped Crow would avenge him. He hoped they would get back to the Heavens and make everything right. He hoped his death wouldn't be in vain.

An angry bolt of lightning struck from the clouds above Jonah's head. A concussive, thunderous *CRACK* jolted Jonah. The monster reeled as millions of volts coursed through its body. Its grip loosened, and Jonah slipped free.

The last thing Jonah remembered was falling toward the ocean.

42

"Avasi, avasi, avasi..."
—The Book of Death. Scholars believe this loosely
translates to "Agony, agony, agony."

75th Storm, Great Flood 1058

Dark clouds loomed overhead. Crow didn't want it to rain—rain would get in the way. They hadn't spilt any blood, so these clouds weren't of their own making. The sky was a wily thing. Crow hoped it would, at least, intimidate Argonaut, but the man did not appear bothered.

Argonaut set a peculiar arrangement of items in a large circle. A monster's bone. A shell from the deepest mortalkind dare dive. A beeswax candle whose flame burned blue. A leaf from the tallest tree in the land.

There was no representation of the sky.

Aeris stood with Elaine atop Mt. Emelle. By the time they arrived, she had set up all the components as instructed. A bone. A shell. A leaf. A feather. Items of every primary Domain except the one to be replaced. Blight, in a mortal form, was bound tight with rope, and though he struggled, Elaine had taken great measure to ensure he did not break free. A spear sat lodged through his shoulder, and by the purple residue on his robes, the weapon had been laced with enough Monster Blood to keep him subdued.

A god, to preside.

A mortal, to ascend.

A god, to die.

Elaine produced a ceremonial knife, decorated with swirling etchings in the blade—sky, fire, tide, and wilds. She plunged the blade, drenched in Monster Blood, into Blight's heart. As his blood flowed onto the rocky plane upon which he lay, brilliant gold faded to sickly brown.

"Arise, Elaine, and take his place," Aeris decreed.

The browned blood of a dying god glowed white, so brilliant and blinding Elaine had to shield her sensitive mortal eyes. The glow did not bother Aeris's divine eyes—they watched as the blood congealed at Elaine's feet. Blight's divinity bubbled to the surface and found its way into Elaine's mortal soul.

When the light faded, Elaine dared open her eyes, a bead of sweat dripping down her brow. Her eyes, once a solid shade of brown, now boasted a rim of gold around her pupils.

Aeris bowed before her. "You are a goddess now."

Crow had never experienced fear quite this bone-chilling and cold.

"You can't do this," they gasped, hands balled into fists. "I won't allow—"

"Sophie," Argo cooed with a twisted smile. "Be a dear and keep the god distracted. I'm not ready yet."

Sophie slammed into them with enough force to knock the air from their lungs. Their back hit the *Godkiller's* deck. She kicked them in the ribcage. As they scrambled to their feet, Crow cursed the fragility of mortal flesh. How could a god be this weak? Is this how Einari felt as he bled to death under a mortal's hand? Was powerlessness what sparked his rage?

"Jonah was always fond of you," Crow growled as they drew their sword. "It's a shame you don't live up to his word."

Crow wished they could know the sister who loved instead of fought. They wished they could know the bright-eyed girl from Jonah's stories, the girl enamored by folktales, but not overcome by them. Sophie screamed and swung her blade. Her attacks were frantic and sloppy. Crow did their best to keep up—while she was strong, rage consumed her. Her recklessness was a polar opposite to Jonah's calculating approach.

Sophie's blade slashed their cheek. Gold dripped from the wound and pooled at their jaw.

Crow slammed their elbow into her sternum. As she stumbled, Crow's eyes darted around the deck—Argonaut kept the *Godkiller* sparse. The deck was the kind of pristine Jonah yearned for but never achieved. There was some steel cable, however, dangling off the starboard rail.

Crow knew they were telegraphing their plans by staring at it. They turned back to Sophie and began the slow, careful process of leading the fight toward the hull. For every step forward Sophie took, Crow took a step back. Sophie, if the smirk on her face said anything, thought she had the upper hand.

They reached the rail. It took one, two, three grabs for the cable before they made purchase. They pulled it off the rail and hid it behind their back. They didn't do well, however, as Sophie's eyes darted from their locked blades to the cable in Crow's hand.

If we make it through this, Crow thought, *I'm asking Jonah to teach me how to be more discreet.*

Sophie grabbed for the cable in Crow's hand. Crow jerked back, but now they were pinned against the railing. *Shit, bad decision.* They glanced over in time to catch sight of Karina climbing onto the deck. Faye, Mouse, then Willow followed.

But where's Jonah? Crow frowned, and Sophie followed their gaze, out over the hulking ship and toward the ocean below. The fight froze, Sophie's fist curled in Crow's shirt. Crow knew she was thinking the same.

Jonah breached the water with the sea monster. It tossed him into the air.

Crow shook free of Sophie and sprinted for the bow. Sophie's footsteps followed close behind. Crow tapped into the blood rolling down their cheek and snapped their fingers. Lightning struck the monster. It—and Jonah—collapsed into the ocean.

Sophie shoved Crow to the floor. She hesitated, then wrenched the cable from Crow's grip and wrapped it tight around their torso. She dragged them over to Argonaut and shoved them to the floor, then dove into the water.

Crow looked around, frantic. Argonaut's crew kept Karina, Mouse, Faye, and Willow busy. They didn't know what Argonaut's ritual meant. They couldn't know. Occupied as they were, they didn't even seem to notice Crow was restrained.

The cable scraped their skin as they struggled. Panic gripped Crow. This was how Blight died. Tied up, weakened.

Crow tapped into their spilt blood and allowed rain to spill from the angry clouds above. A torrential downpour soaked the *Godkiller*. Argonaut's candle went out. The chalk lines he had drawn upon the deck washed away. Argonaut, knelt over a half-drawn line, snarled.

"You little—" Argonaut stood, the chalk in his hand wilting as the rain degraded it.

"You can't kill me!" Lightning struck the *Godkiller's* topmost control deck, where a long antenna extended skyward. Argonaut flinched. He feared Aeris, the true God King. *Good.* "You need another god to preside. You can't do anything without your friend, Death."

"Ha! Death granted Sophie the power to preside."

A monster? Presiding over a godly matter? *No!*

"She's not a god!"

"She's the daughter of a god."

"But—"

"Face it, boy. You cannot worm your way out of your fate on technicality. Tonight, you die. Tonight, I rise."

Argonaut shoved a dirty rag into their mouth and tied it around their head. He disappeared below deck. Crow hated his forethought. They wanted to call out to Karina or Faye or *someone,* anyone, to come untie them.

Sophie climbed aboard with Jonah's limp, unconscious body slung over her shoulder. He was drenched in seawater and blood, the latter of which gushed from the wound in his thigh. Once Jonah was settled, Sophie ran to Crow. She held a knife in her hand, splatters of violet on its blade. Sophie drove it deep into Crow's thigh, mirroring Jonah's injury. Crow shouted through their gag. They bit down on the saliva-soaked fabric.

Sophie slathered Crow's blood upon both her hands, then ran off, leaving the knife buried in their thigh. Crow heaved and sputtered. Sophie pressed her hands to Jonah's wound.

The blood she'd gathered must not have been enough, because she sprinted back to Crow. Her hands were coated in Jonah's blood. She ripped the knife from Crow's thigh and wiped her hands across their wound, frantic to gather more blood for Jonah. God's Blood and Monster Blood mixed. Crow howled in agony.

"*Sophie!*" Argo boomed. Crow jolted. Sophie, poised to run, froze.

"He's dying," Sophie started. "I—"

"I don't want to hear any excuses. We need Aeris *alive!*"

"But Jonah—"

Argonaut slapped her. Crow winced at the sharp *crack* of his flesh across her cheek.

"I don't give a damn about Jonah!" Argo screamed. "Death bound you to me to *assist* me, not *hinder* me!"

Crow could see it in Sophie's face—the way her resolve broke down. The web of tiny cracks in her soul deepened. "You..." Sophie's voice was quiet. "You promised you'd help me *and* Jonah."

Argonaut grunted. Crow almost didn't hear it thanks to the ringing in their ears. He produced a small flask from the inner pocket of his coat and tossed it to Sophie. Sophie sprinted to her brother.

"Her folly is not irreversible," Argonaut mumbled as he knelt at Crow's side. "It's good, even. You'll be a bit easier to handle in the meantime."

Crow blinked. Or, at least, they thought it was a blink. But when their eyes drifted back open, a blue tarp obstructed their view of the sky and Argonaut had resumed his task of drawing the sigil of divinity upon his deck.

Their head flopped to the side and they gazed past the tarp's reach. The rain trickled, weak like Crow was. Sophie and Jonah were at the bow. Willow, Faye, Mouse, and Karina sat back-to-back with one another. One of Argonaut's men stood over the crew, a pistol in his hand.

Crow had always been afraid of Argonaut the Lawless. Now, all they felt was a big, empty black hole of hopelessness, swirling and all-consuming.

So, we've all failed.

43

"Killing a god is permissible if the circumstances are appropriate. If the king deems it just, punishment will not be served. Einari sent to Midir a list of seven gods worth killing. Ione. Sona. Lanali. Riis. Volan. Shivitha. Aeris."
—*The Book of the Tide*

75th Storm, Great Flood 1058

Jonah had no idea how he was still alive. When he opened his eyes, he lay aboard the *Godkiller's* frigid steel deck, Sophie hovering over him with teary eyes. *Maybe I* did *die,* Jonah thought, his muddled mind still taking its sweet time in catching up. *Why else would Sophie be here?*

Right. Sophie was alive. She was also not alive, which was more than Jonah's brain could handle now. Sophie's mouth moved, but Jonah's ears couldn't catch up.

"...onah?"

He groaned.

"Jonah!"

Sophie shook him by the shoulders. His head lolled to the side, and he coughed up water. His sister winced, pulling back from him until they were no longer heartbeats apart. "Oh!"

"G'mme a minute," Jonah groaned.

"How are you feeling? Can I do anything to help?"

"M'fine. Fine. Peachy. Great." The grogginess faded. His leg was sore, but the monster's bite was nothing more than angry violet pockmarks among the tattered fabric of his pants.

"I'll have to admit," Sophie said with a smile. "It's rather convenient, having a god around. I can see the appeal!"

Jonah jolted upright with a gasp. "Crow! Where are they?"

"Over there," Sophie pointed toward a tarp farther down the deck's length. "Argo's prepping for the ritual. It's so close, Jonah! Please, *please* tell me you'll join us."

"...Right."

Jonah looked to his crew. *Most* of his crew. Karina, Willow, Mouse, Faye. They were seated not far away, surrounded by pirates, weapons pointed at their throats.

"I miss you, Sophie," Jonah said.

"Aw, I missed you, too!"

Her smile was bright as the sun, but Sophie didn't understand. He miss*es* her. He miss*es* her kindness, her heart. He miss*es* her empathy for all life, the smallest to the biggest, no matter the circumstance. What had Death said? How had he changed her at such a fundamental level? Had Death's promise to reunite her with her brother done this?

If Karina had not found him in his darkest, rawest of moments, he would have joined her in a heartbeat. His gaze fell to his first mate, who struggled against her bonds. A pirate stood above her, an older man with shaggy black hair and a well-managed beard. He pressed his pistol against her cheek. Despite the threat, she showed no fear.

Her gaze found his.

"Help Crow," she called.

"He doesn't need help," Sophie cut in. Jonah muttered a small *they.* "He's right where we need him to be. We can be happy again, Jonah. You and I."

"What do you want me to do?"

Sophie helped Jonah to his feet. "I want *you* to be the one to plunge the knife into Aeris's heart. I want *your* hand to raise Argo. Prove you're on my side, and we're free!"

"Free."

"I won't be bound to Argo by servitude after it's done," Sophie smiled. "And Death will give us our own Domain. We'll be prince and princess of the Underworld. I don't want to do this alone. All of this— I'm doing it for you. We can mean something."

Jonah knew his worth. Karina had taught him. Crow had taught him. He was not worthless without Sophie. He had grown stronger in her absence. Her memory pushed him forward, but now, Jonah knew what it meant to be alive.

He knew what Sophie wanted him to do. He knew what he needed to do.

"Take me to Aeris," he said.

44

"Life exists not without death. To live is to die. To breathe is to choke. Your veins someday shall bleed, and still, the world will carry on. Act without sin in life, and you shall not fear dying."
—*The Book of Death*

75th Storm, Great Flood 1058

"Jonah!" Karina screamed as Jonah limped behind Sophie. "Jonah, don't!"

Desperation laced Karina's voice, but Jonah appeared to ignore her. Jonah's face, fixed on Crow, was unreadable. Crow shook their head, frantic, panicked. Jonah ignored them, too.

"Jonah's going to kill Aeris," Sophie announced with pride.

"I will," Jonah said. "I'll kill them."

Crow gasped. *No, no!*

"Are you?" Argonaut eyed him with some level of suspicion. Jonah had told Crow, once, that he and Argonaut had a sticky history. Crow didn't know all the details, but the tension between them ran thick.

"I don't care about Aeris." Jonah nudged them with his foot. "I want to be with my sister again."

Crow's heart shattered. After everything they'd been through together? Crow found it difficult to believe—but his loyalty to Sophie's memory had never wavered. It wasn't impossible.

The pirate hummed. "Take the knife, then."

Don't take it, Crow stared up at Jonah with pleading eyes. *Don't take the knife.*

A small pedestal sat to Argonaut's right. Atop it was an ornate shell knife, both its hilt and blade painted with an intricate pattern of swirls and colors. This wasn't the same knife Elaine had used to kill Blight, but it was similar in shape, decoration, and purpose. Jonah picked it up and turned it over in his hands.

"Coat the blade in your blood," Argonaut instructed, "and drive it into Aeris's heart."

Jonah knelt at Crow's side. He pulled the rag from their mouth.

"Please," Crow begged. "Don't do this."

Jonah gazed down at them. His eyes were so warm. So brown. They didn't dare watch as Jonah traced the flat of the knife along his thigh. Instead, they looked over to Argonaut, who smirked, amused. He stood with his arms folded. Sunlight dared peak through the weak layer of clouds and glinted against his prosthetic hand.

Argonaut would rise as the new god of the sky. The thought was horrific. But what was worse: Argonaut failing to wield the might of the sky, or Argonaut paving Death's path into the divine council?

Jonah laid his hand upon Crow's cheek. Despite the pointed lack of expression on his face, Jonah leaned in. His hand was warm and tender against Crow's skin.

His lips met Crow's. Jonah's lips were dry and chapped, but gentle, too. If Crow weren't tied up, their hands would have found his chest. Instead, though, they took what Jonah gave them, his one hand on their cheek, the other gripping their waist as though his life depended on it.

Cruel, wasn't it? That their first kiss would also be their last?

When Jonah drifted away, he stared down into Crow's eyes. His thumb traced the gentle curve of their jaw, from their chin to their ear, then carded through their curly black hair.

"Beautiful," Jonah whispered. "You're beautiful." Tears beaded in the corners of Jonah's eyes, and one dared to roll down his cheek. He blinked them away.

Sophie chanted in Køveni, the rhythmic undercurrent finding its way into Crow's ears. They recognized the chant. They'd performed it when Elaine killed Blight. Sophie started quiet, but grew louder with each passing word, urging Jonah to do the deed. Jonah leaned down and kissed Crow once more. And as his lips met theirs, he drove the knife deep into Crow's chest.

Crow jolted and coughed. Their chest heaved against the shell blade. When Jonah sat back, hand still on the knife's hilt, Crow let their head fall back. Their skull knocked against the *Godkiller's* cold, steel floor. They screwed their eyes shut. A whimper escaped their throat.

As their blood spilt upon the *Godkiller's* deck and Sophie's chanting grew ever louder, they did not feel the acidic cut of Monster Blood. This was nothing like Argonaut's torture, nothing like the bullet they'd taken. No, this agony was bearable. This agony was good. And as Jonah twisted the knife in their chest, as Crow choked and coughed up the blood rising into their throat, they knew Jonah had chosen *them.*

Crow opened their eyes. Their surroundings were dull. Black spots threatened their vision. Jonah still hovered over them, hand on the knife.

"I knew I would have to die, one way or another," Crow rasped, their voice so soft only Jonah could hear. Something wet splashed upon Crow's cheek. Tears. Jonah, above him, choked on the sob he'd been fighting to hold back. He cradled their body in his arms. "But I never expected it to hurt this much."

When everything went black, Crow smiled.

45

75th Storm, Great Flood 1058

The light of distant stars illuminated a sprawling void. Here, there was neither pain nor pleasure. Aeris already missed the sensations of the mortal realm. They missed the agony of the knife in their chest. They missed the way their dying heart had fluttered as Jonah's lips tasted theirs. There had been so much to *feel.*

They supposed it was fitting. Here, deceased souls lined up and awaited their fate. This was Judgment. Here, souls were stripped bare. Every mistake, every decision, laid out for Death to know. Many would be sent to Punishment. Many would go to Paradise. Some of the lucky ones would be resuscitated, brought back to the land of the living, their time not up yet.

Aeris was one of the so-called lucky ones. They would not be resuscitated, but their luck came in the form of ginger hair and amber eyes and rough hands, who had somehow managed to pretend to coat the blade in his own blood. Jonah tricked Argonaut for long enough to get them back to the Heavens. Aeris still wasn't sure how he had done it. Wouldn't Argo have noticed the blade had no blood on it?

They floated their way down the line. Most souls were a ghastly blue, phantom fragments of their mortal forms. Aeris was gold. A few souls identified them as a god and begged them for mercy.

There's nothing I can do, Aeris said. *You're in Death's hands. I am not Death.*

The line was short. There were fewer mortals alive than there were a thousand years ago. Thus, there were fewer mortals to die. The prospect saddened Aeris.

At the front of the line was a construct of Death. The magical projection held enough of the god's consciousness to perform its assigned task. The construct sat at a counter with a stack of papers almost as tall as it, jotting notes as the mortal it had last evaluated floated on her way. Aeris watched the unfortunate soul trudge down the path to Punishment.

Ugh, Aeris groaned as they flopped onto the stool the punished soul had occupied. Something in the construct's eyes shifted. The construct, no doubt, had summoned the rest of Death's awareness. Death stared at them in shock through the construct's eyes. His bug-eyed stare was amusing. *What a drag. Don't you think the paperwork is a bit unnecessary?*

You, Death growled through his construct's lips. *You're not supposed to be here.*

Am I not? Aeris grinned and leaned their elbow against the counter.

You're supposed to be dead! Gone!

I'd argue I am dead.

Death slapped a hand over his construct's metaphysical face. There was nothing he could do now. Here, Aeris reclaimed their throne.

Anyway, they stood from their seat. *Thought I'd drop by. Have fun with your infinity of paperwork. I guess I get why you want to eradicate all humankind. It sure would save you a lot of hassle, wouldn't it?*

If their bodies had been any more physical, Aeris figured Death would have lashed out. They took great glee in the powerlessness of Judgment. They strode past him, offering the construct a pat on the shoulder as they walked by. Their hand phased through its body.

The construct stilled as Death left it to do its task.

Aeris reached the fork in the path. One path led to Paradise. One, to Punishment. Instead of taking either path, they made a sharp right, wading through a sea of never-ending darkness. A soul, should it stray from its designated path, would lose its way and become trapped in Purgatory. Aeris could see a few as they walked. They begged Aeris for help.

There is nothing I can do, Aeris told them. *I am not Death.*

Walk far enough through Purgatory, far past the wayward souls and the invisible barrier containing them, and one could find the gate to the Heavens. The gate was tall and ornate, built like wrought iron but made of brilliant marble. Aeris smiled when they reached it. Their fingers brushed against the gate. This, they could feel. It was cool against their translucent fingers. Under their touch, the gate opened, and Aeris strode through.

Behind the gate was a staircase, which did not appear to have an end. It went up, up, up, past the mortal realm, past the skies, to the Heavens. Relief flooded Aeris as they planted their sandaled foot atop the first step. As they climbed, their divine body rebuilt itself of pale skin, billowing blue robes, and brilliant white hair.

At the top of the grand marble stairwell, Aeris took a deep breath. A mortal habit.

That was the best they could do to prepare.

46

"[No record.]"
—The Grand Catalogue of Last Words: Great Flood
Era. Death #[uncounted]. Stabbed in the chest. Aeris
disregarded leaving last words in the catalogue.

75th Storm, Great Flood 1058

Jonah hugged Crow's body close to his chest. Their blood spilt across the deck, muddling the chalk lines beneath Jonah's knees. Karina, somewhere behind him, screamed. She was far away, but she had a clear view of it all. She didn't know the details. She didn't know what Jonah had done.

Sophie stopped chanting. Jonah was glad for it. He didn't like the way Køveni sounded on her tongue. She shouldn't know that language. "Something's wrong," Sophie said, her mouth fixed into a puzzled frown. "I don't think it worked."

Argonaut's face curled with fury. Crow's blood had not run brown. Their divinity remained intact, and so did Argonaut's mortality.

Jonah should have feared the man, but he didn't. He stared into Argonaut's gray eyes, unwavering and defiant. He did not regret what he did. Crow was on their way home—or, at least, Jonah hoped so. He had no way of knowing for sure.

"You!" Argonaut bellowed. "You wretched, mangy, blasted *son of a bitch!*"

"Jonah?" Sophie's voice was small. "Jonah, what did you do?"

He laid Crow's corpse upon the deck. *Corpse.* He shuddered. He pressed a small kiss to their forehead, closed those beautiful blue eyes, then stood. "I did what I had to."

Argonaut drew his pistol and fired. Jonah leapt to the side, stumbling over his own feet as he found cover. Clumsy. He needed to do better. The bullet grazed his bicep. With a grunt, he reached for his blade. His fingers brushed the leather-wrapped hilt, but he faltered. He'd always hated the deadly precision of a gun. Swords, at least, had a give-and-take to them, but guns? Guns were for people who yearned only to slaughter.

Still, Jonah knew he was at a severe disadvantage.

Sophie had a pistol. He could nick it off her while she was distracted. Her lip quivered. Jonah found he didn't feel guilty for upsetting her. He dove for his sister. She didn't have much time to react as he snatched the pistol from her holster, cocked it, and fired at Argonaut. His shot missed by a wide margin.

Jonah ducked behind a steel crate. Argonaut may be powerful, but his age slowed him down. In a fight between a middle-aged mortal and a half-monster in his prime, the outcome seemed obvious.

Argonaut was, however, a far better shot than Jonah, and in that sense, he had the advantage. He fired a series of four, five, *six* shots, and the crate exploded into steel splinters. Jonah scrambled back as sailing equipment—nets, cannonballs, fishing hooks—spilled to the deck. He needed to get the gun from Argonaut's hands. He leveled his pistol, aimed, and fired.

The bullet smashed through Argonaut's prosthetic wrist. Argonaut hissed—not out of pain, but fury. Prosthesis damaged and disabled, steel fingers curled around the gun and trapped it. Jonah couldn't help but smirk. His pride got the better of him. Argonaut kicked him in the ribs. Slick from the rain, the *Godkiller's* steel surface did nothing to aid Jonah's grip, and as much as he dug his boots in, he slid back.

"You'd be nothing without me," Argonaut snarled. He drew his sword with his flesh hand. "You insignificant brat. This is how you repay me?"

He ducked under Argonaut's blade. "My worth does not hinge on you." Jonah caught the pirate's wrist, stopping his next strike in its tracks. "I am my own man."

"You're no man," Argonaut countered. He ripped his arm free and pressed the tip of his blade to Jonah's collarbone. It drew a bead of blood, which dripped violet onto his gold-stained shirt. "You're a monster."

"Fine. I may be a monster, but in blood, not in soul." He slipped away before Argonaut could slit his throat. "*The God King* said so."

He weaved around Argonaut's back and slammed the hilt of his sword between his shoulders. Argonaut stumbled. Jonah twisted the blade around and poised to stab. He was eager to put an end to this man, but a hand stopped him before he could follow through. Sophie. She wrestled the sword from his grip and lobbed it aside. It clattered to a halt at the starboard gunwale.

"You *betrayed* me!" Sophie screamed as she forced Jonah's hands behind his back. "You said you'd kill the god!"

"I did."

"You didn't! Now Aeris is going to ruin everything! Do you not care about what Death promised?"

"I don't."

"Do you not care about *me?*"

"I refuse to be manipulated to do Death's bidding. You're not *you,* Sophie, you're something else. Something ruined."

"*YOU'RE* RUINED!" Sophie wrenched Jonah's arms behind his back. His shoulders strained, muscles pulled tight. He thrashed in her grip.

Argonaut approached, a scowl wrinkling his face. With the way his lip curled, his nose looked more crooked than it already was. His sunken gray eyes were wild with fury. Fear dripped its way down Jonah's spine, but he refused to acknowledge it. He couldn't. Not now.

Sophie shoved Jonah to his knees. He squirmed in her grip. Her long nails dug into his wrists, not quite enough to draw blood, but enough to hurt.

"Sophie," Jonah tried. "We can still be together again. We can do it on our own terms. I *want* to spend time with you more than anything. I miss reading books together, making shapes out of clouds, the things we did as teenagers."

"Child's play, Jonah. We've grown. You're different, now. I'm different, now."

"You *are* different." Jonah couldn't help but concur. He missed her big, brilliant smile. He missed her hope, her optimism, her vivid imagination. That was long gone. Her lips curled into a nasty, broken snarl. Her long ginger hair was frizzy and unkempt. Death had undone her.

Jonah had undone her, too.

Argonaut's boot slammed against his cheek. The tang of iron flooded his mouth, and he spat blood onto the deck. With a groan, he dared to meet Argonaut's eyes again. His attempt to bargain with Sophie had been rendered a waste of time, and now Argo was upon him, prosthetic hand still trapped around the gun, broken and useless, its exposed wiring sparking. His flesh hand pressed the sword against his throat.

The foreboding chill of the looming frost season was so much worse under Argonaut's knife.

"For your insolence," Argonaut sneered, "I will send you to Death for judgment."

Argonaut's blade pressed against his jugular. Even as he faced his own demise, Jonah couldn't help but prod.

"Don't you think killing me is too merciful?" he asked. He glanced at his crew. Karina had wriggled free of her restraints. The pirate who had held her at gunpoint was unconscious in front of her.

"You're wasting your breath. I will not spare you."

"I mean, how can you guarantee Death will punish me? You may have struck a bargain with him, but you can't control him."

"Silence!"

"You *failed*. Kill Aeris, right? Don't you know if you want the job done proper, do it yourself?"

"It was *supposed* to be Sophie's job. Foolish girl!"

"Death may be more inclined to punish *you*," Jonah continued. "You're the one who failed."

He knew his logic was not sound, but so long as he poked and pushed, he could stall his death for long enough...

Faye slammed into Argonaut. Jonah grinned. She sent the unprepared pirate stumbling. Behind him, Karina hauled Sophie away. Her nails scraped long, ugly scratches down Jonah's arm as she fought to keep her hold—but her grip slipped as Karina slammed her into the deck. Jonah scrambled to his feet.

"What the hell happened!?" Karina shouted as she wrestled with Sophie.

"I didn't kill Crow."

"They look pretty damn dead to me!"

"Not in the way that matters."

Sophie grabbed a fistful of Karina's sandy hair and yanked. Karina shrieked.

Jonah glanced over at the starboard rail where his sword lay—Mouse had it. Their eyes met, and Mouse slid the sword across the deck. Jonah stopped it under his foot and offered Mouse an appreciative nod.

He flourished his sword, then charged.

47

75th Storm, Great Flood 1058

On the rare occasion Jonah spoke of Sophie, he spoke of her gentle temperament. Karina remembered, once, sitting with Jonah in her cabin not long after she rescued him from Argonaut. Back then, his trauma over Sophie's death was raw and fresh. Karina had bundled him up in her fuzzy yellow blanket in an attempt to quell the trembling in his shoulders.

"On Sophie's birthday," Jonah said. *His voice was fractured and weak. "Our adoptive father announced he had saved enough money to take us to an island. I don't think I'd ever seen her as excited as she was then. She spent the whole day babbling about getting to feed squirrels and feel the petals of flowers between her fingers."*

Jonah paused. Karina allowed him the time he needed. A minute passed. Two.

"We—we never went. Someone snuck onto the ship when we were docked at a hub and stole the money. Sophie was heartbroken. She—"

He squeezed his eyes shut, trying his damnedest not to cry. Karina wished he would let it out. It's okay, *she wanted to tell him,* it's okay to feel.

"She didn't deserve to die," he choked. *"It should have been me."*

sSophie was not the woman Jonah had made her out to be. As Karina pinned her to the deck, Sophie snarled up at her with a malice so volatile it caught Karina off guard. Sophie clawed at Karina's face.

Her nails were long and sharp, inhuman, claw-like. Karina peeled the hand away from her face. Sophie kneed her in the stomach.

Sophie grasped Karina's knife from the sheath on her back. Karina didn't have enough time to get away before Sophie slammed the knife into her shoulder. Karina screamed. Blood poured onto Sophie below her. Her fingertips tingled. She rolled off of Sophie, gripping her shoulder to quell the blood flow. Her vision swam.

"I think you and Sophie would have loved each other," Jonah had told her on many occasions. Karina wished she could have loved Sophie. Staring down at her now, Karina hated her with every fiber of her being. It seemed Sophie reciprocated the sentiment.

"What's your angle?" Karina spat. If she were in a better headspace, she could have talked Sophie down, but Karina couldn't keep the fury from her voice.

"I want to change the world." Sophie's knuckles were white with how tight she gripped Karina's knife. "Helping Argo rise was going to be my way up!"

"Jonah said you loved mythology."

"And now I have the chance to be a part of it! I could be a hero! The one who helped replace the cosmic waste of space with a new god!"

"And are you certain you're on the right side of history?"

Sophie screamed in frustration. She stalked in circles around Karina. "You have no right to lecture me! What do you know? Nothing! I've transcended mortality! I've seen things you couldn't fathom!"

"I don't need to fathom anything to know what is true."

"Then, *pray tell,* what is true?"

"Argo works for personal gain. He would make a horrendous god. An evil god." Karina said as Sophie circled behind her. "Death doesn't want you for *you.* You may be his creation, but he sees you as nothing more than a tool for his benefit."

"I'm no tool! He showed me Paradise! He told me I would rule over it! Me and Jonah!"

"Do you *want* to rule? Or are you so desperate for divine gratification you'll take anything you're given?"

"Shut up!"

"Jonah has been a troubled man for as long as I've known him, but he knows what's true and right, too."

"He was a waste of my time," Sophie spat. "I'm done with him. He's no brother of mine."

"Fine," Karina couldn't help but bite. Sophie's rage held the mass of the sun. If she wanted to burn, Karina would let her. "If he's not your brother, he's *mine.*"

Sophie screeched and tackled her.

Karina punched Sophie in the jaw. Sophie's knee dug into her stomach as they wrestled on the deck. Her bloodied shoulder throbbed, but Karina couldn't afford to let her injury hold her back.

Sophie held the knife above Karina's left eye at such an angle that she could pierce straight through to Karina's brain. Karina grabbed her wrist and struggled to push her back. She wasn't eager to be lobotomized by Jonah's shattered twin.

Karina shoved Sophie off her and scrambled backwards. She bumped against Crow's body, limp and unmoving beside her. Her hand brushed against their leg, and she stared down at their slack face. Oh, poor Crow—she hoped they were somewhere better, now, making the changes they'd hoped to make in the Heavens above. She wished they could've returned home under better circumstances.

Guilt flooded her as she scooped up some of their blood upon her hand and held it against her injured shoulder. Was she desecrating their corpse by taking advantage of their divine blood?

Crow would have wanted me to. Tears welled in her eyes. She missed them already. They weren't gone for good, but she still mourned their death. Crow didn't understand what death meant to mortals. They didn't understand how much it *hurt.*

Their blood healed her wound. Her marred flesh knitted itself back together. The least she could do was offer them a prayer for her gratitude.

"Thank you, Crow," Karina whispered as she stood, "I wish I could have given you more. Please remember us up there, okay? You're family."

A gentle breeze answered her prayer.

48

"Any last words?"
—The Grand Catalogue of Last Words: Great Flood
Era. Death #8,903,425,068. Impaled.

75th Storm, Great Flood 1058

Faye and Willow were trying to help. The notion was a kind one, but Jonah didn't want his crewmates to interfere. He needed to take care of Argonaut on his own.

"Get out of here," Jonah barked. "Take care of the remaining pirates. I can handle this."

"We're not leaving you alone with Argo," Faye snapped back.

"This is my fight."

Willow was quick to back away, taking Faye by the crook of her arm. Faye didn't budge. Only after Jonah shot her a nasty glare did she concede.

Jonah turned his attention to Argonaut.

"Good choice," Argo sneered. "I wouldn't want your crewmates to get in the way of your demise."

Jonah couldn't help but laugh. His blade met Argo's. "You're not putting me down easy."

Argonaut shoved Jonah's blade down. Jonah blocked a few blows before he had the chance to counter. Without his pistol, Argo wasn't as efficient a fighter. It looked as though the man wasn't sure what to do with his broken prosthetic hand. Jonah took note.

In his periphery, Sophie's long ginger hair caught his attention. He'd have to deal with her later, and he was *not* looking forward to it. She scared him.

Argonaut's sword caught Jonah's side. White-hot pain shot through his core. He gritted his teeth. *Focus!*

Jonah jumped back to avoid a second strike, and he bumped the gunwale. Argonaut approached with a sinister smirk. He raised his sword, and Jonah dove. He tumbled to the ground with a grunt, and Argonaut's blade slammed against the metal railing with an ear-shattering *screech.*

Jonah scrambled to his feet. He registered another *bang* of Willow's rifle, a body hitting the deck. Whether or not Willow killed the pirates or incapacitated them was not clear to Jonah, but he didn't have the time to appraise the situation.

Pride swelled in his chest. These were the people who gave him strength. Faye and Karina were strong. Willow was compassionate. Mouse was the smartest person Jonah had ever had the fortune of meeting. These people were his inspiration, his drive, his purpose. They kept him moving forward.

He channeled his purpose into every stab and slash. He played dirty. His year at Argonaut's side had taught him how pirates fought: no pride, no dignity. Jonah stomped on Argonaut's foot. He spat in Argonaut's face. When he got close enough, he tore the broken prosthetic off his arm and chucked it into the ocean.

He jabbed his sword toward the man's chest. Argo parried Jonah's strike. Even short one hand and twice Jonah's age, Argonaut was a skilled, formidable foe.

Jonah kicked Argonaut. The pirate king's focus and energy lapsed, but he bounced back quick, bombarding Jonah with a few powerful strikes. Argonaut smashed his heel into Jonah's ankle, and something snapped. Jonah gritted through the pain. He couldn't afford to limp.

Argonaut grabbed him by the collar of his bloodstained shirt. "Any last words?" he sneered with a wide, toothy grin.

"Yeah. Look out behind you."

Argonaut's eyes widened, and he whirled around, expecting Karina or Faye to be behind him, poised to strike. Jonah was the one to laugh, now. Nothing was there except the gunwale and the open ocean. The distraction was enough for Jonah to run his sword through the man's stomach.

Argonaut coughed and sputtered, blood bubbling from his mouth and down his long, scraggly beard. He fell to his knees, and Jonah took a healthy step backward.

"Any last words?" Jonah teased.

Argonaut was a tall, imposing man, but on his knees before Jonah, doubled over, clutching his wound, he looked small. He did not gratify Jonah with a response. Jonah considered granting him mercy. He could slit Argonaut's throat to make it quicker, but Argonaut did not deserve a quick, merciful death. He deserved to suffer. Jonah stood over him. Blood pooled around his boots.

He yanked his blade out of Argonaut's body, and his blood flowed quicker, uninhibited. He clawed at Jonah's feet. Jonah took another step backwards. Argonaut fell face-down on the deck.

Argonaut the Lawless, dreaded pirate of the northern seas, went still.

Jonah shook his hands, letting them flop loose at the wrist. The repetitive movement soothed him. He stood over Argonaut's body. When he was no longer overheated and overstimulated, he turned to Sophie and Karina. Sophie had Karina's arm bent at an odd angle, and Karina's face was screwed up in pain. From the looks of things, Karina had been trying not to hurt Sophie, but Sophie intended for Karina to die.

Jonah missed the Sophie who would never hurt a fly.

He marched toward them, clutching his blood-soaked sword tight in his hand. "Argonaut is dead," he said, dark and low. "There's nobody for you to serve anymore, Sophie."

Sophie looked over in shock at Argonaut's corpse at the bow. She released Karina. "You..."

"It's over."

"*You killed him.* You ruined the ritual, and you killed him."

"Yes."

Sophie released Karina and punched him. Her fist slammed against his temple. He recoiled and dropped his sword. Sophie's brown eyes used to be so warm and compassionate, but now all they held was fury.

"You don't care about me," she snarled. "You never did!"

"Soph," Jonah started.

"I hate you. I hate that damn nickname."

She used to love being called Soph.

"Fine," Jonah whispered. "Sophie. I can't love who you are now. If that means we're enemies, then so be it."

He choked on his words. Turning her away was the most excruciating agony he'd ever endured, more than the broken foot and the gash below his ribs. He could love Sophie in memory, but this was where they parted. Tears rolled down Jonah's cheeks. He made no attempt to withhold them.

Sophie stared in shock. She chewed on her lower lip. There must have still been a flicker of hope in her, and Jonah doused it with a bucket of salt water.

"I have a new family now," Jonah said. "I have a family who wants to do *good.*"

Sophie slapped him in the face. Jonah stood still and took it. A realization hit him like a punch to the gut: he couldn't keep Sophie around. He cast a glance at Karina, who lingered nearby. Jonah extended an arm and waved his fingers. He eyed Karina's knife. Karina nodded, and as Sophie screamed and spat in Jonah's face, she snuck closer and placed the hilt of her knife into Jonah's palm.

His trembling fingers closed around it. He couldn't fathom using his sword. The knife was smaller, more efficient. He looked into Sophie's eyes, memorizing the hurt and the fury shimmering there. He tried his best to imagine the way she'd smiled when she found a little frog clinging to the mast. She had cupped it in her hand and showed it to Jonah with such adoration. She begged and begged and begged their father until he allowed her to keep it as a pet—and when it died two years later, she sobbed with such passion for the thing.

Jonah vowed to remember *that* Sophie. He eyed the long strands of unkempt hair falling far past her shoulders. She would have grown into a fine young woman, had Death not gotten his grimy hands on her soul.

With a solid upward jerk, he shoved the knife into her throat. Sophie deserved a quick, merciful death. She crumpled to the deck, and she was gone.

Jonah's balance failed him. He listed to the side, and Karina rushed to support him. Her hand wrapped around his waist, his arm slung limp over his shoulder. His full weight was in her hands.

"It's okay," Karina whispered. "You're okay. It's over."

Karina guided him to sit, his back braced against the wall that led to the *Godkiller's* bridge. She took Jonah's hand and held it tight.

"Keep breathing," she urged. "You're doing great."

Jonah didn't feel like he was doing great. A tiny, garbled noise escaped his throat. He squeezed Karina's hand as though it were his lifeline. If it hurt, she didn't vocalize it.

She settled beside him, and he slumped against her shoulder. From here, he could see Crow, Argonaut, *and* Sophie, all lifeless on the deck. He choked. Karina urged him to turn away. Like putty, he moved however Karina guided him, until his face was buried against her shoulder.

He could hear footsteps approaching. He knew his crew well enough to identify their gaits. Faye had a long stride. Willow walked at the same pace as Faye, but her legs weren't as long, so her steps were quicker. And Mouse walked soft as his namesake, his footsteps almost undetectable. But Jonah made the effort to hear them. The shift in focus grounded him.

"Doing better?" Karina asked.

"No," Jonah whispered. Regardless, he sat up and turned to his crew. "Is everyone alright?"

"Wounded," Faye admitted, and the others nodded in agreement.

Jonah forced himself to his feet, even though Karina tugged his hand to stop him. "Let's get everyone patched up. I'll find Argonaut's medkit."

He didn't wait for a reply. Falling back into the role of *captain* was easy. Crew first, everything else later. He marched to the trapdoor and descended the ladder, trying to be tender with his injured ankle. He had little success. With every step down steel rungs, pain shot up his leg.

This ship was creepy, between the bloodstained brig and the storage room where he'd smashed the massive tanks of Crow's blood. It creaked and groaned and whirred as he limped through the corridors lit an artificial blue, bright and sterile.

He found the medkit in a storage closet near the bow. The kit was bigger than what Jonah kept on the *Vengeance*. He carried it above deck and sat beside Karina. Placing the medkit in front of him, he popped open the shell case. He struggled as the hinges caught. "Who's first?"

Faye and Karina both pointed at Mouse. Jonah waved him over and urged him to sit.

Mouse was in rough shape. He sported multiple cuts and scrapes across his pale skin. He rolled up a pant leg and revealed how bruised and marred his knee was, so black and purple the boy would no doubt struggle to walk. Was it broken? Jonah poked and prodded at the wound—he couldn't tell. He wrapped bandages firmly around the joint.

After Mouse was Willow. After Willow was Faye. After Faye was Karina. He did not turn to his own wounds until he'd taken care of his crew. Karina helped him wrap his foot as he patched up the cut on his side. He pressed a bandage atop the bridge of his throbbing nose, which wouldn't do much but support it until it healed.

When Jonah finished, he looked up to find Faye and Willow hauling Argonaut over the side of the ship. *Good riddance.*

But then they made their way over to Sophie.

"Wait," Jonah called. "Don't."

Willow shot him a confused glance.

"I want to give her a proper sendoff," Jonah admitted. "Crow, too."

"Yessir." Willow left Sophie's body and moved to the other corpses. The job was a gruesome but necessary one. While Faye and Willow hauled bodies into the ocean, Mouse mopped the deck clean of bloodstains.

In an hour, the crew gathered at the stern. Jonah had laid Sophie atop a slat of scrap steel. Knowing now her death wasn't much more than an inconvenience, Jonah wasn't sure there was a need to send her off, but it felt wrong not to. He had never gotten the chance the first time he lost her.

"I never knew her," Karina said, kneeling at Sophie's side. "But everything Jonah told me made her sound like the most amazing person he'd ever met. I'm so sorry, Jonah. I hope you can remember the good things and forget the bad."

Jonah tucked his hands into the pockets of his bloodied coat. "I hope so, too," he whispered. With Faye's help, he lowered her by the rope affixed to the steel slat until it touched the surface of the water.

"Goodbye, Sophie," Jonah whispered as he let go of the rope. "May things be better for you someday."

She sank below the waves. He wished he could have put her in a dinghy and sent her to sail until the ocean took her. But there was only one dinghy, the rickety wooden one from the *Vengeance*, and Jonah had reserved it for Crow.

He turned to the dinghy. Mouse had hooked it up to Argonaut's release system, which was lacking a lifeboat—Argonaut must have used it for something, once, and neglected to replace it.

"I don't even know where to begin with this idiot," Jonah said. He clenched his fists. "They're the most stunning person I've ever met."

Faye couldn't help but chuckle. "They changed you. They're somewhere in the Heavens, now, and their time aboard your ship has changed them, too."

Jonah combed his fingers through their hair, brushing out any knots and tangles he found. He couldn't bring himself to send them off. Saying goodbye was the hardest part about loving someone.

"You did the right thing," Mouse signed. "If you hadn't killed them, Sophie or Argo would have done far worse. They're still with us."

Jonah nodded. He swallowed back the lump in his throat and lowered the dinghy to the ocean. It bobbed atop the current, drifting from the *Godkiller* at a slow, unguided pace. The rest of the crew wandered off after they paid their respects, but Jonah sat vigil until long after the lifeboat disappeared on the horizon. He didn't move until Karina returned to his side.

"You're in charge of redecorating," Jonah said, and Karina laughed at the absurdity of it all. Jonah couldn't help but chuckle, too. He appreciated the levity. "This is going to be our new home. I'll make sure everyone has a cabin, but you're in charge of making this place *not* give us all the creeps."

"Yessir," Karina affirmed. "I guess I've got my work cut out for me."

"Argonaut's got a massive stash of money around somewhere. Buy whatever you want—we'll stop by the hub to stock up."

"I'm a little afraid of making public appearances on this ship. Folks might think we're pirates."

Jonah agreed.

In the evening, when the rest of the crew was downstairs figuring out their new accommodations, Jonah found some red paint in a storage closet. He tied a cable around his waist, climbed over the side of the ship, and crossed out *Godkiller*.

Below the crossed-out name, he wrote in big, bold letters, as neat as he could, a new name:

Crow's Voyage.

Acknowledgments

Wow. Just... Wow.

I'm awestruck. I've always daydreamed about the kinds of things I might write in my acknowledgments, but I never anticipated I'd actually *get* to this point. It was always one of those things that felt like some far-off daydream. But here we are.

Most authors start off by jumping right into naming people, but I want to start by acknowledging *you.* Thank you so much for buying this book and giving it a read. Thank you for supporting a queer author, for drawing fanart (which I'm so honored to have received, even prior to publishing), and most of all, for taking the time out of your busy lives to read the story I've spent hours, days, months, *years* crafting. I wouldn't have been able to do any of this without you.

To all my alpha readers, a number that remains a mystery to me (though if I were to ballpark it, maybe two or three thousand readers, totaling at a whopping fifty thousand total views), many of whom I will never know by name: your enthusiasm and support of this story in its infancy was what truly inspired me to pursue publishing. What started off as a silly, casual writing exercise has turned into this, and I couldn't be happier, or prouder. Thank you for standing by my side.

To Sarah, my beta reader: this novel benefited so much from your feedback. Thank you for taking the time to read this story back when it was a hefty 150,000 words. What an undertaking!

And to Felix, Kelly, Mina, Alicia, Des, Ryan, Linds, Sarah (again), and everyone else in the Write Spot crew, your presence beside me while I wrote and edited this was so grounding, encouraging, and incredibly distracting (in the best of ways). You all rock.

Despite living an ocean away, Lina has shown nothing but encouragement and excitement for this novel. An eight-hour time zone difference feels like nothing when I'm chatting with you! I'm putting a big hug in a box and shipping it your way.

My colleagues, Jim, Ho, and Valerie: Jim, thanks for encouraging me to follow my passions. Ho, thank you for proofreading my promotional materials. And Valerie, thanks for putting up with me playing character-themed playlists during our commute!

If it weren't for the unconditional support of my parents and my brother, I don't think I'd be here now. My family supported every creative attempt and every failure along the way. I have boundless creative energy, and I can attribute that to them. They've asked me many thought-provoking questions about the world of Midir. Plenty of serious ones, and plenty of silly ones, too. I don't think I'll ever forget the time Dad asked, "Does your story have snowmen in it?"

No, this story does not have any snowmen in it.

Most importantly, though, my family raised me to live without fear. I told them I was transgender at age sixteen and they gave me the permission and guidance I needed to live authentically and honestly. They took those crucial first moments in stride, in the wake of me coming out, and did everything in their power to make sure I knew I was loved.

And, of course, I'd be remiss if I did not mention Nicole Evans (@thoughtsstained) and Charlie Knight (@cknightwrites), my amazing editors. Your thoughts, critiques, and attention to detail improved this work in ways I could have never pushed it on my own.

I cannot thank all of you enough.

Køveni Language Dictionary

History

Køveni is widely considered a dead language. Though early humans spoke Køveni, the gods were quick to design new languages better suited for mortal tongues. A few Midiri scholars have dedicated themselves to learning the language of the gods, though the available materials are severely limited.

Grammar

Køveni follows a simple object-first grammatical structure. This means most common sentences are structured as follows:

Fisig	i	seves	lieni
Kind	is	your	crew

Pronouns

Ejes → She *Ejen* → Her *Ejeví* → Herself	*Eres* → He *Eren* → Him *Ereví* → Himself	*Ennes* → They *Ennen* → Them *Eneví* → Themself
Ø → I *Øve* → Me *Øveví* → Myself	*Se* → You *Seves* → Your *Seveví* → Yourself	*Íen* → The *Íenes* → It *Íeneví* → Itself

Pronouns can take other forms using other suffixes:

Sevej → You are   *Sevai* → You have

Emphasis can be placed upon emotional phrases by including the word *je*.

Kiri → basic apology
Je kiri → sorrowful apology

Kali → Love
Je kali → Adoration

Words and Phrases Used in *Blood of the Gods*

Chapter 20

Shav ejeví Ø davøl. Suhíþ íen cinua. Suhíþ fea silmítha Aeris.
Time herself I call. Lift the spell. Lift from embrace Aeris.
I call upon Time herself. Lift the spell. Lift Aeris from your embrace.

Gí kisiven sevai.
Good friends you have.
You have good friends.

Eren Ø je kali.
Him I adore.
I adore him.

Ili → Sun
Naji → Moon
Noé → Light
Ilinoé → Sunlight, sunshine

Chapter 21

Onasi þídes.
Everything hurts.

Ø geþiel
I need

Chapter 22

Kiri → basic apology
Je kiri → sorrowful apology

Chapter 34

Þides → Pain of the flesh
Kalþides → Pain of the soul

Kaívi → Dog, hound
Sokaívi → Cursed hound

About the Author

Wren L. Rivers (they/them) is a transmasculine and neurodivergent author born and raised in Virginia. They are a jack-of-all-trades type creative. Alongside writing, Wren illustrates their own covers and character art. Everything Wren creates is 100% human-made and untouched by generative AI.

Wren prioritizes diversifying the fantasy genre with queer stories. *The Divine Archive*—a queer seafaring fantasy series—marks their debut.

You can find Wren online at https://linktr.ee/corvidarcana.

9 798993 143736